Bent, Not Broken

Suki Sather
10/22/15

Bent, Not Broken

SUKI SATHER

Bent, Not Broken

Copyright © 2014 by Suki Sather

All characters and events in this book, other than those clearly in the public domain, are fictitious and any resemblance to real persons, living or dead, is purely coincidental.

All rights reserved. No part of this publication may be reproduced, distributed, or transmitted in any form or by any means, including photocopying, recording, or other electronic or mechanical methods, without the prior written permission of the publisher, except in the case of brief quotations embodied in critical reviews and certain other noncommercial uses permitted by copyright law.

For permission requests, write to the publisher, addressed "Attention: Permissions Coordinator," via the contact form located on www.sukisather.com.

Ordering Information:
Quantity sales. Special discounts are available on quantity purchases by corporations, associations, and others. Orders by U.S. trade bookstores and wholesalers. For details, contact the publisher at the address above.
ISBN: 978-0-9967241-1-1
Main category—Fiction: General
Other category—Fiction: Urban Fantasy
Printed in the United States of America
First Edition
14 13 12 11 10 / 10 9 8 7 6 5 4 3 2 1

Dedication

To my husband Brian who is always my biggest, most supportive fan and my inspiration for every love story I will ever write. Love you more than air.

To my daughter Reece for listening to my stories and never getting tired of them. Love you more than the universe.

For Pook, you never left me until you knew I could fly. Not one day passes, that I don't miss your smile. Love you with everything.

Inspiration is found everywhere around you.

A picture, a painting, a poetry verse, the way the sun sets, or how light can play with your eyes, and sometimes the simple notes played on the piano can move you in a way nothing else ever can.

Music is a language that transcends all barriers.

Books are bridges to far away worlds we dream about.

This is the passage to my faraway place and you have been cordially invited to join me there. Please understand when you come here, you may never want to leave. Warning issued.

Thank you for coming. I hope you enjoy what I have created. I should tell you one last thing before we begin:
I love happy endings…without them life would be unlivable.

Chapter ONE

Malik sprang up to the ledge of the abutting building like a spirited gazelle on high alert. He continued moving on the store top until he could observe the shipyard with precise distinction. Awareness danced along the defined muscles of his 6'3" frame until they were pulled taut like a bow string. Malik's feet graced the rooftop with quiet, controlled strides. The adrenaline pumped through his veins while thin ribbons of sweat ran down between his shoulder blades.

My time is coming.

The heart beat appeared weak from this distance, but Malik heard it drumming below on the dry dock. He stopped. After an eternity, he bolted into full motion, continuing his prowl in the underbelly of the darkened city, stalking his prey.

The pungent odor of valerian would not be confused with the natural odors of the Marmaris shipyards, so Malik bided his time and waited for the scent to return on the frosty night air. Valerian was distinct in its potency, much like the man Malik sought.

With great haste, he moved from the rooftop to a Coffee House sign, ascending to a balcony, creaking and moaning when he landed. Malik blew out the breath carrying Caleb's scent and inhaled again. He began to trail him from a distance once more. Malik sprang upward from his crouched position landing on the structure's decaying roof several feet above. His sensitive nose reached farther into the gentle stream of air. He assumed Caleb had to know he was tracking him.

A faint scent hit him like a steely punch to the gut about the North end of the building. He glanced down to witness Caleb crossing the street. The tall figure disappeared in a doorway tucked away from the streetlight overhead. At the last second, Caleb whipped around and his eyes darted from corner to crevice along the darkened road.

Malik ducked behind an air conditioner and waited. He stood after Caleb resumed his footsteps and let the shadow of the adjacent building hide him while he checked the avenue for Stryders.

After setting off with steady foot falls, Malik paused at the periphery of the building and looked to the blacktop below. A careful sigh and he took a step right over the edge, falling the four stories to land on the balls of his feet. Malik stayed in the shadows, remaining still. After a few low, deep breaths, he looked up and down the deserted boulevard before crossing the pavement and making his way to the building.

Malik drifted inside the aluminum door and paused. The stench of death assaulted his senses first, followed by so many other scents tangled together like a kite string in gusty winds that he waited for his nose to adjust. He didn't want to wander in and be blind-sided by a Stryder. The scent of Angelica swept up in a sweet bouquet of painful recollections. Razor sharp thorns encircling Isabeau's image. The picture brought her back alive and vibrant.

Malik's attention turned to memories of Isabeau running free in the meadow filled with Foxgloves and Forget-me-nots, North of the Calia Shore. Isabeau finding a Honeysuckle bloom to push behind her ear, then pulling her waterfall of dark chestnut tresses aside. Even now, Malik remembered her smile and how her scent wafted lazily on the salty ocean breeze.

Bent, Not Broken   3

With blatant reproach, Malik converged on a Stryder standing guard. She stood tall and lanky as if a steel pipe protruded from the earth to hold her in place. Malik advanced in silence and wrapped his arm around her slender neck. With a swift, violent snap he lowered her motionless body to the concrete floor.

"You are already a dead man. Tell me what I need to understand and the end will be quick." A high-pitched laugh permeated the air sending a repulsive shiver racing down Malik's spine. His nerves twisted and tightened while the spark of sweet revenge danced on his tongue.

Malik stared at the man tied to a chair with his head bobbing on his chest. The full length of Trystan's golden hair was soaked with sweat and his skin covered in blisters, burns, and deep cuts. A thick puddle of blood pooled from the stakes driven into his feet to keep him still.

"Let me kill him now." A woman rasped in a ragged, torn voice.

The scent of fresh early morning rain—Trystan's scent—faded into the air.

Anger surged in Malik's veins and fear forced him forward in reckless haste. He stood motionless when Caleb stopped as if his eyes had pinned Malik in place.

"Standing in the shadow is beneath Kindred, is it not? Stop being a coward and face us," Caleb called out.

Without warning, Malik exploded out from the cover of darkness, throwing himself at Caleb.

Vengeance is mine!

An arm caught Malik across his neck sending him to the gritty floor instead.

"Run." The same ragged voice rasped.

Malik whipped around to witness the one man he wanted dead race off into the night. A kick to his chest knocked the air from his lungs. The first punch to his face sent his head into the concrete and she pinned him to the dusty floor.

"It's about damn time." She giggled. Strong fingers grabbed a handful of hair and Malik jerked her to the side. The scent hit him like a knee to the groin. She rolled away from her stunned former friend now lying motionless beside her.

"Fool." The words came at Malik with sharp points.

"You're dead. I…I saw you…I held you…"

"You. Let. Me. Die. And then *he* came for me. Resurrected, I choose to fight for him."

"Isabeau." His head turned away in stunned disgust.

"Did they tell you I radioed in for help? We were overrun and guards were lying dead at my feet. They said they were sending reinforcements. None came to hold the line." She screamed at him.

"When the Stryders found me, what did you think they'd do? I had been a female captain of the Kindred forces. Captured, I became a test subject until he offered me a way out." A ghost of the girl he'd known years before sneered as she spit her words out.

Isabeau flew at him, filled with a fury scalding to Malik's senses and her razor sharp nails dug into his chest. She pushed him backward until a solid surface stopped them dead in their tracks. He threw his head forward, butting her hard enough that she stumbled back. Malik remembered Isabeau was a Boggler and if he fused, she could borrow his abilities and use them against him.

A maroon liquid trickled from Isabeau's nose as she laughed at him. Her eyes paled into a wild purple-black. Her tongue slipped out and lapped the vital fluid from her upper lip.

"Finally." She charged him, her fist catching him in the jaw. Malik jerked too late and his head snapped back.

"You were doing exactly what you wanted to do, Isabeau. You enjoyed the carnage. It is pathetic how you seek justification for your actions. Malik, kill her. She's not Isabeau anymore." Trystan's words raked over Malik's heart.

Malik stepped forward, closing the distance between them.

"You both are fools! They sent us to die. You left me to parish and now I will return the favor." She lunged for Trystan.

Malik interceded. A vicious punch caught her in the back of the head and Isabeau fell face first to the floor.

Bent, Not Broken   5

"You're not the only one to have suffered. You were the only one that turned." Trystan spit the words out.

Malik stood protectively in front of Trystan and stared at Isabeau. His emotions spanning the spectrum.

"All of your blood will run." Isabeau shrieked as she turned to stand and face them. Malik leapt at Isabeau.

She spun around and caught him in the chest with her elbow. Malik hadn't seen the blade but felt it, now buried deep in his thigh. He gulped air as he stumbled down to one knee. Pain spiraled out from the wound.

"Tell Viv and Peyton there are no free passes for them either. I'll see all of you dead before this is over." She turned and fled into the darkness.

The metal door clanked shut and she was gone.

"Poison." Trystan mumbled.

"Don't worry. The Fates prepared me before I left." Malik took out a small jar of honey and applied the contents to the stab wound. The sticky substance felt disgusting, but was an effective cure-all, almost as if it could hold in his vitality.

"Did you know she was alive?" Malik's voice was weak. He forced himself to stand on shaky legs and move closer to Trystan.

"Not until they brought me here. I thought I was hallucinating until she jabbed the spikes through my feet." Trystan's breath was labored. "You should have killed her." The words hung in the room.

"I know." Shaking his head, Malik locked it away somewhere deep inside himself.

"Can you move?" They had kept him bleeding to ensure his weakness. Eventually, he would have bled out. With an injury that could never close, healing was impossible. The spikes holding his feet captive took some time to remove. Trystan collapsed back against the chair once it was finished. Malik fell down beside him, sprawled face-up on the floor.

"What now?" Trystan asked.

"I will take you home."

"And try to track them alone. I'll stay then." Trystan tried to push himself up.

"No. Peyton's expecting you."

"What will you tell Peyton?"

Malik shook his head in response.

"Peyton." Malik called using the telepathic link all Kindreds were connected with.

"Malik." Her voice was hesitant. She sounded in need of good news.

"Trystan and I are on our way home."

"What took so long? You two are supposed to be the bad asses of the group." Her tone was light and happy. Malik hated to imagine the look of despair he was about to put on her face.

"You tell her." Malik looked at Trystan.

"No…Azzure." A soft whisper strayed into the dim glow of the night. Delaney Drake's head turned to lie flat against the wheat colored pillow case. A few more words were spoken through hazy mumbles.

A cold sweat had broken out over Malik's forehead when he slammed back into the present day. He sat frozen while his mind fended off the memories. A heavy sigh of relief and he moved quietly to sit cross-legged on the floor and thumb through the latest books she'd brought home. He cocked his head to one side, his attention drawn back to her. Intent on hearing every word, he listened as she mumbled in that familiar sleepy voice.

In a way, she is talking to me. Or maybe I just let myself believe.

Malik changed the position of his stiff legs and propped himself up against the bed. Briskly, he ran his hand through his hair out of frustration. The ceiling fan sliced the humid air and sent a crisp breeze down on Delaney. She shivered, and instinctively, Malik reached for her oversized comforter and tucked her in gently. He pushed himself up from the floor and walked to the overstuffed bookcase on the left side of the room, tripping over her backpack midway. Her

Anthropology books were stuffed inside and two more sat open on the desk.

"The Mult…alls." Whispering in a sleepy slur.

She stirred and his attention jumped back to her. Delaney's chocolate eyes fluttered open and gazed directly at him. This wasn't the first time she'd caught him watching her.

She never remembers me. That's part of the deal. I have to give her up repeatedly.

"Dream of me, Delaney." Malik spoke softly. Delaney's lips curled slightly up more on one side. A slow, deep breath, and once again sleep came.

Another year passed with him scavenging the shadows for time with her. Malik waited as the days grew tedious. The life he wanted couldn't happen until she'd fused. The possibility of that moment never coming was becoming far too real with each passing year.

The only thing that is growing between us is distance.

His head dipped from the hopelessness of the situation. It had become harder to watch from the sidelines. He wanted to be a part of her life and instead he had become the secret that she had no knowledge of.

I want to be seen, to be remembered. I…miss her.

"Please hurry." Malik whispered.

The alarm would go off soon and the cat and mouse game would continue on for another day.

He exhaled a long, tired sigh and frustration swirled heavy in the room. *It is my own fault, I know that. It is simply too late. I wait for my life to begin with her.*

Chapter TWO

Delaney stopped and listened as fear clawed at her back. Her pulse raced in her ear loud like a sonic boom. The seconds ticked by at a snail's pace while drops of perspiration slid down between her shoulder blades. She perceived her progress to be damn near nonexistent as she crawled within the narrow drainpipes running under the streets of the Vegas strip. Delaney pulled herself through a sea of roaches and her sweat covered skin became an instant buffet for the mosquitoes.

"There are too many Stryders to fight. Run!" The words that sent Delaney scurrying over rocks and chunks of concrete echoed in her mind and refreshed her fear. Her long wet hair smacked the side of her neck as she whipped her head around to confront the darkness swallowing up her surroundings.

How the hell did I get here? The desire to scream raged inside her. She longed to put her hands over her face and pretend none of this was happening, but now wasn't the time. *This is my life, fight or die.*

Delaney pushed through the swirl of emotions and tried to grip another edge to pull herself forward. Her hand slid along the jagged surface, cutting her to the bone. She gasped as pain shot up her arm. The blood on her palms

Bent, Not Broken   9

and runoff water coating the rocks in the drainpipe mixed into an icy slick that rejected her attempts to hurry.

I'm not going to survive this. Fear and frustration surged through her.

Saliva pooled in her mouth and she fought the gag reflux.

Crawl faster, she ordered herself.

A faint glimmer of light emerged through the darkness to guide her out of the tunnel and into the dilapidated concrete wash. She edged a few more paces as the glow of the city fell around her offering a comfort Delaney had at no time imagined would come from living in Vegas.

Delaney sat back on her haunches, exhaled a relieved sigh, and let her arms wrap about her as exhaustion set in. Her eyes fell shut, but she couldn't calm her labored, ragged breaths. She struggled with the urge to cry.

"Who said you could leave the party early?" The Stryder growled in a deep Icelandic tone remitting tremors of panic throughout her body.

Her gaze fell to his military style boots, slowly traveling upward to his calves like Greek columns, thighs like Redwoods, shoulders as wide as an old Cadillac, and his telephone pole-sized neck. She stared up at him until her eyes began to water, too afraid even to blink. *It was already too late to run,* the thought registered like a death sentence. Though her mind raced to find a way out, her limbs remained frozen in place.

A huge brawny hand clasped Delaney's scalp as shivers of fear zigzagged her spine. With a firm handful of hair in his fist, he jerked her up and off the ground dangling her feet over his own. A pain filled scream erupted from her lips, but was cut short by his other hand encasing her throat. Delaney desperately tried to squirm away when their gazes met. Cavernous black sockets with shimmering hues colliding into stunning colors, twirling meteors, and pirouetting comets, as if a supernova exploded where his eyes should have been. She couldn't help but only notice how beautiful those orbs were as his meaty fingers tightened around her neck and the air ceased to flow into her.

Think. The word echoed in Delaney's head while the lack of oxygen took its toll and leopard spots dotted her vision.

"Let's go." His fingers sprang open and Delaney plummeted to the dirt with a heavy thump. She sucked in a mouthful of air and shook her head, clearing away the images that had taken over.

"Get up." He grabbed Delaney's collar and jerked her up to a standing position.

Delaney drove her hand upward, catching him in the chin with the rock her fumbling fingers found on the ground. He stumbled backwards, lost his footing, and dropped his hold on her. Scurrying to her feet, she swung around and fled along the side of the wash. Delaney's tired legs carried her over the rocky landscape toward where Malik had told her not to go, back to the city.

"Fucking bitch!" bellowed the Stryder.

Delaney lost her footing and fell hard against the rocks. She pulled her broken body up and forced wobbly legs to continue moving through the pain. The jagged rubble slowed her.

With a quick jerk of her head, Delaney chanced a glance in the direction she had just raced from. A few feet was all that separated her from the bulky Stryder. They kept coming regardless of how many the Kindreds destroyed. The Stryders were multiplying, an endless supply of hell disguised in a human body.

Her heart sank as she realized there would be no good-bye to Malik. Frustration churned inside her, pulling, tearing, and ripping her apart. Delaney used the fear to propel herself forward that much faster. Her palms stung and her fingernails tore free as she clawed her way up the bank and toward the street. Delaney fought to ignore the pain.

If I falter even one step, he'll have me. Maybe…where I go will in no way matter. Won't they always be waiting for me?

Her eyes darted in search of a place to hide as soon as she crested the edge of the wash. A construction site sat closer than any other buildings. The structure towered over her like a steel giant. Delaney didn't want to think of what followed her a few short yards behind. She fought the shiver rolling down her spine and the fear nipping at her neck.

Where are you? I need you now.

Bent, Not Broken   11

The skeletal foundation swallowed up the yellow streetlights and even the giant neon signs lighting up the night sky. She stared at the enormous concrete walls standing guard, noticing sharp rebar springing from the earth like scarecrows and menacing shadows dancing as she neared. Delaney had no time to rethink her decision as she charged for the metal fencing surrounding the deserted property.

The jagged metallic points ripped at her bloody hands. She pulled her body up, threw her leg over-the-top, and flung herself over to the hard earth on the other side. She landed in a crouch on her feet to absorb the shock of the drop, then leapt up and moved toward WHAT?

"Where do you think you are going?" roared the Stryder from the middle of the street.

The shout stopped her mid-stride. She swung around and saw him barreling straight for her.

"Anywhere but here," she muttered as she continued looking for cover.

I'm alone. She felt like a fist was gripping her insides and tightened just a little more, while a noose cinched snugger around her neck.

Delaney stepped through the opening, darkness enveloping her. She placed her hand on an interior concrete wall and ran shuffling her feet parallel. Continuously moving until she hit a corner, then shifting to the left, she moved farther into the bare rooms of the building. Subtle noises shattered the stillness and echoed, somehow amplified and thundering in her ears. Even the silence was screaming.

A shriek tore through the night sending goose bumps over her skin. It was barely audible to human ears, though undeniable as the distance closed in on her. Her feet stopped moving. She listened hard to every little speck of sound popping up and her hands tightened into fists at her sides.

The Stryders are coming. Trapped. The word flashed like a neon sign, coupled with a dawning realization that a way out was slimming by the breath. Fresh tears filled her eyes and the darkness turned into a blurry mess of kaleidoscope colors.

I'm not ready to die.

A loud growl echoed inside the concrete walls she was navigating. She froze. The snarl thundered so loudly that she lost control of her fear and every rational thought remaining vacated her brain. She would be outnumbered soon.

Panic took over, moving her forward. Blindly stumbling, she reached out but found nothing other than open space. With her arms outstretched in front of her, she advanced. *Shit, the wall.* She didn't know where she was.

What the hell was I thinking? She stood confused in the room. *They could be right next to me before I know they're here.*

Delaney continued walking with her hands spread out until she hit something. She knelt down and leaned against the concrete wall for support. Her fingertips splayed over the rough texture of the barrier near the bottom. The barrier flexed to her touch and a passage way appeared. It was a place to hide and she had nowhere else to go. Her current position was too exposed; the Stryders could find her with no problem.

She lowered herself into an angled shaft. Delaney refused to think about the walls shutting in on her. The passageway continued to narrow until she crept forward on her stomach. Her head became pinned to the side in what couldn't be more than fifteen inches of tight space, and her hipbones ground against the rough unfinished flooring as rocks tore at her exposed torso. Pain seared her senses when something grabbed hold of the back of her scalp as she tried to inch deeper into the shaft. Delaney yanked twice before she became free, pulling out hair and ripping skin. Her skull felt like it had caught on fire. She bit the inside of her check as her nose and eyes burned with tears.

Gunfire erupted somewhere overhead. Delaney waited, focusing every ounce of energy she had left on listening. Muffled angry voices and more firing filled the air.

Whatever barrier had been above her suddenly shifted, allowing Delaney room to crawl on her hands and knees. Her eyes played tricks on her, showing her creamy splashes of speckled color. The darkness magically gave way to the

Bent, Not Broken   13

brilliance of the strip's neon lights and billboards came gloriously into view. Hope sprouted wings and carried her farther.

Immediately, she ran for the shelter of the casino's parking structure and plastered herself up against the rough brick and mortar until the coarse edges scratched her back and shoulders. The hot night air sat still around her as she watched people dressed in flip-flops and multicolored Bermuda shorts amble by with their perspiring beers and half-filled plastic Margarita cups.

Delaney's head pulsated with each movement now. Her fingers gently probed the long gash running the length of her scalp. Blood slowly trickled down her neck and soaked her shirt.

"She couldn't have gotten far. Find her. Alive. No one is leaving until I have the Hynt." A woman spoke from the other side of the concrete pillar, only a few feet away. Delaney's heart fluttered in her chest, knowing her end was closing in.

Hynt. I heard them call my mother the same once. They must think I am going through the change. Delaney couldn't fuse like the rest of her family. She had shown no signs of being anything but human.

She backed up while staying cemented to the rough stucco wall of the parking garage. At no time did her eyes leave the front of the building. She waited for them to simply turn and find her. Though she had not been face to face with Isabeau, Delaney knew she was the women leading the search for her.

Isabeau came for me.

Delaney knew she couldn't stay where she was and combed the area for another way out. She stood as still as a garden statue, watched, and waited for a moment to escape. Sweat trickled down her temples, stringy wisps of blonde hair clung to her forehead.

I have no way out. Maybe…it doesn't matter anyway. Isabeau is in front of me and Stryders are surrounding me on all sides.

The terror was comparable to a physical body pressing against hers, holding her pinned to the wall. She tried not to lose what was left of her mind, but Stryders littered the area like empty beer bottles.

I can't fuse as my family would. I'm different, I have no disguise. Where are you? She wanted to scream her question until he heard her.

Delaney's head pulsated as her heart pumped erratically. Her eyesight twisted and she kept trying to blink the blurriness away. Her hands shook and her knees wobbled; she tried to get herself under some control.

He will find me. That is all he does.

The telepathic link between them had been forged for this reason. But tonight he had whispered for her to stay silent no matter what. Without the ability to Drift from one place to another he would be seen and have no way to locate her position.

He said the Stryders could reach her before he did, and may have meant Isabeau would be able to track her through the link because she too had been Kindred once.

Delaney took a deep breath and tried to think. She wasn't ready to give up. She scanned her surroundings, exhaling the potent frustration. The next building was at least a hundred yards to the right. She would have to run on her bum leg, but had no choice.

A hand snaked out to shut around her mouth. Delaney frantically tried to jerk free as adrenaline shot through her anew. A scream rose up in her throat, then she saw him.

You're here.

She immediately stopped struggling as depthless hunter green eyes stared down into hers. His gaze swept across her face, changing the look on his own to that of relief. He leaned in close, his warm breath danced along her lips. The fight drained from Delaney's body as tears scored her cheeks. She nodded her head in understanding as his fingers brushed them aside. Malik drew her in until her forehead rested against his chest. He exhaled a haggard breath as her fears sliced clean through him.

Malik's hand fell from her waist and he motioned for her to follow him. He rounded the corner of the building and they broke into a jog, running straight for the parking garage lower levels. They climbed over the half wall barriers and landed on the first floor.

Malik pulled every car door handle they passed.

His head felt as if it were being pulled in two, while his shoulder burned from the poison making its way through his body. Within an hour the toxin would overtake him. The accelerated healing of a Kindred still took time. Their only hope was to run.

Finally, the door of a white Toyota sprang open. He pushed Delaney over to the passenger seat, climbed in, and started the truck. They sped off into the night, the threats falling away behind them.

We're safe, for the moment. Malik refused to let his guard down, though. He knew there was no real secure place for her. They drove in silence for a few minutes before Malik turned into an empty parking lot and slammed on the breaks.

"Delaney, are you okay?" His voice strained as he pulled her into his lap. His lips found hers and he pressed her torso into his.

He smelled and tasted of sweet cinnamon. She drew nearer still. Shock kept her body rigid until his tongue snaked out and ran across her lower lip. Delaney's mouth opened to him as she slipped her fingers into his hair, pulling him closer, burrowing into him until he wrapped around her. She wanted more, needed all of him. She grappled for life after being so near death.

He had to make her run and it hadn't come to that before. The fierce grip on his chest only drove the point further home.

"I'm sorry I had to leave you." Malik's hands lingered on her lower back.

"She's here. Isabeau is in Vegas. She searches for me."

"You saw her?" His face drained of color.

"She was looking for me. Not the others, just me." Delaney trembled violently.

His hand gently pulled her mouth closer to his.

"Ouch. My head…it's cut," she said, jerking away. "They won't stop trying to kill me, will they?" Delaney pulled back until her spine hit the steering wheel.

Reality set in. *Malik and I were never to have a happy ending. It's hopeless to want him so much. Yet, that does not matter. He is everything.*

"No." That simple answer destroyed her hopes of a future with him. *My heart...*

"Are they going to send me away?" A tedious and horrible silence followed, one that answered Delaney's question long before he spoke.

Malik didn't want to lie to her. She couldn't stay. The Stryders would find her.

Delaney tried to smile at him. None of this was his fault.

"Yes." The word escaped as a whisper. His hands fell away from her.

It took every ounce of Delaney's courage to raise her eyes and meet his. "My love." She mouthed the words to him. Malik's image blurred as tears clouded her vision. *Borrowed time is all we ever have.* The realization burned through her.

"We could run," she pleaded. She knew that idea to be impossible. The answer already something understood between them.

Malik's face drifted, wavered, and shimmered on the edges of her mind. Delaney tried but lost her hold on him as her dream fell away. She reached out her hand only skimming the murky surface and then he disappeared, replaced by the morning light creeping into her room.

Delaney grew cold from the absence of his body wrapped around her in the dream. She bit on her lower lip nervously and stared at the glow-in-the-dark ceiling constellation, which had comforted her more than once when she awoke from a nightmare during the past four years. Nothing made the loneliness better. Tears slid down the sides of her face, soaking into the pillow. The weight on her chest flattened her until she felt paper-thin against her mattress. Pushing herself up took all of her strength. The dreams made her heartache and her throat burned from holding back the rush of emotions brewing in every cell.

Delaney sat still, one leg stuffed underneath her and the other dangled off the bed. Her head drew to the side as if pulled by a steel rod. Over the last few years, she had been drawn to that one corner in her room. A simple wall and nothing more, yet...

Bent, Not Broken   17

On any given morning, Delaney was normally up and going, but today a puzzled feeling and a long stretch took precedence before she could roll out of bed. She looked around the room, tears still wet on her cheeks. Her heavy stare pinned him in place. She couldn't find him, the action itself unintentional.

Delaney sat on the end of the bed and stared at the bend in the wall, right at him. Her body shuttered as she inhaled and tried to shake the sadness away.

It was wrong to hope; he had arrived at that conclusion long ago. But he couldn't stop himself from grasping for the lifeline. He leaned back, surveying her struggle with herself. Her head shifted to the right, eyes squinting as she tried to discover a truth that had never been intended to become real.

She had no reason to notice him. But she did, on some level she comprehended the fact even before she realized what that meant. Delaney shivered in response. *I know, or maybe I am crazy and just need him to be real.*

Delaney had affectionately begun referring to her sense of never being alone as her guardian angel's presence. She could smell it once more; the sweet cinnamon scent unmistakable. She let her head fall into one hand while the other ran through her wavy blonde hair. He had been haunting her dreams again, making her race to bed each night just to see him, to live a few beautiful hours with him.

Most of the time the dreamy moments happened like last night, horrific nightmares. Her heart took to flight as her mind faded into a deep sleep anyway. She lived another life just beyond her wakefulness. One she hated to leave for long. But she abhorred the dreams too for how much she wanted to stay with him. She longed for what she couldn't explained.

Delaney pushed herself up, her Scooby boxers hanging low on her hips as she yawned and pulled her tank top off over her head.

Malik turned around defeated. His arms fell like driftwood at his sides while he tried to concentrate on something, anything, else. The vivid memories had become medieval torture devices, tearing at his flesh and ripping his insides apart. He drifted downstairs to check on the others rather than subject himself to anymore torment.

"Tryst, we're leaving in ten. Peyton takes Point." He spoke through the cerebral link to the other Kindred's. Trystan and Peyton would keep the residence secure while he and Bowe were gone.

"Copy," Trystan replied in link-speak.

"Copy that," Peyton returned.

"Viv and I are ready," Bowe answered.

Delaney slipped into running clothes folded on the oak chest at the bottom of the bed. She took great care laying them out the night before. To be late would spoil everything. Then again, her mom standing by the door waiting for her was a motivating image in the back of Delaney's head.

Running had become a good thing for Delaney. The activity kept things in their proper perspective. She needed the yellow, straight, defined lines in her life to keep the focus. Without the balance she reeled out of control from the depression and the mood swings. Those lemon colored dashes were easy to follow, no brain required. Delaney fiercely held up the façade of being normal when she ran. The only time of day her head emptied and she felt free and independent. Delaney chose the pace, the distance, and the direction. She controlled the moment.

The therapists referred to her condition as a result of Post-traumatic Stress Disorder. Her childhood had been horrible enough that she had blocked much of it out. Hating being in the state system, pretending to be someone else had become a small price to pay to wake up in her own bed, alone and unafraid of what had been happening to her. When everything around her spiraled out of control and chaos prevailed, she ran. It soothed the nervousness, anxiety, and depression.

Delaney appeared downstairs a couple of minutes later, ready to jog like most days with her foster mom, and unknowingly, with Bowe and Malik trailing behind them.

Malik stretched out his muscles with the first few steps, then the foursome fell into a driving pace. He caught himself watching Delaney as the crisp morning air stung his throat and her legs powered her petite body in perfect form. He shook the desire off; he couldn't afford to get distracted by her.

"Mom." Delany spoke between broken breaths.

Vivianna pulled down her headphones. "You okay?"

They both slowed their pace to a quick walk.

"Have you and Dad talked about the trip?"

Delaney had been asked to be a research assistant to the department head she had a crush on. She had spoken none stop for the last few weeks about her professor.

Bowe and Malik exchanged concerned glances. *No way Delaney goes anywhere near Turkey,* Malik thought to himself.

"We're weighing the options." Viv spoke while shrugging her slender shoulders and averting her eyes.

"Brody and Daphne have both been on digs. This isn't any different. It's only for one semester. This is such a great opportunity because sophomores are never asked to do these things. It means everything to me, please." She had resorted to begging and didn't care.

"We're discussing it." Viv stopped while the words evaporated right out of her mouth, then put a possessive arm around Delaney's shoulder, pulling her closer. Viv took in a long, slow deep breath.

The hair stood up on the back of Delaney's neck. Awareness of the situation struck her: something was wrong.

"Delaney, let's cut this short for today." Viv eyed two men standing on the corner.

"Do you know them?" Delaney asked while touching Viv's arm, trying to force her attention back to her. Viv didn't acknowledge she was speaking.

A shiver of fear crept along Delaney's spine. The two homeless guys stared at them with odd expressions on their faces. *The men are sizing us up.*

"What's wrong?" Delaney tried to sound normal.

Malik couldn't shake the apprehension that had been tugging at him most of the morning. The reason was now clear; the Stryders had been tracking them.

"Mom?" Fear touched her tone as she grabbed for Viv's hand. "Let's go."

"You're right, let's go." Viv never looked away from the two men.

"Corner of Buffalo and Desert Inn, twenty yards from the light, southwest side. Flynn and Peyton are to intercept. Still moving." Malik link-spoke to the others.

Delaney wouldn't be able to perceive the Stryders for what they were. She saw two grungy looking homeless guys you cross the street to get away from. Until she fused, they would appear like all the other humans. After her corneas split and the pupil reshaped, the lens would finally allow in the truth.

Delaney squinted at the two bums.

Malik realized she suspected something about them, her instincts reacted to them. She sensed him, had looked right at him, or where he'd be if she was able to perceive him. A cord had struck in Delaney, an alertness to the other side. The understanding floundered within her, but the last few years, perception grew. She referred to him as her advocating angel. She was half right. Malik doubted anyone who encountered him, even by reputation, would associate him with a celestial being.

Delaney wasn't aware of any of them. She didn't have any knowledge of a guardian standing by her twenty four hours a day. Whatever she did learn had been swiftly taken from her and stolen from Malik.

Viv and Delaney began running up the road again. After a few minutes, Viv increased the pace, then crossed into Delaney's line and drove her to the left down a side street before pouring on the speed again.

The woman can sprint all day. Delaney gulped air and fought to keep up.

"Redirect westbound on Darby," Malik link-spoke.

Viv pushed Delaney in front, forcing her to take first position. The look on Viv's face told him she understood they were right behind them.

Bowe forced Viv to break left with Delaney as a Stryder bared down on them from ahead. Malik exploded forward hitting it in the throat with an outstretched arm. The contact with the Stryder stung his flesh. It was a Copathia. The skin was capable of being acidic, secreting at will.

Bent, Not Broken 21

The strike knocked the Stryder hard to the ground. Malik swiveled to the side as he sprang back up to his feet. Pivoting around, he stood smiling at Malik. The Stryder charged forward catching Malik square in the chin, knocking him backwards a couple of steps, and burning his cheek in the process.

Malik drew a dagger and sliced to the right, then quickly to the left. Finally, making contact on the second try. Malik turned and caught the fighter with a kick to the leg. The action knocked the Stryder off balance. Malik wrapped one arm around his forehead ignoring the sizzling pain of his own skin. Malik pulled back hard and slashed at the Shimmer with the dagger. Before drifting closer to home, he stashed the body to be dealt with later.

Peyton and Flynn took perimeter, running parallel to Viv. Bowe ran next to Delaney while Malik trailed just behind making sure the Stryders had lost their nerve…at least for now.

"Run, Delaney!" The words were wasted on Delaney as she pushed herself just to continue at the same punishing pace. When she finally got into view of their home, Delaney's lungs were burning and her throat was on fire. Breathless, she reached the driveway, glanced over at Viv, and threw up at her feet.

"What the hell was that?" Delaney wiped her mouth. "Who was coming?" She was barely getting the words out as she gulped for air.

"I thought those men were following us."

"Oh, so what, you wanted to run me to death before they had a chance to run me down?" Delaney wondered if Viv was a bigger danger than the two homeless-looking guys searching for a frosty forty ouncer to split.

Walking in the house, still irritated and on shaky legs, Delaney hurried to her room. A dawning awareness continued to haunt her with each step. She sensed that her day had started out crazy for a reason and there was still more to come.

She wasn't sure what the cognizance referred to; it felt ominous, though, and her gut was one thing she trusted. Delaney's heart made all sorts of stupid mistakes, but her intuition was reasonably dependable.

"Malik, Darby, and Cohen. Stryders are still in play." Flynn's voice boomed in his head.

"Copy that." He Drifted into the shadows, coming instantly to the corner and entering the fight at a dead run.

Flynn pursued two retreating Stryders on foot.

Mia and Thistle had their hands full with four Stryders and a Hollower, only two were slated on the ground. Peyton grabbed one and snapped his neck. Before another had the opportunity to escape, she was on him. As the other three began to advance, Malik waited. Three against one was stupid—one man doesn't win a fight so outnumbered. Instead, it became a battle of wits and distraction.

"Hey." Peyton stood next to him. "He got blood all over my hand. It takes forever to get the nauseating smell off," she said.

The middle one broke rank, pulling out a hunting blade and heading straight for Malik. Peyton took the one nearest to her. The whistling sound was a five-inch lance slicing through the air just off the right side of Malik's body. The Stryder was throwing crazy punches and waving the point around. When he came at Malik with the weapon, Malik leaned into the Stryder, using his own weight and the Stryder's forward momentum to knock him off balance. Malik grabbed his fixed blade and threw it, hitting the third one square in the chest. Stumbling back and down to one knee, his target collapsed, still and leaking blood all over the black top.

From out of nowhere a blow to Malik's face spun him around and off balance as the bones in his jaw shattered. He lost his footing and staggered backward. Malik saw only colorful shooting stars, then received a kick to his side. The wind was knocked from his lungs as he landed on his back. He sprang up to his feet and faced the Stryder he hadn't seen advancing on him. Already in the process of another hard kick to his torso, Malik spun around with the Stryder's foot clenched in both of his hands. By using the momentum he created, Malik pulled him into a head butt, then let go and the Stryder stumbled back. The

Bent, Not Broken

action bought Malik enough time to come at him hard with a viscous right and a heavy left punch to the head. Once he went down on his knee, Malik stepped into position behind him and snapped his neck.

The four Kindreds gathered up the bodies and stashed them beside a vacant house until a team of Roq's could be contacted to dispose of them properly.

Chapter THREE

Finger combing her long, wet and tangled hair after her shower, Delaney wandered from the bathroom ready to attack the rest of the day ahead.

On the way down the stairs, she realized the morning's run shredded her leg muscles and some of the wind leaked from her sails. She took each step at a slower, more careful pace. Something important picked at her mind. The idea tickled her brain, words perched on her tongue, and disappeared before she grabbed a hold of them.

"Even my butt hurts. The woman is trying to kill me." Her muffled voice echoed off the quiet hallway walls. Subconsciously hushing herself, so as not to wake the rest of the still sleeping household, she yawned and straggled down the staircase.

She loved crawling out of bed early when everyone but her parents slept. While her siblings weren't present, there wasn't any need for pretenses. She was free to shuffle along without having to worry about how she acted or who may have been watching. Maintaining appearances was exhausting; Delaney attested to that fact every day.

Quiet murmurs reached her as she rounded the corner into the kitchen.

Bent, Not Broken   25

Surprised by only finding her mother and father discussing something in muted ones, Delaney searched the area for the voice she hadn't recognized.

"Stryd…" Vivianna fell silent when she realized Delaney stood behind her.

"Where is the intern?" Delaney inquired. "Did he already leave?" Two pairs of eyes found her. Their weight caused her to clam-up. An uncomfortable silence stretched through the room as her foot falls stopped and she met her father's gaze.

"Intern?" Bannan's brow drew together in obvious confusion.

"I thought I heard another guy's voice." Delaney shrugged, continued into the kitchen, then stood staring into the open doors of the refrigerator.

"Oh, yes. Your father needed some papers from school." Vivianna chirped in an awkward tone, then offering Delaney an empty plate, said, "Scrambled eggs, bacon, and toast?"

"How was your jog?" Bannan asked as he dropped a kiss on his daughter's forehead.

"Mom's training for the Olympics, didn't she tell you?" Sarcasm filtered through her words. She closed the fridge doors, joined them standing around the kitchen island, and accepted the plate but set it down.

Vivianna rolled her eyes and a smirk kidnapped the frown that only moments before rested on her face. "I'm going to take a shower." Viv smiled warmly at Bannan. "Sorry about the run. Tomorrow?" She raised an eyebrow to Delaney before exiting the room.

"Yeah. Hey, want to bring guns with us? That ought to make things more interesting." Delaney offered a sheepish grin.

Her hardy appetite floundered as her thoughts took over.

I live in a vacuum; I can't get away from myself.

Delaney lived inside her head and when it proved too much, she fought overwhelming sadness and lost often. Her eyes swam with tears regularly and she wasn't sure why. She considered going to see Dr. Brendt. Delaney felt her life.

Lately, I'm seeing things, hearing voices I assume are figments of my imagination, and most of the time I forget more than I remember.

Delaney daydreamed of herself with people she'd never met, and they seemed to be memories rather than a result of her overactive imagination.

I can't tell what's real and what's just living inside my head. Perhaps there's no fixing me. I am permanently, broken.

As long as Delaney took her meds, life was livable. She functioned, yet hid everything going on within her. She didn't want anyone to figure out how close to the edge she really was. Or how badly she wanted to plummet off most of the time.

"Are you ready?" Calliope asked, nearly colliding with Bannan as he exited the room. Calliope grabbed a bottle of orange juice and filled a plate.

Delaney studied her rail-thin sister throw down a plateful of food with an expression of envy. She never worked out or ran and her body didn't seem to require any discipline. If Delaney, on the other hand, ate like Calliope and failed to go running, she'd duct tape herself to a treadmill with nothing but water for six months.

"I want to know who your birth parents were." Delaney glanced sideways at her sister.

Calliope cracked a smile and kept eating. "What are you doing to yourself?" She pointed to Delaney's arm.

While Delaney contemplated life in her head, she managed to scratch her arms until the scrapes became red and puffy. She could guess why she'd done it, but she hadn't realized what she'd been doing at the time.

Even college hadn't been the distraction she hoped for when her quirks reared their ugly little heads. The classroom time emphasized her inept societal skills. Until she came to live at the Drake's, Delaney purposefully had been an outcast. Foster homes weren't the best place to be a social butterfly; she busied herself trying to be forgotten.

"Ready?" Calliope asked as Delaney stood up.

"I'm telling you, they're not going to let you go. The trip is over spring vacation and you know how much the whole family thing means to them, especially when we can all spend time together." Calliope spoke as she buckled up in the passenger seat.

"I will be back within one month. You have to help me. I want to go." Delaney replied. She was hoping an amazing plan would pop into her head on the drive to class.

"Stop scratching your arms. You look like you're having an allergic reaction to life." Delaney threw a contemptible glance Calliope's way.

"What do you want me to do, call Santa? You might as well just resign to being here and forget it," she said, slipping Delaney a sincere sideways glance.

"Can't they understand what this means to me?" *It wasn't as if I had been about to pull up stakes and move to Turkey.*

She just wanted to have an extended visit, which included on-the-job training with a certain brilliant and good-looking professor. A month of freedom in a foreign country surrounded by ancient ruins, her mind whirled in anticipation.

Delaney wanted to be an archeologist/anthropologist. She wanted to work with American Indian, Eskimo, Meso American, and South American civilizations. The indigenous population had such similar qualities and characteristics and she believed what she could learn from them might answer many questions.

Delaney could go. She was an adult, but working on a dual degree took up all of her time. The only thing she did besides school was work three shifts a week at the Stinky Sweet. College tuition might not be her immediate problem, a scholarship helped. Living expenses, however, presented an interesting dilemma. Without Mom and Dad's help, affording to live in general would be difficult.

When Calliope and Delaney finally turned up Fort Apache Road, Delaney's thoughts pushed to the day ahead. She exhaled a deep, almost relaxing breath and resigned to having a good morning 'one-way or another' just as her head collided with the driver's side window.

"Time to go, we get second." Peyton link-spoke. Delaney and Calliope would be leaving for school soon. Trystan and Flynn rode in the first car while Peyton and Malik followed.

They patrolled in an Audi TTS Roadster, which Peyton drove as fast as inhumanly possible.

"Not crazy today, I think I have broken ribs." Malik mumbled through a breathless haze of pain.

"Trystan, dark grey Dodge Charger changing lanes fast, on your six, in three, two, one." Peyton jammed the stick into third and roared forward as Malik pressed himself into the seat hoping for some stability.

From the left side, Peyton crossed the multiple lanes of traffic to sit right beside the Dodge. The Charger sprang forth at the same moment. A direct route between Malik and the X-Terra had been shut tight. Peyton hammered down on the breaks hard, tossing them into the dashboard while the Audi fishtailed with the sudden loss of action. The tires squealed as the gas pedal was mashed to the floor. She threw the gearshift into second and they flew forward again, cutting off the Charger and sliding in between the two cars.

"Don't mess with German Engineering." She smiled and put her arm in front of Malik, gave him a quick wink, and slammed on the breaks. The action forced the Charger to crash into their trunk.

The impact tore the back of the car off just behind the seats. They fishtailed as Peyton tried to regain control. Malik wasn't sure what the hell had hit them. Peyton cranked on the wheel trying to even them out, but with no rear tires, it was hopeless.

"Back up eliminated. We're on foot, will intercede in twenty." Peyton connected with Fezz over her com link. She struggled to slow the torn up car to a stop. They exited what was left of the vehicle and moved to intercept Trystan.

Fezz relayed the information to Trystan. He knew he had to get the X-terra stopped for Malik and Peyton to drift in. Kindred's couldn't drift into a mobile transport; there was no way to anchor them to a moving object other than to hope to land on top.

"We're holding. Maybe a minute before the Stryders over take us." Trystan spoke calmly.

Peyton and Malik hastened their steps to catch up with the yellow SUV.

Chapter FOUR

Smack! Pain shot through the left side of Delaney's skull and wrapped around to engulf her head. Out of the corner of her eye she caught a glimpse of a tall man and a pretty Asian woman heading straight for their car at a dead run.

Delaney's eyes locked on the stranger. An odd familiarity about him struck her.

Calliope's hands gripped the wheel and cranked hard to the right. Delaney's foot slammed on the brake out of instinct.

Calliope yelled something at Delaney, but the words flew by unheard. Her eyes stayed glued to the man now only a few feet away, running full throttle directly toward her. He charged the driver's side door, increasing his momentum with each stride.

A small grin pulled at her lips. She sat gawking at him as the same smile tugged at his. "He's…." Then he was next to her. His foot came down hard on hers punching the gas pedal all the way to the floor. The tires screeched and Delaney's body was thrown back against the seat. She grabbed the steering wheel and tried to regain control over as they shot out into traffic.

Bent, Not Broken   31

"Who the hell are you?" she roared at him. He had slid right through her, by way of a solid metal door, to end up sitting in the center of the car, his broad shoulders pushed her body flush against the door, and her head again smacked the window. Half of his big body fell into both seats forcing Calliope over and down into the foot rest area.

Delaney's mind buzzed like a beehive.

Three resounding shots broke up the chaos. The image in the driver's side mirror disintegrated as yellow fibers pulled free of the car and the polished metal plummeted to the road. Two more loud pops and the back window cracked into a giant spider web of tangled, sharp edges.

"My foot. You're breaking my toes!" Delaney cried. "Slow down. Why are we being shot at?"

The hulk of a man scrunched between her drink holder and the roof of her Xterra after appearing out of thin air had knocked Delaney for a loop. Bullets zigzagged into and around the vehicle. To her, the situation seemed surreal, then she glanced in the rearview mirror and received yet another shock. Two people she'd never seen before were staring back at her while a third Asian woman fired her gun out the rear window.

"We have at least three moving threats coming right at you." Leaestra link-spoke hurriedly. More guards would be en route to help. The cerebral connection linking all Kindreds helped expedite coordinated offense and defensive fronts.

"We're sending back up. Will contact with updates." Fezz added.

"In motion with Spyder." Ptah confirmed.

"I will meet up with you two." Flynn informed Ptah.

Delaney peaked into the backseat through the rearview mirror. A Hollywood gorgeous guy tossed Delaney a drop-dead smile before he melted into the fabric of the seat and vanished. She blinked a couple of times, but he disappeared right before her eyes.

"What the hell?" she murmured. She caught sight of another man firing his gun out the other window as his long hair rode the incoming breeze.

"Dispatched Mia and Thistle in the Audi, Thane and Saffron are in the convertible." Leaestra relayed.

"Two Chargers and a Cherokee coming up fast." Peyton confirmed from the backseat. "Get us out of here." Peyton yelled.

"Trying to." Malik answered.

"We need immediate back up." Trystan relayed to Fezz. Leaestra and Fezz had their hands full running the home office. Fezz sent new GPS coordinates as he rerouted everyone to rendezvous with the X-terra.

"Stay on Desert Inn until Hualapai. Back up with intercept at the corner. Hold." Fezz said. The intercom link made their lives easier to have an instant messaging system chipped directly into their ears, but damn it became annoying when too many people wanted to be understood all at the same time.

"You gotta move." Malik mumbled to Delaney. He grabbed her and tried to trade places with her. His fingers swallowed hers as he realized his bulk and the space in the car wouldn't allow them to swap positions. She would have to drive.

"Look, if you don't keep the pedal floored, we're all dead. Okay?" Delaney numbly shook her head in faint understanding. Her eyes should have been on traffic, but she couldn't pull them away from his face.

They sped along the busy streets while Fezz worked on making sure they only encountered green lights as they raced to get out of the city intact.

"Fezz, I need back up now." Malik realized Delaney had become privy to every word of his conversation. He had no time to worry about cloaking his voice, not until they were at least clear of the immediate threat.

"How do I know you?" Delaney asked him when he glanced at her once more. He froze in place as a flicker of surprise flashed through him. He stopped as shock overtook his worried expression. His eyes searched her face.

"You shouldn't remember." For the briefest of moments, Malik moved forward. It had been so long since he had been able to reach for her.

Delaney thought he may kiss her. And the crazy thing about it, she wanted him to.

"Fezz, call Trenton. No more delays." Malik was barking out.

Devastatingly beautiful and a complete nut. What a perplexing combination.

Delaney's grip tightened on the steering wheel as her head swung around and she faced Calliope.

'How the hell do I get us out of this?' Delaney's brain raced.

"You can have the car just pull over and drop us off. You don't need my sister. At least let her go. I'll drive you wherever you want."

"We're here for the two of you." Malik chanced a glance at Delaney. "Calliope, get down." He pushed her forward and moved farther over into her seat.

Delaney's mind was reeling, and then it hit her.

How did he know my sister's name?

"Delaney, follow Sahara find Red Rock Canyon." She shook her head again.

Was that where they were going to leave our bodies? Delaney's thoughts raced faster than the car. *Had he said my name too?* She couldn't remember.

"What's happening?" Delaney's voice shook. She trembled as the battle of losing her calm exterior slipped right through the cracks.

"I'll explain later." Malik tried to reassure her. He understood that Delaney had to be terrified. Strangers with guns had invaded her car. She had no idea who they were, and worse, she didn't understand the significance of the situation.

Delaney's head pounded with each word he spoke. Her fingertips burned while the hair on her arms stood on end. A swift wave of dizziness threatened and bile crested her throat. The yellow lines began to wiggle before her eyes increasing the need to vomit. It became harder to breath with each passing moment. Delaney eased her foot gently off the gas pedal just enough to slow down but not to be immediately noticed. She glanced up to see if she had given herself away.

Delaney's eyes met a huge snarling grizzly bear, stretching and pulling right out of the man's chest. Delaney blinked. On, or rather in, his torso roared a living breathing tattoo as it sparked to life. The animal bared his teeth as he looked around, and its topaz gaze filled with rage as the head of his massive body struggled to get free. The air caught in her throat as she stared unmoving at him.

"What the f...?" Her eyes grew large and disbelief shadowed her face. She gaped at him in obvious awe.

Malik had let his emotions take over and now the grizzly bear in his chest wanted out. The image had been dancing under his skin, the burn unmistakable. He hadn't realized the beast had already half freed itself from his cage. Malik jerked his shirt to cover himself.

"I told you to keep it floored. Are you trying to get us all killed?" He threw his leg over the center console and jammed his foot on top of hers. They shot forward racing towards the desert once more.

"You're...bear." Delaney struggled to find the words. She sat clutching the steering wheel with a vise grip, stunned into silence, and her head stared straight ahead.

"You're clear." Leaestra said.

"You can slow down now." Malik spoke softly to her. The confused expression on her face reminded him how little she understood about her own life.

"Delaney, head home." Malik let her name fall slowly from his lips. He spoke as he climbed into the backseat. Her eyes met his and immediately his brow furrowed as his mouth tightened into a hardline. She held his gaze for a moment longer before the road forced them apart. She scanned the rearview mirror and studied him briefly in between navigating through traffic.

"How do you know my name? Who are you?" Delaney demanded in a shaky voice.

"Flynn, drift to Blue Diamond. We'll pick you up there." Malik climbed over the seat to sit next to Peyton and Tryst while he link-spoke with the others.

"Stryders are more active than normal, not even noon and they have attacked twice." Peyton spoke while staring straight ahead.

"It isn't over yet. They want Delaney now."

"Why do you think Delaney over Calliope or Viv?" Trystan asked.

"She is the common denominator for both attacks. We missed something, she must be close. Either that or…" Malik's thoughts took over. "Is it possible they could force her to transition? What else would be used to trigger the transformation other than puberty?"

"Like…adrenaline or a hormone of some sort? That would make sense. Something triggers the change in all of us. Perhaps the Stryders are tired of waiting." Peyton sighed.

Without a word, Trystan and Malik dropped the touchy subject. Until more information came into their hands, they relied on a hypothetical that had no foundation. His thoughts shot two remarkably different emotions through Malik. Fear, because not understanding what the hell is going on sucks. The other was hope. The idea alone that their time apart had a chance of coming to an end elated him.

"Trenton sent three more teams. They're at the Drake's settling in." Flynn announced.

The ride continued in silence. Delaney would check the rearview mirror every so often, her eyes always settled on him. The Fates had been more than competent; Delaney had no retrospection of any of them. It saddened him to think about how much he'd lost.

"We're okay, don't worry." Delaney spoke in a tender quiet voice to Calliope.

"I know." Calliope replied.

"What?" Delaney sounded astonished.

"It will be okay, Delaney. They would never hurt us." Calliope's hand fell down to her forearm.

"How the hell do you know that?" Delaney blew out a haggard breath.

"It's their job to make sure we are safe. They will die for us if they have to."

"What does that mean?" Delaney shook her head trying to clear it. When she glanced back to check on her three passengers, she found that a heated gaze met hers as she studied the backseat. Liquid green pools holding hers so completely she would forget to breathe.

"Delaney, are you okay?" Malik glanced up.

"Fine. Why?" Sarcasm soaked every word as she eyed him in the mirror through angry slits.

"You just drove past your house." A small smile crossed his mouth.

"Great." Delaney murmured as she flipped a U-turn and headed back home.

"Don't worry. Mom and Dad will explain everything." Calliope squeezed her hand.

"Oh, I can't wait to hear this one." Delaney muttered.

"Fezz, ETA three minutes." Malik had gone back to cloaking his voice. Delaney had experienced more than enough for one day.

When Delaney pulled into the garage, people she had never seen before lurked in every corner. Delaney appeared lost as she sat in her seat still clutching the wheel. *What the hell are we involved with?*

"Perimeter reports with twenty minute intervals, Fezz. Send two teams to sweep surrounding neighborhoods. I want to know where they are." Malik demanded as he noticed Delaney's form still in the car, her eyes focused straight ahead while the confused expression on her face screamed volumes.

Malik knocked on the driver's side window to get her attention. Delaney nearly jumped out of her skin. Her eyeballs were as big as silver dollars.

The thought that her memories could remain suspended in a safe place until she had the tools to deal with them comforted Malik. The Fates would see to it with one simple touch.

Delaney whipped her head around to meet his and her brain began to swim. An image formed in the recess of her mind, of the two of them in a passionate embrace. Just as quickly as the picture came, it vanished.

I know you.

Her skin warmed from the lifelike illustration. Specific mannerisms and the fact that he almost kissed her felt familiar and she couldn't explain why. *They're dreams,* she told herself in a hollow voice that held no conviction at all.

His fingers motioned for her to exit the vehicle, but she just sat still staring at him. The blank stare reflected how far she had receded into herself. Not wanting to spook her any more than he already had, he slowly lifted the handle and let the door swing open. He held out his hand to help her from the car.

She stared at his outstretched palm as if at any moment it would bite her, and still didn't move.

"Come on." His voice carefully reached out and soothed her. Delaney landed on wobbly legs, falling forward into him and her hands grasped at his chest. His arms encircled her without considering the aftermath of the action. Fire pooled in her belly as her fingers clenched his shirt. She couldn't breathe and her eyes flew up to his face. The way he stared at her, *no one has ever taken the time to look at me like that.*

For Malik they had never left the cave. *Those three days. Why couldn't we just go back to those three days?*

Her body laid limp in my arms. Delaney had fallen, hitting her head on the way to the bottom. As her mind cleared, she began to remember pieces of her past. Those memories should have been locked up tight in her subconscious.

Out of the blue, she stared up at me and said my name. The moments stretched around us like a cocoon. I pulled her closer into me; her hair smelled of coconuts and limes.

I realized too late what she meant to do. Her hands fisted my hair. I stared into wondrous hot chocolate eyes and my mouth crashed against hers. Her lips responded and things traveled farther and faster than I had intended. The sparks turned into a blaze before reason could win out.

The moment shattered in his reality. The bustle of where he stood drew him back.

The memories brought such pain, such pleasure, they had become hard to face when he realized those hijacked hours might be all he has left.

I just want to keep her this time.

The idea of telling Dane, Viv, and Bannan everything had even begun to appeal to me. We would be together despite the wrath of her family and the counsel. I might have had something tangible. At the present, I had empty memories that

I could share with no one. I have nothing of her.

Delaney starred at him. He had rugged handsome features until his eyes. A tenderness mingling in the tiny flecks of jade softened him somehow.

Delaney's limbs refused to move and the only thing she had become aware of was when he looked at her.

Everything in my world is aligned. I'm safe with you.

"Let me help you." The way Malik was touching Delaney was more intimate than he meant it to be. It felt right to allow his fingers to linger on her curves.

It has been so long....

He led Delaney into the house as if he had been there a hundred times before. His hands stayed on her, his fingers splayed across the small of her back, the possessive gesture sent a warming sensation flooding through her.

There is something about you, something beautiful and dangerous.

Delaney's breath caught in her throat and her unsure footsteps faltered as she tried to speak. Her mind fell into chaos.

The next course of action Malik had performed seven times to date. When Delaney was twelve, they had to take safeguards. The Fate replaced her memories with those of an adopted child's to explain how young Viv and Bannan appeared. Again at fourteen, when Calliope was attacked at school and Delaney ended up in the crossfire.

Seventeen was the first time I lost her. Twice when she was eighteen I had to give her up again. On two occasions this year already. Soon she would turn twenty and I fear that will mean more waiting.

"Viv, she's here." He spoke while following Delaney into the kitchen. A part of him demanded they not bind her this time. Even knowing all the reasons they had to. He needed them to let her mind heal. *Let her return to me.*

How much he wanted her back sucked the life right out of him. To sit by and watch her every day. Every day he was faced with seeing her and knowing what it felt like to run his fingertips across her hips. A knife in the stomach would have been kinder than being ignored and forgotten.

Delaney overlooked him countless times a day. Right now, he meant nothing to her.

If this war claims me, she may never remember me, remember us. With no memory of how well we fit together. A blazing fire ignited by the simple glances between us. All will be lost.

Viv turned around and smiled at Delaney, though her brow furrowed and her hands were clenching furiously in front of her.

"You okay?" her mother asked as an older and worn-to-the-bone woman stepped into the room.

"This is Josslyn Roaring-Water," her mom gestured to the frail form beside her.

"Delaney, I am most pleased to see you again, little one." In a crusty voice she spoke the words as if English was a second language.

She came closer to Delaney. The woman's small stick arms wrapped around her as if they had been old friends or relatives.

"Do I know you?" Delaney asked while in the older woman's grasp.

"Yes, yes. The last time we saw each other perhaps…eight…no, nine months ago. The Stryders are relentless in the pursuit of you and your family," she said, pausing to look up at the man next to her. "Malik, you have much work cut out for you with this one, yes?" Josslyn's scratchy voice drew him in. Tired eyes stared back at him through long lashes.

The manner in which Josslyn spoke, he knew. The act had already been done. *It is better this way,* he told himself. Malik had no choice. Anger simmered under the surface as he moved closer to say good-bye.

Delaney looked around the room, yawning as a thick blanket fell over her mind. Her mother and Josslyn moved away and began talking to each other in quiet tones. Delaney yawned again and tried to shake her head to wave the sleepiness off. She wavered on her feet and Malik gathered her up. Delaney's head wobbled as she leaned against his shoulder. He carried her through the house and to her bedroom. Maybe for an instant she knew something. A faint acknowledgement in the way she peered at him.

"What? Why?" The utterance escaped her sluggish lips as she fought to stay awake. He laid her down on the bed.

"Don't worry. You're going to fall asleep. It will be like today never happened." The words hardening over his tongue like cement.

Should I tell her good-bye? Coax her into a kiss? Say "I love you". He wrapped all those feelings into a careful touch. His knuckles dragging down over her cheek had to be enough, for now.

Malik. Malik. Malik. The moniker poured through her mind and raced through her thoughts.

"Wait," Delaney slurred as she tried to move. "Malik." His name slid dangerously across her tongue.

"Hi, beautiful. I missed you." He stared at her as his expression became strained. He forced a happier appearance.

"Don't let me go." She pleaded.

"Everything will be okay."

He leaned down over her, his lips brushing over hers before he glanced away.

"No," she whispered against his mouth. He kept his gaze averted, wanted to explain, but nothing came to mind.

"Please," she implored. Malik kissed her once more, while at the same time chastising himself for going too damn far...again. He tried to speak, but it seemed unfair to tell her things that would never be remembered.

I am losing her right before my eyes. No matter how many times it had already happened it burnt him anew. *Ripping through me like a starved animal.* Delaney's hands gripped his shirt. She blinked, but this time her eyes refused to open again.

"When you wake up, I'll be right here. I'll be right here waiting for you." His voice faded away into a new dream.

"I would take you in my arms and never let you go. But we aren't other people and, you're not mine to keep." He looked at her, but she had already disappeared under heavy eye lids. Once again it had been all in vain.

Malik sat on the floor for a while watching her sleep. Delaney's eyes

Bent, Not Broken 41

twitched like windshield wipers during a downpour. Her body lay perfectly still and reminded him of Snow White in the glass casket.

His hands itched to touch her, but frustration won out instead. Resolve wasn't strong enough to hold him in a room with the woman he loved while she omitted him from her life, again.

How *many times do I have to do this?* He wanted to yell and put his fist through the wall.

Anger at the entire situation drove him from her side. He paused in the doorway before admitting defeat, he had been close to turning around. Too close to kidnapping her and escaping both of their fates.

He closed the door.

Soon, he would be watching Delaney wake up. She would begin moving through her life as if she were still the same person and leave for work a few minutes to four.

That gives me five hours to either break everything I can get my hands on, workout until I collapse, or crawl in my bunk and pass out. Today, I want to forget right along with her.

Chapter FIVE

"Wake up, sleepyhead. You're going to be late for work." Daphne's warm breath tickled Delaney's ear as she shook her shoulder. Her exhausted eyes searched the nightstand, the red numbers came into focus.

Three thirty? What day is it?

The jackhammer splitting Delaney's skull straight open continued.

"My head. What happened?" Delaney's tongue had become partially stuck to the roof of her mouth, making the words sound funny. Her brain pounded as she struggled to sit up, a sharp pain shot down her neck. She rubbed her head and found a huge lump on the left side.

"Ouch! What happened?" She blinked, but no recognition emerged.

"You arrived home after your last class and said you felt sick. You asked me to wake you up around three. You crashed hard." Daphne's blurry form cleared and came into view.

"Oh yeah. I did?" shrugging her shoulders, Delaney thought for a second. She didn't remember when she'd last seen Daphne.

"Okay. Wait, what time is it? Shit, I missed my class. How the hell am I ever

Bent, Not Broken   43

going to master Krav Magra if I keep missing the damn classes?" Her words were slurred. Self-defense instruction had become part of her life style, which Bannan made sure Delaney took seriously.

She couldn't remember coming home. This morning, she remembered waking up, running, and then nothing. Not a damn thing after breakfast.

The gaps in her days, the not knowing where she was, or what she had been doing. Feeling like she had no control over her actions and blocks of missing time frightened her.

How much longer can I hold on and act as if nothing is wrong? The questions sat on the tip of her tongue, but her lips refused to let them out. A tidal wave of emotions crashed into her.

The edge grows closer. What happens when I run out of ground?

"You okay?" Daphne turned her head to the side while she spoke. Her long, slender fingers threaded through Delaney's hair and a worried expression replaced the crooked grin she had worn only moments before. "Seriously, ya okay?"

"Yeah, I'm fine. Just got a little headache." Delaney forced a smile at Daphne. Shame is a powerful motivator to keep quiet. For now, Delaney fell silent.

"Hurry up or you're going to be late for work. Move your butt and come Daphne said, laughing down the stairs. Mom made you some soup. You should try to eat something. You look like hell. I mean bad." as she flitted out of the room.

"She's lucky I love her." Delaney stammered as she pulled herself out of bed. She tried to stand up.

I don't have time for this, thinking as she tossed on some jeans and a plain tee-shirt.

"Thanks for the soup," Delaney murmured in a weak and pathetic tone as she tried to focus on the bowl that seemed to move around the table all on its own.

"How are you doing?" Viv asked, placing her hand on Delaney's forehead as she gave her a quizzical once over.

"I hate closing the mall, it's so damn eerie. It's like *Dawn of the Dead* creepy." She paused and glanced at her watch. "I gotta go. Be home around ten." Viv presented Delaney with a quick hug before she hurried to the car and waved good-bye.

When she stopped at the light, a few blocks from the mall, Delaney buried her face in her hands and started crying. Her heart hurt and she wasn't sure why. Depression had resumed with a vengeance. She feared they would put her back on all the meds if she said anything.

Delaney had gone off of them on her own. She didn't want her life to revolve around the pills anymore. Delaney tried to cope, but she hadn't been handling things well without them.

The images, the voices; she was perched at the top of the slippery slope.

Something in the rearview mirror caught her attention. An image flashed in her head, dark hair and intense green eyes.

Malik cursed himself for letting his guard down. The scent of cinnamon rose up and filled the interior of the car. She jerked around, finding the back seat empty with only the odor remaining.

Malik breathed a quiet sigh of relief. He wanted to comfort her. To take away some of the pain. But he couldn't, and that was the most frustrating part.

Delaney gripped the steering wheel to keep her hands from trembling.

It's all unraveling.

Unknown people and images popped into her mind, accompanied by a haunting feeling of knowing something and not understanding why. So much had become familiar, yet unrecognizable. She had to be careful or this time she would end up in the psych ward on a three-day stretch.

Her tired fingers brushed the tears away as she headed into the Meadows Mall parking lot. The giant eye-sore of a parking structure jetted out of the earth like an ant hill and its sea of faces seemed to watch her every move. The yellow Xterra squeezed between the rows of cars and stopped on the second floor. She glanced over at the group of people waiting for the next elevator and decided take the stairs directly to the employee entrance away from the mall's gallery instead. As she headed down the long slanted ramp leading to the back of the Stinky Sweet, Delaney tried to shake the sadness off. The best she could do was attempt to focus on work instead as she walked through the employees only door and out to the sales floor.

"What happened to you?" Lola rounded the counter and stopped just in front of Delaney with her hands on her hips.

"I think I'm coming down with something," Delaney mumbled as she passed by Lola and headed back to the break room to drop off her purse.

"What, the plague?" Half joking, Lola followed Delaney. "Delaney, you should make an appointment with the doctor again. Are you okay?" Lola stood next to her.

Delaney had no idea what to say, so she remained silent.

"Have your parents made a decision yet? Can you go?"

Delaney looked at her with a blank expression. "Where am I going?"

Lola spoke sarcastically because Delaney should have already known. "Trip to Turkey? Hello! Delaney, did the headache leave you impaired? You forgot Professor Declan McDermott personally asked you to go. The same professor you have talked about nonstop since summer school. How sick are you?"

Why would I forget something like that? "Oh yeah. I-I'll speak with them." Delaney wasn't sure what to say. *Did I want to go to Turkey? I have blacked out often enough, I'm lost in my own life?* So many thoughts swirled inside Delaney's head and she became nauseated.

"You okay?" Lola moved closer to her.

"Renna asked me to clean out the backroom." If Delaney kept busy, she could hold it all at bay, at least for a while. This wasn't the long-term answer, it was just the only one she had at the moment.

Lola threw her hands up in the air and huffed as she spun on her heels and left Delaney in the back of the store.

His watchful gaze analyzed her every move from across the walkway. He was loitering in a store that afforded him a good vantage point. *Six years…feels more like an eternity sometimes.*

As he scrutinized her round face, he wondered again what she was thinking. She tossed her head back, and her hair, like a river of warm honey flowing over smooth bedrock, swept about and caressed her cheek. The long, straight strands were like shelter she hid behind. Whenever anxiety peaked, she allowed her dirty blonde tresses to cover her features. The smile that normally lit up her face, and everything in the room at the same time, sank into a sad straight line. Her lost expression told him she needed comfort.

She is always near, so close I could almost touch her.

He watched Delaney glance around outside of The Stinky Sweet. Her gaze traveled right over him. *Nothing, not an indication of recognition, not even a faint pause. It crushes me.*

Delaney appeared to be uncomfortable at best tonight. She acted agitated, shifting from one nervous foot to the other. *The dance of the wild Antelope amidst prowling tigers, which were far closer than she realized.*

She bit on her bottom lip until Malik thought it might start bleeding. Men flocked in to see Lola, often filling up the little store of smell goods with a crowd of chattering voices. Malik sensed how uncomfortable Delaney seemed. Too many people in too small of a place.

Delaney had worked part-time at the Stinky Sweet for a couple of years with her best friend Lola. The friendship still had him confused, though, because the only thing the two girls seemed to have in common was that they both liked Lola.

He forced himself to stop focusing only on Delaney and sweep the area once more. Two Hollowers tracked her from outside the large picture window.

"Fezz." His heart quickened, his muscles became taut and ready.

"South of Dillard's, near the gallery. At least one team of Hollowers." He started walking through the crowded mall, busy with families and friends and store employees rushing to and from the food court for their short lunch breaks, watching for threats.

"Copy that."

Hollowers were trained assassins for hire, and more dangerous than Lopers. He wondered where the Stryders were. The Stryders had made an arrangement with Caleb on their deathbeds to escape their immediate demise. The death deal allowed the human to live if they permitted a demonok spirit to occupy their body. Caleb wanted to create an army of recyclable fighters; killers and followers who needed him.

In his peripheral vision, he saw Delaney leave her store heading for the food court, unaware of the danger about to embrace her. Malik turned into a large department store, moving fast, but still trying to fit in. He doubled around to reenter the walkway behind Delaney as she left the Stinky Sweet. He timed it perfectly and ended up behind the two tracking Delaney. He acted with calculated swiftness when he pushed one's head into an employee only hallway door, opening it to a back alley behind the shops, then pulled the second Hollower into the hallway and broke his neck instantly. Malik was out and searching for Delaney before the lock clicked shut behind him. His eyes darted back and forth to find her. He walked out into the open and Rourke caught his eye.

Rourke moved his hand in several quick motions indicating he would follow Delaney. Malik began moving away to hopefully confuse the Hollowers tracking him.

I hate handing her off, but it makes sense.

Malik moved to the center of the crowd of shoppers to become more accessible to the assassins. He spotted a Dick's Sporting Goods store; the perfect place to eliminate a threat because they had weapons down almost every aisle.

He headed straight into the emporium, finding himself in the shoe section. A pair of dark blue Crampons were displayed center stage. They had twelve razor sharp, angled points.

They're perfect.

He grabbed both and slid down, creeping between the crowded racks of clearance ski clothing. The plan of attack was to lure them away from each other, then strike. A two-man team found their way to him by the time he reached the camping equipment.

A slender built guy with spiky red hair stood guard, peering down aisles with cautious movements. Malik walked up behind him and slit his throat with a crampon. He stashed the body inside a tent erected as a display in the middle of the camping section.

Malik found the second part of the team prowling in the back of the store near the dressing rooms. This assassin stood much taller and larger, with beefy muscles. Malik moved like a ghost to come up behind him. One quick slash severed the bulky killer's spinal cord. He crumpled to the ground like a puppet whose strings had been sliced clean through.

Malik walked around the store until he found an isle with climbing gear and two ice picks stood out. He dropped the crampons for the yellow axes and waited for the Hollowers to find him. This wasn't a movie. He knew that fighting more than one assassin at the same time would be useless and foolish. The opportune moment had to be after dividing the two-man units.

An Asian looking assassin stood near the cycling equipment. Malik jumped up, grabbed the metal rafter bar, and hoisted his torso up. Shimmying along the narrow pipe, hands clenching the duct overhead and feet grazing the rafter below. Like a bird, he remained perched on the scaffolding and waited for the Hollower to find him.

The killer stalked forward slowly, his eyes darting to either side. He searched for a telltale sign that his target was close. His motions were fluid as he moved within striking distance. Malik reached down and snared him beneath the jaw with one ice axe, then hurled the other one into the back of his neck. Spinal cord severed, he dropped the man to the floor. The assassin stared up at him with fixed eyeballs while his body laid lifeless and crumpled on the ground. Malik dropped back to the floor in a hushed thud and pulled the dead body into a dressing room.

Shock registered on Malik's face when he located the last one and realized there were two. They spotted him and began to close in on his position. Like

Bent, Not Broken   49

a pair of large caged cats, they encircled him. He kept his back to the nearest wall, Malik saw what he'd been patient for. They were going to blitz him from both sides. The decision was sealed and Malik made a move, deciding to deal with the one who appeared to be the fastest last. He took off with lightning speed toward the second guy, grabbed a kayak hanging above their heads with one hand, and swung himself forward, ripping at the man's chest with the ice axe. He dropped down next to the fallen assassin's body and leaned down to dislodge the weapon. Quickly, he turned, knowing the other guy would have already begun to advance, but was startled to find he had stopped just short of reaching his goal.

"Malik of The Waiths?" the man called out in a thick European accent.

"Who's asking?"

"That's not important. I'm to tell you Isabeau said hello, and good-bye." He smiled a half toothless grin.

"Well, I'll have to pay her a visit when I wrap this up." Malik sounded cocky while grinning his most dazzling smile.

The European pulled out two rapiers and Malik tightened his grip on both ice axes. The assassin charged, running hard with the blades drawn and ready. Malik waited poised and prepared to adjust. The opponent raised his arm to plunge the razor sharp point into his chest, but Malik lowered himself into a defense position and ducked sideways. Malik took a hard hit to the chin and a cut to his cheek. Quick fists didn't miss their targets, sending them both off balance. At the last minute, Malik moved to the side, swung one axe around himself, and plunged it deep into the man's back while holding off the enemy's attack with the other. The man staggered forward, falling to one knee. His head hung low and he looked confused about what had just happened.

"You're too late to save the girl." Blood spurted from his mouth as he coughed. He fell face first on the linoleum. Gore ran from his wound, covering the cream colored floor in a deep rich maroon color.

With no fight left, Malik abandoned the axe lodged in the killer's back and turned to move away. Malik concluded the rapier had made contact, but with the adrenaline rush, he hadn't realized the blade pierced his back left lung until now. His breathing became labored and shallow.

"Flynn." He whispered through a gurgle. He waited for a response.

"Rourke." Still no acknowledgement.

He knew something had gone wrong. The Hollowers had been a distraction, which meant the Stryders were going after Delaney. His mind filled with questions. He tried to fight the throbbing pain, had to maintain a level head and get to Delaney.

The light flashed off plunging him into darkness. Malik fell to one knee and attempted to take a deep breath. The burn shot through him like razors ripping at his flesh.

"Rourke." Malik called once more, hoping his old friend could answer the call. His hope was dashed when no one link-spoke back. His lungs struggled to get air. His body wanted to fuse—it was instinct, but in his condition it would be impossible. He pulled himself up to stand, lumbered to the front of the store and broke the metal fencing as quietly as possible, and moved out into the dimly lit mall.

Chapter SIX

"See you tomorrow," Lola waved as Delaney walked off in the opposite direction toward an employee's-only hallway, passing by a bathroom. Delaney hated stopping especially when the overhead lights were out, but she didn't think she could wait to get home. The heavy door creaked open and she slid into the first stall. Back out and rushing to leave the restroom, she stumbled and bumped into the porcelain sink with her hip.

Delaney was so busy chastising herself for being clumsy, she never looked up. With no time to react to the hand closing around her skull, her head snapped forward and smacked into the mirror with incredible velocity. A loud crack and a sharp sting to her forehead, then her face bounced like a rubber ball off the side of the basin and she fell to the cold, dirty tile floor.

His sweaty fist closed around Delaney's throat, squeezing hard, cutting the air off. Seconds ticked by before Delaney realized she was about to die. Her hands pinched, scratched, and pried at meaty fingers. Oxygen didn't come and his grip never gave way. Big black spots clouded her vision in a polka-dot pattern. Delaney swam in the sprinkles.

"Why?" she wheezed, trying to grapple with him, thrashing around. Her fingertips fumbled over clammy skin. Delaney dug in her nails managing to draw blood from his pudgy face and throat.

Delaney grabbed at the bear claw knife hung from her neck. The one she thought her dad had been crazy for buying and making her wear. She wrapped her fingers tightly around the grip and jabbed the point into his jugular, aiming for his carotid artery. Delaney felt hot liquid roll down over her palm as he yelped.

Her forearm snapped like twig under the pressure of his foot that had been pinning her down. Pain, so much pain, she was dumbfounded. She hadn't detected his hand coming, but something hit her nose and blood shot out similar to a pyroclastic cloud exploding. The blow stunned her into submission. She lay unmoving and staring blankly up at him.

The knife loosely hung from her fingers. Thick, metallic liquid ran down Delaney's throat making her gag. Her head jerked to the side, smacking the floor. Dizziness started to win over her senses. She fought to get a breath. Delaney tried to spit out the blood, instead the liquid leaked out of her mouth, dripping along her cheek bone and mixing with salty tears.

"Die already." His words bounced around in Delaney's head before making sense. His knee dug into her chest, her ribs beginning to give way as her breast plate cracked. A muffled pop and her sternum collapsed under the pressure. Breathing became near impossible as her body burned with each attempt at inhaling. To get his point across, he punched her in the mouth. Her bottom lip exploded as her teeth cut through. Her face felt on fire. Crack, pop, crunch, the punches continued to crash down on her.

"They said you gotta die." The words slithered down and pressed against her harder than his brawny fists.

She coughed and choked as the metallic flavor of her own blood flooded her mouth, She watched the bubbles spew into the air like little red balloons at a birthday party. She attempted to speak, but her words drowned in the bloody stream running down her throat; she couldn't choke them out. Pain shot through Delaney's arm all the way into her shoulder with bone-crushing pressure. She wanted to cry out, but only silence followed. His hand began crushing her larynx again.

He picked Delaney up by the throat for just long enough to slam her head back down into the floor. She gulped at whatever air she pulled into her lungs while her eyes swam in their sockets. She tried to focus on the room, but everything became a blur. Pain blasted through the back of her skull as the world spun out of control. The only sound she recognized was like heavy breathing that soon drifted off into the rhythm of her pulsating heartbeat.

Delaney inhaled the filthy stench that swarmed her senses. Every punishing blow to the side of her face sent her swirling in starry circles. As blackness enveloped her, she heard the hefty white doors burst open. A figure came charging forward. A deafening roar screamed out into the silence. A flaxen mane flew over her as her eyes slid shut.

Blink.

Where am I?

Blink.

The overhead light shined through and Delaney realized she lay on a wet, sticky floor. She tried to sit up as pain spiraled within her. Her sight cleared and startling realization of a dead body sprawled next to her sank in. Adrenaline forced Delaney to move.

The scene developed as she studied the corpse. Bite marks, torn skin, and one ocean blue eye stared vacantly back at her. Blood covered the floor. The man's body had been broken like a marionette with no one pulling its strings.

She reached for the sink to pull herself up, but met searing resistance. Agonizing pain stifled her senses. With her lower lip trembling, she clenched her eyes tightly closed. The darkness increased her discomfort. Delaney's hand grasped a shard of shattered mirror. She looked into the sliver and found someone she didn't recognize; a person broken and battered. Blood streaked her face and coagulated in her tangled blonde hair. Delaney's cheekbone protruded through the epidermis just below her eye that was rapidly swelling shut. Her bottom lip was caked over with dried gore, tender and quivering. Her tears stung as they ran the gauntlet of ripped and raw flesh.

Delaney's t-shirt had been partially torn up the front. The small leather backpack still hung over one shoulder, but the contents were strewn across the floor. Thoughts started to tumble over her like violent waves from a perfect storm.

Vomit rose in her throat. Her head flopped to the side as the dizziness won full control. Random pictures Delaney couldn't identify flooded her brain again. People she didn't know or recall pushed forward into the forefront of her consciousness. Within her racing mind, a slide show took the form of a little girl with her parents all cuddled together. Delaney came alive in the illustrations.

A man laughing with her. Happiness resonated from her with fuzzy warmth formed the next picture. The images began flashing so quickly she couldn't gauge them all. Her mind reached out and she grabbed the depiction of the mysterious man. He gazed at her with deep emerald eyes. His arms pulled her closer and Delaney melted against him. His name sat on the tip of her tongue and then fluttered away like a bird. Adrenaline coursed within her veins, making her limbs tremble and jerk. Without warning she threw up on herself.

She sucked in a quick, ragged breath through the contraction.

Just calm down. A slow exhale. *Hold it together.*

Delaney's hands quaked like dry leaves in the wind, pain shot through each finger as she tried to flex them.

He said 'they', they were still out there. The room blurred as her eyes rolled back in her head.

"Peyton, does anyone have Delaney?" Malik coughed, spewing blood at the same time.

"Malik? I'm on my way."

"Secure the house. Hurry, Peyton." The act of breathing made his lungs burn in protest.

"I'm on site and need immediate back up." Flynn wheezed.

"Spyder, Delaney's alone, find her. Rourke's missing, I'm down. Start with the store. Bring reinforcements. I'm not sure how many teams. Have extra guards sent to the Drake's house and locate Delaney now." Then he fell silent as the trickle of blood dampened the right leg of his pants.

"I need help, one of them had…well, ah fuck…I got blown up." Flynn sputtered.

Malik stopped when he arrived at the Stinky Sweet, still trying to ignore the pain. The black spots in front of his eyes were a clear sign he was in real trouble. Shortness of breath slowed his progress and muddled his thoughts.

He wanted to yell in frustration. *I'm taking too long. By the time I get to her I'll be finding her dead body.*

Malik changed his tactics and went to her car in the parking garage. He couldn't drift in this condition, he had to trail her on foot. He coughed up blood and spat the red liquid on the blacktop while trying to stay focused. Sluggish and stumbling, he bounced off parked cars like a pinball.

Rourke not answering means things went south. He is a formidable fighter, it would take a lot to bring him down.

Delaney could be dead too, for all he knew. His mind filled with picture of her being tortured, which only fueled his seething anger. The fight wasn't gone from his brain, but his body had been broken. He battled to keep his droopy eyelids open as he reached Delaney's car. Weak hands gripped the overhead rack to stay upright. The locks popped and he fell into the backseat. Barely getting the door closed before his surroundings became hazy. He cursed himself for the weakness as the light blurred and then nothing.

Am I dead?

Probably not.

It doesn't seem to be anything like what I would have thought being departed felt like.

Instead, everything hurt like hell. Surely death should have provided a form of serenity, and not the kind of torment now tearing through Delaney with an undeniable force. Her body suffered in such agony and she began crumbling from the inside out. She didn't understand why she had experienced a sense of loss or even what it was she grieved for. The sensation so palpable, the weight pushing down on her chest suffocated her.

I'm lost.

Delaney closed her eyes and concentrated to remember Andrea Bocelli's "Time to Say Goodbye" for comfort. The notes strummed their way along her tattered soul from the instruments fluttering like a subtle breeze through her mind. They became an anchor and she relished the tether. Her heart reached out for the perfection of the strings and the voices of the lovers aching for something beautiful to come of all the ugliness.

I can sense you unfurling under my skin. A gentle warmth and breath-taking beauty. I can't explain how I know you are here, but I know you exist somehow, just beyond my denial.

Time to say goodbye. She accepted what the words meant and sensed them down to the deepest parts of herself. She didn't understand why the concept applied to her, only that it did somehow.

I'm broken. Only shaky ground sets beneath my feet and only falling sky overhead. I wish for nothing more than for this night to end.

"Let's go, people. She's in and out. Get her to ER three," one of the hospital staff roared in a bullhorn voice mentally jarring Delaney back into the moment.

"Her blood pressure is spiking and her heart rate is elevating," someone else shouted. "What the hell?" The question hung over the room.

"I need an IV. Bring her upstairs for an MRI. Definite head trauma," a female spoke with authority.

"Hey, don't you worry, okay." Light contact flitted over Delaney's arm firmly, and with enough compassion that she distinguished the touch from the pain of everything else. The voice became a kindness in the storm, and Delaney tried to attach herself to the tenderness.

Nurses came in and out, discussing her injuries as if reading from a grocery list: dislocated shoulder; broken nose, wrist, fingers, and ribs; fractured ulna, radius, clavicle, and sternum; punctured lung. Deep lacerations and contusions. She might still lose one of her eyes. He had stomped on her skull until her right eardrum had ruptured under the trauma. They found a boot print on her scalp.

Delaney stopped listening and started sobbing.

The horror flick replayed in her head. She smelled his rancid breath against her cheek, stinging her nose with its malodorous odor. His creepy utterances echoing all around her. She imagined the ocean blue eye staring forward with a hollowed flatness, and she couldn't escape.

Delaney's recollections had to be forced away as a woman's voice came closer. The sound was high and thick with worry; she recognized the tone immediately. Relief washed over her.

"Where is she?" Her adopted parents demanded in unison.

They were both in their early thirties. Her dad, a college professor of anthropology at University of Nevada Las Vegas, and her mom, a curator at the Nevada State Natural History Museum and Chairman of The Southwest Historical Educational Institute. Vivianna and Bannan Drake looked much too young to have girls in their late teens and early twenties. They had adopted them because children hadn't been possible for the couple. The details were private and Delaney never had the heart to ask why.

Delaney had three sisters who had also been adopted. Brody was the oldest, then Daphne, Delaney the middle child, and Calliope the youngest.

"Delaney." Viv's voice cracked as she said her name. Delaney caught her father's sharp intake of breath, then pictured them in her mind: her mother's beautiful face, tears filling her depthless sky blue eyes while she chewed on her bottom lip, and her father, with his pale skin and warm, broad smile. His handsome expression would be distorted, with a creased forehead and lips flattened into a thin, hard line. His hands were tight fists at his side.

Delaney had no idea about all the specifics. She began fading fast.

It is okay to sleep now.

Chapter SEVEN

Malik found his way to the obnoxious clanking sound. Troubled steps through swirling darkness brought him out into a bright beam of streaming light. He blinked several times, a female silhouette appeared, shining a huge blue-lite into the window as she alternated between the clanking.

Relief washed over Peyton's face.

For a few minutes, Malik had been lost and disorientated. His muscles had tightened and the joints creaked from holding the same position for too long. He peered at his surroundings and realized he'd collapsed in Delaney's car. The memories washed over him as he grabbed for the headrest of the chair in front of him; he swung straight up in the grey leather backseat. Dizziness consumed him as his chin rested on his chest.

He turned and hit the automatic door locks to let Peyton in. Malik tossed his set of keys into the front of the car for her to start the engine with.

"Where is she?" He whispered in a hoarse mutter. He forced his head to stay still fearing the dizziness would claim him again. *There are only so many things you can argue your way out of. Some things are just bigger than you or your sense of invincibility.*

"At Sunrise ICU. The adrenaline surge or the injuries forced her body to compensate. I believe the earlier conclusion involving Delaney and why the Stryders have increased their attacks has been proven correct. She's going through the conversion now." She spoke while holding a bottle of water out to him.

"She's changing?" Relief flooded his foggy brain. Peyton glanced at him in the rearview mirror as his head bobbed up. She only nodded in response.

"Why didn't you just drift in?" Malik asked through practiced slow breathing to keep from getting sick all over Delaney's car.

"You're always so cranky when I wake you up. Besides, everyone's already in place." Peyton inhaled a deep breath. "Delaney took a hell of a beating. Viv's with her now, Ptah and Bowe are guarding them. Four additional teams at her door and the hospital entrances. Reinforcements are on standby awaiting instructions." Peyton tossed the bottle of water on the seat beside him.

"Buckle up, let's get out of here." She pulled the car out of the parking space.

"Rourke?" Malik kept his eyes closed and tried not to dwell on the continual motion of the vehicle.

"Tryst had me go to the mall and do a second sweep, but I found nothing. I don't think he ever got to her, she was alone in the bathroom." Peyton ground her teeth so harshly he heard the crunching.

"Flynn?" He concentrated on breathing in and out rather than the swaying of the SUV.

"He did get blown up. One of them tried to light him up with a Bic and a can of hair spray. We had to cut the clothes off him. Viv and Daphne are treating him now. He will be out until day after tomorrow. And you?" Peyton asked without taking her eyes off the road.

"Punctured lung, I'm almost healed. I lost a lot of blood, I just need to eat. I'll grab something later." He realized they were passing by the hospital.

"Where are we going?" He sounded more forceful than he'd intended to.

"The Drake's. In your current condition you will not be able to guard

Delaney. I'll take you to her when you can protect her." Peyton wouldn't acknowledge the sour expression on Malik's face.

"Peyton." His voice raised while lifting his head to stare at her, the activity requiring more energy than Malik would ever admit to.

"Malik, be reasonable, she needs someone who can defend her. Look at yourself, you couldn't guard a lemonade stand on the corner, let alone Delaney. If you don't approve, fire me. Or suspend me. I need the time off." She smiled at him.

At times, his sister drove him crazy beyond reason. *The thought of her knowing me so well bugs me to no end. I would never tell her how right she is.*

"Dane needs to be contacted. You need to go to Naroke. Trenton should be kept in the loop, and the council must be compelled to react against the latest threats and developments. Delaney's on the radar now and immediate response is required. That is the job, remember?" She understood the chain of command had to be completed in Rourke's absence.

"Fine, hurry up. Under any other circumstances, you'd drive like the road is falling out from under the wheels."

Back at the Drake's, Peyton made Malik something to eat at her insistence. He hated to admit it, but she'd been right. An hour had passed and he was almost healed.

"Trenton." Malik waited patiently for his response.

"Malik." Trenton link-spoke in reply.

"I need two extra teams sent up. Have four more standing by, just in case. We've had some problems arise. I'm contacting Dane about a meeting with the Counsel. You are requested to attend." Malik spoke.

"Copy that." Trenton stated.

"Dane." Malik's nerves frayed when it came to affairs of state. The fighting was the easy, straightforward task. The politics, he didn't like. As he waited for a response, everything replayed in his brain.

Rourke, my friend and commander. I sense the loss of you.

"Malik." Dane's voice sounded unconcerned, unaware.

Bent, Not Broken   61

"I will be there in twenty. Please assemble what you can of the Counsel, some problems have arisen and should be dealt with as quickly as possible." His attempt at trying not to sound grave only sounded worse.

"Peyton, I'll be on Naroke if there are any more developments." Without waiting for a reply, Malik was gone.

Within seconds, he stood on Naroke surrounded by chatty seafaring birds. The wind coming up off the tide blew across the cliffs. The spray from the ocean coated the black Basalt rocks. The creamy sand leading to the patio appeared smooth like polished stone. Malik paused and studied the surf. The way the waves slapped against the shore calmed him somehow and right now he needed to be distracted. A large part of him wanted to run into the chaos, let the weight of the water pound him into the rocks, and allow the jagged edges to claw at his skin and pull him under. The thought of some peace tempted him. The cost mattered little.

Malik fell to his knees struggling with his thoughts and obligations.

Maybe enduring lifetimes of living is wrong. The life span of a human being is condensed in comparison to ours. You can only endure so much in a short amount of time. I have lived far too long.

Malik glanced around the place where his life had been put on hold and his thoughts depressed him further. Rourke wouldn't be coming home. The Waltz of the Mariners to honor him would not happen. Without a body, there was no way for anyone to pay their respects or say good-bye. He felt bone tired as he pulled himself up the hand carved stone steps.

This is my house, where I keep my belongings, but this isn't my home yet. I had found the perfect spot to build. Trystan and Peyton arrived later and moved in. All the Kindreds were here before I realized what was happening. We just kept carving more bedrooms out of the rock cliff.

He left the French glass doors hanging open and glanced around. The house was quiet. Trenton probably told the other Kindred's that he was en route to the island. Malik walked over to the couch and sat down for a moment. Out of frustration, he dropped his forehead into his hands. Rourke had been his mentor and a close friend, even fatherly. The weight on his shoulders felt enormous, pressing down on him until his bones would give under the pressure.

He sat upright and let the cushions cradle his neck as he stared up at the tall ceiling. *There is no time for this, but I needed to be here.*

Out of the corner of his eye, he saw the H. R. Giger's print of *The Birth Machine* framed and hung on the adjacent wall. The little aliens in a row, all ready to go.

I am the one about to be discharged from a gun. Shot into the atmosphere, spiraling forward with pinpoint accuracy, incredible velocity and purpose. One goal to accomplish no matter what I encounter or have to endure along the way. I will find my target, and burrow in at the expense of myself. Sacrificing all and everyone for one objective, one person.

Reluctantly, Malik pulled himself up to stand and turned to go. The door clicked shut behind him as he said a silent good-bye. One day this would be his home, not just where he housed his belongings. Malik found himself with only the Kindred's and Dane in his life. He would never complain; they were family. He knew better than to hope for the pitter-patter of tiny feet, or for someone standing at the door awaiting his return.

People like me, we don't receive such gifts. The horrendous acts of violence keep others alive. We sell ourselves to the all-consuming darkness that comes so naturally with the career choice. I have lived my life as a killer. The cost would be paid one-way or another. I had no doubts about the payment being required tenfold in boiling blood and tormenting screams. I'll join Isabeau in hell when the time comes.

"Dane." Malik forced himself to face what he'd come to do.

"Malik." Dane knew something had happened.

Malik walked to the Council's meeting place. "Old friend." Malik grabbed the large outstretched hand firmly in his own.

"Son." Dane addressed each of the Kindred in such an intimate style. Malik knew he had been the first to earn the name, all those years ago in the rain forest. All of the Kindred took the reference as an endearing compliment from a man they held in the highest esteem.

Malik turned from him as he approached the Council and lowered himself down on one knee, bowing out of respect for the law makers he stood before. He awaited to be called on as Dane went and took his place among them.

"Malik, what's the urgency?" Ky asked. He was the second oldest of counsel and served as their Harbinger.

"We fell under attack yesterday. In the scrimmage, we've lost all contact with Rourke. In his absence, I've assumed responsibility of the Kindred teams until a suitable replacement can be appointed. The events have driven Delaney to finally begin the transition also." He left emotion out of his voice. He bowed his head once more and waited to be readdressed. To keep his breath steady and even, he focused his attention on the hard rock flooring.

"Delaney has begun to change? Why after so much time has passed?" Fury asked.

"We aren't exactly sure. I think this is what the Stryders were attempting to accomplish with the constant blitzing yesterday. I believe they planned this." The confusion added weight to his already furrowed brows. With no answers to provide, he only had supposition.

"We require more information about this." Malik continued. "What course of action would you find acceptable?"

"I need to time to make inquiries of my own." Fury fell silent, and he nodded at her in understanding.

"A strong front has to be maintained," Ky communicated in an even tone. Malik sensed those gunmetal gray eyes boring into his torso with each word.

"I respectfully recommend the Counsel establish Malik as Commander of the Kindred," Dane declared in his quiet man-big stick voice. Anyone who understood Dane, also knew this was more of a directive than a recommendation. "Delaney will be joining us soon, she'll need an instructor as well as a guard."

"Are Caleb and Isabeau behind the attacks?" asked Fury in her musical voice. She rarely expressed herself during these meetings.

Rumors that Fury was the oldest of them had been spoken between the

Kindred for years. They suspected her to be the first Kindred to The Spirit People and guardian to the Relics.

"There's been no confirmation of this information," Malik said. The Intel they had was sketchy at best, but it had become the most obvious conclusion to draw from the events.

"Is the family returning home?" Dane inquired with an authority in his voice Malik knew well. Naroke was their stronghold and it made sense to reign everyone in to keep them safe.

"I will raise these questions and concerns to Vivianna," Malik responded. He was confident Dane knew what the reaction would be from Vivianna before the words left his mouth.

"Dispatch guards to check the other families just as a precautionary measure." Ky's eyes narrowed while she was deep in thought for a few minutes. "Anything else to discuss?" Ky glanced around the floor looking for others to express their discord or opinions.

"I think that we're finished, yes?" Fury loudly asserted. She ended the meeting when no one spoke up directly. Rising from her seat, she walked to Dane as everyone disbanded. The two had a brief but heated exchange before Fury hastily departed.

"Son." Dane declared as he hugged Malik.

"I'm going to see her injuries for myself. Whatever happened, there must have been a lot of them to bring Rourke down." Malik didn't even attempt to hide the anger and regret from his expression.

"Only so much can be done before it's no longer in your hands. I'm happy and relieved you are unharmed. I'd have no one to play Othello with. Peyton suffers from a lack of patience for the game, and Trystan has nothing else on his mind but my other granddaughter." Dane smiled at him as he let his hand rest on the other man's shoulder.

"Delaney's special to us all, no?" The French accent from years past reappeared. Giving those who conversed with him the sense that they were carrying on a conversation with a gentlemen from mid fifteenth century

France. *Hell, I wasn't sure how old Dane was. He could probably remember when France had been ruled as Gaul and the Franks may have been chew toys.*

"She'll be kept safe at any cost." Malik attempted to carry on with the conversation.

"Is there anything between you and my granddaughter?" Dane wasn't a noncommittal type of person. He said what he meant and expect truth in return.

"No." He swung away while he prepared his gear to leave. He felt Dane's eyes boring into him. Malik tried to abstain from directly lying to someone who had never lied to him. *I'm not willing to reveal what is in my heart, not yet.*

"We'll talk tomorrow. If anything develops, you'll be made aware of it." He pivoted back around and Malik noticed the wide arrogant smile, one of a cat right after he had eaten the canary. It irritated Malik to no end.

"Good-bye." Malik nodded as he drifted to the Drake's residence. Standing on the landing at the top of the stairs, Malik heard Peyton.

"Malik?" she called out to him.

"Yeah, I'll be ready in five." His nerves were frayed. He couldn't stop thinking about Delaney and how they had beaten her. Torture wasn't something he enjoyed participating in.

This one time I will make an exception.

Malik drifted to the hospital a few seconds later.

Viv, Bannan, and Calliope were fussing over Delaney. Standing off in the corner, Malik stayed in the shadows. He wanted only to be present in the room with her.

Chapter EIGHT

Time bended and blurred in the small sanitized cell. When Delaney pried open the one eye which hadn't swollen shut, she realized night had slipped into daylight. Crisp white walls stared back at her with a cold expression. Machines beeped, chirped, and hummed in an arrangement of ugly harmonies Delaney wished she didn't have to hear.

The fog of confusion hung thick over Delaney's head. Most of her brain remained comatose, her senses numbed by pain meds and exhaustion. The phosphorescent light filtering through the twists and turns of Delaney's mind, began waking her up to a whole new world.

"Mom." The one single word burned her throat.

"Right here, Delaney." Viv's voice resonated by her ear. The concern dripped from the silky words like maple syrup, thick and heavy.

What happened?

Delaney concentrated on the last thing she recalled. Work, she remembered she had been at The Stinky Sweet. The night's events began to tumble over her with grotesque realization. The bathroom…the man…the blood. Of all the things she had forgotten, what happened last night was unfortunately not

Bent, Not Broken   67

among them. The memories came back in clear, bright colors with a perfect picture.

"You're safe, sweets." Delaney's father walked towards the bed. He acted as if nothing had changed, her regular everyday pop. The action comforted her in ways she didn't fully comprehend. She wanted normal at the moment more than anything else.

"I'm here for you, sweets, I promise," her dad mumbled into her ear. "I'm so glad you're safe. Don't worry, everything will be fine now." Bannan attempted to ease the arduous moment with unmistakable tenderness.

Delaney's throat grew tighter and that had nothing to do with her injuries.

"Is she okay? I came as fast as possible." Brody burst into the room. Surprise that Brody had come at all registered in Delaney.

"Damn, your head. You're a comic book character." She tried to joke in her unfunny way.

Her words didn't carry concern or compassion; instead they communicated the same emotion a five o'clock news broadcaster would. Brody acted as though she were about to order food from a giant clown's head at a drive-thru.

The door burst opened and Delaney's third sister marched in. Her anger directed at each of them with panted breaths.

"What the hell, people?" quipped Daphne. "One of you could have waited for me. I've been wandering around this damn place for thirty minutes." Daphne's annoyance still swirled through the space.

"Daphne, you would get lost in a bathroom stall with a map and a flashlight. This hospital is like walking the Titanic to you." Calliope laughed, followed by their dad's chuckle.

"Is she all right?" Brody didn't come to the bed. The best Delaney could do was shut the one working eye and pretend she no longer existed while they conversed.

"We haven't spoken with a doctor yet," Viv finished.

"How long…have I…been down here?" Delaney's breath sputtered as her voice broke and faltered.

The memory of his tight grip on her throat still too fresh.

"Since last night. We came as soon as they called. I stayed to make sure if you woke up you weren't alone." The warmth in Vivianna's words provoked many welcome emotions that left Delaney with a tangible embrace.

Delaney would be okay, but Malik needed to observe her for himself. He moved to stand beside her bed. Against the plastic railings, her frame appeared small and broken. Covered in bandages and gauze, one arm in a cast. Her face ignited such anger in him, he began to choke on it. The image still managed to startle him. He hoped Peyton had been misinformed. Delaney's right eye had become swollen shut with deep purplish rings surrounding the oval shapes. The other lid hung low, black and dark blue bruises hovering around the base. One cheekbone had collapsed in on itself. Her nose had been set and packed with gauze, the upper lip distended over her lower one.

"Okay, everybody out. I don't want anyone late for class, or work, Bannan. I'm playing Mommy, so I get to stay. Your sister needs her rest and I demand to have her all to myself for a while." Her mother used a commanding tone, sending everyone on their way. The room began to clear as they said their goodbyes with hugs and kisses.

Viv moved a chair closer to the bed and sat down. The rustle of her skirt as her hands smoothed over her lap echoed through the silent room. Viv stole a deep breath and exhaled in a deliberate, slow manner. She opened a bottle of water and took a drink. Delaney became sure she was stalling, but not aware of why.

"Delaney, we never told you things because there had been no reason to tell you, not yet, anyway. We thought maybe you were different. Most of the time our change happens around puberty, but you never showed even a single sign of changing." Viv paused as she searched for the right words to continue. Still lost in her own world, Delaney struggled to pay attention through her thoughts.

The pull is nothing explainable. A tether, or a life jacket, it will not release me, or let me slip under. I cling to the comfort the safeness offers. The allure, I can't break free of, or more aptly, I don't want to. There is something beside me, all around me, someone beyond my sight and touch, but it's here drawing me near. I am a moth to the flame.

Delaney let her head fall to the other side of the bed. The cinnamon scent wafted over her. She inhaled and tried to keep hold of the spicy fragrance she associated with protection; the security made her insides warm. She wondered what her protector angel might resemble. *Is he terrifyingly ugly? A brutal, fierce warrior knee-deep in a battle for my soul. Or does he possess an unearthly beauty?*

A Seraph. The idea seemed ludicrous and Delaney almost laughed out loud.

After what happened, the thought of being unattended terrified her, even though she had always been alone in some form or another. She couldn't help but have faith in an existence infinite to this world. Was the presence she sensed an angel? Had her mind made up the guardian to offer her comfort as the loneliness had grown too overwhelming? When fear had taken over her life, Delaney wished she had sure footing on anything.

Even though the room appeared to be empty and there was no one she should see, nothing tangible that she could explain, Delaney understood someone stood next to her now in the hospital. It felt like the same someone from the corner in her room at the house too.

Her scent, spicy Juniper, filled the room. The fragrance fit her personality. Juniper Trees are the symbol of the warrior. The thought made Malik smile. As his hand held steady, floating adjacent to hers, the heat from her skin washed over his. Her fingers stretched up as if reaching for unknown contact. This was as near as he could safely be and it would never be close enough.

The tightness in Malik's chest constricted his lungs, breathing became difficult. The protector in him wanted to make her safe always. He needed to touch her, to sweep the strands of hair away from her face. His fingers itched to brush her cheek, to run slowly across her lips. Regretfully, he pulled his hand back from her and massaged the tension from his forehead.

Delaney's eyes never left his. Tears rushed down the swollen skin and was soaked up by the gauze. Malik held the edge of the bed so tightly the plastic began to buckle under his grip. Her voice would catch and Malik's temper flared.

The heat over her hand comforted her, though she didn't understand why. She found comfort in nothing but a void. The thought established a free-spirited streak within her. One that wanted to throw caution to the wind and fling herself into the shadows with pure abandonment, having no inclination of what may await her.

That's so unlike me.

Viv's voice brought Delaney's thoughts back, but her eyes remained looking up at a nothing that felt much more like a most important something.

"With your sisters this was easier. They had acceptance and adjustment time. I'd hoped it would be that way for you too." Delaney listened to Viv without turning her head from the empty space that held her gaze with a lifeline she didn't wish to sever.

"What do you remember about last night?" Viv asked Delaney cautiously.

With just that one sentence Viv had deflated her. *I don't want to look back.* Delaney squeezed her eyes shut. Why live the ordeal twice? Once had been more than enough.

"I need you to try and remember what happened. You don't have to be afraid. Whoever did this will never hurt you again. If he tried, believe me, he'll die before the thought forms." Viv attempted to soothe Delaney with gentle words and reassurances. This particular course of action should have worked too, but Delaney had been aware last night when she woke, he wasn't coming for her, not now, not ever. The only place he could force her to run for her life was in her nightmares and that would be enough.

"He's dead," Delaney admitted, breathing the words out slowly, not wanting to face Viv. In staring at the empty space, a certain amount of sanctuary developed. Delaney wanted to reach out and touch the air, to hold onto the sureness. She knew it wouldn't let her go. She clung to it until the darkness had been chased away and all was safe once more.

Delaney tried to make herself see clearly. "No, I mean, I don't know,"

Bent, Not Broken

Delaney forced the heavy words out. "He was trying to kill me." She gasped for air through tightly clenched teeth. Why couldn't it just be a distant memory fading into the nothingness of her head like so many others?

Delaney's hands began warming from the inside out. Her fingers strained upwards, trying to grab something corporeal to hold on to and make the bewitching sensation a reality. She wanted to curl into the warmth and forget the nightmare that played in her mind. She didn't want to be dirty anymore, alone, lost, angry, or broken.

When does the despair ever end? Can an angel fix me? Can anyone? Where had he been when my childhood had taken a turn for the worst? Where had he been when I walked into the bathroom?

Delaney struggled to take a breath. Her heart began breaking, shattering, exploding. Why did the silly organ hurt so much? The sentiment itself became ridiculous, to yearn for what she couldn't even detect as real.

Then, words flowed out of her like the rushing water from a broken damn. "He broke my nose, arm, and…the pain. He wanted me dead…said I had to die. Had to! I couldn't breathe, he held my throat so tight. He fell on top of me, forcing me to the floor. I tried to struggle, but he kept overpowering me. He snapped my wrist. He punched me in the face, banged the back of my head against the ground. I must have passed out then. I don't remember anything else." Delaney inhaled a few strained breaths. The sharp-as-barbed-wire air scratched at her raw throat as it filled her lungs, stretching at her broken ribs.

"When I came to, he was lying beside me, his head ripped apart, covered in scratches and bite marks. Blood flowed everywhere. I was happy he was dead, and relieved, because I had been so scared. I didn't think I would ever walk out of the bathroom alive." Delaney interjected.

Viv handed Delaney a cup of water, helping her sip from the straw. The relief was too short-lived, though.

"There could have been another man, I think. Someone else in the room with us, I am sure of it." She tried to swallow, but her throat cracked like dried, chapped skin.

"I heard voices. They might have fought. I woke up to whatever was left." Delaney stopped because of the noises in the hallway. A nurse came in and notified her mom that a doctor needed to speak with her. Viv squeezed her hand and kissed her forehead before walking out the door.

Delaney's eyes drew back to that spot next to the bed once more, as if for some reason, if she glanced away, the world might shatter and the shards of life would rain down on her. The emotions bubbled to the surface and she couldn't hold back the rippling effect.

"Is someone there?"

The question took Malik by surprise.

Delaney peered at a blank space, yet, somehow she sensed his presence. Why had she even said the words out loud? Delaney questioned her actions. In the back of her head, she recognized the action made no sense, but didn't resist the urge to hold the connection.

"Delaney, I have to tell you a story." Vivianna settled in the seat next to the bed, pushing her thick ponytail of curls back over her shoulder.

Delaney hadn't heard Viv reenter the room.

"I know you're there. Please don't leave me again," Delaney whispered. She had to say them, the driving force behind the sentiment such a strong compulsion. *With no reason why, no explanation for the need, other than I am compelled.*

Malik wanted nothing more than to stay beside her. But he also knew that wasn't possible. He had a responsibility to Rourke.

The sensation began to fade, receding into Delaney's head or heart or wherever the awareness had come from; she was left empty and hollow. The presence's sudden absence left Delaney with an intense emotion of being all alone once more.

Vivianna's voice was soft as she began to tell Delaney the story of where she'd come from, why they'd hid her from the world. Why the truth had been kept from her. She started with Bannan's history. About the Amalgamates and what they are and can do.

Bent, Not Broken   73

"I understand you're tired, but this can't wait any longer. Our story starts generations ago. Bannan's family have been archeologists for hundreds of years. They went digging in the dirt before archeology became popular. They were always off on a dig or cataloging what they'd found for museums. Some of the most amazing discoveries, groundbreaking finds for Meso-America, are the products of his family." She declared it all with such pride.

"One of those explorers was named Sebastian. At that particular time, there was an influenza epidemic ravaging Mexico and South America. So many were sick and he too came down with a fever, almost dying. Most people couldn't survive the pandemic influenza infection or smallpox. It became an immediate death sentence." Viv took a sip from a bottle of water.

"Mom, I'm confused. How long ago are you talking about?"

"Right around the time Cortez landed on the coast of Mexico, bringing with him his diseases and weapons." Disgust seeped from Viv's voice.

Viv blew out a lengthy sigh. "Influenza, smallpox, and a handful of other infections were quickly spreading. The Spaniards didn't even need arms. They had something far more sophisticated and brutally efficient; disease has no qualms about who it kills. Most of the population of the coastal tribes were wiped out. Then the disease began spreading to the interior of the country.

"Sorry, I'm a little off the subject. The story irritates the hell out of me that all those people perished and we understand nothing of their lives.

"Anyway, Sebastian spent years traveling extensively throughout South America, Central America, and Mexico. It had taken months, but word finally reached him that his younger brother had contracted tuberculosis. People simply didn't recover from illnesses in those days. Sebastian hurried home while his brother's condition continued to deteriorate. Sebastian stayed, nursing him back to health.

"When he'd made a full recovery the gossip began. Talk that Sebastian had acquired and used magic that he'd found on his travels. The changes that became noticeable couldn't be ignored. Sebastian's bother seemed healthier than he'd been before the Tuberculosis.

"They soon left the States all together, to travel the world." She stretched her neck from side to side. Viv appeared both tired and relieved at the same time. She yawned and stretched her lower back in the process. Finally, halting her pacing at Delaney's bedside, Viv realized Delaney needed her rest.

"I'm sorry. It's so easy for me to become entangled in something that is so personal. Get some sleep, baby. We still have a lot of ground to cover. We'll continue this little story later when you have more energy and can stay awake. Feel better and if you need something before I get back, call home. Love you, and I'm so happy and relieved you're safe." Viv held Delaney's hands tightly in hers while bending down to kiss her forehead. Viv lingered for a moment longer than she had to. She pressed her cheek against Delaney's head, Vivianna's face crinkled as she began to smile.

"See you in a little while. Right now, just rest and get some of your strength back." Viv brushed a lose strand of hair from her daughter's forehead.

Delaney's eyes drooped, her mind clouded, and before she drifted off to a drug-induced stupor she let out a giggle. *I'm crazy and this makes perfect sense.*

The dream began peacefully as Delaney walked around the fountains at the Bellagio. The dancing water shot high into the night sky on a mission to reach the moon. Music played in the distance, the same measure always seemed to find her. A dolphin swam through the spray as it danced in time alongside the composition. The magnificent being had not been part of the show and yet he played amongst the shallow waves.

Delaney watched the majestic creature break free of the water. No longer a dolphin, a stunning Native American man stood, with golden skin and shiny black hair hanging wet down his back and flapping in a swift breeze. He walked straight toward her, mesmerizing, flawless and beautiful. He raised his hand and gestured to Delaney to follow.

The breath caught painfully in Delaney's throat. She found herself compelled to be in his arms.

"Come with me," he said in a husky tone, arm still stretched out.

When she glanced up into his face, Delaney saw the familiar depthless green eyes and started to run to him. But the image wavered and she found herself alone and left knee-deep in the fountain, overcome by emptiness.

"Peyton, can you watch Delaney; I am going to the mall." Within a few seconds, Peyton stood beside Malik, gently reaching up and touching his shoulder.

"You okay?" Concern was etched on her soft Asian features and her voice filled with compassion. How she had any sensitivity left within her was a miracle. To withstand such a terrible captivity and yet not be a monster was a true display of her nonhuman condition.

"I'll be back to relieve you for the night shift at the latest." Malik disappeared before she'd answered. He arrived at the mall only moments later.

The corridor had been blocked off by yellow police tape and several uniformed officers at the mouth of the hallway. A short, balding man tagged blood smeared fingerprints with thick, clear cellophane patches.

Malik drifted forward to get a firsthand view of what they had found in the bathroom. He moved into the doorway. His hands fisted at his sides, he wanted to beat the piece of crap himself. Thick, dark red, calcified gore covered the floor as if a stuffed pig had been slaughtered and hung to drain. The crimson liquid caked the sink and smeared around on the linoleum in smudged shoe prints. Blood stained fingerprints appeared on every surface, like a craft project from a kindergarten class. The mirror had shattered, Delaney's hair hung from the pieces still attached to the wall. The sink had small bloody handprints on the outside of the bowl.

Malik found her in his head, the panicked expression, the tears running down her face. The only thing he thought about was putting his fist through the wall.

Malik walked back out and turned to leave the crime scene behind. The emergency exit off to the right had more bloody fingerprints calcified on the propped open door leading out to the parking area. He refused to allow hope to die as he walked the perimeter of the mall looking to find a clue as to where Rourke had gone.

Chapter NINE

Delaney had been stationary for hours or so it seemed to Malik. Each slow breath eclipsed into subtle twitches, seizing his attention one at a time. Puffy eyelids fluttered in ping-pong championship motion below her swollen lids. Those petite legs moved with tiny spasms as if at any moment, she would spring into action and bolt from the room. Her fingers shuddered involuntarily from bent to straight and back again. The fixed, vulnerable body trembled while death waited to claim her.

No large or sudden movements. She never once tossed or turned. Malik's torture lay in her relatively static appearance.

Those sleepy words are all I had left from her. They are what I carry with me. Will she survive the transition? Her slumberous voice in those moments she almost knew he was there while waking, and he knew she felt something for him, had been repressed.

I am a powerless bystander who isn't able to do anything to help her find her way back to us, to me.

With an inquisitive gaze he waited, lingering in the hope that Delaney would have her memories intact. The door cracked open, startling Malik and forcing him to abandon his thoughts. He studied the threat with critical vigilance.

A tall man with short blond hair stood a few steps from the bed. The man's brow furrowed as he surveyed her with an intensity that bothered Malik.

"Hey, how are you?" The guy whispered into the darkness. He pulled out a pen flashlight and held it between his perfect white teeth. He reached down and picked up her chart, then browsed the pages until pausing half way through. He returned the medical records to the footboard of her hospital bed.

The sweet smell of cologne became so strong that it stung Malik's nose and his eyes watered. He repressed a sneeze by breathing through his mouth. After a few minutes, the man turned and walked out. A burning sensation formed in Malik's throat and his physical reaction to the visitor stumped him.

"Flynn. Get someone to check out the tall towhead that left Delaney's room." Malik issued the order.

"Copy that." Flynn affirmed. Malik stared at her when her unexpected gaze went to the open space where he stood.

She found him again. A smile pulled at his lips. A flash of recognition, maybe. Or simple curiosity held her watchful gaze to his as if a steel rod had been welded between them, yet no more substantial than a cotton thread.

Delaney released a deep sigh and her eyelids fluttered shut. She sensed that she was safe as if she understood he was there to ensure her protection.

I am always here beside her, but that still doesn't mean she is mine. Not in the sense that I want her. She's never mine to keep.

Malik's fingers hurt from being in tight white fists at his side, though doubtful he'd ever admit it. Out of frustration, he threw himself in the chair by the door.

I'm nothing more than a shadow. Someone who has stood next to her a million times, but in moments she'd remember only as being all alone.

My arms are always only inches from wrapping around her. My hands tingle to touch her velvety skin. She is so close I can scent the Downey on her clothes, the ever-present coconut lime shampoo and the Kenneth Cole fragrance lingering

Bent, Not Broken   79

on her neck.

He had sat beside her countless times, holding her hand while she had her troubling dreams and terrifying nightmares. Those moments when he put the Kindreds on the line for her, he'd told himself it was the job, nothing more. Truth was, he would lay down his life for her because he couldn't imagine an existence she wasn't part of. He understood her as a person. He was drawn to her, and believed she was his only hope of deliverance. In her arms, he thought to find the desire to live and love.

"Hey, I thought you might want a break. You should check in with Dane. Vivianna and Bannan need a minute with you too." Peyton had entered unnoticed while his thoughts distracted him. Now she stood next to him.

He turned his head to stare at her. Exhaling a deep breath, he let the thoughts go and refocused his energy on his duties.

"You look as if you require a holiday. Did our dog die? Oh wait, we don't own a dog." She kneeled down beside him and rested her hand on his knee, then squeezed.

"Dane wants me to take over the guard. He recommended it to the Counsel," Malik confessed with absolutely no enthusiasm.

In less than two days, what he'd been waiting three and a half years for had finally happened. Whether it would be good or bad once Delaney completed the transition was yet to be seen. Everything he knew would be different, one way or another.

"I know you didn't want to lose Rourke." Peyton paused as her tone filled with emotions she never allowed out. "Neither did I. He was like a dad to me. Him and Dane are as close as I'll ever come. I'll be as proud to call you my commander as I am when I refer to you as my brother." She continued to look at him.

"Peyton." He wasn't sure what he wanted to say next. "What if being in command isn't something I want?" Malik hadn't meant to glance at Delaney. The action had been an automatic response to every situation, and one that hadn't escaped Peyton's attention.

"Is the reason because you will be in a position to deal with this? Do you want a life with her? You can tell me what's going on in your head. I'm here, talk to me."

"I'm not sure what you mean." Malik was not ready to disclose his feelings for Delaney.

Nothing was real until he told Peyton.

His reaction seemed normal under such an extraordinary situation. The assassin succumbed to the temptation, attached to the principal and balked at the concept of letting her go. Malik had never been close to anyone besides Dane, Peyton, and Tryst. He hadn't any inclination of what to do next.

"Just because you guard her doesn't mean you are conscious of who she is. Eavesdropping on her life isn't the same as a friendship." A sad smile crossed her face.

He didn't respond. He had nothing to say.

Malik drifted out of the room to a place where he could leave the discord behind. He stood near the edge of the rocks watching the surf crash against black volcanic rubble far below. The water leapt high into the air as it crashed into the cliff face and salty mist caressed his face. The chatty birds talking back and forth soothed him.

Malik sat down, defeated, and his head fell into his hands.

How did it all get so screwed up? I knew better than to let my feelings grow for her and yet, I never attempted to walk away. I needed to request out over four years ago, should have seen the direction things were heading. I tried to compartmentalize what I wanted, keep it apart from my duty.

He sat for a while, the wind howling in his ears and stinging his face. Once his mind calmed, he forced himself to concentrate on the surf far below and not Delaney, waiting in a hospital bed.

Maybe if I stare long enough, answers will ripple to the surface and I can understand what to do.

"Malik." Dane's voice link-spoke over his thoughts.

"Yes." He hoped his words didn't sound forced, then took a deep breath and tried to collect himself.

"Are you coming home?" Dane inquired as if he was aware of Malik's location. He stood up and drifted into the Drake's kitchen.

"Everything's good. Delaney's healing and Vivianna already began educating her."

"Will they leave Vegas?" The question held a hopeful tone. Dane appeared worried. This time the attack had come too close for comfort. The activity had dredged up the past and made Dane realize how much he wanted his own family closer.

"I'm about to discuss the issue now. I'll get back to you with any new developments." The person Malik needed to speak with entered the kitchen just as he responded to Dane.

"Malik." Vivianna's face lit up in a wide smile. She leaned over and placed a kiss on his cheek before going to the refrigerator.

"Your dad wants to know if you'll consider bringing everyone home." *Might as well get this part done*, he thought.

"No, they need to be normal." Anyone who had ever met Viv understood the answer before the question was even asked.

"Extra guards were issued for each of the girls." Malik left out the part about Vivianna's own additional protectors. The subject would cause an all-out battle he didn't want to begin at the present.

"Peanut Butter and Jelly sound good to you?" She spoke and then flashed him one of her cover model smiles.

"You know they're my weakness. Toasted bread and extra crunchy please?" He asked while he attempted to relax a little. A deep breath later and he stood in front of the toaster, waiting.

"I'm glad you're with Delaney. I feel better knowing it's you." Her voice broke. "Do you think we need to go home?"

"Yes…and no. If enough of the Stryders come, it won't matter where we are. There's safety in numbers. Going to Naroke would stack the odds in our favor and jeopardize an entire community seeking refuge from the war." He eyed the glass of milk she was pouring for him as he spoke.

"I think the Stryders hoped the stress of multiple attacks would send Delaney's body into overdrive and shoot her into the transition. I wonder if adrenaline can be used as a catalyst." Vivianna had only paused for a second and then glanced at him speechless.

"Wish we had considered that."

"I'm off to see Delaney. You're taking the night shift?" She asked while gathering up a cup of hot water and a tea bag.

"Yes. I have to talk to your father first." Malik turned to leave, but stopped mid stride.

"Any of Delaney's memories begun to resurface?" The question burned inside of him.

"Nothing yet. Please contact Josslyn? She will need to come if Delaney remains resistant." Her brow pursed as she spoke.

Viv left for the hospital.

Malik needed rest. He never had personal issues until Delaney. With ties to only Kindreds and the Drakes, everything had been straightforward until he started adding things to the private list. The complications were growing right before his eyes. Now he had stuff that mattered, the outcome of which would affect him on levels he didn't realize he even possessed.

He shook his head at the whole stupid mess, then fell asleep thinking about Delaney.

The dream began in a rolling wheat field under a clear midnight sky dotted with iridescent diamonds casting shadowy monsters onto golden stocks. Delaney lay on the ground intertwined with me. I pulled her against my heart thundering unrestrained in my chest and wrapped my arms around her body.

Her soft hair blew in the flurry, smelling of coconuts and lime as it brushed across my cheek. Burying my face in her mane, I nipped at her neck and she shivered wildly from the tantalizing act. The spicy Juniper became intoxicating as it swept around me.

She stared at me with those hazel green eyes slicing right through me. The breeze turned into a barreling wind, twirling her shirt sleeve and pulling at her hair. She vanished from my embrace, sucking all the warmth away with her.

Off in the distance, a light laughter rang out and I raced in that direction. She called out my name. I sprinted towards the shimmering image and musical tone, but found nothing in all directions.

Later in the evening, Malik awoke in a cold sweat. He had fallen asleep wrapped in Delaney's sheets, staring up at the glow-in-the-dark universe covering the ceiling.

Was being in her bed inappropriate?

He didn't care.

Malik always had so little of her to call his own; today he needed more.

He realized he had tread into Delaney's dream on accident. The setting seemed real, because to them it had been. Delaney was the only person he had ever been able to link with in such an intimate way. The dreams they shared had become a reality that kept him feeling alive while waiting for her.

After a long, hot shower, he checked on each of the guards. Back up plans, new strategies, and ulterior escape routes had to be considered and formulated.

"Viv wants to talk to you." Fezz link-spoke before Malik left the office.

Chapter TEN

Delaney witnessed the tenebrous night sky peeking through her open blinds. The absence of light in the room gave way to menacing shadows withering on the floor and leaping from the walls. A shiver tore down her frame and she snapped her eyes shut.

Her imagination picked up where her vision left off. Grey and yellow spots detonated on top of each other, creating scarred faces, rainbow brilliant eyeballs, and blurred lines. Fear kept her lids stapled together. She minded less that her imagination created the blips—a limited amount of terror seemed controllable.

The rustling whispers she swore she heard turned out to be her own breathing, ragged and irregular, not monsters under the bed or hiding in the closet. She became desperate to take another look, but the beast in her mind refused to release her. In the end, impetuosity had the final comment.

"Hello?" She whispered to no one in particular. She couldn't shake the thought that something waited in the dank shadows as she strained to catch a glimmer of it first.

Delaney felt relieved when the door opened and someone chased away the supernatural eeriness.

"Are you awake?" Muddled words pulled at Delaney to fully wake up.

"Sort of," Delaney mumbled through a yawn.

"I wish you were home right now. We'd sit in your room having a mom and daughter conversation about our world, and everything would be okay. I wonder, had we been honest earlier, if any of this might have been avoidable. We wanted to protect you from the bad. Now I am not so sure our chosen course of action was the right one." Vivianna's voice was gentle, yet troubled.

"I understand you've got inquiries. But let me continue with my story. Some of the questions might be answered along the way." Vivianna her things down on the tray table and put a warm paper cup in one of Delaney's hands.

"Apple cinnamon?"

"Of course, darling. That's your favorite, right?" said Vivianna. "I figured you are bored, so I brought some things to keep you busy while you're stuck here." Delaney's iPod fell into her other hand.

"Thanks for the tea." Delaney tried to sip the warm liquid and realized with utter sadness, her mouth was too mangled to enjoy her favorite drink.

"Get on with the story." Delaney croaked.

Viv smiled at her. "Okay let's see… The two brothers spent the next few years back and forth between Mexico and South America, searching sites and looking for more information about the origins of the texts. They searched for Lucas's people, the ones who had cared for Sebastian in the beginning, but they had vanished.

"They emerged in Spokane, Washington. Each man had taken a bride, in the meantime." Vivianna chewed on her lower lip with a faraway look in her eye. "It is harder than you can believe for us to find someone special. Much more difficult than finding love is for the humans. We wait lifetimes to find our significant others. When we fall in love it is more profound than a simple bodily function and a release of chemicals in the brain. It is as if you have been waiting for that particular person to arrive. I hate to say something as contrived as destiny, but we are meant for someone and they are meant for us. It is referred to as the Echo Principle. Two people created of one another for the specific purpose of finding each other."

"So what happened with Sebastian's brother?"

"His name was Bannan." She answered without glancing at her.

Wait! Had she just said...?

"Both Sebastian and his brother had found their Echoes while traveling. Sebastian had married Candace, an Italian-Brazilian beauty, with deep cocoa colored eyes and cascading wild black hair." She walked to the other side of the bed. Her shoulders pulled forward in a long breath. Viv was stalling.

Delaney realized there had to be more of a bombshell still to come.

Viv turned her back to Delaney and went on. "Sebastian's brother, Bannan...married Vivianna, a native American from Naroke, an island off the coast of Chile." Moving away from the window, she carefully avoided looking at Delaney.

"I get you're swimming in a hundred feet of questions, but please be patient." Viv slowly paced the room, her expression guarded.

"When Sebastian traveled through Argentina he became deathly ill. He stayed with a small tribe living high up in the Andes. The chief, Ny, liked and respected Sebastian immensely. Over time, they became good friends. Ny had Sebastian nursed back to health by his own son, Lucas.

"At first, Sebastian didn't understand what had happened. Lucas began explaining how his tribe managed to exist when everyone around them perished from war or disease. Lucas told him the old stories.

"Sebastian had been fused, becoming a Gabled Amalgamate. No longer fully human. Lucas advised Sebastian that if the transition hadn't been brought on him, he wouldn't have lived. He soon learned the small tribe consisted of what the chief called 'Amalgamates'. Amalgamates developed the ability to fuse with different animals, taking on their physical characteristics and then fusing back to their human forms. This process accelerated healing properties keeping them from succumbing to disease and trauma.

"Sebastian stayed with the tribe for a short time, learning about the new life that had been thrust on him. The clan's elders retold the history of how they had been entrusted with caring for the animals, but the fables didn't explain what they were. So, the senior tribesmen explained their deviations from the human race, a few myths and other just terrifying facts about their people. They spoke of the dark side of the nonhumans." Vivianna looked somber as she finished the sentence.

"I'm a recent divergence from the line," Viv said, smiling at Delaney. "We... you, I, and Calliope are abnormalities. Not dark, though. I'm an Amalgamate also, nevertheless different from Bannan and Sebastian. More abilities than any other Amalgamate incorporated inside me. They believe this is because of my bloodline. I was born this way." She stopped to take another breath and paced around the room silently for a few minutes.

"So, Gabled is someone who was something else and then turns into an Amalga-thing." *I don't understand any of this.* Pain lurked just behind Delaney's eyes as everything began to sink in.

"Sebastian and Candace conceived two children, both girls, less than a year apart. Their names were Brody and Daphne. Vivianna and Bannan had two amazing little cherubs known as..." She paused, but didn't glance directly at Delaney. "Delaney and Calliope." The words bounced around the room like flares while Delaney processed the information.

"Wait. Just stop for a second!" Delaney's gaze pinned Vivianna in place. "You...You're my real mother?" Her voice became a hoarse whisper.

"I am." Viv sighed in relief as went to Delaney and sat down on the mattress next to her. "I have held that painful secret for far too long. Not a day went by that I didn't want to tell you everything. It wasn't possible. If it was a choice between your life and the truth, I chose for you to live. You deserved the opportunity to do whatever you wanted, not the future everyone has planned for you." Viv exhaled a deep breath.

"I understand what it is like to be kept under a microscope. To grow up with people watching and waiting for you to turn into something different altogether. I hated that for you, any of you. Your father and I took you away from our home to give you a chance at a normal life. To be like everyone else, not a super hero meant to save our world from a man who could end us all.

"I always wanted you to be mine. I thought about what our life would have been like if we had been a real family. I never believed—" A pounding headache thundered behind her eyes.

"You should go on with the story. I need the rest of it." Delaney murmured softly.

Viv shook her head and began once again.

"Brody and Daphne came to live with us when Candace was murdered by Seeley, he's Isabeau's partner. They were sent to kill the entire family, but only Candace died. Sebastian was never the same, so I took them in and cared for them as my own.

"Because we don't age, we've had to lie and call all of you our adopted children. Otherwise, people would want to know how a couple in their thirties had children appearing to be in their late teens or early twenties." Viv took a deep breath. "I'm your real mother." Hesitating, she locked eyes with Delaney, who was still too dazed to speak and too stunned to move, to think, or to breathe.

"When Bannan was sick, Sebastian came straight home, telling Lucas he'd return after he'd seen to his brother's health. Sebastian helped Bannan by rushing him. Once he became a Gabled Amalgamate, he healed himself. That's how they've lived so long."

"Delaney, you and I are unique, even more so than the rest. Thanks to your grandfather, we all got a little something extra tucked away in our DNA. Also, because of your father, Calliope and you possess some human characteristics, as well. You and your sister are of Gabled Amalgamates, Do-La-Roux, Demi-Wraith blood.

"The three of us are known as Hynts by our people; we are what humans would call hybrids. So far, I retain the strength and the acute senses of an animal even when my symbols are not filled with energy and life. Brody and Daphne harbor no physical evidence of being able to fuse. We are still waiting to see if any abilities will surface in them." Delaney nodded.

Bent, Not Broken

"Those men from last night were sent to kill you. Malik managed to take them out. But he was injured badly in the process. Malik knew he couldn't protect you by himself, so he called for backup guards. They have been with you while he's still recovering. Someone is always next to you. If you need anything, just say Malik's name aloud. He's linked telepathically with you and he'll be here immediately." The reassuring tone made Delaney feel better.

"This is all real?" Delaney's timbre faded into the nothingness again. Fear, confusion, and jubilation were so close; her bed felt crowded.

"Why do they want to hurt me? What threat do I pose?" The words rose up through her anxiety and sounded shrill.

"Who you are is enough for them to need you dead. To some, we're abominations, mixed blooded miscreants. We are something to fear." Viv blinked and let her eyes flutter downward.

"You… We have no idea what you'll be capable of. The change is happening so late, and now you are making up for lost time by racing through a process normally taking days to complete. Your body's already healing itself." Viv scratched her face as she pulled wispy pieces of hair away from her forehead.

Delaney's chest felt like someone was sitting on it. She heard the blood thundering within her veins. Her hands began to sweat and her head spun.

"Can…'t…brea…the."

Viv handed Delaney a paper tumbler. She put it over her mouth to help slow her breathing.

"What's a Demi-Waith?" Delaney asked with raised eyebrows and into the Styrofoam cup.

"My mother, grandma Dasha, was a Relic pureblood. A Demi-Waith is the result of the mixing of the Relic DNA with any other breeds.

"Originally, the Relics were shifters from the North. None of us are familiar with the history. For whatever reason, the tribe acquired the capability to alter their appearances. They could shift into animals. We call the ability 'fusing'.

"Grandma Dasha was the last of the original clan; the Relic line is gone now. When the Relic bloodline was mixed, the Demi-Waiths became a byproduct.

The tribe fractured into different clans for whatever reasons. We are members of one.

"We're like humans. Consider the amount of American Indian tribes there are. All maintain their own cultures, just as we do. Separate, but the same. My father lives by the old traditions given to him by my mother's people. We differ from the Relics because they were only able to fuse to a single animal, which had been decided at birth for each one of them. No Script or Prints. But—"

Delaney exhaled confused frustration. "Script and Prints? What are they?"

"Prints are of specific animals, insects, organic material, etcetera, and indicates what you animals you can fuse into. A living tattoo that penetrates the epidermis and lies dormant underneath the skin until you fuse. A script describes you as a person. It tells your story and what you can do. Like if you have psychic powers. A still picture with moving parts. Like a waterfall, water actually falls, trees blow. " Vivianna glanced down at her own arm.

"Will I be covered in spots or stripes or something? Will it hurt?" Delaney didn't even try to keep the fear from her voice.

"I don't know and no. These identifiers can land anywhere on the body or lie dormant under the dermis. When you need the mark it will emerge. We can't know what it will look like until it appears, but there is no pain, though a little itching is normal." Vivianna didn't want to lie anymore. The truth may be confusing and sound absurd, but it was the truth.

"Anyway, as evolution stepped in and the breeds began to procreate, they developed stronger pedigrees, more defensive and protective stances, and fewer weaknesses. My mother changed the bloodline even further when she married and mated with Grandpa Dane. He was not of Relic origins.

"No one understands how the distinctive breeds came to be. I suppose if life wants to succeed, it finds a way to do so. Physically, we change into different animals. But over the years we evolved again to include Scripts and Prints from the mixing of the different bloodlines, each generation developing more abilities as we developed. Prints and Scripts are how we identify who and what we are.

Bent, Not Broken   91

"We believe the idea that your heart will never deceive you. Your mind and body can be fooled, but not your spirit. The heart searches until it finds the one true match because you were made of one another.

"Either your Script or Prints will lead you to the one that matches your marks, your spirit's twin, your Echo. It's like being drawn to someone, a literal gravitational pull that's unbelievably strong and unbreakable once connected." Vivianna turned to look at Delaney, then smiled.

"Our clans came together when the wars got too close to home; the battle for survival resulted in our city being taken from us by the Stryders. My father took everyone who wanted to go, to the original stronghold, Easter Island. Our people are all unique, coming from different backgrounds and ethnicities. Some are Fusers, equivalent to us. We include Pikes, Tracers, Trackers, Pickets, Sentinels, Dares, and more.

"Our tribe is the largest of its kind anywhere. When we ran, we all gave up our old names and took on new ones. Now we are memorialized as the Leonawa Aquana Tallulah Waiths among the other families. In our world, we are addressed as Ghosts of the Leaping Water." A half smile reached her lips, and her eyes became soft and watery. A strong sense of pride hung heavy in the room.

"Who are the guardians you referred to?" Delaney asked.

"The guards are Kindreds. They are an elite band of assassins and protectors who are unparalleled in their skills. The Spirit People assembled them. The Sighmeran Guard is another militia force my father put together in order to guarantee the safety of our tribe. We are personally guarded by the Kindreds. They're the most trained and best equipped to carry out a variety of missions. They're held in the highest of esteem. Without them, none of our family or our people are safe." Viv glanced at Delaney.

"Who are the Spirit People?" Delaney asked.

"Every culture incorporates a belief system. The Spirit People are our answer to God." Vivianna answered with a slightly sullen expression.

"What about the rue thingy you said?" Delaney racked her brain trying to remember the name of something Viv had mentioned.

"Doux-La-Roux. Calliope, you, and I are also part Doux-La-Roux. They are the original wolf shifters from Gaul or present-day France. None of the traditional characteristics show in me, but it is possible for them to still manifest within you or Calliope. Another one of those things we aren't quite clear on," she said, shrugging.

"Doux-La-Roux, okay. Great," Delaney mumbled, half to herself as she carefully shook her head in bewilderment.

"Archaeology is our family business. The occupation is the only way to search for answers and not draw unnecessary attention to ourselves from the humans and other enemies. Collegians are allowed access to countries which allow scientific excavations to take place. It provides us with much more latitude to find our answers than the alternative." Viv took a break and grabbed a long drink of water.

"Where did we come from?" Delaney asked her.

"We don't know. There are stories handed down. But the truth is, we aren't sure how we began. The Haunts, the Relics…who knows? The origins of most night creatures are still widespread mysteries. Created or born, we're all here for whatever reason, though." No solid answers presented themselves.

"How long ago did Calliope change?" It suddenly occurred to Delaney.

"Calliope began changing when she reached twelve. You never showed any sign of the changes. We sent Calliope, Daphne, and Brody away to summer camp every year to be trained. They were being schooled at our clan's home." Viv stopped when Delaney raised her hands.

"Viv, I'm going to pass out, my head is killing me. I need time to think. A mountain of questions, I don't even know where to begin. Come back later when I'm not swimming in painkillers and exhaustion, please." Delaney closed her eyes and passed out immediately.

An unsettling sleep consumed her. She tossed and turned in restlessness seeing visions of wolves, coyotes, and peace pipes. She dreamt of beautiful

Indians and fires burning bright against the night sky. Her dreams filled with symbols she didn't understand.

"Did you know she was seeing a psychologist?" Viv raised an eyebrow as Malik approached.

"I found out she was talking to a school counselor about a year ago. It seemed harmless to let her work through some of her feelings."

"I think I understand why Delaney never changed." She exhaled a long breath. "The therapist told her she was suffering from Post-Traumatic Stress Disorder. Her mind was shielding her consciousness because she couldn't handle it. The memories would resurface and Delaney believed she was going crazy. She thought she had a chemical imbalance or something. The therapist prescribed antidepressants, which could have acted like a deterrent. The built-in catalyst would have been nullified. The medication changed the brain's chemistry just enough to delay Delaney's fuse.

"She told me she believed there was something wrong with her. She was convinced she had been abused as a child." She shook her head in sadness. "We drove her to think she was crazy. What kind of parents do that? She'll never forgive us for this. We have stolen her past and her future is in jeopardy." Her lips pursed tightly. "I don't even know how much she lost. How many private, important moments are now gone. We took things from her."

"Viv, it may take time. She will understand. When she fathoms what the Stryders are capable of, she can comprehend the reasoning behind our decision to protect her." Malik hoped that was the way it turned out. He still hadn't told Delaney their truth.

"I'm going to relieve Peyton. There is only so much we can do to keep Delaney alive. If she lives and her anger is a repercussion, fine." He left for the hospital.

Chapter ELEVEN

The sun was hiding behind the Spring Mountains when Delaney finally awoke in her sanitized cell. Her eyes fluttered open to find her father sitting alongside the bed. An immediate sense of security wrapped around her, pushing a distorted smile to her face.

"Hey, my little girl." Her dad, full of warmth, spoke to her as he pulled the headphones down off her ears.

"Calliope and your mom are on their way up. You're in for it now. Also, I'm popping the bubble of serenity and telling you Daphne and Brody are coming too." He laughed at her.

"Be sweet Delaney, they're family." Bannan pushed the hair from Delaney's face. Kissing her on the forehead, he leaned over and gently hugged her broken frame.

Her father sat next to her in the chair closest to the bed. Neither verbalized their thoughts, they didn't need to. He reached out and took her hand while Delaney searched for something in his silence.

"I'm sorry you needed me and I wasn't there." Bannan exhaled loudly. His voice cracked and collapsed.

Bent, Not Broken

My dad is more like I am than I realized. This festers in him as well.

"I fought hard. I tried to stay focused. Every self-defense move I have been taught went right out of my head. Despite the training, I got lost." Delaney's brow furrowed. "All the classes…I couldn't remember a thing to help myself. I should have reacted, instead I fell apart." Delaney's tone grew softer. "Daddy, the fight didn't happen the way I thought it would. In some ways, it had been just a game until now."

"Those classes were for helping to save your life because you couldn't be trained like Calliope, Brody, and Daphne. I hoped to arm you with enough knowledge to understand what to expect. Delaney, you survived, and that's all I ever wanted." He exhaled and his shoulders fell forward.

"Your mom has told you some of our history. She hasn't brought me up to speed on how far you've gotten. So let me say this, you will have to become the strongest version of yourself. You've learned the hardest lesson: sometimes you can't win. You acquired the skills to survive." He tossed her a small grin. "Learning to fight in a controlled atmosphere is one thing. When confronted in a real-life situation, there is no control. You can use this to be better prepared for what is coming next." Bannan's words didn't comfort her.

"Delaney, more are already on the way. They will never stop. Until you, your mother, and, Calliope are dead, they view you as a real threat. They want to eliminate the prospect of any saviors. You have to be on guard every minute. Be aware of everything going on around you. Choose who you trust carefully," Bannan paused as Delaney watched him in awe.

His voice became soft. "I wanted you to come face-to-face with the truth, but you were safer before." He looked distraught. Delaney couldn't think of anything to say. He struggled and she didn't understand what to do.

"When you came into this world, you were so small, your little body got lost in my hands." Bannan's words lapsed as he stared down at his fingers. "I needed to protect you from everything. I would do anything to ensure your safety. I am helpless now, and I'm not sure how to keep you alive." His gaze fell to the floor. Delaney witnessed him wipe his cheek with his index finger and her chest tightened around her heart.

Her life had been taken from her and a new one created. A mountain of lies tied up tight with a big fat bow. Even through the anger and the pain of knowing she never really knew any of them, she understood their motive and tried to release the resentment. Everything they had done was to ensure she had a chance to live.

By not knowing, she couldn't be expected to lie.

Bannan bore such a burden. Delaney found anger to be the one emotion she wasn't able to conjure as she realized the years of his carrying this weight— the years of lying—had aged her dad. She understood her father had helped them steal her past to ensure her future.

Their tender moment shattered when four distinct female voices erupted in the once quiet hall and began to draw closer.

"Daddy, I love you. You being here makes me safe."

Bannan smiled broadly at her and somehow everything became right between them.

Delaney welcomed the distraction her family would bring. The closeness felt perplexing and any attempts at intimacy with anyone had always seemed difficult, so this moment stumbled in the same familiar direction. Only now, she felt more vulnerable than ever. The truths she had been faced with incited feelings of inadequacy, insignificance, and a sense of divergence. Delaney had always suffered from never understanding what she's supposed to say or do. Now was no different, but more profound at the same time.

The four women came piling through the door talking a mile a minute and driving all thoughts from Delaney's mind that didn't immediately pertain to them.

They love me and I them. That realization made her smile.

Delaney looked around the room at the faces she adored, even Brody. They were all really strangers she didn't recognize at all. Her eyes were drawn back to Viv. *Mom.*

Delaney had always wanted to be able to offer more of herself, but fear of rejection had kept her distant and unreachable, even to Viv. Personal attachments were just another awkward sentiment Delaney had always tried to avoid.

The next few hours passed with giggles, sarcasm, and tenderness. Calliope and Daphne helped Delaney take a shower, because as they lovingly informed her, she smelled similar to a piece of fruit seconds away from rotting. Neither of them would shave her legs, though. She was sure she would gain status as a national forested area any day now.

After cleaning up, Delaney felt human once again, sort of. Brody assisted by drying her hair and even straightening it. Because Delaney and Brody had the greatest distance in age between them, they seemed like distant relatives to each other. When Brody finished with her hair, she stared at Delaney for a long moment.

"You don't look as bad today. Next time, fight with your hands and not your face, moron." Brody laughed as she smiled at Delaney. This is the closet Brody had ever come to hugging her.

Progress, if you could call it that.

Brody was working on her master's degree in Forensic Anthropology. She was interested in Meso-America and the Chinchorro Mummies in South America had become her current interest. When Brody graduated she wanted to be a Forensic Anthropologist. She had a fantastic sense of right and wrong and her own life mirrored the concept. All things were always clearly marked in dark and light for her. She believed lending a voice to those that no longer had one to be an obligation every person should accept. Delaney found her view point precarious because in some ways Brody understood more about the dead than the living.

Brody engaged people with brainy ideas, not one for frills, she liked the basics. Her boy-cut jet-black hair was always hand ruffled. Her lanky body suited a model. Brody's intensely serious nature kept most everyone at a distance and made Delaney believe everyone was socially inept in some way. Tonight, she portrayed a sweet and caring sister. Maybe Brody had suffered an incredible blow to the head rendering her loving.

I can dream.

Brody depicted the polar opposite of Daphne in many ways, which made little sense because they had such a strong bond of sisterhood. Daphne was girly and fun to hang out with. Fire engine red hair shot straight down to her lower back, contrasting against her translucent white skin. She was stunningly beautiful and genuinely sweet, but with a temper that could scare the hell out of any drill sergeant.

It was hard not to be jealous of Daphne. Most men's heads spun like tops when they heard Daphne speak with her articulate Mensa styled vocabulary, if her looks hadn't already rendered them under her spell.

Daphne followed in the footsteps of her father, right into the family business. She was an archeologist in the making, and resident dinosaur junkie. She'd gotten back into town only hours before after spending the day at a dig site in St. George, Utah, researching something about a new breed of Raptors.

Calliope was the soon-to-be paleontologist. She was the youngest and had deep mahogany tresses flopping down her back in giant soup can curls. She was the one always doing the right thing, never caused trouble, and was always the dependable, straight-as-an-arrow responsible one.

"Girls, time to go. I need to finish talking to Delaney and you guys are just too disruptive." Viv looked at them all serious, but winking and smiling.

Everyone said their goodbyes. Within a few minutes Vivianna settled into her new favorite chair on the side of the bed.

"I've probably overloaded you with information in the last twenty four hours. You have a bunch of questions, I'm sure. I'll get to them, I promise. First, let me finish, please?" Delaney nodded and Viv jumped right in.

"Delaney we're not alone in our world, there are other families like ours, more groups of nonhumans where individuals have come together forming sects for safety and survival. A war has been going on since the original tribes walked over North America. A peaceful ending is far from sight." Viv took a slow breath.

"Delaney, I had to tell you everything because you've finally begun your transition, and this fact changes how we proceed. A steep bounty is attached to you; one that will bring assassins. I understand you're tired and it's late, so we'll talk more tomorrow. Get some rest, baby girl." She floated out the door before Delaney could even say good-bye.

Delaney's mind tried to swim through the sea of questions from all that Viv had revealed. Her eyes drooped and before she realized it, Delaney was back in dreamland. Where the earth exploded in fiery volcanoes and demons filled the sky with beautiful black gossamer wings.

This can't be sleep, Delaney thought when she woke to darkness later in the night surrounded by menacing shadows that seemed to be coming for her.

"You're right. I hate to admit the fact, but I do have feelings for her. There is something between us pulling at me like a physical need I cannot escape. As stupid as I am being, I can't seem to help it." Malik put his arm around Petyon's shoulders. They stood together, both quiet and left to their own thoughts.

"Does she know?"

"What does that matter? Whatever had been between us is locked away in her head. She doesn't remember…yet. Once the fates unbind Delaney's memories we can figure things out."

"Malik, be careful." Peyton smiled at him as her features disintegrated into the open space and he found himself alone.

Deep into the night, Malik realized the solution wouldn't come as easily as he had hoped. Delaney held the answers and without her, nothing could be solved. Frustration settled between his shoulder blades like a festering wound.

Malik grabbed Delaney's hand and traced small circles on her palm with his fingers before pulling her lifeless limb up and kissing the inside of her knuckles. He held her velvety skin to his mouth longer than he should have. Before he had given it too much thought, he leaned over and kissed her cheek, then gently and carefully crawled into bed next to her. He positioned himself on his side to watch her sleep.

Her face turned into his chest, her warm body curling close to his. She burrowed into him. Malik wanted to reach out and pull her closer, but he didn't. To lay next to her was enough, for now.

Delaney is a greater danger for me than I ever realized. Because, after so many years of loneliness, the wanting to be no other place than with her seems more important than anything else.

Hours passed as he stayed perfectly still next to her, watching her eyes flutter behind closed lids as she dreamed.

The door opened and a bulky man with raven black hair in a ponytail and wearing a medical assistant's uniform poked his head in. He strolled over to stand next to Delaney, unable to detect Malik under his cloak of shadow. An unrecognizable scent alerted Malik that the orderly wasn't human.

The imposter pulled out a syringe from the pocket of his white jacket and stepped closer to the network of machines. Malik's hand shot out to grab the arm holding the needle and knocked Delaney's IV rig to the ground. It broke open and flooded thick liquid all around the man's feet. The next thing Malik knew, they were on the Helipad deck on the roof of the hospital.

A Traveler can mimic another's attributes once they are in close enough proximity to them. The only thing they couldn't mimic was another's instincts and reactions. Malik's ability to drift from one place to another was the trait he mimicked and the liquid from the IV provided a Halo for two to travel within. When any of the guards brought along a passenger, he required a liquid to complete the link because the aquifers they drifted through wouldn't allow a hitchhiker without a catalyst.

Scarlet strobe lights flashing in a slow rhythm gave a blood-red tint to the night sky. The balmy wind blew the Traveler's scent to Malik once more. He smelled of fresh cut pine trees and Malik wondered what had made a forester take a job like this. The man had journeyed far out of his element for this particular hit.

"A Kindred now are ye, laddy?" He spoke in a thick Irish brogue.

This one is going down the old fashion way.

"Peyton. Delaney's hospital room now."

"Can we get this done already; my girl is waiting." Malik hoped the assassin failed to think things through and he could throw him off his game. The Traveler could borrow any of Malik's abilities that were in use.

"Would it help if I spoke in Gaelic and showed you pictures as to what is supposed to happen now?" The Traveler's nostrils flared and his eyes narrowed. Then he stood there, staring at Malik.

He wasn't a subordinate, he had been trained. The Traveler wouldn't allow any verbal assaults to waiver his self-control. He was waiting for Malik to do all the work for him.

The slayer's eyes flashed around. A lead pipe caught Malik's attention as the man ran at him. They tumbled to the tarmac as Malik's back hit the landing pad hard. The surface tore through his shirt and ripped at his skin.

Road rash, perfect.

The assassin tried to pin him to the platform. Malik punched his arm in the bend of his elbow. The guy crumpled forward rolling into Malik, who forced his weight to the left. Malik sprang back to his feet. The Traveler came at him again with a right and Malik dodged it, then struck him down with a left. Malik's fist connected to the man's jaw and sent him backwards a couple of feet. The man shook his head, looking angry. He whipped around into a high round-house kick. Malik jumped back at the last minute and a swish of air grazed his face. Malik grabbed for his outstretched leg, gave a yank, and pushed forward trying to knock him off balance.

He caught a glimpse of the shiny blade in the assassin's hand as it extended. The Traveler launched himself swinging at Malik with the knife. Malik moved back while grabbing a chain holding nearby plastic trash cans in place. This time, the assassin came at Malik leading with the shank. With a few quick jabs he left Malik with a deep gash in his arm. Malik wrapped the chain around his hands to use as a deflector to the blade and went in again. The man kept coming at Malik's torso and managed to hit him hard with a punch. The Traveler stumbled back when Malik caught him in the jaw with his chain-wrapped right hook. Blood sprayed from where the links tore skin away.

The assassin advanced again, but Malik managed to dodge to the right at the last minute and wrap the chain about the hand holding the knife. The move dismantled the Traveler's offensive. A series of punches to his mid-section knocked him down to one knee, gasping for air. The Traveler tried to lift his head, but his energy was spent on breathing instead.

As Malik went into snap his spine, the Traveler plunged the blade deep into Malik's stomach. Malik wrapped the chain around the assassin's neck and pulled tight until the Traveler's movements ceased all together.

Malik took a few minutes to get back to Delaney's room. As Peyton turned to see who approached, the color drained from her face. He leaned against the wall; his pullover was shredded and clinging to his shoulder, blood soaked.

"You're lucky you can't die from this, but that doesn't mean I won't kill you, stupid."

"I need a team of Roq's to the roof of the hospital. One body." Malik sputtered over small gasps.

"You can't call for assistance before the fight? Why do you wait till you want a cleanup crew to contact someone on the radio?" Anger coursed through her words.

"Peyton, it was one guy. Can you help me now? Please call Fezz to come get me. I'm too weak to drift back to the Drake's." The knife handle still poked out of his front.

She took off her hoody and tossed it to him, then helped him dislodge the weapon and tug the shirt over his head to hide the wounds. Malik looked up and met her gaze.

"One of the Stryders got the drop on you. Are you slipping? Getting too old for the fun stuff, huh?"

"It was a Traveler." *Sometimes I wished I'd never learned to speak.*

Peyton swung at him. Her fist hit him dead center in the face. Landing on his butt with an embarrassing thud, his brain exploded with colors as his nose spurted blood.

"What the hell, Peyton?" He remained on the floor as she leaned close to his ear.

"You and Trystan are the only family I have. Why are you trying to get yourself killed?" She whispered as Malik stared straight into her eyes.

"Pull this shit again, and *I'll* stab you." She pushed back until he lay flat on the floor.

Malik decided it was safer for him to remain lying still on the ground until Fezz came.

Chapter TWELVE

Delaney cracked a small smile as she pushed the sleepiness away; if not a grin she might give into the tangle of raw emotions swirling under the surface and fracture into small pieces.

She had believed her birth parents voluntarily abandoned her. *Hell, I modeled my whole way of life around the idea something is infinitely wrong and nobody wanted me. I've been in foster homes, under terrible conditions. Or so I thought, because the past had appeared to be real. Didn't they understand what giving me those memories would do to me? I even managed to make some of the retrospections up myself, building on what I couldn't explain.*

The drugs...did I ever need them?

Delaney had heard the excuse, and rationally, she understood. Emotions still rattled around inside her and she had no idea what to do with them. The lies had caused her pain, whether they had meant to or not.

In the last twenty four hours enough had happened that Delaney believed she had the right to be leery of everyone and everything. Even family.

How much had I missed? Am still missing?

Vivianna appeared in the doorway. Delaney wondered if reading people's thoughts may be another hidden talent of her mother's. Viv slid into the room with a small brown paper bag and a thermos of hot tea.

"Do you feel better? You seem as if you do. A little color back in those checks is encouraging. Along with some deep, dark black circles under your eyes, though. Are you not sleeping well?" Viv stopped abruptly. "Oh, I guess that could be from the broken nose, huh?" Vivianna rolled her eyeballs as she spoke. Delaney erupted into laughter with Vivianna following suit.

Delaney thought about telling Viv all the things that had been on her mind most of the morning. She figured the anger itching under her skin might be misplaced. The wounds were raw, fresh, and she knew she needed time to clear her head and form a reasonable opinion. The timetable factor, or lack thereof, served to increase her agitation. For the moment, Delaney decided to let herself heal a little while longer before confronting anyone.

"Why don't I remember my childhood?" *When I consider the future may be short-lived, I should at least be granted the knowledge of my past. Years of memories have to be stored somewhere, locked up tight in my head? Are they gone for good?*

Delaney wondered how she got to be this person. Had another path been offered, which road would she have chosen if all the facts had been available? The back and forth banter inside her mind had gotten her no closer to figuring out what to do. To deliberate what could only amount to an increasingly frustrating circumstance was pointless. All the debating in the world would change little.

"We didn't take your memories to hurt you. We thought we gave you a chance at a normal life. All these years…. I'm sorry. I couldn't understand how much our efforts would cost you. I should have ended the charade a long time ago." Vivianna finished sadly.

"I can't figure out what's real or what I want to be real." Delaney tried to shrug off the varying emotions. "Go on with your story." She didn't want Viv to be sad.

"Okay, we need to finish up the family history. But, either you come home and we care for you, or your healing properties are going to be a medical phenomenon in another day or so. Even your eyes are becoming unusu—."

"What do you mean?" *How much of myself will I lose with this metamorphosis?*

"They aren't brown anymore, baby. They're green, hazel, I believe. They'll be a brilliant color when you finish the transformation. Before, your eyes had a brownish membrane sitting over the top of the cornea. This sheath prevented you from seeing other breeds.

"Now you'll receive an unobstructed view of people as they are, and not what they project themselves to be. Only the most powerful Hellme—a dark fairy—can distort their image from another one of us. This skill set is a rare talent and even the highly practiced would deliberate before attempting to use it.

"Delaney, being able to see the truth around you will allow you to defend yourself when a threat approaches you." Viv smiled at Delaney.

"Why don't you look different to me then? Shouldn't your appearance be nonhuman?" Delaney asked, a little confused. She found there to be a lot of rules, and this particular one didn't make much sense.

Viv pulled her long-sleeve cardigan off. "The imprints don't jump off my body, not until I want them to, anyway. I have practiced self-control in order to limit how much of them show. I'm different from any Amalgamate because when I fuse, there is no totem, no animal, no Prints at all, only Script. But, an unidentifiable language that lies under my skin. That's why I'm called the Archetype. I am the first. Calliope, you, and I are considered Hynts. No one knows what we will be capable of.

"I possess the skill-set many believed had vanished centuries ago. My Scripts reflect those abilities and they're visible only when in use. They float along my exterior."

She closed her eyes and took a deep breath. Her skin began to dance. When she opened her eyes, the whites were bright and glowing around an azure blue core. Her skin had an unusual hue, partially glowing as swirls and curves formed substantial grooves. The intersecting straight lines became distinct symbols. Solid black pieces swaying back and forth from side to side, traveling the length of the exposed skin and finally disappearing under her clothes.

"Only one of my brands are visual for anyone to witness." Viv turned around in the chair, grabbed her hair, and raising it above her head, showed the back of her neck.

In the brightest hot pink and most vibrant violet was a symbol, more like parts of alphabet letters, surrounded in a cobalt blue outline. The lettering materialized in a rather beautiful form of calligraphy sitting under her skin. Swirling lines grew into an intricate frame similar to a 3D graphic picture. The sweeping characters appeared to be a capital I with a side of a V on the right and a small O on the left. The O part was where the fuchsia initialized. When it hit the middle of the neck, it began to turn violet and continued to darken as it made its way across to the end of the V.

"They are beautiful. What do they mean?" Delaney traced the odd mark with her eyes.

"None of us have ever seen anything even close to it." She lowered her hair and turned back to face Delaney. Viv smiled a half-moon grin while shrugging her shoulders.

"Oh, I can't lose you yet, baby doll. There's still more for me to tell you. We're just getting started. Each Amalgamate discharges a specific odor, a pheromone. You'll start to notice a distinct perfume coming from all of us. Our scents are impossible to hide. Usually, the bouquets are unique, but family members can share the same scent. This act doesn't happen often, though.

"Your body is emanating Juniper. Brody exudes Geraniums, Daphne is Blackberry, and Calliope radiates Jasmine. Your dad emits a sort of Downey fragrance. Maybe it's because he's Gabled, who knows." She laughed, rolling her eyes while she smiled.

A thought hit Delaney. "Sometimes I detect cinnamon. Whose does the scent belong to?"

"Cinnamon?" Viv questioned with wide eyes sending bolts of confusion through Delaney.

"I catch a hint of it everywhere I go. My room, out running, school, even here in this hospital sometimes. Who is it?" Delaney tried to pin Viv into an answer.

"How long have you noticed this?" Raising an eyebrow, Viv searched her face.

"For five or six years. I smell that spice most of the time. I used to think you burned cinnamon as an incense in the house." Delaney appeared breathless.

"Your markings will show up any day now. The impressions are only visible while you're using them and humans can't envision them at all. When an Amalgamate fuses, whatever they're borrowing is inclined to peak on their skin, moving as if a separate entity within itself, essentially like the marks are alive. A living, breathing tattoo. Calliope, Brody, and Daphne show no sign of fusing traits other than that their eyes have changed. They display no Prints, and as of yet, no Scripts." Viv's lips pursed together. "Um, let me think…how far did we get last time?" Vivianna squirmed from side to side.

Delaney allowed Vivianna to avoid her question about the cinnamon, for now. *He's real and that is a start.*

"Your body will attempt to adjust to the new strengths and abilities. You'll be stronger, faster, and more agile; those are breed traits. You'll age at a much slower rate, if at all." She hesitated for a quick drink from a large bottle of water.

Delaney turned and squirmed around, trying to ease the irritating tingling in her limbs. She let her leg fall along the side of the bed. An obnoxious itching sensation crept up her thigh.

"I'm glad you know the truth. The constant lying took a severe toll on us. I hated the deceit, but to keep you safe, we did it." She stopped as her eyes got big and round like saucers. "Well, this changes things."

She stood and stared at the mark now swirling around on Delaney's thigh. The brand resembled a bruise first forming with slight indentation developing in the tissue, and then the impressions disappeared. "I couldn't discern what the imprint was." Viv blew out a long breath. "We don't have much time now." She pushed a rueful smile forward and worry crept into Viv's eyes.

Chapter THIRTEEN

After Vivianna left, Delaney lay still, thinking until the moon emerged on the horizon like a giant eyeball examining the world. Alone in the imposing darkness, the chilly shadows swept too close to her bedside, as if death decided to check on who would follow him first.

He is coming for me too. Though in her case, packs of raging assassins were trying to beat him to the punch. *I am alone, bodyguard or not.* Fear sat beside her, taking up most of the space on the single mattress. *They found me before, they can find me again.*

All the ideas and beliefs she'd been so sure of, everything she believed she wanted, all seemed menial now and she wasn't sure if any of it mattered anymore.

A loud, boisterous noise interrupted Delaney's thoughts; the pandemonium unmistakable. She could hear them coming, and possibly the rest of the hospital wing did also, or so she concluded. No more time to think and maybe that wasn't a bad thing.

Bannan bee-lined right for her, running his fingers over her still-swollen cheek as he stared at Delaney. A warm smile and a kiss to the forehead said a silent hello.

"Well, you're starting to resemble my lovely daughter again. Sorry we're so late. Daphne got lost and we had to locate her." He laughed as he spoke.

Delaney listened to the hearty laughter with a peacefulness she hadn't experienced in a long time. To find something to laugh about eased her mind and soothed some of her earlier concerns.

"This is a big hospital with a lot of twists and turns. I'm not the only person to get lost in this place." Daphne tried to defend herself.

"It's okay to be lost, as long as you can always encounter a man willing to help a gorgeous woman," Brody joined in the conversation with a lighthearted smile, which was not like her, ever.

"Um, not to interrupt, but when we're all finished ganging up on Daphne, can someone help me take a shower?"

Relief washed over her as much as the water and soap when Daphne and calliope had her in the bath five minutes later. There was a girl under all the bed head and bad breath. After Delaney's family cleared out she put her headphones on, descended back into the under stuffed pillow, and closed her eyes with a deep sigh.

Life is good, she thought to herself while a small smile.

Delaney wasn't sure how much time had passed when she caught faint sounds from one of the bustling nurses. Her brain was still heavy with sleep, her senses dull to everything except the music waltzing through her earphones. A pillow was jammed against Delaney's face, pressing her head into the mattress. A heavy torso followed, pinning her down. Delaney lay helpless while fighting to take a breath. Her will to live couldn't budge her tangled limbs from the weight of the body holding her down.

Delaney forced open her lips to cry out, the material sunk into her mouth. In her mind, the scream became deafening, but inside the room, no sound other than a muffled proclamation easily lost and overlooked. She sucked the pillow farther down her throat as she choked and struggled for air. Her eyes rolled around in their sockets like marbles on the floor as she suffocated to death. The lack of oxygen took its toll. Delaney's already weak limbs ceased fighting. Her shoulder twitched twice. Her body lay lifeless as her brain began to shut down.

The pillow shifted from her face; the pressure of someone lying on top of her evaporated. Delaney sucked in a mouthful of air in a long gulp as her body sprang up into a sitting position. Fear pulsated through her as she struggled to get out of the bed sheets she had become tangled in. She quickly scurried to the head of the mattress dragging her blankets with her.

Delaney gasped at the sight of a crowd of strangers fighting in her room.

She froze as a blonde guy darted in front of her, charging full speed at a man up against the door. He charged into the burly male and they both disappeared into thin air. The quick movement of a petite person grabbed Delaney's attention as she questioned what the hell had happened to other two men.

A small woman clutched a nurse against her chest. Her long black braid danced across her spine as the two struggled for the advantage. The medical assistant stomped down hard on the floor while throwing her crown back in a quick jab. The small lady moved faster than anything Delaney had ever seen. She mirrored the other woman's every movement, avoiding any damage the caretaker had a chance to inflict.

A snapping sound and the nurse went limp. The smaller woman turned enough for Delaney to witness the curve of her face. The dark haired lady whipped about and searched the room, her eyes finding Delaney curled into a ball at the top of the bed. Exotic almond shaped orbs found hers and pinned Delaney in place. "Okay?" the woman mouthed the words at Delaney, who sat quietly with a stunned expression.

In a thick haze, Delaney surveyed the room.

An enormous man wrestled with a blonde female. Her face twisted in a mask of frustration and pain. Her arms flailed above her, rushing down in a chopping motion to land solid against the big man's shoulders. His thick body turned away from Delaney. She stared on as he broke the hold the woman had on him. She reared her head back and slammed her skull forth, missing his face as he ducked to the side. The nurse's forehead hammered against his broad shoulder instead. He pushed the woman's body forward and wrapped his hands around her slender neck, pushing her up the wall and pinning her in place.

The buttons of her shirt ripped open and the head of a lion broke free in a 3D explosion of flesh and hair. The predator shook its thick mane and snarled while snapping razor sharp teeth at the man's face, grazing his cheek. A husky growl filled the room.

The massive fighter's body contorted as he dropped the woman to the floor. Delaney couldn't see the woman's frame blocked by the man's big body. She noticed his arm shoot forward and begin ripping backwards. Blood spattered across the room in tiny droplets, spraying the side of Delaney's face, the wall, and ceiling.

Delaney didn't move. She sat motionless trying to figure out what happened. The headphones still lodged in her ears, she focused on the soft melody and fought the blood stained horror of the scene in front of her.

She stared at his back as he rose up to a standing position. His frame stood tall and he appeared like a giant to her. She noticed his breathing, quick and erratic, as he towered over the lifeless body now bleeding on the linoleum floor. Tight-fisted hands hung at his sides, blood covering the right one. He didn't turn around. Instead, he moved into the bathroom. He came out with towels and a trash bag. He stuffed the bloody head of the corpse into the garbage sack, wrapped a towel around the neck wound, and began wiping the floor clean.

Delaney sat in a daze as she observed him clearing away any evidence that anything had ever happened. He paused, stood, and without warning, whipped around and met her gaze. Sparkling emerald eyes met hers and she gasped again. Blood trailed across his face, shock creeped into his expression but soon was swallowed up by a blank stare.

Delaney was watching as I ripped her throat out. I am ashamed at how

callous I have been right in front of her. Our first meeting enveloped in blood and death. Already, nothing is going as I hoped.

He envisioned a romantic reintroduction. Instead, he broke a woman's bones and flung her around like a toy. When he'd finished cleaning up the mess, he gazed up and she stared back at him. Her mouth open in what he assumed to be horror at the scene she'd witnessed.

My high hopes of grandeur, or at least a clean shirt devoid of any signs of blood splatter, crashed and burned before me. We are supposed to be starting over and I wanted to rekindle all the feelings she had for me. I needed her to crash into me again, not run screaming from the room.

What he must have looked like in a rage had never occurred to him until now. Face twisted with fury, limbs shaking with adrenaline, he wondered if she could pick through the crap and find him, feared she would discover nothing more than the violence he had grown accustomed to. Her gaze pinned him down and his steps fell short.

I missed her steamy hot chocolate brown eye. They had become a consolation of sorts. When I saw the cocoa spheres, I knew where I was. The nights she'd looked at me through those sleepy orbs, things had become dangerous and wild. In my arms, she burned with a tenacious hunger. With her body wrapped tightly around mine, I developed an obsession with her. I loved her before we connected physically, became consumed once I had experienced being with her.

She noticed me tonight for the first time with breed eyes. I cringed at what she might discover. This is a critical initial impression for her and I blew this chance. I fear we are hopeless.

Malik experienced an emotional exhilaration at being near to her. Excited and smiling like a fool, and none of it could be helped. He had always been in deep.

She is like quicksand. I have been consumed.

Malik moved towards the bed with cautious steps and leaned over to balance one arm on the bed railing, he smiled at her. *Hopefully my grin doesn't appear creepy like an I-just-killed-everyone-in-the-room sort of menacing smile.*

Malik decided to stop smiling all together.

"Are you hurt?" Malik asked in a velvety smooth voice.

Their gazes met. The chocolate was gone, replaced by a hazel green with gold highlights at the edges. She had the ability to envision the breeds for what they are; no more blinders to cover up reality. Delaney still hadn't answered his question. Her head was tilted to the side and she stared blankly at the wall. She tried to lick her lips, but found her mouth dry and her tongue got stuck halfway across. The lump in her throat silenced her, but the events of the last few minutes had kept her from forming the words to begin with. Tears filled her eyes and slowly cascaded to wet her face.

Malik stepped back as blood dripped from his nose and the long gash down his cheek. Her gaze fell to the dark navy blue shirt pulled tightly over his chest and she noted the blood splattered down the front of his pants. Somewhere in the back of her head, Delaney understood she should be terrified, and perhaps she was just a little.

He was the most intimidating man she had ever seen. His face was rugged, handsome on some level, but not beautiful. The way he looked at her disturbed her also. His eyes were sharp like a predators and she felt like prey before him.

He took a step forward and her gaze immediately fell to his chest. He stopped.

"Delaney, are you okay?" he asked again. The question reached her more clearly than the first time. The catch in his voice as he spoke caught her attention as well. Any sort of emotion seemed awkward for someone like him.

Delaney swallowed hard and still couldn't speak.

"You're safe. I protect you. Do you understand?" He kept his tone low. He didn't want to upset her any more than he had. Not a word came out of her mouth. She sat still as if the grip of shock held her in place.

Did he fear she would scream? She had considered screaming her head off, but for some reason, she hadn't uttered a sound. Delaney's mind began to swim through foreign images that seemed familiar. So lost in her consciousness were the answers to questions she wasn't aware she had. But they pushed forward

Bent, Not Broken 115

and she couldn't thrust them aside. She didn't want to.

She was in her room at the house lying on her bed. Her arm draped over the edge and hung down across a man's chest. His head leaned back, hair tickling her shoulder as the clean smell of spice, wood, and cinnamon lingered in her nostrils. Delaney read out loud while she squirmed to change positions. She laughed as he pushed her over. Slowly crawling up her body, his face hidden by his long hair as his hands braced on either side of her ribs.

The laughter died on her lips as the air caught in her throat. Heat pooled in her stomach and her hips twitched upward. Her lids fell shut as her body grew sensitive to his nuzzling finger tips.

"Look at me, please." His breath whispered across Delaney's cheek. His lips caressed hers. A slow trail of kisses set her skin on fire and she instinctively reached to bring him closer.

"I'm always with you." Delaney spoke as she opened her eyelids and a smile tugged at her mouth.

Delaney blinked and she was back in the hospital room staring at the same man. She closed her eyes and tried to find the images again, but the image fluttered and disappeared. Delaney shook her head as her gaze darted around her.

"Who are you?" Her tone was harsher than she had intended.

Delaney's coarse voice raked over his skin like a cat scratch. *Right now, I would give anything to hear her cackling laughter, or for her to sing a Sheryl Crow song badly, as usual.*

"My name is Malik. I'm..." *Does she know who I am?*

He took another step toward her. She didn't flinch or try to move away. He wondered if the shock of it all kept her in place.

All those years ago, their being close had seemed harmless to him. She had been crying so hard one night and he hadn't understood why. He had no explanation for being so aware of her, no reason to get involved, but he had.

That night, he only held her hand and spoke to her after she a slept. Her fingers clasped around his and wouldn't let go. She needed him. He had the power to make her safe. Malik spoke to Delaney that first night and they had linked somehow. When he would sleep, he would find himself in her dreams. Time spent with her had become addicting from the start.

Whenever he wanted to be alone with Delaney, he would search for her in those dreams. They held his happiness and chased away the loneliness. The uncertainty of the future hadn't mattered to him. He knew when she murmured in her sleepy voice about green eyes and cinnamon, she spoke of him. He had proof she liked those stolen moments as much as he did. For Malik, her words were enough.

"Do I know you?" Delaney's straining voice pulled Malik closer.

Malik stared at her for the longest moment. He hoped to see some recollection pass over her features, but they stayed blank and even. His chest constricted as he realized she didn't remember him at all.

"I guess you don't." Malik meant to keep the emotion from his voice, but failed. He leaned over.

Delaney's breath caught in her throat as he peered down at her. The air pushed down on them heavy with anticipation as Delaney struggled with her racing heart. Her lips tingled from the pressing urge to kiss him, the need coming from nowhere she understood. The thought came as somewhat of a shock because she didn't know this man, but wanted to. It became all she could think about while he leaned entirely too close for her to have a clear head.

What would he taste like? Delaney tried to shake herself out of her wonderfully naughty thoughts. "Your eyes, they're so… familiar."

He couldn't pull his eyes away from her slightly faded red lips when she spoke. While standing so close to her, he also began noticing how much her body had begun to heal.

"Delaney." Her name caressed his tongue.

"Yes." The word was so softly spoken, Malik leaned in closer to hear. Butterflies flitted through her. His breath was warm on her cheek, she licked her lips again.

"Delaney, do you remember me?" The catch in his voice annoyed him.

He asked with such softness that his prior actions seemed impossible to her. He was overwhelmingly violent, terrifyingly dangerous, and breathtakingly beautiful in some crazy way.

She shook her head in answer to his question; her voice seemed to have deserted her, leaving him empty inside. He wanted to bellow in frustration.

Is there no hope of her coming back to me this time?

"I'm sorry you had to see what I did. You understand my actions were necessary, don't you?" He had to keep talking, or fighting, anything to keep himself from crawling into bed next to her.

"Why do they want me dead?" Quick, short ragged breaths shot between her words. Her hands fidgeted.

I just iced an assassin, a woman no less, in full view. I hated the way she looked at me, like she could never make it to the exit before I had her in my clutches. This time I did manage to look away.

"They're associates of Caleb and Isabeau." He gave a nonchalant shrug of his shoulder. There was no point in lying to her about the situation. She had been told there were people who were hunting her and her family. If nothing else, she should be armed with the information.

"They've been waiting for your family to leave. They almost had you with a needle in your IV last night." Malik hated making her aware of her status as a target.

To find out everything you've believed to be the truth was nothing more than a host of carefully crafted lies from people you have implicitly trusted. He definitely had to give her credit for not having a nervous breakdown.

He turned away, walked to the door, and opened it to slip out.

"Wait," she blurted out.

Malik heard the terror echoed in Delaney's voice.

How do you sooth someone's fear? How do I make her feel safe? "I'm coming right back." *It is haunting the way she looks at me.*

"I'll get rid of this and come back so we can talk." He slipped out the door.

Malik walked down the ultra-white hospital hallway and looked for a mode of transportation to move the body. Down two more long ridiculously white halls, he finally found a wheelchair pushed off to one side. He walked quickly taking the chair back to her room, unable to shake the nervousness that swamped his senses.

Fighting felt more natural. Those movements had become like writing and talking. The interaction with Delaney felt more uncomfortable than he believed possible. Perhaps she would be asleep and he wouldn't have to talk. Then I could dump the trash and just finish the night.

Just grab the body and leave, he thought. *No commentary needed. I knew the face-to-face talk wasn't going to be that easy. Call it a hunch.*

She watched him like a hawk as he entered with the wheelchair. He scooped up the body and covered it with a blanket. Malik pushed the chair to the door and waited for a chance to move with no hospital personnel in the vicinity.

Relief washed over him when she remained silent. Within a few minutes, he was at the back of the hospital dumping the body. Stopping beside a white van parked close to the door, Malik dumped her to the ground and rolled her under the white monstrosity.

"Fezz, I need a team of Roq's at the back entrance of the hospital in ten. A body under a white fifteen passenger van closest to the exit." He link-spoke quickly while walking back.

"Copy." Fezz said gruffly.

Malik was frustrated with himself. He knew he had to go back and talk to her. He just had no idea what he was supposed to say. If they were going to discuss how to murder and maim, or how to track opponents, then they would have a hell of a conversation. The little stuff people talk about from day-to-day irritated Malik.

If only we could discuss hand-to-hand combat techniques, I would be immensely engrossing.

Chapter
FOURTEEN

Malik approached the door with sweaty palms. His breathing had become erratic and his fingers fidgeted. *This moment...*he blew out a slow breath attempting to calm his nerves...*a lifetime in the making.* The hospital door seemed incredibly heavy as he pulled the thing open.

"Declan," Delaney murmured in her sleep. *The towhead occupied her dreams instead of me tonight.* He realized his window of opportunity had been slammed shut right in his face the moment he had let her go.

Do I have the right to expect her to fall in love with me all over again?

He had been defeated by his own thoughts and lack of action when the moment presented itself. He gave her up. How should he argue the point? Malik fought the battle raging inside himself and wondered if she would ever know or understand the magnitude of the situation for him.

I have never loved any other person as I do her. My life has become possible because she can see me as a good man. The thought humbles me like no other.

He wanted to hold on and revel in the idea he had sacrificed to save her, though the reason his surrendering of his most prized possession mattered little to him now. He was alone and she was moving on.

Malik grasped her arm, jostling her gently until her green eyes flickered open and she gave him a familiar sleepy grin.

She lurched up, her full attention drawn to him. Fear showed bright in the way she studied him. Malik pushed backward and landed a few feet away, frozen. She appeared terrified.

"I'm sorry. Do I frighten you?" His voice became hard again. Malik's irritation with himself grew for not thinking before he touched her. *She didn't recognize me, doesn't remember who I am.* Malik let out a heavy sigh. His eyes fell away from hers in self-disgust.

"Just a minute, please." She slipped out of the covers and disappeared into the bathroom. Delaney brushed her teeth and tried to primp.

"Dead people are more attractive than I look right now," she muttered to herself in irritation.

The flannel nightgown her mom brought made her resemble a nun. At least she'd showered and her hair smelled cleaned. She opened the door and shuffled back to her bed. Delaney wrapped the one unbroken arm around her legs and hugged herself. Malik walked towards the bed and she noticed the sweet fragrance of cinnamon once more.

"You. You're real." Delaney gave him a half dreamy glance. *Malik might be going to save me from the bad guys, but who is going to save me from him?*

The aroma seemed to intensify, as if the spicy mix rolled off of him in thick, hot billowy gusts. She slammed her eyes shut and inhaled deep. *He is strangely intoxicating, drawing me in while doing nothing in particular.*

"What do you mean?" he questioned Delaney as he took a seat on the bed next to her.

She met his eyes and felt a rush of lightning and thunder. Her cheeks flushed bright crimson and his smile grew larger. She began fidgeting from nervousness. He found her enthralling, until her gaze dipped down to the scar on his neck. She drew in a hard breath. The moment fluttered to the floor,

Bent, Not Broken   121

lost and forgotten, or so he wrongly assumed. He shifted uncomfortably, then reached up and adjusted the collar to cover up most of his scar. Delaney became mortified that she'd caused awkwardness and inspired him to feel embarrassment.

"I recognized the cinnamon. I've detected the scent in the hospital since I've been here."

He saw the wheels turning in her head and her nose scrunch up.

"And at the house. Actually, in my room, and then the other day, I noticed it on a run with Mom. But, you already know that…don't you? My whereabouts are something you keep track of most of the time, right?" As the words came out, a smile formed on Delaney's lips.

He'd never seen Delaney look more beautiful than in this moment. Their eyes kept meeting, like two moths drawn by the porch light. No matter how many times they tried to turn away, they sought each other out again. A certain level of intimacy unfurling with every glance. Her knowing gaze captivated him. Malik missed the steamy chocolate color, but found aquamarine eyes suited her well. He wanted to dive in and drowned carelessly, find redemption for his sins in those eyes, or in her arms. Something in the way she held his gaze fascinated him. A painful truth reflected deep in the emerald flecks. She still had no idea who he was.

"I know your new life is a lot to take in. The possibilities are probably confusing and upsetting." He wondered if she sensed his discomfort. Malik was a calculating man of action not words.

Relief washed through him when her expression softened and she ceased looking at him with what he interpreted as her wanting to run. Malik reached out and took her hand in his without contemplating what his response may mean to her.

Heat she didn't fully understand radiated as if her skin would melt against his touch.

What am I doing? He shifted his body away from her.

"Will you be sleeping with me tonight? I meant here in my room, not here in my bed?!" She wanted to kick herself. *He makes me so nervous.*

The inquiry almost made him laugh out loud.

With both feet stuck in her mouth, talking became near impossible.

"I've been staying here with you since I healed." He moved his arm toward the chair by the door. "I will never leave you." His voice took on a sexy sweetness, like maple syrup, smooth and sugary.

"Um…what am I supposed to do?" Delaney crinkled her nose.

He stopped to think about his next statement. "Don't worry." He wasn't sure what she needed to hear.

"Is all this a mistake?" Delaney shrugged her shoulders, then settled back into the pillows.

"You believe we have miscalculated your importance?" He stared at her.

"Everyone making a fuss over me. They could be wrong, you know. I'm still just regular me." Delaney's stare fell to the blanket and she fidgeted with tucking it around her legs.

"Delaney, there's no mistake. What makes you think you're so ordinary to begin with?" His curiosity laced voice made her glance up to see his expression.

"Be real! Daphne can stop traffic. Calliope's smart like a nuclear scientist. Brody is driven to do good and make the world a better place. I'm only the cute one. It's okay, I'm used to it. There are worse things."

"Just because you don't *stop traffic*"—he made air quotes—"doesn't mean that you aren't beautiful. Perhaps traffic has been traveling the wrong way. Now, go to sleep."

"You're staying with me, right?" Delaney tried to hide the touch of panic she felt behind a shaky grin.

"Of course." Malik slipped off the bed as he spoke, a subtle smile playing on his lips.

Without a word, he made himself as comfortable as possible in the visitor's chair by the door.

He disappeared, melting into the armchair like a daydream slipping away.

Her mouth stayed open until she passed out. Dreams of haunting green

Bent, Not Broken   **123**

eyes replaced surprise when sleep finally settled over her. Malik was lying on a bed next to her. His chest rose and fell softly with each breath. Delaney turned towards him and moved closer, seeking comfort in the warmth of his body. He rolled toward her, his arms drew her in, and he tucked her tightly against him. Delaney discovered contentment in the circle of warmth he provided. Against his warm skin, Delaney realized she had found her place. She rested her palm on his chest. It all felt preordained, or like they were repeating something they had done a thousand times before.

His face was inches from hers. Delaney watched as the scar on his neck rose and fell with the beat of his heart. Without thinking, she ran her fingers along the braided tissue. Malik grasped her hand, pulled it to his mouth, and kissed the center of her palm. With his eyes still closed, a peaceful look settled on his face.

Everything about him excited her. Craziness and comfort mixed into one. If she could hide away from the world with him, she would be perfectly happy to never come back.

Chapter FIFTEEN

Malik returned to the Drake's to find himself swamped with guard reports, loose ends, and an absent commander. He received updates from Fezz on issues demanding his immediate attention. The most important communication was from Grey and Louden. They hadn't acquired Sebastian's location and were instead leaving Italy, heading straight for the Greek islands. Malik hoped the data gathered might lead them to a still living Mr. Drake.

Malik wasn't worried about Sebastian, not yet, anyway. When Sebastian decided he didn't want to be found, they would have a hell of a time tracking him. Ever since Candace had been murdered, Sebastian hadn't been right. Malik wondered if the guilt had become too much.

Parker and Valentina had checked in with three of the old families and all members had been accounted for.

One less thing to worry about.

The Doux-La-Roux proved to be quite elusive. Dane hadn't been in contact with several affiliates of the consortium. Two teams of Kindreds were sent to France to investigate further.

Bent, Not Broken   125

"Viv reported a mark forming on Delaney's thigh. She revealed the tattoo isn't a regular Script or Print. The brand is like Viv's." Fezz informed him. The news came as no surprise, but did change how they should proceed. Additional security would need to be added for the house and Delaney.

"Okay. I'll be in the barracks." Malik chewed on the inside of his cheek as he went to contact Dane. After a detailed debriefing with Dane, Malik wanted some alone time to think. "Peyton, I'll be back within an hour."

Malik headed home to Naroke. He needed to clear his head. He examined the swells crashing into the basalt rocks lining the cove he referred to as his front yard. He stood on the sandy beach and took a deep breath. Stripping down to his boxer briefs, he ran into the exploding surf. Malik cut through the breakers, exhilarated. His muscles began to relax. The water enveloped him, cool and crisp, washing away the stress and strain of the last few days.

This is the one thing that actually helped him forget the anxiety and pressure in his life. His mother and father had both been imprinted with the blue whale. They had found solace in the surf too. To him, his love of the ocean made perfect sense.

Here in the wild water we are once again a family and I am not alone. His mind drifted into the past with each swim stroke. Cusco had been a bustling metropolitan and they lived just outside the city. His mother acquired employment as a teacher, his father as a peace officer. He relived their time together as he swam. Twenty five minutes out, he turned around and headed back in. He was rejuvenated by the break.

His thoughts returned to the previous night with Delaney. *I'm not clear what the conversation really accomplished. I am sure I have a better chance of surviving ocean predators than Delaney's questions. I should stop guarding her. It seems wrong to continue. She doesn't know me and I am taking advantage of intimacy we have shared that she doesn't remember.*

Of course, none of his thoughts stopped him from being excited at the prospects of the coming day. He would face her and she would see him.

Within an hour, Malik stood in the kitchen of the Drake's house, leaning against the archway dividing it from the living area. Everyone was home for breakfast and gathered around the kitchen island and nearby dining table. Vivianna had gone all out making a colossal feast to welcome Delaney back. The scent of blueberry wheat pancakes invoked a hearty growl from his stomach. Most of the guardians were settled near the front and rear doors to the residence and the fragrance tantalized their senses too.

She will see me, and the others, from now on.

"What are you doing?" Trystan had been behind him before he'd realized his privacy had been encroached.

"Shhhhhhhhh!" Malik waved at him to be quiet. He listened for a short break in the heated discussion between Viv, Bannan, and Delaney before acknowledging Tryst's presence.

"Bannan and Vivianna are attempting to talk Delaney out of the Turkey trip. Bannan's trying to be reasonable, but I think he's losing his patients." Malik smiled and breathed a deep sigh of relief.

"You're enjoying this aren't you?" Trystan looked at Malik with a raised eyebrow and a smirk.

Everyone's gotta have something to say. It's downright irritating.

"So? Don't you have somewhere to be? Do you need extra work?" Malik turned his back on the other man. Trystan remained behind him.

"You're sick man." Trystan laughed.

"Calliope may be watched by someone who isn't so damn annoying? Maybe Flynn, he's handsome and flirty. You can have Brody instead." Malik knew he was needling Trystan and didn't care. *He started it.*

"That's low, man. I'll take Delaney. You're so busy now and she might like me. I can be smooth." He loosed a soft chuckle and a friendly nudge to Malik's back.

Trystan would never leave Calliope.

"Trystan, want to take over for Fezz?" Malik link-spoke a touch of acid mixed with sarcasm.

"No, I'm not the house mom, thanks anyway." Trystan laughed.

Bent, Not Broken   127

Malik heard Fez move forward.

Fezz growled. "House mom, that's what you call me, you fu—"

"Shhhh! I can't overhear what the hell is going on with you all talking like a bunch of teenage girls. Shut the fuck up for five minutes," Malik said.

When they wanted to be quiet, they were perfectly silent. When they wanted to talk, it was like the damn Today Show.

"Yeah, Tryst, he needs an update on Delaney," Peyton said from right behind him. Malik's back stiffened; she was going to make him suffer.

"Trystan and Malik are in the same tugboat and it's sinking faster than the Titanic. Peyton, Bowe, and me, we are the only ones left unattached. Flynn keeps trying to cozy up to Daphne, who wants nothing to do with Errol Flynn here.

"I'm not watching the house on date night for you fucking losers." Fezz pushed past Malik and left.

"Why look at me? It's your fault he's here." Tryst followed Fezz with a dumb grin.

"I just don't think running off to Turkey is a good idea. You are asking for trouble!" Bannan's voice rose above their conversation.

"I wouldn't be alone, though! Malik would be with me, right?" Delaney scrutinized her dad. "Only now, I'll actually know he's there and be aware of the danger!"

Malik became nervous upon hearing his name. He wasn't covered in blood and no violent acts would ensue, he hoped. He'd spent most of the morning trying to appear perfect for her. Newer jeans, burgundy pullover, and a pair of Cole Haans, and even taking an extra-long time shaving.

I am becoming Barbie Flynn and need a strong right to the face. My grasp of lucidity has become fleeting at best.

Shaking his head, he took a deep breath, stepped forward, and drifted into visibility.

Chapter SIXTEEN

I missed home.

Delaney found acting sick around the hospital staff so they wouldn't realize she'd healed so fast to be exhausting. This discovery also meant she wouldn't be able to go back to her classes or work for a few days. The plan her family and the guards had constructed teetered on whether or not she could succeed in portraying a pathetic woman who had gotten her ass handed to her.

Delaney had to admit, she had not been blessed with the ability to perform.

Since returning home, her parents had been attempting to convince her not to go to Turkey. Delaney heard all the arguments and understood their concern. The opportunity ate at her still. The chance to work with a world renowned professor thrilled her.

"I wouldn't be alone, though! Malik would be with me, right?" Delaney scrutinized her dad. "Only now, I'll actually know he's there and be aware of the danger!"

"When did you meet Malik?" Viv stopped turning the pancakes and faced Delaney with a concerned expression.

"Last night, after you guys left."

Bent, Not Broken   129

"Good morning." Malik made direct eye contact with Vivianna, then Bannan while standing in the bright light of day after walking out of the shadows as if he was nothing more than an apparition.

Delaney forgot to breathe.

A fitted, cotton burgundy pullover framed his broad shoulders and baggy blue jeans sat over his black shoes. Malik's face was clean shaven and his still damp hair tumbled half over his eyes.

He isn't anything like the guys at college. They only made Delaney nervous; he terrified her.

If she stared too long, she thought her heart might stop, her lungs fail, and her mind combust with sizzling, irrational thoughts and sexual images. He had the power to make her crave him.

Malik gave Daphne a quick smile and tossed respectful nods to Brody and Calliope. He didn't want to avoid Brody, but any attention he gave her always seemed to give her the wrong idea.

Malik wanted a glimpse of Delaney's expression, but refused to allow his gaze to fall on her. If he acknowledged her, he might never turn away. He fixed his view to only include Vivianna and Bannan.

The strain of their way of life had taken a toll on each of them. Bannan's physical appearance drew Malik's scrutiny. He appeared ragged, beaten down, like someone had kicked him right in the gut. Tight balled fists fixed at his sides, face twisted into a mask of indignation, his pensive gaze pinned the distance to some invisible line in far-off space. Fine lines surrounded his mouth and eyes where smoother skin had been only days ago. He'd lost weight too, the stress and anxiety having waged war with his appetite.

Malik understood on an intimate level what bothered Bannan the most. The girls were his children, his family; he had raised and cared for them. Though he had no part in Brody and Daphne's existence, he protected them as if he had. Four young women shared ownership of his heart. Not to discount Vivianna's place; she was his everything. Theirs souls were so intertwined that one could not live without the other.

Vivianna took her strength from Bannan as she went to stand next to him. He immediately put his arm tightly around her. Vivianna faired about the same as her husband under the stress. The color had been driven from her face and her complexion had taken an ashen hue. Deep-seated, dark circles shadowed her eyes and concern marked her beautiful features in deep ridges and valleys.

An intensely real threat awaited them, with an uncertain ending they all worried couldn't be stopped.

The universe had all but fallen away while Delaney waited for Malik's gaze to fall on her. When he finally glanced her way, his eyes locked with hers, her breath caught in her throat, and everything except the two of them faded from her mind.

A whole new undiscovered world stared back at her from depthless aquamarine pools filled with endless potential.

The contact too brief, Malik glanced away. The unfulfilled moment slipped through her fingers and settled beyond her reach.

This is the part I'm not good at.

"We realized the hospital would become compromised at some point. She was in no real danger. We had additional security at the individual entrances and exits." Malik spoke in a calm voice. "I decided to wait until everyone came home today to speak with you both on several matters.

"Possible breech situations have drawn our attention and I want to discuss the potential problems. We need to focus on either an immediate retreat to the island or an increase in the efforts to defend of our home front. I'll leave the decision up to the both of you." He nodded to Viv and Bannan.

"Additional guards have been put in place and there's more on the way. Two will shadow Vivianna going forward." He held up a halting hand gesture to Viv, who'd already begun to protest. Malik hoped a quick overview of his plan would bring the level of concern back down to their version of normal.

"No arguments. Your safety as the archetype is paramount. Please understand this is a directive from the Counsel and our community. No discussion on this matter will take place. Either you agree to the new security measures or you will be confined for your own safety." Malik stepped closer as his voice became softer. "Please, accept the extra security without altercation." Malik whispered and nodded his head low to her in a show of respect.

"Peyton has assumed the lead in the house for now and Leaestra will be directing communications with Fezz." Malik stood with one leg crossed over the other, leaning back against the counter with a serious expression on his face.

"Will Bannan also be assigned a protector?" Vivianna peered at Malik.

"If you wish, of course. One will be dispatched within the hour."

"I don't need a guard. I can defend myself. Hell, I trained with the Sighmeran, remember?" Bannan turned to his wife and grabbed her hand in a reassuring gesture.

"Bannan, please. Your safety is peace of mind for me." Viv's eyes were soft with a thin sheen of tears threatening to fall. Her upper lip quivering, she quickly pulled her bottom lip between her teeth to steady herself. Such emotion had not been representative of Delaney's mother; she always appeared strong, so impenetrable, like granite.

"Is this what you want?" Bannan brushed his lips softly over her cheek.

Viv closed her eyes and leaned farther into him.

"I will send for Dahallan. Don't take him out and get him drunk, though." Malik smiled at Bannan with a hint of laughter Delaney didn't understand.

Bannan glanced toward the floor with a sheepish grin. In that small moment Delaney realized there was a whole lot she didn't know.

"Immediate backups for every one of the Kindreds have been arranged. Teams are preparing for deployment. We will have a debriefing later," Malik said.

"Do I get to be in on this meeting?" Delaney asked.

"No," they all spoke in unison.

Malik looked directly at Delaney.

"Why? I've got a vested interest in staying alive." She pushed her back into the chair, squaring her shoulders. "If you people had trusted me to begin with,

I wouldn't have been trapped in a bathroom with some creepy man and almost beaten to death. I have a right to be present, especially since I seem to be in harm's way at every moment."

Her temper flared and anger surged through her. *What if the truth had been revealed sooner, would I have fared better in that bathroom?* She blamed not being prepared for making her experience life as a target.

Delaney sat staring at Malik, and he sensed the wrath radiating off her, gnawing at her spirit. He was sorry she perceived her treatment as a punishment. He didn't feel guilty for wanting to keep her safe.

Malik smiled at Delaney with warmth in his sea green eyes. His rugged face had faint whitish scars along his cheek, his nose sat slightly off center, and his right eyebrow was separated in the center with a faded welt. Still, he was beautiful. Delaney swam through a wave of delirium, nearly faltering mid-stride. Malik rendered her useless in the speech department, and she had only been aware of him for twenty four hours.

Malik turned to Bannan and Vivianna.

Bannan's voice filled with regret and sadness. His eyes were cast downward and the lines in his forehead were deep. "Maybe you're right. We were trying to protect you. We hoped you would have a normal life, to grow up like everybody else. I'm sorry that we placed you in more danger."

Delaney wanted to kick her own ass for the sorrow and guilt she witnessed on her father's face. She got to her feet, walked over to her father, and hugged him. He smelled crisp, like clean clothes from a laundry line hung out for most of the day. He held her tight and everything fell away.

"I'm sorry, Daddy, that was stupid of me," she whispered to him alone.

While her parents discussed her future, Delaney returned to her breakfast. Malik seated himself next to her and she studied his every movement out of the corner of her eye, trying not to be obvious. Delaney felt like her insides would come unraveled with Malik sitting next to her. She accidentally spilled her glass of water into her plate and stumbled through the morning meal with positively no grace or elegance, almost knocking her breakfast to the floor twice. Her cheeks seemed to be a permanent shade of scarlet.

An intimacy existed between them that she didn't understand and found to be unnerving, to say the least. He knew her, intimately understood her, though she had no real understanding of how, or how she knew that to be so. Her imagination flexed its own muscles.

It was a feeling she couldn't shake and the most unsettling part for her was that she possessed the same knowledge of him too, and actually appreciated him in a way she knew to be impossible.

Why do I know this to be true?

Every time she licked her lips, she imagined his tongue slipping across them. Everything about Malik made her want to be alone with him, and breathless.

From the edge of his eyes, Malik realized Brody peered at them. Her gaze focused on the way he observed Delaney. His smile evaporated as the realization washed over him that one of these days he needed to tell her there would never be anything but friendship between them. Going on for years by now, he figured she would lose interest. Brody was a sweet girl, though more like a sister. If only she visualized him as a brother.

Every other bite, his eyes drew back to her. *She is here, right next to me, in the daytime.*

Delaney stole glances at him each chance she got. At one point, she examined him with such fascination, it had to have been obvious. He never let on that he detected her scrutiny, or cared. This only made her need to get his attention more.

Malik smirked in between bites, leading her to think he found it amusing having her act like she'd never been around a guy before.

"Malik, do you want anything else?" Delaney whispered to him as she leaned closer. Her saying his name made him grin again.

She became deflated; not even a glance in her direction. Disappointment fell over her. Though his lips curled into a slow half smile, the expression didn't say 'thinking about ripping your clothes off too.'

Delaney felt curious at how much she wanted his attention. She decided his lack of interest was infuriating and he'd become agreeable to her because he had to. The fact that she still couldn't pull her eyes away from his mouth drove her crazy. His full lips made thinking of anything else unfeasible. She could only contemplate running her fingertips over those crimson edges.

"Do you need something?" Malik meant to lean over far enough to be close, not to touch. His shoulder brushed hers and they both moved away. His thoughts fell more along the lines of pulling her into his lap and— *Stop!* His grip tightened on the fork and knife.

"No, thank you." As Delaney spoke, her cheeks exploded into red delicious apples. Her hands were on her thighs and she was fidgeting like crazy. Her stomach quivered and she became lost in the sweet cinnamon scent.

He is a stranger. Delaney couldn't help wondering how her body knew exactly what it wanted, or how she understood the way he would touch her and she would respond with fiery passion. The heat of the moment scorched her skin, stoking her into a frenzy she hoped she could conceal within herself. Delaney unconsciously demanded more than a protector from him. If her hands touched him, he would understand what she searched for.

Malik longed to grab her hand and never let go. He needed his fingers to touch her palm and trace tiny circles all the way across. His body craved hers in any contact she might allow. The Juniper scent became a surging cloud of the most welcome scent around him. His nostrils filled with the spicy fragrance.

She shifted in her seat.

He quickly pulled away.

"Is Delaney going to Turkey with the hot professor or not?" Brody's snide tone cut the air.

Delaney gripped the wooden edge of the kitchen table so tightly one of her fingernails cracked.

Malik sensed the daggers shooting from Brody's eyes, but he would not be swayed. Maybe he should retreat and excuse himself, but…how could he? How could he throw away this rare opportunity? Sitting beside her—and her finally aware of him as a real person, not a dream—was too precious.

"This topic is open for discussion. Wait, hot professor? The guy, *he's a man*, and he's good looking?" Bannan threw his hands up in defeat and shook his head. "I gotta get out of here for my sanity," he muttered as he turned away.

"Going to Turkey isn't a big deal, Daddy." Her voice grew soft, no longer carrying the conviction of how badly she wanted to go as before.

Malik's gaze stretched to the curve of Delaney's face, then her caramel colored hair in its messy bun at the base of her slender neck. He glanced down, noting her fingers were twitching in her lap. She appeared so vulnerable.

To imagine her one day commanding as her grandfather did. She will take control of the same power her mother possessed and wield it against their enemies.

The urge to kiss her was almost irresistible.

"I'm off to class." Bannan grabbed his briefcase.

Malik wondered what Bannan might say if he knew about his feelings for Delaney. How betrayed would he feel because the man who gave his life up to safeguard his daughter also fell in love with her? Her parents trusted him to do whatever he believed best for Delaney. In their world she was untouchable, unattainable royalty.

Malik issued his apologies, left the kitchen, and headed to the back room home office to get some work done. The back corner bedroom was designated specifically for the Kindreds. A large panel of computer hardware inhabited most of one wall, three flat screens occupied another, and a world map dotted with push pins was opposite the computers. A sizable mahogany table took up the center of the room, with two smaller versions against the back wall. One was presently occupied with guard rosters and training schedules. The middle one had a weapons diagram on it that Bannan had been working on.

A matching pair of yellow ice axes.

Bannan was attempting to customize them from Malik's specs. They were a versatile weapon, easily trained on. The crampons were another intriguing idea he had asked Bannan to look into. Bannan had an extensive knowledge of blades and how to fortify them and had been laboring on smaller handheld versions for the girls. He was trying to figure out a plan for his women to carry weapons.

A large portion of Malik's day would be spent right here. He had training schedules to make, debriefing to finish up, and strategies to formulate. He collected the guardian reports first.

"I'm tired of sitting around like an old woman." Fezz link-spoke startling Malik from his attempts to get into work and lose the daze Delaney left him under after breakfast. "I will kill you in your sleep if you don't do something about this current position."

"I'd welcome the break." He replied with a long sigh.

"I'll take Peyton out instead." Fezz threatened, having drifted in to stand across the table from Malik.

"Thanks. I'm sick of having roommates." Malik smirked.

"You're all dead." Fezz turned and headed out of the room as he mumbled under his breath about the ways he was going to "pick each of them off."

Like we didn't have enough crazies, I had to bring one with me.

After two hours of checking on his staff, Malik checked in with Dane to give him a heads up on things. Next, he contacted Trenton. The island was secure and there had been no breeches in security. He had Trenton put Spyder, Bast, Poe, Kiernan, Ptah, and Riven on standby to fortify the home front as needed for what was surely to come. He also asked him to send Dahallen up to keep an eye on Bannan.

Malik finished the schedules, then contacted Louden and Grey. They still hadn't found Sebastian, but were following a lead on him in Marmaris, Turkey. That alone made him want to be sick.

What is it with Turkey?

When he spoke to Basil and Devlin they were on their way to Cypress, Greece. He reminded them to contact him with frequent updates for the rest of the afternoon.

Chapter
SEVENTEEN

The police came and informed Viv and Delaney of a male body discovered in a public bathroom in the mall. Two different blood types were found all over the room. Those facts led to more questions. Delaney told them all she remembered, which entailed almost nothing.

Maybe they'd attribute her memory gaps to prescription drugs or brain damage from her injuries. She had enough to deal with. The cops only created more stress.

Vivianna didn't appear nervous, thankfully. She was an excellent hostess, both calm and reserved, as if having over old friends over for afternoon tea and crumpets.

After an hour, the cops finally left. Vivianna headed for the kitchen to prepare dinner, or so she said, Kindred guards in tow. Delaney sensed they were still not comfortable about the situation including her knowing about it, so she went to her room and flopped down on her bed. She decided to call the one person who listened to whatever she had to say.

The phone rang three times before Lola answered. "I came to the hospital, but they said family only."

"I got attacked in the bathroom by someone. I wish…" She wanted to confide in Lola, but knew she couldn't.

"You might have been killed." The ring of distress in her voice made Delaney appreciate her friendship with Lola even the more.

"I know." Delaney understood all right, up close and personal.

"Are you okay?"

"Do you need anything?" Lola had always been there when she needed her and Delaney realized how lucky she was for her friendship.

"I want to talk, but not here." Delaney tried to relax, but found that every little thing and every little nothing annoyed the hell out of her. Nothing seemed right.

"Sounds good, but your parents are never going to let you out."

"I'm stuck here for a while, but I'll tell them I want to go back to work as soon as possible."

"Go out the window, I'll help you sneak away."

"I'm still healing." Delaney thought about telling Lola the truth, but decided against putting her friend in danger. It struck her that she'd just made the same decision her parents had.

"I'll come over if you want. I think we should meet. You need someone to talk to."

"No, my parents demand family time right now. But thanks for offering."

"Call me later? I'll break you out of your house whenever." Lola spoke like a veteran in sneaking out warfare.

"Sure." She hung up the phone.

Delaney had hoped talking to Lola would make her less restless. She still had all these unresolved feelings bubbling around inside. The frosting on the cake had been the moment she realized her new found ability to lie her ass off.

Delaney stared up at the constellation ceiling, attempting to clear her head. She jammed her headphones on, hoping to find some peace. Adele began singing her heart out; Delaney screeched right along with her. The words walked all over her too-sensitive skin. The energy inside her bounced around, making her crazy.

What's wrong with me now?

Stupid Malik wouldn't stay out of her head. In two days, he moved into her brain and took up permanent residency in her every thought. Frustration swallowed up more space in her room than she did. She needed to get lost in something other than him. She grabbed one of The Night World books, settled her feet on her pillow, and submerged herself in reading.

It didn't take long for Delaney to lose herself in someone else's emotional fulfillment. This series of books kept her fairy tale love life beautiful and perfect. Poppy and Ash were among her most favorite. But the books only drove her to want a love of her own even more. They reminded her no matter how screwed up she seemed, there was someone for everyone. She'd never had the nerve to find out and her only experience was someone else's love story. At some point Delaney realized, she needed to participate in her own adventure or stop dreaming about falling in love altogether.

The hair on the back of her neck suddenly stood on end. An eeriness settled in her stomach. She sensed she was no longer alone. Delaney had no idea how or why she had become aware of a presence close to her, but she had. She got a whiff of sweet cinnamon, and excitement surged through her.

He's here.

Her stomach lurched with anticipation. She longed for him to kiss her as much as she craved to touch him. She took a deep breath of cinnamon, savoring the aroma. He smelled sweeter than ever.

"Stop creeping around. Don't you ever knock before you barge into someone's room?" Delaney didn't bother to turn around.

"I've heard you sing before. Unfortunately, you have not improved with time."

She wondered if Malik had the same smirk he wore at the breakfast table when she dumped her food like some freakish clumsy weirdo. Malik puzzled her in a way she had no idea how to cope with.

The bed dipped as he sat beside her.

"I just wanted to check on you. See if you're okay?" He lied, trying to make the moment last. He realized his actions were dangerous. If he stayed this close, he wouldn't be able to stop himself.

Malik reluctantly withdrew. He stood up and walked to the door before Delaney realized he had moved off the bed. She followed him just as quickly, though she hadn't grown reaccustomed with moving so fast and almost fell over from the rush. She reached out and touched his arm instinctively to steady herself.

"Please, don't go." She crashed into him.

"Sorry. I'm not used to this yet."

Her teeth sunk into her lower lip.

One look at her and he knew it was another mistake among so many he'd made when it came to Delaney Drake. The aquamarine color in her eyes seemed to swirl like the raging sea, pulling him in and drowning him. Malik went into the depths willingly.

Tiny explosions tickled her palm and her fingertips twitched where her hand had met his skin. It was smooth and the muscles hard; her brain failed under so much sensory overload. Her breath caught in her throat. It was like an electrical live wire was drawn between them, taut with energy. The hair on her arms danced as her lips quivered with wonder. Delaney couldn't seem to pull free of the tether connecting her to him.

Malik's mind screamed at him to vacate her room, but his legs wouldn't work. All he imagined was his body crushing hers beneath him.

A natural disaster couldn't have separated them. The room was silent and calm, like the eye of a storm before havoc explodes and consumes everything.

"Do you remember anything of the past yet?" His mouth was dry as the words tumbled out.

"What? No. I, um…get feelings of déjà vu most of the time. But nothing concrete." She rolled her eyes in frustration. "Will it be much longer before my memories come back?" Her eyes searched his face.

He mumbled something unintelligible, running his hand through his hair in a gesture of discontentment.

"I need to go." He tried to move away from her. *I can outrun Delaney, but not myself.*

He forced his lungs to inhale. The bells going off in his head became louder until he unwillingly glanced away. He wanted to bend down and kiss her with such an intensity that would create a spark and ignite them both—making her melt up against him, destroying the binding—and bring her back into his arms for good. Too much time had been spent apart, the intensity of the moment too strong, too profound. This time he wouldn't let her go without the fight of his life.

Watching her is somehow more provocative now, because she knows I am here. To let my mouth dance down her skin. To pull her lower lip between my teeth and feel her shiver with lust against me. I learned what would send her body into a frenzy. There is nothing I wouldn't do to hear her cry out my name again. Her body was made for me to love. There are no words for how much I miss her. The thought makes my skin burn and my insides ache with a need that only she can fill. All I have to do is see her and I want her. Every time I turn around, everything between us escalated higher and higher.

A slow, bitter smile crept over his face. An acid burn was racing over his body, leaving in its wake a feeling of absolute need. Smoldering ashes of restraint were teetering on the weakest thread.

I have to get the hell away from her.

He made his mind up just then; Peyton should take over as soon as possible. Malik hadn't thought any of this through. If Delaney whispered his name right now, or moved any closer, in a simple act of desperation, he would get lost inside her. He was strung tight with anger at the thought of her never seducing him again.

Motionless, they stared at each other in piercing silence. She sucked in a small breath of air. The subtle noise reminded Delaney of glass shattering on a tile floor.

"I don't understand why you look at me like…" She never finished the sentence. Delaney had no idea how to sum up what she saw in his expression.

"How do I look at you?" He understood exactly the way he looked at her, but was shocked by having unknowingly allowed her to see his emotions.

"Like...like you want something from me." She inhaled his scent and felt like is pure essence mingled with her own.

"I do." Malik hesitated for a moment. "I want you to be safe." She realized he had left something paramount out.

The next thought smashed her flat and she gasped. "I could get you killed?"

"This is what I've been trained for. I will lie down my life to ensure yours. I made the choice years ago. I am a Kindred. You should have faith in me and my abilities to keep us both alive." Anger radiated off of him like arctic cold.

"I don't give a damn how glorious you are. I don't want you to die. This isn't about being a Kindred." Her voice shrank to almost nothing. Her bottom lip quivered as tears spilled over and ran down both sides of her face.

What if I lost him? I don't even know him. Confusion sliced through her. "I don't want you to die. Don't you get it? Dead, as in not coming back." *Stupid man, stupid damn man.*

"I'll never leave you." His arrogance didn't sooth her. Death could change his plans; dying had a way of doing that.

"What if the choice isn't yours to make?" Delaney appeared broken as she sank down to her knees. The stress of the last few days came barreling into her. *I'm not cut out for this stuff.* "Maybe, I should leave?"

"They'll find you, torture you, and kill you. Afterwards, they will come for Calliope and your mother, and do the same thing to them."

The truth could not be sugar coated. Delaney running wouldn't even be considered an option, but a death sentence. She needed to get that fact through her head The Stryders were coming for them all, Death Watchers included.

She wiped her tears away with trembling hands while he stood observing her. His checks seemed hollower since she first set eyes on him, and he appeared exhausted. She realized her life weighed heavily on him. So much danger lie ahead. People died in war, she understood the weight he carried.

Bent, Not Broken   143

"If you tried to run, I'd find you. There's no place you can go I won't search for you. I will find you and drag you back." He spoke with such softness. He couldn't let her leave, not now, not ever again. Even if they had to run together and without the Kindreds to help them fight against the Stryders. None of the risks mattered to him anymore.

"Where is everybody?" Vivianna called from the kitchen. Malik should have left Delaney's room right then, though he didn't.

"I need to go and talk with your mother." He didn't budge.

"Should I come with you?" As Delaney finished the sentence she realized the answer. She didn't want the moment to end, not yet.

"No one died today, my report is short." He stood only inches from her, his scent cocooning her in soothing fragrance.

"Oh, you don't want me to come along, huh?" Delaney chewed on the inside of her cheek, glancing up, then dropped her eyes to her toes.

Still frozen in their stolen touch, neither of them moved.

If Delaney became any more weightless, she might have defied gravity and hit the ceiling. Her fingers curled tenderly around his and she lifted her gaze to meet his. Malik's hand didn't return her pressure, though he didn't let go either. Slowly, his face moved closer to her. Glimmering pink lips became like magnets to his. She leaned forward, his mouth drew hers in.

The kiss began painstakingly slow and he had to think about the Dodgers or ice axes, or anything else to keep distracting himself ever so slightly. He wanted the moment to remain soft and special, but his want to strip her naked and continue where they had last left off was something Malik had to keep a tight leash on.

He pulled back and brushed his lips to her cheek, reveling in her closeness, her hunger. The need to crush her to him became overwhelming as if were he to let go, the world would fall right off its axis.

Delaney pushed into the length of his body, wanting more from him. His lips pressed against hers and the heat from his mouth made her tremble. He delivered slow nipping kisses across her check, forcing her body to arch farther into his. Malik's hands covered the small of her back, pressed firmly in place.

His mouth moved below her ear. "Delaney." He rested his cheek against her forehead and pulled his body away from hers.

Instinct told her to grab and pull him close, but his reaction made her hesitate. Then, she decided it no longer mattered what she should do, and did what she wanted. Her arms tightened around him, refusing to let him go. She nestled and sighed against his chest and tightened her embrace. Her palms slid under his shirt, then over the smooth skin of his back, taut toned muscles quivering under her touch.

"This is a bad idea." He took an unsteady breath, so little self-control left.

If she kissed Malik again, it was going to end in them tangled together on her mattress. He couldn't stop thinking about the bed, and her. He wanted her to touch him, loved how curious she could be.

"I am safe with you. It's more than that, though. I…I…" No words came to her rescue. Delaney only knew she needed him here, now. Whatever there was between them was a driving force. Her arms fall away because that was what he wanted from her. She didn't want to let him go, but what choice did she have?

He moved toward the door.

Her eyes never left the point where he had been. "I don't understand, but I know you." She slowly met his gaze. "I know you."

Saying nothing, he retreated and closed the door.

Trystan sat next to Bannan, Malik across from them with Peyton, and Bowe right behind him. For some strange reason, Peyton flanked him as if at any moment an attack was eminent. With all the years of sparring together and battling their enemies, he possessed no clue as to why she now treated him like he was fragile.

Trystan had Malik's back every bit as much Peyton, and he had theirs. The three Kindreds had logged the most damage inflicted and were as close as siblings. Under normal circumstances, Kindreds worked in two-man teams in the field, but the triad made one outstanding team and refused to be broken up.

Flynn caught Rourke's eye a few years earlier. He'd said Flynn fought with his head as much as with his hands. Then during a training session, Bowe brought Peyton down to the mat like a pro. She admired any woman who got the drop on her as she usually kicked the crap out of anyone of the rest of them, Rourke included. She asked Rourke to bring Bowe aboard.

Fezz was a mean old guy in a young viral body. Luckily, he looked like Tom Selleck because his personality was angry little troll. He managed to needle you until you wanted to break him in half.

Dahallan was a Sighmeran Guard, not Kindred, and a skilled fighter more than anything. He and Bannan got on well.

Tanner was a late addition, one of the most proficient assassins they possessed. His mother was of Aquana descent. While Tanner's dad tried to smuggle his family out, his mom was murdered. Tanner's father received a mortal wound during the escape and died a short time later. Tanner was raised by his father's brother and his wife. Parentless like the majority of their group.

Trystan discovered Poe when he was taken into custody by Isabeau; he and Malik brought her back with them after they escaped. She had no idea who she was, so Tryst began calling her Poe because she was like the knight always searching for El Dorado, from an Edgar Allen Poe poem.

Isabeau had chained Poe and bogeled her ability, then Caleb let the Stryders torture her and who knew what else. She remained strong until her end came when she tried to help Trystan escape and paid dearly for it, repeatedly. As she lay dying on the ground, Tryst and Malik had agreed to take her home with them. Trystan took on the responsibility of training Poe and made her into a valued member of the Kindreds. She carried the ability of a Raver to move with incredible undetectable speed. She couldn't fuse, being the only Kindred not an Amalgamate by either parent. She was still a fierce soldier and had stealth on her side.

They started taking on recruits not long after finding out about Isabeau, developing a small army of Kindreds, who in turn established a more secure way of life for the Waiths.

Caleb and Isabeau acquired a new partner in the meantime, of that Malik felt certain, and the Stryders' numbers grew at an alarming rate. Defeating them seemed impossible. The Kindreds needed to cut the head off of the snake to keep it from slithering forward. The Stryders would follow them right back to the Naroke. To go home was a death sentence because the island would easily be turned into an all-consuming fire pit.

They couldn't even find refuge at Maripesa. The beloved stronghold had already been invaded once. With Delaney beginning the transformation, the stakes rose yet again.

Chapter EIGHTEEN

Reluctantly dragging herself off the fluffy comforter, Delaney pulled on black running pants and a t-shirt, then headed for the door. The enticing aroma of dinner drifted up from the kitchen, making her mouth water.

"Calliope, dinner's ready," Delaney yelled down the hall.

Calliope fumbled around in her room while she waited, then blew past her and Delaney chased her down the stairs. They giggled while grabbing and pushing each all the way to the bottom. They laughed as they entered the kitchen, still shoving each other.

How Delaney wished Calliope liked running; the two of them could probably run until one puked or died and it would have been entertaining.

"Can we help?" They asked in unison through the giggling.

"Um, let's see. Calliope grab the silverware. Delaney, put this stuff out on the table," Viv said, gesturing to a large green salad and dishes of green beans, asparagus, and sweet potatoes. Calliope collected glasses and a couple of pitchers of iced tea and water and took them out to the table. Viv scattered fresh parmesan cheese on the hot lasagna.

"How many of us are eating?" Delaney joked as Calliope walked back into the kitchen. They always ate outside when the weather turned nice, which wasn't often because of the heat. A slight refreshing breeze blew across the backyard tonight. Palm trees offered speckles of shade and the waterfall off the pool created a soothing din.

"We have guests this evening," Viv answered in a whimsical, lighthearted tone Delaney found surprisingly calm, all things considered. "Delaney, will you grab your dad and our guests from the back?"

Viv was finishing the Greek yogurt platter with mixed raw veggies and fruit. Calliope helped with the rest of the food as Delaney walked out the French doors.

Bannon was deep in conversation with a group of men and women. They spoke in hushed voices, so she couldn't understand what was being said at first. A man sat next to her father with magnificent purple and shiny gold flecked eyes. His honey-colored hair hung long and free, moving with the breeze. He wore a solemn expression that robbed her of the frivolousness of only moments before.

A large man who could've just walked off a Viking ship stood beside a young beautiful blonde whose celebrity good looks would make anyone take notice. On the other side a tall, like NBA tall, young guy wearing a scowl occupied a large space. Across from him stood another male with midnight black hair cropped close to his head. He wore a warming, radiant smile. His expression held something open and inviting despite severely scarred skin covering his arms. A tall replica of a real-life Tinker bell stood with her hands resting on the small of her back. A petite Asian with waist-long onyx hair fixed and braided close to her head stood next to a guy seated with his back to Delaney. When the man spoke, his velvety voice was one that she would find hard to forget, maybe even impossible. Malik had become imprinted on her brain, making her stomach swirl like a tank full of hungry piranhas.

The group spoke in low voices, she couldn't distinguish what was said until she was almost upon them.

"I know they'll come. Caleb's anger knows no bounds. Isabeau's revenge will thrust her right into the middle of the shit. Don't underestimate them." Her father looked at Malik.

As Bannan spoke, it occurred to Malik how much of this was his fault. He should have taken care of Isabeau when he'd the chance. All those years back, Malik wasted the only opportunity any of them had ever had to take her out. Seeing Isabeau after all those years of believing she died just shocked him. Who would have thought it would have driven her to this? Hate and derision had fueled her into the evil ugliness consuming her. Malik wondered if things might have been different.

"Their hatred makes them dangerous." The man next to her father entered the conversation with a sad expression and grim tone.

Scent hit Malik hard, knocking rational thought right out of his head. In place of them drifted in an image of Delaney, dressed in her blue jeans and t-shirt, hair falling down her back like honey. Wild spices swirled around like thick billows of smoke, rendering him altogether useless. He wanted to turn and examine every inch of her. Let her know she'd been caught spying red-handed. The hungry expression would give him away, so turning around and ogling Delaney as if he wanted to devour her was a terrible idea. He threw himself back into the conversation with all he still had control of his remaining senses.

"I fear they'll come for Viv first. I've begged her to let us all go home, but she refuses." Bannan fell silent as he ran his long fingers through his thick hair. His voice turned raspy, filled with raw emotions.

"We can't go home. We have to make a stand. An offensive position from the island would only get more innocent people killed. We fight here." Malik was on his feet and pointed to each person as he called out their assignments. "Flynn and Tanner will continue to watch Brody and Daphne, and Peyton and Bowe will follow Viv. Trystan will stay in place watching Calliope, and Dahallan is here to keep you company. As a precaution, I've already spoken with Trenton, and everyone else is standing by.

"Also, Trenton is shadowing Dane, just in case. I'm more convinced they'll come for Brody and Daphne first. They're the easier targets to acquire. I've dispatched Basil and Devlin to Sebastian's last known location in Greece. No trace of him has been found as of yet. Grey and Louden haven't yet checked in with an update from Turkey—"

"Marmaris?" Bowe asked.

Malik glanced up to Trystan in time to see fury pass over his expression before he once more appeared calm and collected.

"Figures, Isabeau's reliving fond memories," Trystan muttered not even trying to hide the bitterness in his tone.

"Trenton reports the island appears to be secure and all is well, at least for now. Still, I think no one other than Kindreds and family travel on or off, for the time being. Disregard of the circumstances would allow too many variables that can't be anticipated or dealt with." Malik sounded like a military general planning the invasion at Normandy.

He glanced around the circle of faces, realizing they all had reasons to succumb to rage. Isabeau and Caleb had taken from each of them in some way.

Delaney didn't mean to overhear so much, or maybe she did, but felt bad she had. All their talking made her realize this wasn't some sort of training exercise. People had died and more would follow. This was war.

"I'm sending Riven for Rourke. She's a skilled tracker. I think she'll find whatever is left behind. I had considered sending Poe," he said looking to Trystan.

Malik had discovered Riven when on out patrol. She was living in an alley in downtown Vegas and had the same story as the rest of them. Her mother was human and her dad an Amalgamate. Both had died and she'd survived on her own.

"Poe's a Raver. She could be in and out before they know she's been there. Riven takes after you with tracking, though. You're right, if there's anything left of him, Riven will find it," Trystan answered.

"Why not make them a two-man team, send them together?" suggested the pretty woman standing behind Malik. The way she stood flanking him reminded Delaney of old mob movies, this woman the body guard to a Don.

"Good idea. I'll speak with Trenton and have them dispatched within the hour." Malik must have considered the man next to her father and the Asian woman's comments to be reliable.

"Dad, I'm sorry to intrude, but dinner's ready." Delaney called out as she approached. She sat down beside him, facing her dad's guests.

Delaney's voice broke Malik's thoughts and even brought a small smile to his face. She glanced at her father with such affection, green eyes warm and the curve of her face brighter for her sweet smile.

"You're eating with us?" Delaney turned to Malik. A wide smile tugged at her lips.

He had meant to say something, anything, but no words came out. He sat staring at her as if he had missed place his voice or lost his mind.

Her long hair was pulled back in a ponytail and he got lost in how much he wanted to nip at the place where her neck met her shoulder. Malik forced out a deep sigh, commanding his eyes to look away from her and back to Bannan.

"Hi, I'm Delaney," she smiled with a polite nod.

She held out her hand to Trystan first, and he hesitated briefly before grasping it in his own.

Delaney reminded him of her mother, never standing on ceremony. Viv had always done what she believed to be the right thing in her mind. Delaney had adopted the same mind-set. People want to protect someone deserving of protection. An obligation becoming something you do out of respect, not only duty. Delaney wanted to make friends among the people who would give their lives for hers.

"This is Trystan Anise. I forget you haven't met any of the Kindreds. That's Dahallen Boggs and Flynn Descoteaux on the other side. Fezz Minzy and Tanner Forestier over there. And over here, behind Malik, Peyton Aadiamo and Bowe Shanks. Everyone else is out on patrol now, so you can meet them later." Bannan made the introductions and Delaney smiled politely at each of them.

In return, each nodded to her with a pleased expression. Her eyes reached out to each one of them with a purposeful gaze. Malik wondered if she knew how much the little gesture would be acknowledged and appreciated.

"Will everyone be joining us tonight for dinner?" Delaney kept her eyes on her father's face.

She wanted to peer at Malik, but fear got the best of her. Rejection encompassed such power, Delaney was too afraid to chance it. The only person she still hadn't glanced at was Malik. Though her body language gave away little, Malik assumed he had upset her.

Her brows tightened.

A part of him wanted to get her attention, to force her to acknowledge he sat right across from her. He pushed the thought away.

Her gaze dropped to the ground and a thin frown replaced her warm smile, her whole demeanor changing in an instant. Delaney sat in stony silence, sad eyes pinned to the floor, and her hands cradled one another on her lap. The stillness caught him off guard; Delaney always fidgeted.

The group began moving about and talking among themselves. Malik took the opportunity to sit beside her, being careful to hide his feelings from everyone, especially her.

With Delaney, I was foolish. Kissing her had been downright stupid. But I have missed her for too long. I can think of nothing but being back alone with Delaney in her room. How she held my face while she kissed me. My blood races at just the thought. I am foolish. This affair will endanger us both even more.

Delaney began to chew on her lip. She looked past the pool decking to stare into the abyss of the concrete, wishing the ground would open and swallow her whole.

"Oh, you're still out here. Dad, dinner is ready." Calliope stepped out of the house. She appeared cheerful and lighthearted. A look Calliope rarely wore.

"It's good to see *you*." Brody threw herself at Malik, hugging him as the group moved toward the other side of the patio where picnic tables holding

Bent, Not Broken   153

their feast waited.

I have to do something about Brody. By ignoring the problem, I have only made the situation much worse. The thought of hurting Brody didn't appeal, but the idea of her upsetting Delaney wouldn't even be considered at all.

"Do you need more help, Mom?" Delaney asked as she stepped back into the kitchen.

"Here's the last of it," Viv pulled out condiments from the refrigerator and set them on the countertop.

"I got them." Delaney stumbled at first, then made her way out to the picnic tables before she fell to the floor. *Man, the dizziness.* She wanted to puke. She closed her eyelids hoping to stop everything from spinning while the back of her neck began to smolder as if she were burning from the inside out.

"You okay?" Warm hands gripped her shoulders.

Delaney cracked her eyes open a fraction, caught her mother staring at her with concern stamped across her face.

"Dizzy. Sorry. Guess I'm not as healed as I thought."

Vivianna pulled Delaney up. "Are you hungry or would you rather go lay down?" Viv asked as she rested her head against Delaney's.

"I'm okay. Sorry. Really, I'm okay," Delaney attempted to make it the rest of the way to the table without drawing any unnecessary attention.

Her hands burned as she moved away, itching and tingling like her limbs had fallen asleep. She rubbed her fingers together, trying to relieve the numbness. The temper Delaney had become known for lit up and she wasn't sure why. A sudden rage gripped her with a ferocity that shook her to the core. She became short of breath and her eyesight yielded a poke-a-dot pattern. She tried to wipe her sweaty hands on her jeans and took a seat. Delaney's eyes began to close to a tunnel vision that made her shake her head from side to side, attempting to clear away the confusion. Pain shot through her brain as if her skull might pop under the pressure.

Why am I so angry?

The back of her neck burned and itched. Too much talking around the table, the noise irritated her. A muffled buzz Delaney couldn't banish from her mind grew louder until the assibilation blocked out the chatter.

She sat next to her father, digging her nails into the skin of her neck. The itching so intense she couldn't stop raking her nape. A loud pulsating heart beat in her ear sounded more like the drum during a rain dance. Her left hand closed into a tight fist in her lap. The energy she projected made the hair on Malik's arms stand on end. She scratched at the back of her neck again like crazy. He almost stopped her when she began tearing her own skin.

"Well, a Script is visual." Delaney's father's voice broke through the buzz and she opened her eyes. She turned to focus on his frame. The tunnel vision began to fade and she could see him clearly. Daphne quickly got up to catch a glimpse of the mark at the nape of Delaney's neck.

"It's an ankh. Oh, the Script is beautiful. A shimmering gold and deep violet brand." The sudden jubilation from Daphne surprised Malik.

To witness her experiencing genuine feelings after everything she had been through brought a smile to his face. The Stryders may have been after Calliope, Delaney, and Brody, but Daphne was the one Malik worried about. She had been lost ever since her mother was murdered and her father fell apart.

"It's begun." Daphne said with uncontainable excitement. Daphne giggled and began rambling so fast her words were tossed together. She touched the spot on Delaney's neck softly, tracing the outline while grinning like a fool.

"I've been waiting for you to hurry up for…forever." She bounced around behind Delaney. When Malik moved closer, Delaney's stomach tightened.

Damn, the man smells delicious!

"There is something on Delaney's thigh, too. It's like mine," Viv spoke from across the table.

"Is the brand identifiable?" Malik asked.

"Hello, still in the room. Stop acting like I'm not." Delaney's outrage had come out of nowhere.

The glance she shot Malik made him want to get up and move over at least one seat for safety reasons. Delaney stared down at her plate, anger simmering through her. Her skin pulled so tight, her bones hurt as if they were grinding together at the joints. The muscles in her neck screamed in her head.

"Don't talk about me like I'm not in the same room with you. It's creepy, like I'm dead and the only person who doesn't know it is me." Delaney couldn't shut her temper down. She had no idea why and she didn't care. Every action, each word, every damn breath being taken in the room, seared her skin and grated her nerves. Her eyes stung and burned.

What's wrong with me? "Can we eat?" Delaney demanded as she snatched her fork up from the table.

"The mark on your leg, I need to know what it is." Malik didn't believe in beating around the bush when he needed answers. Even if the responses weren't what he wanted, at least he'd have them and walk away with the truth. She didn't understand how crucial the information was to him.

Malik's green eyes shimmered like pools of liquid lime Jell-O as he starred at her.

She needed to scream at him. At the same time, she wanted to hurl herself at him and head-butt him in the face, raking her fingernails across his chest, biting and kicking in a frenzy.

Just breathe. Exhale slowly. She closed her eyes and tried to calm down.

"I need to know what markings show up." Malik was beginning to sound irritated. A cool air of exasperation weighed down his features.

As determined as Delaney was to ignore him, he was just as obstinate about letting the issue go. He had to shut up, though. Her head pounded as if at any moment an explosion would rock her. Then the little bit of resolve she had left fled and her temper exploded for no reason. Their eyes locked and both of them refused to given in. He watched as the blaze died in hers first. She shut them tightly and closed out the world, but most of all she forced him out.

"Okay, should I drop my pants right here at the dinner table or do you want to follow me to the bathroom?" Delaney slowly opened her eyes. Anger bubbled under the surface.

He stared at her, eyes widening slightly.

What am I so angry about? What's wrong with me? Her eyes narrowed into slits. Silence fell on the group of awkward observers.

Malik's temper burned and his normally full lips formed a tight straight line.

Shut up! Everyone shut up! Delaney closed her eyes tight, but the thoughts remained, echoing through her. Her ears were ringing like the microwave timer. She got up from the table, unsteady on her feet, pushed back hard, and her chair fell to the ground. Dizziness threatened to take over and send her to the floor right next to it.

"Everyone just shut up. This stupid voice is screaming inside my mind. You're crowding me. Leave me alone." Delaney shouted, though she hadn't meant to.

The anger burned so passionately she couldn't help herself. Her head throbbed with shooting electric currents. The burning shot to her hands and her fingertips blazed. She stumbled back from the table, staggering toward the French doors and grabbed the door handle thinking, *I have to get away from him.*

Her fingers hit the metal and pain seared her palm as light erupted in front of her, blinding her. Thousands of tiny shards of glass burst into the house with a loud boom!

"What the…" Delaney gasped as everything took on a silvery hue. The pain shot through her hand and up her arm, scalding hot bursts engulfing her shoulder and reaching for her back. White light traveled up her forearms.

Malik flew out of his chair and ran for her; crashing into her, he brought her down on the deck. Under him she bucked like a wild horse.

Trystan was right behind him and worked on getting her hand off the door that had fused to her palm. Her body became an inferno. Everywhere his flesh touched hers soon smoldered.

Peyton grabbed her head and forced her face first to the floor. White light burst from her eyes with a blinding shimmer. Screams ripped from Delaney's lips in thundering successions. The noises crackled loudly in Delaney's ears.

Bent, Not Broken   157

Hands gripped her and she was being yanked backwards hard. Delaney's palm still wouldn't relinquish the metal doorknob. The next thing Delaney knew she landed in someone's arms as they wrapped firmly around her upper body, restraining her. A tremendous pressure on Delaney's right hand and forearm pinned her flat. Someone grabbed her head and forced her face to the ground. Delaney's nose smacked the floor. A female voice spoke softly into her ear from what seemed like millions of miles away. The sound too garbled, it boomeranged around before the words began to make sense.

"Be calm." Someone screamed. The comments toppled over into themselves until the only thing Delaney became aware of was a high pitched type of ringing, but nothing she could describe.

Voices all talking at the same time distracted her. Some familiar and others were angelic and peaceful. Those celestial ones sounded different, chanting words Delaney didn't understand. Even through the pain, Delaney wasn't afraid. She was drawn with a fierce intensity further into the moment.

"Dayata siama heoway bayarone siadona kia imaway..." Unidentifiable phrases rushed from Delaney's mouth.

Delaney sensed waves tickling the hair on her arms and legs, the sound of her words becoming similar to vibrations. The words like a liquid form of Braille: long bumps, short bumps, medium bumps, with blanks in between, all colliding in her head, somehow forming back into words once inside. The burning traveled across her back and reached around for her other shoulder. Delaney heard her own screams in the distance.

Someone was next to her. She could see nothing more than the bright white light, like a solar eclipse blocking out every trace of luminescence except for the rich violet and shimmering gold.

"Your eyes." A voice fell over her, soothing and calm. Viv, at the other end of the universe. Her speech muffled, but somehow Delaney felt it.

The sounds scrambled and then reformed into a scream. Delaney clamped her eyelids shut and tried to hold them closed.

"Trystan!" Calliope's words sounded strange and breathy.

"Malik!" Brody called out.

Viv's voice became a lifeline Delaney tried to hold on to, but she was lost in an all-consuming darkness.

"Is Malik dead?" Those were the last words Delaney heard before the light was fully extinguished and blackness fell over her.

Chapter
NINETEEN

For the briefest of moments, Delaney was back in the mall bathroom. His hands were on her throat. Warm breath swept over Delaney's face. "You have to die" echoed loudly in her head. A tepid, feathery touch ran across her forehead, pausing briefly and finally trailing away. Delaney awoke with a jerk to her mother's soft voice.

"Delaney, can you hear me?" Viv whispered into Delaney's ear. The smell of gardenia wafted forth.

Delaney reached out for Vivianna, searching for a life preserver to pull her from the depths of darkness. Her eyes were heavy with sleep and felt as if sandpaper were glued to her lids. Her mouth was unusually dry and she couldn't swallow.

"Finally." Her mother sucked in a deep breath, then exhaled in relief. "You're definitely coming around. This change is like none I've ever seen before." Viv's temperate touch spread across her forehead soothing her hot skin. She'd been checking on Delaney every fifteen or twenty minutes for seven hours.

"Sleep for now. You'll need the strength for whatever comes next. We can talk in the morning. The sticky stuff on your right hand is honey, don't wipe if it off. The thick substance will speed the healing process and seal the burns from infection. Rest and try not to move too much."

Delaney quickly returned to oblivion, the last of her mother's words trailing off barely heard. She awoke again with some of her strength restored. Delaney felt the extent of her body's aching as she rolled over on her side to soothe sore muscles. Her arm brushed against something hard and a groan came out of murky shadows. Her eyes flew open to a phantom figure less than a foot away.

"What happened?" Her words came out of the darkness, startling Malik.

"Not sure." Malik gulped air greedily as he spoke, his coarse voice seeming to scratch her skin. His throat was raw and it felt like he was inhaling fire balls with each breath. He was weak from being lit up like a hundred million watt light bulb when he'd touched her. No recollection of what happened the previous evening, he only remembered the pain of what laying his hands on a branding iron, scorching hot from the open flames, felt like.

He turned his head to the side, her silhouette inches away. Delaney's once neat ponytail was a messy flop of pulled free hair. She sounded sleepy, but more confused than anything.

"Why are we sleeping on the floor in the front room?" Her mind was snowed under, but searching and concentrating on remembering.

"You were like an electrical current—" He coughed and took a gulp of air. "—reacting to the metal. An explosion throughout you…doorknob fused with your hand—" He gave another cough and his voice cracked, so he continued in a much softer voice. "…overpowered you, shot out your eyes and through your hands." He stopped, instinct driving him to protect her from what must have sounded horrifying.

Delaney forced herself to roll on her side and face him. "Once you realized I was burning you, you should have released me." She was only partially speaking to him, and mostly thinking out loud. *Why the hell would he hold on?*

"You began convulsing. Couldn't let go." He tried to clear his throat.

"Are you bipolar or something? You're constantly pulling me forward and pushing me away."

I guess passionately delicious and undecidedly biting are normal behaviors for us.

"My choices are never easy. I am torn." He stared up at the ceiling. It wasn't often he spoke the truth to her. Misrepresentation had become less of a choice and more of an inescapable fact of his life. Speaking such a deep, inner truth that laid him vulnerable to her was even more difficult for him.

"Torn between?" *Every word he says is evasive.*

"What I must do and what I want to do are rarely the same." He brought his gaze back to hers.

Delaney's eyes adjusted to the darkness of the room and she caught a glimpse of the side of his face. His expression was hard, almost angry. In the dim lighting, a sorrowful truth hid in the way his eyes examined hers. She didn't understand what his scrutiny meant.

His eyes swept over her face searching for an answer to his conflict.

No one has ever looked at me like I'm something so incredibly special. Her thoughts sent shivers dancing up her spine and goose bumps down her limbs.

I would curl up in his arms and forget everything else if he'd only offer his embrace to me.

"What's going on between us?" She stared at him, inviting his response.

He only wanted to give himself up to the pain and pass out. To dismiss what had gone on with Delaney and escape the reality of his existence.

He isn't my lifeline; it's more like he is my life. I don't even understand what that means.

The butterflies patrolled Delaney's belly in anticipation of whatever came next as she held her gaze on him and waited. To explain all the hows and whys of what she understood to be a truth about her own emotions.

"Please tell me." *Are they only dreams, snippets of my life with him, or fantasies that I just want to be real because I'm attracted to him?*

"Are you okay?" A cough racked him and a low groan escaped.

"Don't change the subject. Answer my question."

"I told you, I'm always with you. In the past, when you had been hurt or stressed out you would remember things."

"Is that what it takes for my memories to find me?"

"Do you recognize me at all?" Unmistakable desperation rang through in his voice.

"How do I know such intimate things? I dream about you, about us." Her voice fell as she said, "I understand how to touch you. How is this possible?"

He turned away to hide the sadness on his face.

"What was on your thigh at the hospital? Is the mark one of ours or one of Viv's?"

He is pushing for his own answers, so the topic must mean something. "Explain all of this to me and I'll tell you whatever you want."

"Please, go back to sleep."

"How much did I hurt you?"

"Not bad. You're okay, that's what matters." He coughed so hard he gasped for air again.

Delaney forced herself to stand up, which was a huge error in judgment. The dizziness downed her to one knee before she stood fully erect. She lowered her head and closed her eyes, waiting for it to pass. Slowly Delaney rose once more, walked carefully to the kitchen, grabbed two bottles of water, and returned to her spot on the floor next to Malik.

"Here, I brought you something." Delaney offered him the drink, but he didn't take the bottle from her. She fidgeted for a moment, then set it down on the floor between them.

"I can't."

"Why not?" Out of the corner of her eye she caught another figure moving at floor level a few feet from them. Delaney pushed herself up and crawled to the coffee table, grabbed the flashlight velcroed to the bottom, and crawled back to her spot. She switched the searchlight on and dropped the beam to the floor almost immediately.

"Oh." Tears sprang to her eyes and her hands clenched into fists. Her family was mistaken, they were all very wrong. *I am not in danger, I am the danger.*

Bent, Not Broken   163

"Did I do this?" Her face went pale and a different pain registered in her eyes as she saw the extent of Malik's injuries, and the other Kindreds laid out on the floor around them.

Malik had been burned over most of his torso. His skin hung loose in large sections. Small pieces of his shirt were imbedded in the dermis of his shoulders and chest. A light sheet covered the rest of him. His hands were raw, the skin blackened and charred in places. Trystan had burns over his hands and forearms. Peyton's fingers resembled raw meat straight from a grinder.

Her bottom lip quivered and she blinked to clear the sting of coming tears away.

"Please, stop trying to help me. Stop protecting me. You're going to get yourself killed. *I* could have killed you." Delaney sniffled. Smothering in her own guilt for how she'd repaid him for all of his sacrifices, she had to try and help him.

"Can I help you get a drink?" She picked up the water, needing to do something for him.

"Hold the bottle for me."

She moved forward, poured a little of the liquid into his mouth, then waited to help if he wanted more.

"Delaney, the reaction wasn't your fault. You didn't hurt us on intentionally."

"I'd never do this to anyone on purpose. What is wrong with me?" *I am a monster hurting the ones who keep me safe.*

"The cellular interaction and chemical submersion is taking over. You're not going through our normal Amalgamate transformation." Shame washed over her again and she scooted back, distancing herself from him and the others.

"Please, don't go away from me." He tried to move towards her, to touch her. She jerked her hand away.

"Don't!" *What am I becoming? What am I even capable of?*

"I want you to stay with me." Unable to have a visual on her, no way could he take the time to recover adequately. He needed to listen for her, to make sure she was okay and didn't need him. "Please stay here with me." Malik tried to lift his hand.

A part of her needed to be close to him, too, to lay down beside him and dream in his arms of something better. Even his beautiful face was burned on one side, yet all he worried about was her. Witnessing what she'd done to him, to any of them, caused her to chicken out and scoot another inch backward instead. Whatever the hell had taken up residence inside of her wanted out, and she was afraid the chemical reaction was going to consume her and everyone around her.

"I can't stay here. I'm sorry, I can't." She scurried backwards, got up, and tripped over something, half falling, half stumbling away. Escape was the only thing she wanted.

She ran to the kitchen and plopped onto a barstool at the island dividing the room into preparation and dining areas. Delaney's hands came up to cradle her head and she started to cry. Burying her face in her fingers, she let the pent-up emotions rage out.

"They won't die," Daphne's voice materialized from behind her.

Delaney jumped at the noise, falling off the seat to the ground.

"Don't touch me. Look what I've done." Delaney jerked away before they made contact.

"Delaney, stop, burning the hell out of them wasn't your fault. Your body is testing the waters. They know you didn't mean for anything to happen. Your body is filled with a lot of different DNA fighting to figure out what traits are coming forth. You're a wild card." She put her hands on Delaney's arm and sat down next to her on the floor. Daphne forced Delaney to remain still when she tried to pull away. "And being a complete reversal of fortune bites." Delaney exhaled heavily. "I love you just the way you are."

"I could have killed them; I could have killed you all. What if next time I go nuclear and it goes further? I have no control."

"Delaney, we'll get through this. There will always be things to deal with. This isn't the end of the world. No one loves you less because you're finally changing." Daphne rested her head on Delaney's shoulder.

"I like Malik. I like him so much."

"I know. So does Brody. You both have excellent taste. Malik's a good guy." The expression wasn't pity but understanding that made Delaney accept Daphne's comfort.

"Malik is hot. He's too serious and aloof for me." Daphne bumped Delaney forward.

She turned her face to look at Daphne. "What should I do? If I were you, he'd be eating out of my hand."

"Trust me, after tonight he noticed you." Daphne giggled.

Delaney pushed into her with her shoulder, and couldn't hold back a small laugh. "Great. I'll stand out in his memories as the human torch who tried to fry him like a Christmas goose." Delaney expressed a long sigh of frustration.

"I'm serious, help me, Daphne. I like him. I can't stop thinking about him. I…." Delaney let her head fall forward in obvious despair. "Look what I did to him for not paying attention to me as a girl, but as a potential problem."

"Delaney, you are a good hearted person. So, you got mad. Did you have any idea you may be capable of that? You were trying to walk away, remember. We all know the lighting up was an accident. Malik has stayed by your side for five or six years now. He understands what kind of person you are." Daphne insisted.

Delaney had no memory of how she caused Malik's injuries. Reaching the glass door was all she remembered.

"He can't become attached to anyone. Emotions put you in more jeopardy and he knows that. You're valuable to him, but if he cares too much, he puts you both in danger. His judgment would be less than impartial. Malik is big on doing the right thing. His honor and duty will keep him lonely. Delaney, let it go for tonight. Come on, you need sleep to continue healing."

Delaney stood and followed Daphne from the room.

Chapter TWENTY

"Unknown number of threats two hundred yards out, moving fast from the North."

"Stryder's converging from the Southwest."

"They're coming." Peyton took control of the situation. "Track them, don't make contact without back up."

"I've got six Stryders in front of the house and more on the adjacent street. Should I engage?" Flynn echoed in Malik's head as if he had used a bullhorn.

Peyton responded. "I'm on my way to Flynn. Chase and Bardot move to the upstairs. Tanner and Dahallan remain in the backyard. Bowe wake Bannan and Vivianna, have them readied."

"Malik, I'll take point. If we need you, I'll call. Otherwise, stay put, you're a liability," Trystan said, then disappeared.

Malik forced himself up, ripping the newly healed skin back open and revealing fresh blood and tissue. He understood Trystan's opinion, though the knowledge didn't make his being put out of commission any easier to accept. He was useless in his current state. A grown man covered in honey, he looked like a Halloween treat.

"I have six in the backyard."

"Flynn hold position. Fezz head to the front. Leaestra relay and reposition as information is cleared. I'm moving to the back. Trystan takes the house. Bast find the girls and move them to the second floor. Keep them separate from Viv." Peyton was out of breath.

"Ethan and Teague head to the— Trystan, I need help." Peyton sputtered.

"Trystan, I'll take the girls, reroute Bast." The pain from sitting up made him dizzy. Malik forced himself up the stairs and took position in the hall. He would hold his position until someone took him down.

"Trenton." Malik gurgled out the words.

"Malik." Trenton retuned.

"Send Kiernan, Thorn, Wade, and Fiona. They'll be active on arrival. Have the others readied."

"Copy that. Seven minutes." Trenton replied after a short pause.

Calliope abruptly shook Delaney awake. She began speaking so fast that Delaney only caught part of what she said.

"They're here." These words echoed clearly, like thunder.

Calliope sprang up and out the door before Delaney asked a single question. Delaney should have moved, jumped into action, but she didn't even get out of bed. Panic had her shackled right to the mattress. She appreciated what being terrified meant. Having his sweaty hands wrapped around her throat, knee pressing down on her chest had made Delaney understand the terror of almost dying. She hated the fear, but couldn't shake the memory of trying to breathe and having the air denied from her. Someone else had control over whether she lived or died. The experience changed life for her.

Calliope burst in with Daphne and Brody right on her heels. Brody wanted them to go outside and join the fight. Calliope and Daphne argued with Brody to stay put, but she refused to accept their logic.

Delaney agreed with Brody. Malik had already been injured because of her.

She believed he would find a way, though; he'd die trying to save her family.

"Quiet." Delaney crawled off the bed, went to the window, and gazed out through a crack in the wooden shudders. Flynn fought in the street with two big men. The one named Fezz ran over to help Flynn.

A loud knock made them all jump.

"Keep quiet!" Malik growled through the door.

Finally, someone Brody would listen to.

"Peyton. What is going on?" Malik heard the fighting. They were lucky the whole neighborhood couldn't hear the fight, but the Astasia had secured the house with spells. A nuclear bomb could go off and no one would be aware.

"Later." Peyton struggled to speak.

"Flynn and Fezz hold the front. Bowe move Vivianna and Bannan to the tunnels. Once they are secure, I'll follow with the girls." No more chances, if nothing else, Bowe and Malik could reach the underground water springs and catch a Halo. The family would be moved in under five minutes.

"Backyard." The voice was unrecognizable. The strain so pronounced Malik pivoted on his heels and stopped just short of running down the stairs.

"Bowe, how much longer?" Malik gritted his teeth.

"Leaestra, contact Trenton, five more teams. Now!" His hands fisted so tightly they began to cramp under the pressure.

"Copy that," Leaestra returned.

"Malik, ready." Bowe shot through the incessant chatter back to him.

"We need to help them. Calliope, Trystan is fighting right now, we may already be too late." Brody goaded Calliope and her tactic worked. She turned to Delaney. "And you have feelings for Malik. He's half dead because you lit him up like a Christmas tree. Are you going to let them die in vain?"

Delaney's gaze fell to the floor. She had to give credit to Brody; she'd become

Bent, Not Broken   169

a master manipulator. No matter how much Delaney hated to agree with Brody, she did. The Kindreds would keep them alive or die trying.

"I'm unstable. You saw what happened. I go nuclear without warning. I might bring down the damn house." Frustration pulsed through Delaney's words.

"You've been training in those classes your entire life. You mean to tell me you never learned how to fight?"

In a flash of anything but genius, Delaney climbed aboard the sinking ship of fools.

"We bypass the door altogether, use the window. The absence of knowledge will keep him out of the battle." Brody weighed the odds like a pro.

Delaney's gaze slid to Daphne arching her eyebrow at them.

"Once out where we have no protection, then what?" Calliope sounded almost scared.

"Kick Stryder ass." Brody moved forward.

Delaney grabbed six of her fixed blades, the Sig Sauer P226, and the polymer tipped ammo. Once they realized she wasn't exiting until she had some way to help herself, everyone got in on the action.

I can fight without weapons, but why go empty-handed?

The four young women escaped out the window, being as quiet as possible to keep from alerting Malik. They found the tile coverings slippery when they reached the roof, making the climb over the edge treacherous. With nothing to grab on for leverage, they had to push and pull each other up.

Delaney watched from the roof as Flynn and Fezz fought in the street. Two others fought beside them now. From their vantage point, they witnessed more Stryders coming over the fence in the backyard. A few assassins had become a full blown invasion.

"Let's go." Brody approached the side of the house.

Delaney grabbed her arm, forcing Brody to look at her. "How the hell are we going to get down?"

Brody grinned as she hurdled herself over the edge.

"Don't worry, you're immortal. You'll bounce." Daphne smiled, and then followed.

"Tuck and roll." Calliope grabbed Delaney's wrist and pulled her forward.

Once on the ground, Brody engaged a Stryder in hand to hand combat, while Daphne sauntered up to another. He stopped dead in his tracks, stared at her, and let her approach. When he got close enough, she snapped his neck and took off in a run to help Brody with a second woman who had joined the fight.

Delaney became shocked and appalled at how cavalier Daphne's actions were. She always seemed like the loving one. Not really the snap-your-neck sort of girl.

This is war.

A punch to the side of Delaney's head focused her attention. Her feet became entangled in each other and she stumbled, nearly toppling to the ground before she righted herself. The Stryder advanced on her. For a split second, she thought about running. Fear ruled her emotions. The human fraud coming at her was frightening. Stryders were something she didn't yet understand.

"Peyton, we're moving the family." Malik pushed the door open and had the wind knocked right out of him.

The room was empty.

Malik stood stunned in the doorway. There was no way the Stryders had gained access to the bedroom and kidnapped four girls without a witness. Yet, four women he guarded had vanished. The partially open window caught his attention. Fear crawled up his spine like razor-sharp fingernails digging into his heart.

"Delaney!" Malik roared. He tried to drift, but his cells were still too damaged.

Malik ran down the stairs and his mind shut everyone out as he searched to find her. So many scents mingled in the room, he couldn't zero in on hers alone. He picked up speed as he moved, and his surrounding became a blur of light and shadow. The pain clouded his thoughts, but he forced his feet forward. He flew through the house and found no evidence of the four of them. Malik hit the backyard at a dead run. Adrenaline silenced his pain as fear fueled his anger.

A Stryder came out of nowhere and threw herself in his path. With no time to stop, he grabbed her with his forward momentum, wrapped his arm around her neck, pulled hard, and let her dead body fall to the ground, all in a single motion.

"Delaney!" Malik bellowed.

To be honest, she'd rather have faced the horrifying one with the black holes for eyes than the handsome one looking for her. Delaney's feet wouldn't listen and they continued moving backwards as the Stryder advanced closer.

Her hands went for a blade and she gripped the cold metal. Delaney raised her arm and took a deep breath. She awaited his move to use his strength against him. Delaney planted both feet into the ground and waited.

"I won't hurt you." His words slithered over her skin just like the ones from the man in the bathroom.

Without warning, he charged. Weapons warmed each of Delaney's hands and she threw them, aiming for his chest. The Stryder fell dead at her feet. The Stryder lie on his side, her knife protruding from him. Delaney flipped him on his back. His face looked peaceful now. She starred into his eyes as the labyrinth of colors faded into nothing but the darkness within him. She pulled the knives free, but glanced away as his body returned her weapons. Delaney cringed, but knew it would be harder to defend herself without a blade.

More assassins came from everywhere. Delaney threw two additional knives and dropped a female ten feet farther out. She moved towards the house, trying to encounter a face she recognized. Lifeless Stryder bodies littered the ground like dried leaves from a Maple tree in autumn.

"Hey, come and play with me." The voice sent chills up her spine just as the scent of sweet Angelica swept around her. Delaney turned and a beautiful woman stood a few feet away. She wasn't sure how or why, but Delaney understood this woman wasn't like the other Stryders.

So, what are you?

Without another thought, Delaney threw two daggers at her. One lodged in the woman's shoulder and the other she caught midair. The assassin fired the knife back at Delaney. She had no chance to react, no time to think, as the dagger embedded itself deep in her chest.

Delaney couldn't help her stunned reaction to the events. The woman caught the blade, picked it out of the air like a baseball. Delaney fell to her knees as tears blurred her vision. The skilled killer began walking towards her. Delaney gasped as a quick burst of memory pulled free of her forgotten past.

I clung to someone who clutched me, holding on as if our lives depended on it. The fear, so tangible, a subzero chill frosting the night air. Malik pulled away from me, moving toward the rocky wall. We exchanged words, but with no volume, only the images screamed. Something had happened, though without sound I couldn't figure out what.

I stormed up behind him, forcing him to confront me. Malik's face looked sad, beaten, as his eyes fell to the ground. I think I screamed at him.

He raised his arms before him. He didn't want me to come any closer.

Desperation swirled through the space. We stood inches apart, but the distance seemed greater. Tears streamed down my cheeks as I glanced away, insides burning like a raging inferno. His hand brushed the moisture clear with a gentle sweep. Arms closed around me, pulling us into a bittersweet embrace. Sadness stood between us.

His breathy words swept across my neck. He shuttered in my arms and then tried halfheartedly to break away. I couldn't let him go. And somehow I knew that he didn't want me to.

"Back away from her, Isabeau." Malik's voice shattered the images and Delaney flew back into the present.

"Malik, how rude of you to show up. This is a girl thing." Isabeau chided him with a wicked smile pasted on her blood red lips. She wrenched Delaney's body up by a fistful of her hair, her arms lifeless at her sides, head bobbing only with Isabeau's movements.

His heart stopped altogether.

With no way for him to get in between them, Isabeau took the chance to finish what she had already started. Malik couldn't tell if Delaney was alive or dead.

When Isabeau jerked Delaney's head back, she coughed and blood droplets sprayed out and up into the air like tiny balloons. Delaney got woozy and only caught a few of their words.

"I win. Pity I don't get the satisfaction of seeing Vivianna's face as her precious little girl dies at my hand. The irony, I murdered her mother and now her daughter. This family cannot survive me." Isabeau's voice became sickly sweet and dangerously sour at the same time, and a snicker escaped her lips as they curled into a sneer.

Malik's mind sputtered, trying to figure out a way to get Delaney away from Isabeau.

"Forget the child. Take me. I'll leave with you now." The only thing to occur to him had been to barter his life for hers, thinking Isabeau and Caleb would love torturing him again.

He been there before, for nearly three months, with Isabeau wielding every tool and technique she could think of. Isabeau was ruthless in ways he had never imagined. Electrocutions, branding, dunking, flaying, beating the soles of his feet.

"Is she special to you?" Isabeau jerked Delaney around like a ragdoll. "I won't just burn you this time. I'll let rats nibble on whatever flesh is left when I'm done slowly roasting as much off as I can. I will prolong the inevitable for as long as I want. Not for years, not until you beg me. You will plead with me this time, Malik, I promise you."

The acidic words stung his ears. An involuntary shiver crawled up his back. Malik knew she meant every word. This time, no chances to escape, no reprieves. Peyton and Tryst would never find him—there'd be nothing left behind to discover. If he were lucky, Malik could provoke Isabeau into killing him quickly.

Thoughts of Delaney mixed with the cold, hard fear of what they would do to him. All he thought about was always losing her. They were damned in more ways than he wanted to admit.

"Are you going to beg for her life?" A slow smiled curled on Isabeau's wicked lips.

Delaney's weight shifted, but she still dangled lifelessly. Her arms swayed and she fell further forward. Malik shot a few feet towards her without a thought.

"She's already bleeding. I can make her scream." Isabeau tightened her grip on Delaney.

Malik froze. There seemed to be nothing to do but watch.

Isabeau stared at Delaney's face. Her eyes rolled around her head, then the other woman came into view through speckled vision. Pulling air into her lungs seemed impossible and she knew there was a hole in the middle of her chest.

Isabeau jerked her from side to side, enjoying the reaction she received from Malik. Delaney's arms swished in every direction, her fingers brushed the gun butt she tucked into her clothes on the way out the window.

A way out! She jerked the gun free from under her shirt.

"Get away from me!" Delaney hurled the words at the woman as she pulled the trigger.

Delaney doubted she could kill Isabeau, but thought she might be able to buy Malik time to get to her. She hoped the dagger stuck in her chest wouldn't end her either, but was scared by the amount of blood drenching her shirt and jeans. Everything about her transformation made it so unknown how, or whether or not, she could die.

The woman stared in shock at Delaney. The dagger slipped from her grasp and she dropped the other hand tangled in Delaney's hair. Delaney fell like a domino, flat on her back. The night sky became a kaleidoscopic of color as she fluttered off into unconsciousness.

"What...?" Delaney mumbled.

The assassin turned her back and jumped on the block wall behind her.

"You're both mine one way or another." She paused and stared down at Delaney, her mouth hung open in obvious surprise. "She's the map. She shows the way. Tell her we will see each other soon." Isabeau stood staring down at Malik for a brief moment, and then was gone.

Running to Delaney, he saw why she had been lifeless. One of her blade handles poked out her chest. Kneeling down beside her, he checked for additional visible injuries.

"Delaney. Delaney, can you hear me?"

Her eyes flickered open slowly.

"This is going to hurt." Malik grabbed the hilt of the blade and jerked it free.

A whimper escaped as her eyeballs rolled back into her head. Malik sat down beside her and waited.

"Trystan, Report." Malik said through troubled breathes. *Tonight has been an unmitigated disaster.*

"Fezz and Spyder are tracking the retreating Stryders with Bast, Ptah, Mia, and Thistle." Their link-speak intercom system went quiet for what seemed like minutes after Malik was brought up to speed.

"Isabeau was here. She attacked Delaney in the southwest corner." Malik spoke.

"I need a word with my sister." Peyton said.

"Peyton, I don't think..."

"I'm not asking for your permission."

"Trystan." Within a few short seconds, he stood next to Malik.

"Send three more teams to track Peyton. I don't want her hurt. She's running on emotion," Malik said with his eyes still focused on Delaney.

"How bad is Delaney?" Trystan asked as he nodded towards her still body.

"I just dug one blade out of her chest. Isabeau was going to kill her. She was about to slit her throat. Then out of nowhere, Delaney pulls her Sig and shoots Isabeau." He heard the echo of surprise in his own voice.

"She shot her, huh? I like this kid." Tryst laughed out loud.

"How bad was it?" Malik asked, but didn't actually want to know. Somewhere inside, he knew it was beyond terrible.

"We lost Kiernan, Tanner, and Dahallan. We need a team of Roq's for clean-up. Scratch that, send multiple teams." Trystan replied breathlessly.

"Tryst, keep ours separate. I'll take them home." Malik's head fell forward, chin against sternum.

Malik glanced to the side, Trystan had already gone.

"Is it over?" Delaney breathed out the words softly. The question caught him off guard.

"We're on lockdown." His breath whispered across her lips. An eerie quiet surrounded them, like the noises of the night knew better than to interrupt.

"What the hell were you thinking? Why would you leave the safety of your room?" Malik demanded in a soft voice, dragging his knuckles gently down her cheek. The vein in his neck looked like it was going to jump from his skin.

"I had to. I couldn't let you fight." It was all beginning to sink in for Delaney. "What did she mean by 'showing you the way'?" Delaney asked.

"Don't worry about it." Malik felt foreboding, like he had missed something crucial in the exchange. Isabeau now knew Delaney possessed more information. If they were to get a hold of her, they would torture her for intelligence she had no idea she had.

"I killed two people tonight," Delaney whispered, more tears threatening to fall.

"Isabeau isn't someone to play with. She is an experienced assassin and would have ended you tonight. You have to take this seriously." Malik said as he brushed her hair behind her shoulder.

He looked better than earlier. Skin no longer hung from his wounds.

He gently hoisted her up and cradled her in his arms. The movement made more blood trickle and slide down her stomach. A groan slipped out and her eyes rolled around in their sockets, attempting to focus on him.

"Don't leave again, okay? When I walked into that room and realized you were gone... All I had to go on was an open window." Scrubbing a tired hand down his face and exhausted, Malik stumbled. His earlier injuries had not healed adequately enough for this much exertion.

Delaney reached for him, needing him. His heart pounding and his blood racing all in her name told her he was hers.

"Malik."

His anger all but disappeared. The way she spoke his name made memories flare up in full color inside his head. Malik could almost taste her. The heat of her skin mingling with his own. The vivid recollection came alive in his mind.

"Yes." Malik leaned down to be close to her.

"When were we in a cave?" Delaney asked.

"Malik." Leaestra interrupted.

"Go ahead."

"Josslyn's missing. Trenton's already sent two teams after her."

Was that what the Stryders were doing here tonight? Was this all to cause enough of a distraction to slip in and claim Josslyn? "Copy that. Have someone try to pick up her scent. She might be wherever the retreating Stryders end up."

His head was only just beginning to throb. He gathered Delaney up and took her inside, passing the bodies in the backyard. He noticed the down-cast eyes of Kindreds he passed, then his gaze found Tryst and he nodded.

Delaney said nothing as they moved through the carnage. Malik was thankful for her silence.

Peyton was chasing down her lunatic sister, possibly running headlong into a trap. Joss had vanished and, if Delaney's memories didn't start to come back, without Joss they wouldn't return at all. Malik had lost three friends and anger swirled within him.

He walked through the house, carrying her up to her room. Laying her tenderly on the bed, he pulled the comforter up and tucked her in, still in complete silence.

SUKI SATHER

"Delaney," Malik breathed her name.

Grabbing her hand, Malik held it loosely in case she wanted to pull away. He sat down on the floor and she turned to face him.

Malik needed time to think. Now wasn't the time to go into this. He had way too many pressing matters. Despite everything going on, he was tempted. He needed her. Desired something stable even if only for this brief period of time.

"A year and a half ago, you and I became trapped. We were both injured. I had a concussion. I couldn't drift or make contact with the Kindreds. Three days later, we were found and rescued." He looked so tired. Deep, dark circles swallowed his warm emerald eyes.

"What else do you remember?" he asked.

"I get flickers of moments. I can't tell if they are real. I...I don't know." *I know there is much more to the story, the images dancing in my mind are more like memories than dreams. The figures I saw—*

"Get some rest. This conversation will require you having a clear head." He rested his forehead on the comforter next to hers.

Cinnamon wafted around her, butterflies dive-bombed her stomach, tears slid down her cheeks, and a silly smile that couldn't have been removed with a sledgehammer played on her lips. Malik snuggled his head next to hers on the pillow, allowing silence to take over. She fell asleep within a few minutes and Malik reluctantly went back to work.

He abandoned Delaney's room for the backyard to assess the casualties. Trystan waited for him by the door. He spied Tanner's remains first. What was left of him sagged against the entrance' they had cut him to shreds. Tanner had said, "No one gets inside." He died making sure.

Kiernan's body rested in a pool of his own blood. The bastards took his head with them. Dahallan's torso slumped against the stucco wall of the house about ten feet away. With so many stab wounds, he resembled a pin cushion. The Stryders tried to enter through a window. These men stood their ground and continued to fight until the end.

"Want some help getting them to Naroke?" Trystan peered around at the carnage.

"Let's go as soon as Bowe and Peyton get back." Malik scrubbed his hand down his face as he walked away.

"Dane."

"Malik." Concern thick in his voice.

"The family's fine. An attack by an unknown number of Stryders and Isabeau made a brief appearance. We requested multiple Roq teams. We lost three. Trystan and I will bring them home." Malik didn't elaborate further. Dane would grasp the extent of the losses soon enough.

"I'll meet you at the Pickets. How long before you arrive?"

"I'll call when we are ready to depart."

Malik waited anxiously for news of Peyton. They had already been gone over an hour. Peyton's good, but no one was infallible.

"Are the girls going to school?" Thane stood behind Malik.

"We're on lockdown and I'll need to speak with each later. No one leaves, not today." Malik nodded at him.

"Are you going to be able to take them home? You're still burned badly. Maybe Vivianna should have a look at you." Trystan gestured to his chest.

Malik ignored his concern

Spyder and Fezz returned not long after Peyton. They had followed three Stryders back to an active nest. The Kindreds were all in agreement that an attack had to happen immediately.

"I want to come." Peyton said.

"Trystan is going to help me. I need you to stay here and take point. Fezz and Leaestra should search for more information on the area where the nest is located. Make sure everyone is covered. New teams are arriving within the hour, and staying indefinitely. The tunnels will need to be prepared." Malik turned from Peyton. "Trystan, let's go."

"Dane, ETA ten minutes at the Pickets." Malik sighed.

Kiernan Veroff had been raised like the rest of the Kindreds. No one awaited his return home. His mother was a Sinera, a psychic vampire, and one of the most skilled contracted assassins until she went rogue. Kiernan's dad was an elder Amalgamate. Instead of killing him, she fell in love with him and they ran. Their plan worked for a few years. Isabeau and Seeley were dispatched to correct the problem and Kiernan watched his parents die from the inside of his mother's wicker trunk. She'd locked him in to save his life.

Rage boiled within Malik. Kiernan had been his friend, his brother in this war.

In less than a week, three Kindreds and a Sighmeran Guard had been annihilated. Now Malik had to go home and explain to Trenton he lost one of his too.

Dane waited for their eminent arrival. Ministerials awaited their dead. They were assigned with the task of caring for them and preparing the bodies for the Waltz of the Mariners. As guards, they would receive the highest degree of respect during their funeral processions.

"Son." Dane shook Malik's hand, pulling him in for a hug.

Malik tried to keep rigid, not wanting to sway from his chosen path.

Dane turned to Trystan and did the same.

"We need to talk away from public ears," Malik said.

"Walk to your house." Dane gestured to the right.

The three of them walked in silence until they slipped out of sight of the Pickets who helped guard Naroke. The giant statues stood tall near the sand beach only feet from the water.

"Isabeau went after Delaney and I don't believe she got lucky. There was no sign of Seeley anywhere." They hastened their strides as they spoke.

"Delaney is changing into...I'm not even sure what she's becoming. She exploded last night. Her body became a white-hot, burning light. A live wire current shot through her and she redirected the energy."

"You mean like electricity." Dane glanced away, then walked a few more steps before breaking the silence. "She's a Rafe. How incredibly odd. Generations have passed and one has never made an appearance. I thought they were extinct. The last one was well over a thousand years ago. The Rafe must be in my bloodline." Dane smiled wide.

"What exactly is a Rafe?" Trystan slowed his pace.

"They wield pulses of energy. Because the fluctuations are hot as lava, they can manipulate heat also. We need to be certain of the Rafe connection. If that is in fact what she is to become. Once she's at full strength, she is capable of destroying anyone in her path. Could the Stryders have obtained information about Rafe lineage?"

The three men walked quickly, each one of them deep in their own thoughts.

"Malik, is she showing any of my other traits?" Dane said.

"I'm not sure. She has one identifiable Script on the nape of her neck."

"Viv remembered the brand from the back of her mother, Dasha's collar. Another is forming on Delaney's thigh, but she refuses to speak of it with me." The frustration of the situation came through.

"She is much like her grandmother Dasha. The woman attacked me while I was out for a run, and once I saw her, to keep my mind on anything else became pointless."

"She would drive me to distraction...such determination, and stubbornness..." Dane turned away.

"She broke into an archaic language during her meltdown. We recognized some of the phonology, but not the meanings. Bowe copied down what she understood. Delaney chanted like the original priests from the Channels. I remember the sounds from my youth," Trystan said.

"Stellanic...how odd. Dasha is the only one I recall speaking it fluently. That is the language of the ancient rites. The speakers disappeared centuries ago. Delaney is quite unique, no?" Dane shook his head as he spoke.

"I think my mother spoke it...it sounded familiar. There was one word that stuck out. *Bayarone*. Something to do with the old festivals. Remember when Maripesa used to hold the seasonal balls and the breed celebrations." Malik spoke of when the old galas were once so alive.

"Bayarone was the Ball of the Tracers, Ryders, Fates, and Summoners. It was when they would celebrate the earth and all that it offers." Dane's mind was working so hard, Malik heard the wheels turning.

"Have Bowe deliver to me what she wrote down immediately. I might be able to have it translated." Dane's eyes traveled the distance to Malik and Trystan's home.

"How should I proceed with Delaney?" Malik asked Dane.

"We must find out about the possibility of her being Rafe, foremost. She will have no control yet over such an ability. She is dangerous. Take extreme care to keep her calm." Dane began chewing on his bottom lip.

"Dane, we're hitting the Stryder nest tonight. I demand Kiernan's head back. While I'm at it, I want a few of theirs hanging on my wall by morning." Malik shrugged as he stepped through the front door.

Chapter
TWENTY-ONE

Delaney spent most of the day in her room, mostly by her choice. After the stunt they pulled the night before, she was told she would be lucky to leave the house ever again, even with a guard.

To keep her mind busy, she finished reading the first book from *The Morganville Vampires*. A part of her wondered about Malik. She hadn't seen him yet and thought better than to go in search of him; she valued living more.

A loud discussion occurred earlier between her parents, Daphne, Brody, Malik, and a couple other familiar voices. From the sound of the argument, her sisters had been lucky Mom, Dad, and Malik had different people nearby to restrain them.

The events of the preceding night continued to resurface. Delaney pushed them away, but her thoughts would boomerang around her room and always find their way back home.

The previous evening she had a vision of something that left a nagging awareness the story Malik told her was missing some significant details.

Why does he appear as lost as I do when I am with him? The manner in which we stood together, the way I touched him.

"So, is your head near exploding or what?" Daphne appeared smiling in the doorway and chased away Delaney's thoughts.

"You're concerned too. I am worried about you, and surprised none of the neighbors called the cops. Usually something big draws the authorities." After the struggle spilled into the street, the spectacle had been loud enough to wake up most of Vegas, not only their neighborhood.

"Where were the cops? Why weren't they circling the vicinity, asking questions at least?

"We are . The Astasia put something similar to a soundproof bubble around the house. Whatever goes on here, no one fully understands but us."

"What about the fighting in the streets?"

"The police will attribute the violence to rowdy kids or gangs. They had all dispersed by the time the uniforms drove by, so who are they going to question?" Daphne shrugged with a smirk. "I'm sorry Brody and I drug you along last night. Malik is right, we acted stupid. Sometimes I want revenge for what they did to my mom, my family. They shouldn't be allowed to attack people in their homes. You don't go after families and little girls who don't understand what's going on." Daphne sank down on the bed next to Delaney. "A child shouldn't witness their mom's death." Tears filled Daphne's eyes, but she held them back.

Delaney wanted to say something, to offer Daphne comfort. "Do you remember your mom?"

Daphne's shoulders shook while tears cascaded down her face. Delaney moved to sit closer to her and put an arm around her shoulders. Daphne opened her mouth to speak, but clamped her lips shut. She remained quiet for a while, trying to find her voice, and Delaney held on to her. The way she stared off into nothing saddened Delaney. Daphne appeared shattered and lost like a little girl or a woman who wouldn't allow herself to get past the tragedy she suffered as a child.

This war takes and takes and none of us are left whole. Does winning matter if all we achieve is a long life filled with loneliness? What are we fighting for?

Bent, Not Broken   185

"No." Daphne shook her head to the side before continuing, "The only clear memory I have is when the man told her to step away from me. She kept begging him to let me go. The two of them stood silently facing off. I experienced a driven need to examine his face. I couldn't resist." Daphne's voice shrunk to a shallow whisper. "I peeked out from behind her leg and he glared at me." Daphne shivered, closing her eyes. She wiped her nose with her sleeve and struggled to take a deep, calming breath.

"He is beautiful. Ironic, huh? Like an angel or something. Seeley Delacroix is breathtakingly gorgeous. I found out his name later, researched him until I became as familiar with him as I am about dinosaurs. What he is, what he can do, how to end him.

"He had these jet-black eyes that penned me where I hid behind her. His expression softened as he took a step toward me, then he reached for me. My mother threw her hands up in front of us. She must have done something, because she fixed him in place without moving or touching him. He never took his eyes off me and didn't even try to fight her. I thought he would let us go." She fell silent.

Delaney waited for Daphne to catch up.

"She whispered something to him, I'm not sure what. I had never heard the language before and I have never heard the words since, until you went all iridescent last night. You chanted in the same dialect they used with each other the night my mom died." She turned to look at Delaney.

"I needed to go with the stranger. I wanted to stay with him over my own mother. Her last thoughts must have been of her daughter's betrayal. What's wrong with me?" She looked so broken. "Out of nowhere, he told her to run. She grabbed me and ran so fast my feet never touched the ground. I glanced back to find him watching us flee with this odd expression on his face. He made no move to stop us or give chase." She paused and swallowed painfully.

"I didn't want to leave him. Crazy, huh? An undeniable pull I couldn't fight. I wanted to let my mother's hand go and run to the assassin who had been sent to end me. She gave her life for me, and all I had been concerned with was him.

These moments haunt me every day. What had my mom last thoughts been? Her treacherous daughter was willing to get everyone killed because she drug her feet to stay with the stranger who wanted to kill her. I can't explain why I needed to remain with him. I wanted to, though." Delaney understood the crippling pain by the blank look in Daphne's eye and the hollowness in her tone.

"Isabeau appeared at Seeley's shoulder. I turned back and my mother fell to the ground on top of me." Daphne closed her eyes. "She told me not to move, everything would be fine as long as I stayed motionless. No one checked, they assumed they killed us both." Her head turned slowly from side to side, as if her thoughts consumed her.

"I was so afraid and freaked out. When I talked to her, my mother didn't answer and I thought we had to be quiet or be found out. I sang 'Dream a Little Dream' to her. She would wonder around the house singing that song. When darkness fell, I attempted to push her off me. She was too heavy, so I tried to wiggle out. I wondered how much time had passed while I lay underneath her. Her blood had soaked my hair, I smelled her death all around me. Later, someone pulled her torso half off of mine, but when I slid out, I was alone." Daphne sighed.

"When I stared into her eyes, I realized she was no longer in there. I crawled on top of her and hugged so tight. With each passing minute I grew more afraid. At some point, I must have passed out." She buried her face in her hands and cried.

Delaney had never seen Daphne lose control of her emotions. She wrapped her arms around her sister.

"In the morning, I woke up in a forest, under a big pine tree, alone. I didn't recognize my surroundings. I had her blood on my hands…all over me and my new dress she had bought me to wear for Sunday dinner. The scent of her had dwindled into a metallic stench. My mom's body disappeared and I had no idea how I got to the forest." Daphne stared straight ahead as if reliving the moments.

Bent, Not Broken **187**

"I found a bundle of clean clothes at my feet. I cried for my dad, but he never came. I called for Brody, too, but she never answered. I figured, my whole family… With no idea where to go or what I should do, I curled up under the tree and waited to die too. I awoke later and found cheese, crackers, and a bottle of water beside the clothes. Someone had brought them to me. Some person I didn't know took care of me, but they wouldn't take me home.

"When night fell again, a woman appeared out of thin air to stand before me. She said she had been told where to find me. She brought me to your mom's." Daphne took a slow, deep breath. "I've never recited the whole story before."

They spent a long time in Delaney's room, each girl propped against the bed, their individual thoughts allowing silence to envelope them some of the time. It was comfortable between them, more so than ever before. Delaney couldn't think of one thing to say that didn't sound stupid.

Daphne fidgeted her hands. "This is a lot to deal with. But, all is not lost. We…are just a different sort of found. You discovered a distinct version of yourself. Not worse, not better, unique."

"How can you be so sure?" Delaney asked.

"I don't think we get definitives in life. Under normal circumstances, I choose to accept what I can reason and touch. We have to believe in something more, though. This is my act of faith. A larger reason sent my mother running with me, away from Seeley and Isabeau. I don't understand the plan involving all of us. My dad, Brody, and I all survived for a reason. I won't waste my chance."

Daphne's words gave Delaney pause. Without realizing she was doing it, she traced the floating continuum mark on her thigh, through the leg of her jeans, as it came and went. Delaney hadn't told anyone about her secret. She needed to know what the symbol meant before she could reveal it to anyone.

"Daphne, what does the infinity symbol mean? I have only seen the pattern associated with math." Delaney glanced down at her thigh.

"Infinity is one of the oldest emblems. Everyone claims its origin, but I don't think anyone knows what the truth is. In ancient India and Tibet, infinity represents the unity between male and female, perfection and dualism. In tarot, the symbol means balance of forces, maybe even harmony in nature." Daphne leaned her head back against the mattress.

"What does all this stuff about Prints and Scripts mean?" Delaney slumped farther into her pillow.

"Two types of brands exist. They sort of tell a story about you. They're called Scripts and Prints. Your markings tell who you are and what you can do. Except the women in this family are different. We possess no marks yet. Mom bears the blueish-black symbols. To me, they look like the continents shifting around. None of us girls show any signs of the brands, except you. For instance, an Ankh is a Script, a self-expressive formatted symbol. Some sort of ability will be attached to the Script. With the forming of a Script, you experience burning and a lot of itching." She touched her pointing finger to Delaney's thigh, just where Delaney had been circling the pattern underneath the fabric.

"You encountered the side effects last night. The skin rises permanently, but only slightly…enough for other Amalgamates to be able to identify you. Human eyes can't see the marks. A Print is different because it shows what you can fuse with, but only becomes visible when you're about to change. It resembles a real-life tattoo, but burns when coming to life. Your skin warms to the touch too. Remember this: a Script tells a story. A Print explains how you are going to exist with your other half." She shrugged.

"I don't understand why you possess the Ankh, you'll need to ask Mom. It's Egyptian, meaning eternal life in their culture. Our Script symbols come from many of the ancient cultures in some form or another." She continued to talk, but all Delaney could think about was the word Echo.

"How does the Echo thing work?" Delaney interrupted.

"One of your markings, either a Script or Prints, will match your Echo. I wish I understood how the idea worked. Somehow you scribe with another person to perfection." She seemed sad.

Daphne had always wanted to fall in love more than anything.

"The waiting drives me crazy. I want someone of my own. I want…" Daphne leaned in, letting her shoulder brush Delaney's.

Daphne was a romantic, and Delaney loved her for her strict beliefs in happily ever afters. She had been planning her wedding for as long as Delaney could remember. Daphne knew how many kids she wanted, and even what their names would be. She wanted to be a part of something special, a love that life would stand still for.

"Give yourself time. Things get easier." When Daphne spoke in her motherly tone Delaney smiled.

They both sat quietly, their minds thousands of miles away.

"Dinner is ready," someone called from the kitchen.

"Hungry?" Daphne grinned.

The girls scrambled away from their depressing reverie and joined everyone in the kitchen. They ate amidst light, happy talk. Delaney sat with them for a long time during dinner, watching them laugh and tease each other, studying their gestures and imprinting them in her mind.

The future is promised to no one.

Her head was too busy for much participation; Delaney's mind became an overhead projector for memories playing like snippets of some old home movie she had no actual recollection of.

I haven't been daydreaming. I existed in those moments, but couldn't remember enough to place them. With no physical connection to them, no sense of familiarity, I am detached from my previous existence. Real moments were stolen from me, to save me. How ironic.

Dinner felt like strangers sitting together, suffering through awkward silences as Malik realized he and Delaney ate silently, and he was the only one in discomfort.

She was sitting next to him, or rather he had made a point to sit next to her.

She was more of a stranger than ever before. Not so long ago, Malik read her moods in the way she did things. All her tells had vanished. Malik had no idea what was going on in her mind.

Bannan excused himself after dinner, motioning for Trystan, Peyton, and Malik to follow him to the backyard. He wanted to know what they found out from Dane.

"Malik, we need to talk in private." Bannan spoke as he stood up from the table and began pushing his chair in.

The trio followed Bannan, then joined him side by side as they strolled the length of the evening dew covered grass.

Malik began their conversation. "Based on what happened the other night, Dane believes she's a Rafe. He believed they existed until about a thousand years ago. Rafes can manipulate pulses of energy and heat. They can consume power and redistribute the flow. She can absorb heat and redirect the intensity of it, as well. The fluctuations are searing hot and ignite farther while traveling through her. Until she learns how to use the ability and control herself, she's dangerous. She might light up like a flare and take us all out." He replicated bombs exploding with his fingers.

"Dane wants me to notify him the minute any of the other characteristics appear, especially anything weird. He thinks she's chasing his bloodline more than Dasha's, which makes sense. According to him, if she adopts anymore traits, she'd be a force that could destroy everything in her path." Malik's voice became more serious the longer he spoke, and quieter, so it didn't carry beyond their small group. He thought it best to keep the information from Delaney for the time being. Once she settled a bit more, he planned to sit her down and tell her everything.

"We need to tighten the ranks. I don't want anyone to know about the Rafe blood except for the five of us, including Viv when you tell her, Bannan." Malik had a grim expression set firmly on his face.

"The words Delaney chanted the other night, Dane wants them." Malik link-spoke to Bowe at the same time.

"Looks like an Austrian's last name to me. I copied down as much as I understood. Should I take my findings to Dane now?" Bowe link-spoke in response.

"Leave immediately."

"Dad, can I interrupt and speak with Malik for a moment?" Delaney called from the doorway.

Bannan cut his eyes at Malik; a warning or just a fuss over being interrupted not clear.

Malik walked to Delaney.

"I need to get out of the house for a while. I know I can't go by myself. So can you find someone to go with me?" Delaney was trying to be courteous. Just because she wanted him to go didn't mean he did.

"I'll take you. Give me a few minutes." Smiling, he walked back to her father.

"Tryst, we'll be in the immediate area. I'll call you if I need you." Without risking a look to find concern on Bannan's face, Malik turned back toward Delaney with a smile on his face.

"Why are you going with me?" Delaney needed the walk to be calming, not irritating with lectures from Malik.

She stood on the defensive though he had done nothing more than agree to her wish, and step in her direction. He took a long, deep breath. "Because I'm supposed to be with you. You're my respon—".

She waved the rest of his speech away, thinking his explanation would hold none of the answers she hoped for. "Yeah, yeah, let's go. I don't need the details." She rolled her eyes as they walked to the front door.

They made their way down the sidewalk while Malik's eyes constantly surveyed the area. He persisted in glancing around, prepared for an attack at any moment. His actions encouraged her to wonder about the man walking by her side, so distant one minute and then a ball of fiery, longing looks the next. Delaney still considered getting him meds for his whacked-out behavior.

"If you're always with me, you know what happened at the mall, right?" Her words were a punch to his gut.

"I watch you most nights." He felt uncomfortable as they walked in silence for a while.

"I never leave you unless you are protected by another Kindred. I failed to keep you safe that day, though, and I'm sorry." His eyes found hers briefly, then wandered back to surveilling.

"Are we being followed?" Malik looked at Delaney as she spoke. He quickly studied all around them, eyes darting, taking everything in.

"Why? What did you see?" Malik became jumpy and grabbed her hand.

Delaney stilled and just stared at him.

"No one, nothing. You are practically jogging, though. I figured you had a reason." Delaney said with a giggle.

"No, I am...no. Sorry, I'll slow down." Malik began to walk, still holding her hand. His fingers had interlaced with hers and for a brief time, they were nothing more than two people on a romantic stroll during a beautiful night.

"I'm glad you killed the human." He tone was fierce.

"I'm not sure I did. I don't remember killing him. Things got fuzzy after he threw my head into the mirror. I woke up to his body laying next to me, face torn up and torso bloodied. I don't remember anymore." Delaney shook her head in disbelief.

"I possess no excuses for not getting away from the Hollowers."

Hollowers? Another question to keep for later. " I believe more than one was in that bathroom with me. I heard a second voice before I passed out."

"I took out the other man before you left my line of sight." Malik sounded bewildered.

Still hand in hand, they walked in silence. She noticed the large rough callouses covering his palms.

"Have you murdered a lot of people?" The words sprinted out of her mouth before she thought to sensor them.

"Yes." He answered without hesitation or emotion. "I have never killed anyone who didn't deserve to die, though." He spoke with such conviction.

"Have you ever murdered anyone you didn't want to?" she asked as they turned down another street.

In the oddest way, she reminded him of what a conscious may have

Bent, Not Broken   **193**

sounded like.

Kindreds aren't comparable to the police. They didn't arrest the people they were sent for. They always used deadly force. Those who posed a credible threat were prejudged, convicted, and sentenced to a visit from a death dealer. Kindreds were simply the facilitators, dispensing an inevitable ending in order to save whomever they could. That was the easiest way for Malik to look at his job.

Most of her questions deserved more than simple answers. If Malik said no, he had never killed anyone he didn't want to, he was a liar. If he said yes, how would one explain or justify a solitary existence where life became irrelevant? These questions went deeper than yes or no. Some were just too personal; they needed to stay buried under the ten feet of concrete he had poured over them.

"I have been given the task to kill people I was close to. Kindreds who didn't survive the torture they'd endured. Isabeau likes to experiment on us. She does things to us, unnatural things we can't undo. I'd never leave anyone behind who changed into something monstrous. They wouldn't want to live as a research project gone wrong. Those kills, I'm not proud of, but they had to be." Fire sparked in his words.

"So what happens with me now?" Delaney asked, now staring up at him, though he wouldn't meet her eyes.

"You'll start training as much as possible. We'll fit you with more sophisticated weapons." He kept walking, his eyes fixed straight ahead. Shrugging, he let the subject fall to the sidewalk, hoping to lead her away from topics he found uncomfortable.

"How do you live the way you do?" Delaney wondered what shaped him into the man he was. His life seemed so opposite to hers. She was a college kid with a part-time job. He was a bodyguard and she didn't know what else.

"There isn't an easy answer to that question." His voice was low.

The fact was, he had never lived any other way. So, although it appeared to be unnatural to some, as a Kindred, it was the only thing he understood. They grew up with violence. When chaos was erupting, they reacted the most efficiently.

"Do you have family?" She pressed, hoping he would open up to her.

"Not in the traditional sense, no." He shut her down again. She didn't know how to draw him out; how to make him notice her as more than just someone constantly in need of saving.

"Am I doing something wrong?" Everywhere lay land mines with no safe passage through to him.

"What do you remember?" Desperation rang through every word.

"Pictures of myself or other people will hit me at odd times. But it's more like watching a movie. I possess no memory of the moments or the sentiments. Sometimes whole scenes will play, but with no sound and I can't figure out what is going on. I can't tell if they are memories, dreams, nightmares, or my imagination running wild." Delaney answered him as honestly as she believed possible. She tried to smile, but the action seemed hollow.

Malik hadn't given much thought to how her unknown life affected her. She didn't understand why or when, or who she may soon be.

My Delaney is locked somewhere inside her mind and I can't reach her. Standing right next to me and I can't find her, can't pull her into my arms. My nerves fray at the very idea my Delaney is gone for good and that this woman will never feel the same way about me.

"Are you angry with me? You come close and push away at the same time. I find your actions confusing and without merit. Have I done something to offend you?" Delaney squinted her eyes at him.

"I…I'm not angry with you. We are complicated." For a moment, he considered relinquishing her hand, but instead tightened his grip.

I'm frustrated and it's killing me. All I want is walking right next to me. Always close enough to kiss, yet not mine to touch. All we ever possess are stolen moments pieced together and I was so willing to settle for them. Anything to be with her. Echoes or not, I know I need Delaney Drake. In the chaos of my life, she makes sense when she shouldn't and, I love her for no reasons that make sense in the rational world.

We have spent hours in each other's arms. I have traced every inch of her with my fingertips or my tongue and I want to spend lifetimes continuing the detailed exploration. Mere days of being thoroughly immersed into one another was all we had.

Days are not enough!

I need a lifetime, or several in our case. Passion filled moments should be ours to share. Hers to remember. Ours to relive. Instead, I cling to them alone.

She carries nothing of me. Our time forgotten, for her, the time never existed.

In the past two and a half years, she's found her way back to me countless times. I have to believe she will find me again.

"Like the other night when I thought we had been in a cave together. The image seemed so clear in my mind. But I couldn't tell if the picture was something real or something I made up." Delaney said, shaking her head.

"What was the image of?" His demeanor softened.

She was trying to remember. He witnessed Delaney concentrating on fractured moments that were yielding nothing but more questions.

"Um…we were arguing, I think. You turned away and I followed you. I think I did something to force you to turn around, made you face me. Then you reached out your hand and I think you touched my cheek and that was it. The picture blurred and fell away." Delaney tried to recreate the image in her head.

"We *were* arguing. The Stryders had come for Calliope at the end of your junior year. They attacked us on the way home from school. We weren't as prepared as we should have been. It was just the four of us. Trystan was watching Calliope and I was watching you. We made a run for Red Rock Canyon." He cleared his throat, buying time to pick and choose his words carefully.

"You lost control of the car and crashed. We were near Black Velvet Canyon and headed out on foot. The four of us made it to Whiskey Peak when the Stryders descended like locusts. In a rush, you fell partway down the rock face and hit your head. When I drifted to you, you were disoriented. Next thing I knew, you decided to club me in the head with a rock. You knocked me out and gave me a concussion. Tryst and Calliope went for reinforcements. It took them another two days to hike out and make it back to your house without being captured. Then they came back for us."

Malik's head was ready to explode. *Either I tell her or I leave. I can't do it anymore. Losing her every other minute is tearing me apart.*

She had a right to know the truth.

"This conversation is one that I have put off on purpose. You needed time to see things for yourself. I didn't want to get in the way of you being able to get comfortable with so many changes. I have been hoping your memories would come back on their own, but I can't wait anymore."

Delaney wondered if he meant to continue.

"We sat in your room, up late at night talking for hours about everything. We became friends. And then we became more. The next time we had four days together. Then we were trapped at Black Velvet Canyon for three days and things went as far as they could go. We…I wanted you to remember this on your own." Malik looked away.

"What are you saying? What? We were like together or something?"

I want him now. I wanted him in the past too and that does not shock me because of how much I want him now, how familiar he feels to me. She stopped walking and just stared ahead. Why didn't anything he was telling her spark even a little bit of recognition in her head?

"How close *were* we?" Delaney demanded harsher than she had meant to.

"All we ever had together was borrowed time. A few days at the most, here and there. Then Joss would come and I would have to watch you forget me. You would wake up a few hours later and I wasn't even a memory. Your mind is strong and you would force yourself free of the binding eventually. Sometimes it would take months for you to break through. But you always found your way back to me. This time you're different." He was struggling with the words. For once she thought he had no idea what to say next.

"What happened in the cave? Why were we arguing?" She wasn't sure why that question seemed so important.

"You wanted to give me something that you couldn't ask for back. I wanted to wait, but you were so adamant, so determined, and I was weak. You were all I wanted." It was hardly a whisper.

"Did we have sex?" Her nose crinkled up.

Malik realized she didn't understand what he was trying to tell her. It felt strange to talk about her sex life, or lack thereof, with a stranger.

"Yes, I was your first." He said softly.

Her brows pursed together as she buried herself in thought. For a minute, Delaney didn't get it. She couldn't remember her first time, now that he'd brought it up. She remembered her first kiss; that went to Logan Michaels. She remembered her first date was with Brad Doyle. But the first time she had sex was a blur.

"Was I in love with you?" There were no feelings in her words, making them hit him with the force of a physical blow.

"We are, I mean were, in love with each other. I started guarding you over six years ago. After three years, I realized I was in love with you and you didn't even know I existed. It was never my intention to let you know. I kept you at a distance at first. I wanted to avoid being alone with you, but how could I without raising suspicions? It was easier to hide when you didn't know about me." He sighed.

"It was when you were hurt and would cling to me that I let my guard down. I wanted to comfort you, you wanted more. Then it was too late. You were all that I wanted too."

Delaney felt even more lost than before they started talking.

Releasing her hand, Malik let her go in more ways than he could deal with.

"I've hated lying to you these last few days. It felt like that was what I was doing by not telling you about us. I'm sorry if you feel like I took advantage of you. I let my feelings sway me and it won't happen again. But I'm not sorry that we were together. I'm just sorry you don't remember." He glanced away before she could discover his expression.

"Why did you let them steal my memories of being in love for the first time? My memories of being with you?" Delaney was so angry and hurt. She felt so cheated. Losing her virginity was supposed to be significant and she couldn't even remember the moment.

"You believe there are choices that I could have made? Like what?" His voice was an angry whisper.

"You could have told them to leave me alone. We could have stayed together." She wasn't even sure what the options were.

"I wanted you safe more than anything."

Malik unconsciously took a step away from her, putting physical distance between them to match what he felt inside.

"So you just gave me up? You let them play with my mind, steal moments that weren't for anyone else to have, but were for you and me to share?

The question caught him off guard. Anger surged through him.

"Yes, Delaney. I am a selfish ass that decided to watch the woman I love forget me again. Callously dismissing that she had just given me her virginity with a casual wave, that we had spent the better part of three days so wrapped up in each other that Trystan walked in on us before I realized he was even there. I chose for you to live over keeping you for myself."

Her gaze fell to the street. She had been so busy thinking about what was taken from her that she hadn't even begun to consider what Malik had lost in the process.

"How could you do that to us? If you loved me, then we should have…" She struggled, as if there were an easy answer to be found.

"What would you have had me do? Should I have left you unprotected and vulnerable to an attack by the Stryders? As long as your memories where hidden, you were safe. No one came for you. So my only choice was watching you leave me, and carrying around our memories in my head while for you it never existed, in the hopes that you would one day fuse and make your way back to me. I couldn't watch them come for you. What if I hadn't gotten to you before they did? Or wonder what Isabeau was trying to turn you into."

It was then Delaney knew why she had cared for him to begin with.

"We should get back." Malik held his hand out to her. Delaney hesitated for a split second and he let his arm fall away. Malik turned back, but waited for her. He didn't hold out his hand this time. He knew that watching her decide she didn't want him to touch her again would hurt too much.

They walked in silence for a while.

In her heart, she knew he spoke the truth. Delaney had fallen for him and perhaps always loved him. Malik said she found her way back to him every time. Her past continued to rise up and surprise the hell out of her. The one emotion she couldn't deny was her anger.

Delaney felt cheated. It wasn't fair that she couldn't remember. She needed time to put things into perspective, but knew somewhere deep inside herself she had already begun forging a new path back to him.

"I *am* drawn to you, that much makes sense now. I can't recall our courting and we went right to sleeping over." Delaney couldn't help sounding sad. She'd missed the fundamental moment of falling in love.

"You have no idea what this is like…to love someone so much." His voice grew faint. "Only a handful of times do you recognize me for who I am. The other ninety five percent of the time, you walk right by me," he swallowed hard, "and not even a glimmer of recollection passes over your face when you look at me. You think I let them take something from you? They took everything from me." He lengthened his stride, leaving her just behind him as they walked back.

"Malik." He stopped, but didn't turn to face her.

"I'm so sorry." She whispered.

"I don't need your sympathy."

Chapter
TWENTY-TWO

At one a.m. the Kindreds left the barracks, drifting two houses down from the Stryder's nest and into the shadows of a large Weeping Acacia. Trystan stayed behind and took point and at 3 a.m., if the members of that squadron hadn't returned, he'd contact Trenton and have an additional five squadrons dispatched immediately. Two units were assigned to search for stragglers. Three squads remained behind at the Drake's in case of retaliation.

Three teams would take the house doubling as a nest. Bast and Spyder had collected pictures and solid Intel about the set up inside the building. Analyzed data showed fifteen to twenty Stryders manning the property.

Infiltration through the front would be by one covert pair, followed by the main assault coming in from the back and side. The team assigned to go in the front door would approach as undercover Stryders. Bowe's ancestry included being half Zooza; she had the ability to manipulate her appearance. She would enter the nest as a Stryder and link-speak vital Intel to the rest of the teams. Flynn, who was partly Shell, would cover his scent, and drift in to support Bowe.

Bent, Not Broken 201

The other teams had Kindreds whose fuses were less for fighting and more for recon, or undercover work, to support those who were better suited for fighting. A team had been dispatched just to watch the neighborhood, too.

The street was eerily quiet, disturbingly silent. Had the Stryders already moved on? The Kindreds kept to the shadows. Though the Intel remained reliable, the idea of an ambush struck Malik. A trap waiting to be sprung had to be considered a valid threat.

Everyone began moving into position. Bowe and Flynn stood ready to enter through the front. Malik and Peyton headed for the rear of the structure via the yard, while Spyder and Fezz picked up the side entrance by way of the garage. The rocks of the desert landscape gave way under Malik and Peyton's feet, lending a slight gnashing sound to the silence.

A sliding glass door with a flimsy single bulb light shining dimly over the concrete patio was the rear entrance.

"I'm going in. Hold position." Malik believed the possibility of a trap too likely to be ignored, and losing a commander had been enough for one week. He deemed it his responsibility to go in first.

If luck stood on their side, clues as to Rourke's disappearance and Kiernan's head might be discovered.

Malik disappeared into the house. Up against a wall in a small laundry room, in the far south corner of the little two story, sorely neglected residence he hesitated long enough to allow his eyes to adjust. A pair of banged up Maytags sat staring back at him. Time being limited, he remained methodical and refused to rush as he glanced around, assessing everything.

An old ironing board haphazardly hung from the tattered wall. Kiernan's skull had been propped on top. Blood soaked the material covering the board and was dried on the metal in thick chunks.

They used his head for target practice with cigarette butts and blunt knives.

Anger coursed through him anew.

Malik remained as still as stone and listened.

A TV boomed from somewhere upstairs, along with jagged shallow breathing and a vacant hissing sound he couldn't identify. Loud cursing in a room only feet away. Dishes rattled in the kitchen. Noises came from where the front door opened and closed.

Malik moved forward to the threshold, peering along the adjacent wall. Crusty wallpaper flaking off in strips covered the hallway walls, but otherwise, the corridor appeared empty and dark. A smiley face night-light halfway down smirked at him.

He crept out into the hallway.

The acidic fumes of various bodily fluids and the strong stench of decomposition stung his nose. He passed a bedroom with a lavender painted doorway and pink flower decals on the door. At least one dead human inside was indicated by this being where the decay smells became the strongest, most offensive.

An opening on the right had Chuck's Do Not Enter sign on the door. He saw two large holes in the bottom of the door, and the handle was missing. The door flew open, almost hitting him. Malik jumped back and immediately stilled. The door swung wide into the hallway. Malik waited on the opposite side, his back pressed against drywall.

Two Stryders walked out. Grabbing one by the collar, Malik snapped his head around quickly. The second one stopped, and before he could turn or make a sound, Malik had his arm around the Stryder's neck. He pulled his head back and the blade slid through his skin as if he had cut into tender filet mignon. The Stryder flexed his back muscles and Malik had just enough time to think, *This is going to hurt.* Thorny spikes jammed past the Stryder's vertebrae and pushed through Malik's skin. They punctured his torso as the corpse slumped against him. Malik continued to hold on despite the pain. A little something the demon got to bring with him into the human suit now poisoned Malik's body.

A hand fell on Malik's shoulder. He whipped around, dropping the lifeless torso to the ground with a small thud, and reached, grabbing for whoever had touched him. Peyton stood with a sly smile on her face, her eyes dancing with amusement. She lifted her right arm and tapped her wrist with smooth movements, and then an eyebrow shot up in surprise.

Peyton raised two fingers and motioned Malik to move forward. Instead of acknowledging his annoyance, she smiled wider. She spun the same pair of digits around counterclockwise, indicating to him that the teams had already begun moving through the house. Peyton pointed to the holes in Malik's torso and he quickly waved her off. He refused to debate his health and whether he should leave the op with her.

The tips of the King Tryad spikes had been poisoned with a toxin capable of penetrating the body's natural defenses through the bloodstream, effectively using it as a superhighway to the heart and brain. Malik had about thirty minutes to get back to the barracks and be treated before paralysis over took him.

They came to the foyer. The entryway opened up and three more dead Stryders lay at their feet. Peyton found a doorway to the basement. She drifted, Malik closely behind her. The room had stacks of paper filled binders, rows of boxes with black and white pictures crammed into them, and crates littered the floor, filled with everything from limestone chunks to medieval swords. Stone instruments cluttered one corner. In a large wicker basket sat a collection of tools for uncovering human remains; Malik had seen similar gadgets at the Drake's.

What the hell is all this stuff doing here? How is any of this relative?

While Peyton secured the area, Malik searched to see if any of the paraphernalia would be relevant to them. He noticed a strange grouping of symbols on a torn piece of paper. One of the same marks currently resided on the back of Vivianna's neck. He grabbed the stack of papers and pictures. When Peyton followed beside him, he instructed her to call for help and drift as much of the material as possible to the apartment they held in Turnberry Towers.

Peyton got to work and Malik drifted upstairs. The first floor remained quiet, except for the kitchen.

A dead Stryder lay sprawled on the dirty carpet just inside the living room. Beyond the entryway, Malik moved through a swinging door. Bowe had changed into her "street clothes" and Flynn was forcing an assassin's head into a bowl of cereal.

Death by Fruit Loops is a new one for me.

Bowe waved a quick hand over her throat. A noisy Stryder jogged down the stairs and pushed the door open. She struck him in the larynx with her forearm, seized his falling corpse, and dropped it quietly to the carpeting. The team moved out of the kitchen and up the steps.

On the second-floor, Flynn and Bowe went one way and Malik the other.

The first door he came to stood open. Malik caught sight of a bathroom, where he found Fezz making use of his blades.

Malik continued down the hall, to the closed door of the next room. Malik waited and listened intently.

Fezz and Malik drifted in. A small figure lolled in the center of the floor. Chained and filthy, the form smelled of vomit, urine, and feces. Fezz approached the unmoving frame, blades readied. He pushed the being over on its back and the smell got worse. Dead eyes stared at them, irises black like a moonless night, until they blinked and a shimmer of white peeked out. The face was covered in bruises and chunks of skin hung free off the torso and limbs. Under all the stench, contusions, dried blood, and whatever else was a young girl.

Malik couldn't believe what he witnessed.

A hissing sound came from where someone had done some kind of surgery to her throat.

She stared up at Malik as if waiting for something. She coughed and blood trickled out of the opening behind the cloth duct taped around her neck.

Malik turned to Fezz, arching his shoulders in confusion. Fezz returned the sentiment.

"Spyder." Malik link-spoke.

A second later, he drifted in to join Fezz and Malik.

Spyder went over to the girl and studied her for a moment. Without a word, he disappeared from the room.

Bent, Not Broken   205

Malik and Fezz waited. They stared at the broken body, then at one another.

Peyton came in, raised her right hand, and tapped her first two fingers against her head. The house had been cleared.

Fezz and Bowe took strategic positions on the main floor. Peyton contacted Trystan and let him know how the operation went and when they would be returning.

Spyder drifted back in with a different Kindred by his side. The newer man stood taller than most of the Kindreds, at six-five or six-six. His muscular build moved gracefully while resembling a block wall.

Darko kneeled down next to the figure. She didn't try to get away from him, which Malik found interesting. The big man intimidated men twice her size, but instead she stared up into his face. Darko's Manage lineage came from his mother's side, along with her gentle nature. His ability included breaking down the walls and scanning people's minds and witnessing truths, lies, and hidden details they may not even understand are important.

After a few minutes, he stood and turned to Malik. "She can read the history of inert objects. She senses information about places and items by physical contact. They're using her for research. She says they are out in the desert getting more for her to examine. A woman who tortures her until she does what they ask usually stands guard. She hasn't been allowed to eat or bath. She's terrified and asked if we would take her with us."

"So she's a Stellar? How does she know we aren't a worse fate than her current situation?" Peyton's expression remained unreadable as she spoke. Darko paused and glanced down.

"She said there isn't a more fatal consequence than her present predicament and she's willing to chance things might get worse." Darko explained, shrugging his shoulders in confusion. "She wants you to know she has nothing left to lose."

"She speaks to you?" Malik asked with a raised eyebrow.

"I can hear her in my head, her voice is…musical. She shows me where to scan for things I want. She wants me to trust her based on her honesty and willingness to help." He shrugged again.

"What do you think of her?" Malik stared at Darko, the question he really wanted to ask pasted clearly on his face.

"She's been assaulted, sexually, and repeatedly. Apparently there's a human who comes here too. He abuses her. She asks if we won't help her to escape that we take her life. She's tried, but couldn't move enough to finish the action." Darko's expression hardened while the tick in his cheek worked overtime. He waited to hear the verdict for the broken body still lying on the floor like yesterday's trash.

"Is she sure the man is human?" Malik's eyes narrowed in suspicion.

Darko turned his attention back to the figure.

"No. She just assumed." Darko pursed his lips.

"Take her to Dane. The Fates will need to heal her. Have her watched like a hawk, though. If she does anything which seems odd, leave instructions to have her killed immediately. Go now. I want to hear from you the moment you have any information."

Darko bent over and lifted her up, jerking the chains free simultaneously. He tucked the small form tightly to him, and they all left the room behind Darko and his package. Darko couldn't drift with the girl without liquid, so he went into the bathroom and turned on the bathtub faucet. He filled the basin more than half-full and stepped into the tub. The Halo appeared and they fell down through the water and out of sight.

Before the remaining Kindreds drifted out of the house, Malik grabbed Kiernan's head from the laundry room. Flynn and Fezz set charges on the doors. A two-minute delay and then the structure would blow. The rest of the team drug the fourteen bodies down to the basement, to make sure the blast would effectively hide them. Peyton had been busy; she'd loaded all the papers and boxes to the Turnberry with no problem.

Within ten minutes, the Kindreds sat around the office back at the Drake's. Everyone had been posted for the night. Retribution would find them soon; perhaps not tonight, but within the next few days. Malik instructed Trystan to call three teams for the mid-morning shift. Thane and Saffron were sent to the

Bent, Not Broken   207

Turnberry to begin investigating the information found at the nest.

Sometime later in the morning, Malik stiffly awoke, sore all over. A thin layer of beaded sweat covered him from the quiet battle ragging inside his subconscious. Recollection rose up and laid claim to him once again.

Some things...no escape is possible. Memories are the steadfast and most tangible examples.

No matter how many lifetimes pass by, regardless of the skills you perfect... the ability to outrun the destruction laying in your wake is an accomplishment I would trade almost everything for. Memories...so sharp...so clear.

Faces, smells, and even textures worked to send his mind hurtling back into days gone by and moments purposefully banished because his brain knew to self-protect.

A lot of time had passed since he last dreamt of Isabeau. He experienced a familiar twang of sadness. The unshakable sense of loss for what his love, or what loving him, had done to her. Malik relived this particular truth more times than he wanted to remember. Isabeau had been replaced by the witch and no salvation awaited her now; she had chosen her path. Peyton endured the same torture, barely being able to crawl from the wreckage. She chose to fight the darkness, while Isabeau gave in. Isabeau had been lost to the depravity inside herself. Malik left the girl he knew far behind, or rather she discarded him and the others, or maybe they all abandoned each other. Malik no longer could be sure of the specifics. The children they had been, those who ran wild on the Calia Shore, now lay dead, for all intents and purpose.

Malik wanted to let go of the memories, or force them to release him. The viselike grip on his mind became relentless. At least it had ceased to squeeze his heart. Time healed that wound. Years of blame and guilt lessened the pain of loss, or maybe the emotions were better camouflaged underneath everything he could pile on top of them.

His Isabeau had disappeared; he'd learned to live with it.

Malik's mind found contentment in the one person who offered a hand in a time when comfort seemed unthinkable, unimaginable, and perhaps undeserved. Dane and Fury sought them out individually. Maybe fate intervened and led Fury and Dane to each of the lost kids with a purpose already clear in mind. The warrior class needed to be regrouped to prepare for the last stand. This was no longer the shifter's war alone and the end was steadily coming in crushing bones and hell fire. A conflict could be won only by those who had nothing left to lose. The forgotten children of the Calia Shore would stand up and fulfill the harbinger's last declaration.

With shaky but firm hands, he mentally slammed the door on the past. *Now isn't the time to stroll down Elm Street and resurrect the demons which wouldn't be slain.* He couldn't have saved Isabeau from her choices.

He needed to find a way to force his mind to think about something else. Malik went in search of Fezz. They discussed the situation at Turnberry. Thane and Saffron had been cataloguing the items found at the nest. They suffered from being understaffed and hadn't gotten through even half of the materials.

Black and white aerial pictures of Central America, Turkey, and the Southern Cypress. Every ancient site in Egypt and Greece. The Andes in Argentina near Cosco. New Zealand, the Faulkner Islands, England, Scotland and Ireland, Canada, and the Pacific Northwest. Digital close ups of ancient ruins from all over the world. Only the Faulkner Islands and New Zealand had no archaic relics. They broke the pattern.

A few of the photographs hadn't yet been identified. Dense forested areas and ice fields. A couple of large bodies of water. Two desert shots, maybe the Sahara or even the Gobi.

Five mountains, three of which are snowcapped with puffs of smoke exhaling from their tops. One may have been Rainier in Washington, another may have been the baby in Iceland. Mexico City's Popocatepetl seemed to be a reasonable bet. Malik guessed the last two might be Mount Baker or Hood.

After they finished with the photos, they began on the boxes. On their own, the parts made little sense. When trying to piece this puzzle together, Malik hoped the Stellar would be willing to help.

Cartons contained old world maps depicting the ancient boundaries of the Persian and the Hittite empires. Others were fairly detailed and mapped out most of Europe. Papyrus sketches leading through the desert to an oasis—considering how much markers change from sand storms—would be useless. More crates contained everything from basalt to onyx pieces. A third had stone implements and chunks of flint. The fourth held bottles by the dozen, stuffed with mortar plants and something organic. The fifth appeared to be blueprints for weapons. Swords, daggers, and other blade tools mixed in with books suffused with Chinese characters. A chest cluttered with fossil and geology textbooks. Several over loaded golf bags brimmed with staffs of varying heights and widths. Some had headpieces and others had grooves as if something was meant to be attached. The bags also held more charts of the tunnel systems running underneath different cities. Hand drawn pictures of all of the gods and goddess of ancient Egypt, Greece, and Mesoamerica. Hindu beliefs along with lists and descriptions of the Inca guardians and earth bound spirits. A separate box contained American Indian and Inuit replicas of totem poles topped with Thunderbirds.

The entire puzzle was rather complex and an enormous amount of research. They hadn't even started on the binders full of papers yet.

Malik needed to find them help. The task could take weeks, maybe months, to sort out.

"Trenton, send two additional teams to the loft. I need you to have someone uploading images around the clock. Assign a couple of teams to begin looking at them with Dane, Ky, and Fury." Malik exhaled heavily.

"Copy."

"Malik, Riven, and Poe haven't been heard from. Should I activate their beacons?" Fezz's fingers flew over the keyboard as he spoke.

"Find them." Malik walked over to the main table and sat down with a guard roster. He noticed the prototype of the weapons Bannan had been working on for the girls to use.

"Will you sweep the house and find out if Bannan is still up?"

Fezz punched a few keys. "He's in the study grading papers."

"Ask him to stop by the office?" Malik picked up a small bullet and rolled the cylinder between his fingertips while he waited.

"I finished them up earlier today. The bullets have a hollow point containing a combination I came up with myself. The chemical will react with the Core of the Stryder. I call the synthetic mix Lacid. Once mixed, the base has an adverse reaction to the Stryders core DNA. Because their makeup is different from fuser, or human blood, for that matter, bullets cannot do enough damage. They don't die unless you penetrate the demon inside.

"I filled the hollow tips with the Lacid. On impact, the bullet fragments, filling their system with the poison. The Lacid interacts with the properties of the DNA, becoming a combustible inside of ten seconds. The Stryders will catch on fire from the inside out. These should buy the girls time to get away." Bannan couldn't restrain his excitement.

"How can they pack enough of them?" Stryders always came in droves. They would require multiple clips to make a dent in the onslaught of assassins.

"Hold that thought." Bannan moved onto another weapon.

"For the girls." Bannan drug out a Sia blade and its customized holder.

"This will fit each of them like a backpack. The cartridges are on a rotational wheel that winds the ammunition to the bottom, here. I saw this in a movie and thought the contraption might actually work with a few minor changes." Bannan pointed to the underside of the pack.

There were clip holders attached to both sides running along the back. When one munition cassette is extracted another is freed to drop, ready for deployment.

"Bannan, this is good work." Malik studied the housing closely.

"I'm not done yet." Bannan laughed as he tugged out black Lycra packs. "I've been experimenting with the idea of somehow making the blades smaller while maintaining the deadly purpose of a larger blade. Also, trying to construct a type of holder that's easy to wear, lightweight, and how to maximize the amount carried. So, I came up with these."

Malik opened up one of the packs and pulled out a black set of biker gloves

Bent, Not Broken   211

fitted with bear claw knives attached to the back of the hand. Three pouches shaped in a half-moon, each equipped with a barb, stood out.

"These are artery slicers. Great for hand-to-hand. They are featherweight and easy to handle, and aren't going to come off too easily. They fit right on their fingers, so quick jabs at the neck and thighs should cause enough damage to make a getaway." Bannan looked rather smug.

Malik had to give him credit for being so determined about ensuring every available resource was at the girls disposal.

"I have one additional thing to show you. I'm still working on these. I'm having a hard time with the weight." He pulled out a five-or- six inch blade that looked more like a scalpel than a dagger. They were double-sided and the part held in the hand was only made for fingertips.

"The handles are so small compared to what Fezz carries. How will they hold it?" Malik asked as he cut his finger twice just holding it.

"Their fingers are smaller than yours, for one. Plus, I want to be able to strap them to their thighs. Like this," he pulled out another Lycra piece with long leather inset holsters. He positioned it over his thigh and pushed one of the knives into place. By his calculations, each girl could be fitted with between eight and ten blades on both legs.

"They are thin. They may not cause adequate damage to be useful." Malik said.

"Oh, wait there's more." He pulled his arm back and launched the daggers into the cork board above one of the tables. Then he walked over and ripped it free. A hole about two inches wide was left in the drywall.

"What? How?" Malik sputter the words out as he stared at the gap.

"Look." He pointed to the side that was implanted in the wall. It was like a quill. Once it made contact, the submerged point became bigger than the entrance hole. "So if the victim attempts to extract it, the exit wound will be worse than going in. The other option is driving it out through the wound. Oh, and I dipped the quills in the Lacid. Their dead either way." Bannnan smiled proudly at Malik.

"I'm so glad you're on our side." He returned to the table and started reviewing each weapon. They spent the next hour fine-tuning. The girls were going to begin training with them the following day.

Next order of business was to talk to Darko about his progress with the Stellar. She must be important or the Stryders would have been allowed to kill her.

"Darko, update on the Stellar's status." Malik hoped he had something.

"Her name is Acantha, but call her Ace. She's from the Faulkner Islands. An extensive population of Stellars have amassed in the location for safety."

"Where is she from?" *Too many coincidences in one day.*

"The Faulkner Islands. Her grandparents had relocated there into a large community of like breeds. Her parents and grandfather were killed when the Stryders took her. She's asking if I could contact her grandmother and let her know she's alive. So far, I sense she is telling the truth. Caleb tried to turn her the same way he did Isabeau. When he was unsuccessful, they chained and allowed everyone to abuse her." Darko's voice was hoarse as he spoke the last sentence.

That confirmed Malik's thoughts on a human accomplice. Stryders physically couldn't have sex, leaving only one alternative. Malik knew what they had done to her. She was lucky they hadn't begun the experiments. The Stryders needed her mind or they would have. She may not feel blessed, but she was alive, so that counted.

"Hold a moment, Darko." Malik turned to Fezz.

"Fezz, who do we have that can go to the Faulkner Islands?"

"Grey and Louden just got back from Greece." Fezz returned after a few keystrokes.

"Send the next three teams on rotation."

"Darko, ask Ace to make contact with her grandmother. If she's willing to help us, let her know I'm sending two squads to keep an eye on things. Check to see if the grandmother will allow them to stay with her. Make sure she understand that we are at war." He ended his conversation with Darko and refocused on Fezz.

"Relay the message to contact Darko for arrival coordinates. I want everyone accounted for twice a day. Send a team to meet up with Valentina and Parker. Two crews from now on at each location." Malik decided to try and get ahead of the loss he feared were still to come.

"Malik." Darko hesitated for a few seconds. "Caleb and Isabeau have a human accomplice, Ace has seen him. He was the one that would come every day and torture her. She said that there was something off about him, she believes he is of creatural nature. A half breed would explain why she isn't sure." Darko spoke in a quiet voice.

"What does Dane think?"

"Malik, she'll never talk again. They cut the girl up too. Some I have seen, others are hidden by the girl's clothes. The one on her neck is healing, she'll always have plenty of reminders though. Dane thinks she's damaged but salvageable. Dane said it's hard to get a read on her when I do all the talking, but he is trying. He wishes to discuss this further with you. He wants to train her as a Kindred, says she's strong to have survived them."

"Ask him if tomorrow afternoon is soon enough. Can you have Ace ready to meet me?" Malik wanted to get to know this Stellar. It was late, almost four in the morning.

Malik drifted up to Delaney's room. He decided to catch an hour nap before they all went running when the sun came up. He sat on the floor next to the bed and watched her for a moment.

She was smiling in her sleep, which made him grin in return. He wanted to know what the smile was about, but knew better than to dream walk anymore. He wouldn't invade her privacy now, unless he had to. He would try to keep his distance as much as possible.

She tossed and turned, then her eyes began to open and she looked directly at his face. They slid shut as she moved towards him. Her hands reached out to curl around the nape of his neck. Holding on firmly for a moment, they loosened and her arm slide down across his shoulder. He placed them gently back on the bed where they belonged.

Within a few seconds, he lay sleeping on the floor.

Malik laughed softly as Delaney's alarms belted out "Shattered" by O.A.R. A personal epitaph for both Trystan and Malik. It didn't matter what direction Trystan went in, every path led back to Calliope. Just as his choices all led straight to Delaney.

She didn't get up right away, instead stared blankly at the glow-in-the-dark stars just overhead. At this precise moment, she was peaceful for a change. Lazy eyed as she softly sang along to the song.

When the little half grin appeared, Malik let himself smile too. She was happy this morning.

A soothing emotion swirled around Delaney like the Juniper scent that filled his nostrils. It seemed to be pulling him in, closer and closer to the center of everything, which was always her.

It was nice to see Delaney vulnerable. It reminded him of only weeks before while things were still anonymous. When she had nothing more than tests and decisions about what book to buy next.

She leaned up abruptly, bracing herself on her elbows, and scanned the room slowly. She lost her smile while she looked for him. The way her eyes narrowed and her happy mood dissolved into a grumpy wrinkle that fell across her forehead saddened him.

Delaney took a long, hard look. She stopped at the corners, staring there for a few extra seconds. She knew where he would be. Her eyes paused on his position and, for a moment, he thought she might call him out. Malik was about to drift into sight, but her eyes moved on.

She had a feeling, but couldn't pin it down yet.

"Malik." He didn't want to fight or have a discussion that went around in circles. His energy was spent from lack of sleep and a full night of work that left more questions than answers, and today would be just as hectic.

She must have given up because she yawned and rolled out of bed. Delaney stumbled over to the dresser where she kept her running clothes all folded and ready to go.

When she started getting dressed, he headed downstairs. It was against his better judgement, but the privacy matter kept gnawing at him. She needed time alone, so he was giving her some space wherever possible.

"Darko's waiting for you in the office. I figured you would want to meet with him directly. Peyton will take point, okay?" Tryst threw back the last of the orange juice.

"Thanks. Is the Stellar with him?" Malik asked as he grabbed some of the scrambled eggs and two bottles of water.

"Dane and Darko."

"I didn't know they were coming."

Malik exited the kitchen and treaded down the hall to the office. He found Darko sitting at the large table. Dane stood behind Fezz, watching him on the computer.

Darko's large form made the grand Mahogany table look more like a small dinette. He stood when Malik entered, remaining so until his superior nodded to him. It was a show of respect Malik appreciated.

I wish Fezz had been watching.

"Malik." He took his chair back as he spoke.

"Darko." Malik set the plate of food down. He placed a bottle of water right in front of him, then took a long swallow from another.

"Son." Dane said as he held out his hand.

"Has something happened?" Malik took his hand.

"I needed to speak with you in person about the language. Stellanic is older than Sumerian. Fury translated only half of it. 'Siadona kia imaway' transcribes loosely to 'the way of the dead.'" Dane spoke seriously.

Silence fell over the room.

"I need to return. We will talk later, no?" Dane stood and held out his hand to Malik. They stared at one another for a brief moment before Dane made his exit.

"Since allowing the Kindreds to settle on the Faulkner Islands, Ace's grandmother demanded to see her. They are together on Naroke, going through photos and copies of the research information. The box of feathers turned out to be deadly weapons. They were used by a breed known as Rainers. The breed is known for manipulating organic material. The feathers, once thrown became sturdy like an arrow. Rainers were thought to have perished as long ago as the Rafes." Darko explained.

"Ace says a woman would bring her things to identify accompanied by a human. She's trying to help get their faces on parchment. She remembered symbols too. When I saw this one, I recognized it. Look familiar?" Darko handed Malik a creased white piece of paper.

Malik unfolded the sheet and sucked in a breath as the character glared up at him. It was the same symbol stamped on the back of Vivianna's neck.

"What can she tell you?" Malik asked, never glancing away from the sketch.

"She said they'd found the mark at Mount Hood in Oregon, in the area of the Chinook Indians. The symbol is carved right into the mountain, at the base of the most Northern point. According to Ace, the mark means walkway." Darko spoke with a confused expression on his face. Though Malik had no idea what it meant, he sensed this clue would be important.

"Fezz, send three team up to Mount Hood A-S-A-P. I want eyes on the peak twenty four seven. Have them do a work up on the area's history and known-breed activity." Malik turned his head to frown at Fezz.

"Three teams will be in route within half an hour." He reported back.

"Darko, good work. I'll be back around four, relay the information to Dane." Malik spoke as he stood and offered his hand to the other man. Darko vanished a moment later.

Malik stood thinking about Darko. He led the seventh Brigade when they all had come of age, back when everything was different. Peyton, Trystan, Isabeau, and Malik all had their own squads to lead then. His thoughts turned to Tanner and Rourke, who'd been present on the front lines as well. Malik thought of how many of the inceptives had disappeared. Immortality only presents an opportunity for an extended life to be possible, it was not an indefinite or guaranteed outcome. Some of the original Kindreds had simply been "taken"; the missing's whereabouts were unknown and they were eventually presumed dead.

"Malik, anything else?"

His name brought him back. He left the past behind, the days held nothing but pain and sorrow.

"I need Viv's and the girls markings all catalogued. I want to record every Print and/or Script on each of them. Bowe and Peyton will help you gather the information. There may be solitary symbols on one of them they aren't even aware of. Ask Bannan about Sebastian's." Malik sat back down and ate his cold eggs.

Chapter
TWENTY-THREE

Delaney stopped the Nissan in the parking garage at the mall. She leaned her head back, collapsing farther into the seat. The music played soft like a lullaby around her. She imagined the haunting notes encircling her in silky strong webbing, sensing the pitch gliding over her skin with such infinite purpose. For the moment her, mind stayed still. She considered taking two of the pills that used to help her get through the day when she noticed her white knuckles holding on for dear life to the steering wheel.

My hands tighten and yet I continue to spin so fast. The threads are weakening the tighter I hold. What is there to anchor myself to? All I want is to not feel crazy and alone.

"Malik," she whispered into the car, then closed her eyes and struggled with the noose cinching tighter around her lungs as she tried to pull in a breath.

"Yes." The single utterance echoed softly in the space. The word slipped in between the melodious warmth and tugged at her heartstrings. Delaney closed her eyes and sighed faintly. *Peace.*

Delaney perceived his presence, she always knew when he was near.

Has the attraction been automatic? Is wanting to be close to him something I could ever have resisted? Echo principle?

Malik wanted to drift into the front seat, sit beside her, and ask her what is wrong. A horrible premonition that he already understood on an intimate level stopped him. Hundreds of things needed to be said and he wanted her to know all of them. Yet, no words came to mind.

The song continued to play, so formidable; the music had become a physical presence between them. Malik had listened to the piece before, echoing Delaney's mood when she hid from the world inside her room. He realized she had purposely put the song on now, too. Beethoveen: Piano Sonata #14 in C sharp minor, "Moonlight". Delaney allowed the symphonic harmony to resonate. The notes swirled through the car like eerie ghosts encircling them both with arms of barbed wire satin, comforting and harrowing at the same time. The music swept over him while permeating the air with a desperate poignancy.

He thought of running his fingertips down her cheeks, wiping the tears away, kissing her until he swallowed the sadness drowning her and kept her safe and protected. He wanted to pull her from the depths and save her for himself.

He sat in the backseat, wondering what now.

"You say you loved me. I might be a carbon copy on the outside, but I'm not her on the inside." Her voice faltered, the rest of the words dying in her throat like thoughts she lacked the strength to speak.

"Am I?" Delaney wondered how long she had been crying too. Through a sheen of tears, she forced herself to find him in the rearview mirror. It was an empty point she knew he occupied.

"No. You are different. After the last few days, I expected our way of life would affect you." She voiced the identical doubts echoing throughout his own mind. Instant pain spiraled inside of her. She wondered if having her head smashed against the dashboard may have caused less tenderness.

He understands the difference, presumes whatever part he once had feelings for is gone. I am all that is left of her.

"Do you still think you love me?" Her eyes fell to her lap. This was the question she didn't want an answer to, but the inquiry needed to be made.

"Yes." Without hesitation, the words ping ponged through Delaney's mind and ran thick lines around her heart. She remained silent, fighting the urge to speak. *He isn't sure what to say. I perceive the point, and that says enough. It conveys everything.*

Delaney pressed her head back into the headrest as hard as possible. She dug her fingernails into her palms until her skin was slippery from blood and bit the inside of her cheek until she tasted the metallic flavor. Something else had to hurt, because Delaney's insides had caught fire.

I can't handle it.

"What if the part you loved is gone?" The words flowed out easier than Delaney thought they would. Her sense of attempting to do the right thing nudged her forward. To offer him a graceful exit seemed appropriate. *He's given up enough for me. To sacrifice for him appears fitting somehow, it is my turn. I can do this.*

"Delaney." Out of nowhere he emerged sitting right next to her, whispering her name. "Is that why you're crying?" He caressed her face with his fingers.

"While you're gone, your absence is like a dull knife ripping through my skin. I don't know who you are, but I do…somehow. I sense you when you're near me. I'm not supposed to, though, am I?"

She wanted to get lost in him, to crawl across the car and hide in his arms. Delaney needed him to understand the depth of her feelings, however misplaced they may have been. Should something happen she wanted no regrets.

Malik gave Delaney a warm smile and her wounds began stitching themselves back together. She found incomparable comfort in the moment, such hope that a future with Malik could be possible.

"All the things you are experiencing, I struggle with them too. At first, I only protected you and your unawareness of me was fine. Before I knew it, I was closer than I should be, cared more than I am supposed to. I could have walked away, gone back into the field. I couldn't leave you. If there was any way to change things so that I didn't have to hurt you, I would, no matter the cost to myself. But I still wouldn't give up the stolen moments that we have shared. They are all I have of you." The relentless rock hard lump in Malik's throat choked him.

"I'm not her anymore. This relationship may never measure up to the connection you experienced with her. Those feelings you possess are for a ghost and I am only a shadow of her. What if you loved a part of her that is gone and may not be coming back?" Delaney sniffled again.

Malik realized how much time she had put into analyzing all of this.

"Concern yourself with what is important, stay alive long enough for us to start again." Malik gently chided as he whiped the tears from her face.

"You seem more content than you have been in awhile. What's up with that?" Lola asked with a raised eyebrow from across the isle of the Stinky Sweet. "Are you going to tell me why?"

"I'm happier," Delaney answered, rolling her eyes with a shrug and a quirky grin.

I think it's all a state of my mind. I am sick and tired of being sad and lost. Either way, she had begun looking at Malik as if he were a lifeline pulling her to safety. *With him, I'm found.* In a life filled with chaos, everything began to make sense.

"So...?"

Delaney took a deep breath before answering Lola. "He's sweet to me. He looks at me as if I'm something to treasure." A half giggle escaped. With all seriousness, Delaney whispered, "No one has ever looked at me like he does." Delaney glanced around the quiet store. "I like him. I never expected... I figured meeting someone who could be so special would be impossible. What man would want to deal with all of my baggage?" Delaney shrugged.

"The issues are not your fault," Lola spoke. "You have faulty wiring in the genes." Lola tossed Delaney a silly half smile as she reached for the strawberry lotion.

"Are you still taking the pills for depression?"

"No. I need to make another appointment." She was the only one aware Delaney had been to a therapist before she confided in her mom. The idea had been Lola's. Delaney's memories were like scattered pieces from so many different puzzles. Lola hoped the doctor could help put things in perspective.

Lola appeared in most of her recollections of junior and high school; they must have been close for a while. Lola had suffered from depression and thought the medication would help Delaney when her lows had become so low she couldn't see up. At her ultimate bottom point they had talked about a suicide pact, doing it in a pill-induced haze. The idea sounded strange to her now.

"Hey, have you check out the guy at Spots over by the gelato place? He's very cute, started a few days ago. In fact, I'm going to get my lunch and walk by. Want anything?" Lola laughed as she stared at herself in the mirror.

When Lola came back, an attractive blond man walked her to the store entrance. Lola moved closer until her hand was perched on his polo shirt, resting in the middle of his broad chest. She batted her eyes at him before saying goodbye with a quick peck to the man's cheek. She stood in the doorway watching the blonde walk back down the gallery towards his own retail shop before turning with a triumphant smile. Men seemed to fall unconditionally in love with her anywhere. Another reason Delaney envied her.

"He's meeting me here after work and we are going to get a bite to eat." Lola winked at Delaney.

The night passed quickly.

"I missed working with you. When you were gone I got stuck with the know-it-all. She's loud and finds herself far funnier than anyone else. If I ever become Aderin, shoot me," Lola poked Delaney in the shoulder as she locked the metal pull down gate.

"Is she that bad?" Delaney was counting down the cash register.

Bent, Not Broken   223

"Worse!" They both stopped when they heard knocking on the glass door. The blond guy had returned and was waiting impatiently outside.

"Can you let him in while I grab my stuff and change?" Lola called as she disappeared into the storeroom.

Malik hadn't seen Delaney this lighthearted in such a long time. A broad smile had been stapled to Delaney's face that an industrial piece of steel wool couldn't have scrubbed off.

The weight pulling Malik down had finally lessened. There was hope for a future where none had been before. A smile played on his lips as he sucked in a deep breath.

"Hi, I'm Delaney. Lola will be right out."

"Thanks."

Delaney moved to the rear of the store to grab her stuff.

"Want me to hang out until you're ready to go?" Delaney asked Lola.

"Do you mind waiting?" Lola spoke while dabbing lip gloss on her lips. "I'm so glad you're back."

"I vow never to allow myself to be attacked by a psycho ever again." Delaney laughed out loud.

"Don't be so sure, flower," Lola said in a husky, unfamiliar tone. For a long moment, Delaney stood staring off to the far wall. Even before she turned around, Delaney became fully aware something was about to go terribly wrong.

Lola spun in reverse and Delaney's mouth fell open. *How did I miss this?*

"Why you?" Delaney spoke sadly, looking at the new and frightening version of someone she loved and trusted as a sister. Delaney's lips formed into a tight straight line. Her tears became hard to conceal.

"Why didn't you kill me before now?" Delaney stood looking dumbfounded in front of Lola. She couldn't explain her needing to understand the reason.

"If you would have continued to take the pills, this would never have been a problem. You're a headstrong pain in the ass. You had to keep fighting the aftermath of the Gare. The pills would have kept you from the transformation for as long as you took the medication. But you always had to find your way back to him. The damn guard!

"Stupid self-professing prophecies. You just don't fucking get the problem. You wouldn't leave him be. This situation may have all been avoided if you would have let go of the fucking guard. He isn't meant for you, anyway." Lola's surface flushed red with anger. "Stupid whore. Why couldn't you die the other night? Do you understand how hard it is to set up something like that?"

Without warning, Lola punched Delaney. She stumbled back and fell down on one knee. Her hand went to her cheek to ensure the eyeball hadn't popped right out of the socket to roll around on her cheek bone.

"What are the pills I have been taking? Did you set up the doctor too?" Delaney attempted to shake off the effects of her punch.

"Oh, those, they are for depression. They are custom-designed to block the nerve endings from sending messages inside a non-human brain. Every time your central nervous system began to change, they stunted the process. Those pills should have bought me more time. We could have finished you after Mom and Sis were disposed of. No loose ends, nice and neat. Instead, your body fought the effects. I got stuck here baby-sitting your stupid ass. Do I seem like the fucking baby-sitter type to you?"

Delaney doubted anyone with a brain would mistake the pointed ears and long claws for a caregiver. Pink irises looked more like marbles with jet-black pupils glaring in tiny feline lines down the middle.

"I couldn't leave until we became certain you wouldn't begin your transition. Now you can die before Cali and Mommy instead." Lola spit the words at Delaney.

"I should be given more credit. Making you believe that you were nuts, not an easy task. I even gave you overdoses sometimes, hoping it would kill you, but you don't die. Fuckin' invincible little pain in my ass." Lola licked her lips and took a step closer.

Delaney still struggled to comprehend everything Lola was saying.

Why had I never seen her true form? Lola fooled me, my family, and even the Kindreds.

Bent, Not Broken 225

"Seeley, let's get rid of her and get something to eat. I'm starved," Lola shouted back toward the door.

"I told you, she remains alive." The voice startled Delaney. She whipped around to observe the blond casually standing in the doorway. "If you kill her, I will take you to Isabeau instead."

"Fine." Lola rolled her eyes.

Lola whispered something under her breath in a language Delaney didn't understand. Without warning, several ghostly figures began to appear and walk toward Delaney from a wall across the room. Large men with distorted faces and disturbing bodies, all of them closing in on her.

Lola grabbed Delaney by the neck and squeezed tightly. She pulled Delaney up off her feet until Delaney's shoes dangled above her Manolo's. She lowered Delaney's face to within inches of her own.

"You will die this time, bitch." Lola hurled Delaney away. Delaney smashed through the piping running the length of the ceiling. Water rained down her limp frame as her torso returned to the floor with a solid thump.

Delaney's body, bloody and broken, smacked the ground hard enough to knock the wind right out of her.

Malik, why didn't I call for him from the start?

Blood spilled from her lips. Through hazy vision, Delaney witnessed her hand resting in front of her, the phalanges had become twisted to resemble an olive branch. Like quills from a Porcupine, jagged bloody bones protruded from the skin on the back of her hand.

"Mal...k." Half of his name fell out of her mouth as a whisper, with a steady stream of thick crimson liquid mixed with saliva. Delaney prayed she had said enough for him to find her.

"Poor little Delaney, are you hurt, flower? Don't worry, I get to play with you for a few more minutes. This isn't all about you, I've come for your guard too. Isabeau will be playing with Malik soon enough."

Delaney blinked, but her vision remained cloudy. "What are you?" Delaney asked with amazement as she coughed up chunks of her insides and spit them out.

How had Lola hidden her real identity after I started to fuse? I should have seen her true self.

"My mother, who left soon after I was born, was a Hellme. My beloved father a Zepho.

"He drew fire through his hands, like torches. I adored watching him coach me about how to catch the little townie children and burn the flesh right from their little bones."

Again Delaney witnessed the symphony of crazy laughter erupting from her. Lola leaned down close to Delaney, laying her hands on her back. The flow of sweeping heat danced across her spine like nuclear coils. A scream of pain ripped free.

One of the men came to stand next to Delaney. He put his foot on the side of her head and smashed it into the floor to keep Delaney from flopping around. Her back sizzled and burned as if she were trapped with wildfire raining down on her. Pain came in waves, stealing her breath. Delaney's eyes fluttered as she fought to stay awake. *Once I pass out, I am never coming back.*

"We're here to prolong the pain, flower. I'm going to make you suffer, but don't worry. You are an immortal. You will heal and we can do this all over again."

"Malik. We've lost contact with Peyton and Bowe. How should I proceed?" Leaestra spoke directly.

"Hold." Malik tried to wrap his mind around what he had been told.

"Tryst, what's going on?" Malik asked as he began to pace the small storefront.

"Bowe had been checking in with Leaestra when she was interrupted and contact was never reestablished. I have sent four teams after them already. Are we going to get her?" Tryst's voice was strained and Malik understood his fear.

When the Stryders had taken Malik, Peyton and Tryst found him. When

Tryst had gone missing, Peyton held everything together so Malik had time to find him. They had to go and get her back.

"Leaestra, send two teams to shadow Ptah and Bast. I'm going to Mount Hood." Malik said as he rounded the corner.

"Copy." Leaestra returned without delay.

"Bast, Ptah, you have Delaney." Malik drifted to Mount Hood. He was surprised when Tryst stood waiting for him.

"Anything?" Malik asked as they looked for tracks.

"Here." Malik caught sight of a broken branch about shoulder height for Bowe. Blood dripped down the leaves and formed a puddle on the ground.

Tryst immediately took the right and Malik the left.

"I'll fuse." Malik began to shed his clothes.

His senses heightened as the dog. He could hear everything, pick up smells barely on the wind for a couple of miles. Malik could track them faster this way.

His heart thundered in his ribcage, blood roared through his veins as Ranger shook his head and breeched the lining of his chest. One last deep breath and the mongrel howled as he sprang forward and Malik became lost inside of him.

If anything was left to find, the dog would discover it. Malik understood what Trystan was thinking. The gnawing concern ate at him as well.

Malik searched for four miles to the south, bobbing and weaving to guarantee he missed nothing. He found no sign of Peyton. His gut twisted at the idea Isabeau had her. Peyton was strong, but Isabeau would never let her survive. The sun began setting and Malik's nerves wobbled ever closer to an implosion if he couldn't ease the tension building within him soon.

He lifted his nose, barked loudly into the direction of the sunset, and then made his way to their original location. He detested the helplessness encircling him. He lifted his head and howled at the sky.

Deafening silence the only reply, it chilled him to the bone.

"Malik." Tryst's words rolled around in his mind.

Malik drifted to him without delay. He got dressed.

On the ground lay two dead Kindreds. Both burned to ash. Malik got the impression they had been shielding something or…someone. Perhaps whoever they shielded had gotten away unscathed, or only wounded.

The muscle in Tryst's jaw began working overtime.

"Now what?" Tryst muttered angrily.

"Leaestra, send the Roqs. Two of our own need to be brought home. No sigh of Peyton, Bowe, or Bannon.

"Post updates with Trenton, Dane, and Fury immediately. Put the house on lock down. Find the other teams. Activate the beacons, I want a location on every one." Malik's head exploded in sensation, a nagging awareness he couldn't seem to shake. "Delaney."

"What are you talking about?" Tryst turned and found himself alone.

"Torture is my specialty and I've learned from the best. I know you called Malik. We were to let you. This little trap is for you *and* your guard." Lola turned to her men.

"She's not yours to play with, Lo. Leave her alone," Seeley chimed in from the doorway.

"Put her in the van," Lola said as she swung her leg back and let it rip into Delaney's ribs.

"Move it, let's go!" Lola scolded her accomplices. "We'll wait for Malik. If anything should happen and I don't show, take her straight to Isabeau."

Lola reminded her of a soldier. The wounds in Delaney's back burned as if acid had been poured into them. Warmth blistered and scorched inside her, slowly scalding her. She sensed her anger rising to the surface through the pain, and it centered her. Delaney knew if they got her into a van, she'd be finished. She needed to fight.

A searing awareness slowly took hold. Delaney's skin pulled like the sheath was too small for her body. A tingling sensation pulsated under her surface, followed by a collapsing consciousness, as if crashing throughout space with no

Bent, Not Broken   229

end in sight. Delaney rose and fell back into herself, everything started to rush forward through burning sensations. The room stretched into a panoramic view narrowing by the second.

Lola made the mistake of turning her back on Delaney when her survival mode kicked in, and regret had to be forced aside.

The need to lay eyes on his face once more became a primal reason to push her body up despite the pain, against stiff, sore muscles screaming "no" and crushed bones refusing to work properly. An unswayable instinct ripped at Delaney. She closed her eyes and tried to concentrate.

"What's wrong with her face?" The sound came from across the room.

Delaney turned to pinpoint the location of the voice, finally seeing the images that had been hidden her entire life.

He had dark greenish blue, thick scales instead of skin, with dark gaping eye sockets as empty as the remnants of a supernova.

"Lo," he called out.

She turned and stood staring at Delaney. All of them watched the change come over her. The blond man took a step forward with his hand outstretched, cautiously approaching Delaney.

"Calm down, Delaney. You're different than the other animals. You are like me, a mixed blood." He raised his fingers to touch Delaney's face and she quickly shifted away.

Delaney's movements became so accelerated, she lost her footing and swayed to the side, falling to her knees when she attempted to slow down. The air fractured with each movement she made, crackling loudly with the instantaneous exchange of lethal energized strikes.

"You're new at this. I can teach you how to use your advanced strengths. You'll need to take a deep breath and calm your blood first." His velvety voice fluttered against Delaney's skin.

For a moment, she found herself wanting to listen.

"What the hell are you doing, Seeley?" Lola said with pure venom in her tone.

"Shut up, Lo. Delaney is much more important than I first realized. Those are Stellanic symbols of a dead language that hasn't been spoken for more than two millennia, flashing across her skin." He stepped closer. "I'll bet there hasn't been one like you in a long time." His voice lowered for only Delaney to hear. "What exactly are you? What do they want with you?" He spoke as his brows drew tightly together. Concern rippled through him.

Malik's name had been so drawn out, said through broken breathes, his heart stopped. His mind broke free of his current predicament. All he knew in that moment was that Delaney was in trouble and from the sound of her voice, she was critical.

Malik drifted back to the mall and found Bast laying on the ground unconscious. Blood ran down the side of her face.

Trystan stood next to Malik before he could begin moving.

"Bast called to me as she went down." Trystan was already talking.

"They have her." Malik gritted out.

Bast pulled herself up to stand next to them, wavering on unsteady feet.

"Ptah?" Malik's eyes narrowed. Bast shook her head and glanced away.

"We need immediate back up at the Stinky Sweet," Malik said to Leaestra as he looked around.

"Where would they take her?"

"Who cares, Seeley, grab her and let's go." Lola cranked her head at two of her men.

Delaney had lost her sight and now only registered visual hot and cold signatures. Her viewpoint had become comparable to peeking through night vision goggles. Someone approached her and she saw them by the thermal image their body gave off. When she took a step, the atmosphere seemed to fracture with electrical activity. The energy danced along the hair on Delaney's arms, sending tingling waves across her eyebrows until they stood on end.

Delaney flew forward and grabbed one of Lo's men. His skin pulled free, stuck to her palm, and he erupted into screams. There were popcorn popping sounds echoing throughout the room. She raised her broken fist up to a second guy. A pulse propelled through her hand and thrust from her fingers. The red dot of body heat was shoved back and up against the opposite wall. A lightening quick flash of light jumped from Delaney's grip. The cardinal speck began to fade, leaving only a faint pink color for her view.

Trystan kicked down the door and Malik rushed in. Shock slowed his steps. The sight of Delaney fusing took him by surprise.

This time is different than before, she reared into a full transformation.

Delaney became a brilliant white glowing light resembling a star in the darkest night sky. Her eyes were popped open wide with blue sparks fluttering inside. Her skin pulsed with the black symbols buried under the surface, as if tattoos rolled along her in stormy cloud swirls.

Puzzle pieces?

Delaney moved rapidly through the area like lightening, attacking everyone within her grasp. Bodies were torn apart and arterial spray covered the walls, while the scent of burning flesh and hair permeated the space.

The door to the break room burst open and in rushed more figures. She drew her arms back and pulled them close to her body, thrusting them forward and letting the energy shoot through the space. The red dots dispersed, resembling confetti before bouncing off the walls and gliding to the floor.

Someone hit her hard from behind, knocking her to the ground. Nothing in Delaney's line of sight registered as anything more than a blur of movement as the figures quickly surrounded her.

"Stop. Don't fight me. I won't hurt you." The words ground out from whoever sprawled atop her.

"Let her go, Seeley."

Delaney's heart stopped and her vision cleared. She found Malik standing only a few feet away.

Seeley still lay on top of her, holding her in place.

"Malik." Delaney's anger cooled further.

"I'm here, Delaney."

"Seeley, you aren't walking out with her. So disappear and save yourself."

Seeley tightened his grip on Delaney. He pulled upright while keeping Delaney against him. She sagged, helplessly pinned to his chest. The room began to spin in full circles. Her eyes involuntarily flickered and all the perfect points became swirls and swooshes.

"Isabeau will be disappointed in an infinitely dangerous way. She wants Delaney more than she desires you." Seeley leaned in and brushed his face across hers, smelling her neck as he moved his hand to pin her body adjacent to his.

Malik inched closer.

"She's more like me than you." Seeley smiled at Malik. "Give me Daphne and you can have the girl. We'll call the whole thing even." The rich tone swept soothingly along though the words were explosive.

Delaney wondered if Malik would consider the trade. She didn't want to be free if Daphne was to be given over to the man who murdered her mother right in front of her.

"Juniper, you smell good. We will meet again." Seeley inhaled deeply and spoke quietly to her. In another instant, he disappeared.

Delaney fell forward on her hands and knees, gasping for air while forcing her head up to see what may come at her next.

Lola attempted to stand. Delaney watched her with perpetual interest. Lola raised up a dagger as she moved to the right. Malik's back faced her and he didn't realize she was coming. She charged, knife poised and ready to carve Malik into pieces.

Delaney understood what she intended and sprang forward, propelling herself on wobbly legs with pure adrenaline rushing within her veins. Delaney hit Lola hard, falling on top of her to the ground. The women stared at one another, neither moved.

Bent, Not Broken   233

Fond memories flashed inside Delaney's head, giving her pause. Slumber parties where they had stayed up all night talking about boys. Two best friends crying when Delaney had gotten her feelings hurt at school by that loser Jared. Delaney studied her from new, wild eyes.

This thing was my friend. I can't do this.

Delaney didn't move fast enough, nor did she realize Lola had been playing her again. She experienced a white-hot pain shooting up both of her hands, lighting up her arms and shoulders.

"She's a Zepho." A voice rang out, obviously recognizing the immediate threat.

Delaney looked like someone had doused her with gasoline and tossed a match. Chaos erupted as flames flashed and wiggled higher on her skin. Malik rolled Delaney back and forth until the flames calmed and finally were extinguished all together.

Delaney started screaming as she fell to her side. She blinked.

The smell of burnt skin hung thick in the store while thick blood clots spilled from her mouth like fresh jelly. Delaney tried to get up, but only managed to slip on shredded skin and fall back down each time. Another anguish-filled cry ripped right out of her.

Trystan charged forward, grabbing Lola by the head, jerking hard to one side.

"Delaney." Her name sounded like a desperate cry.

"Bast, get to the Drake's, have Fezz drive you back here. Call when you're right outside. Go now." His eyes never left Delaney. "Wade, take the mall's perimeter. Fellene and Asher, drift to my location. Find Ptah. Peyton, Delaney needs her mom home now. Spyder, get Daphne to the Drake's. Fezz. What the hell is taking you so long?"

"I'm still five minutes out. Move, it will take you a few minutes." Fezz sounded out of breath.

Tryst's hand on Malik drew his attention.

"Okay, let's get her out of here," whispered Malik.

He picked her up, resting her head on his shoulder. Skin hung in tangled blotches right off Delaney's forearms. The air on her exposed tissue stinging and burning her until her eyes rolled around in her head like marbles.

To blink was similar to raking barbed wire across the surface of her corneas. To take a breath became a branding iron being jabbed down her throat. The pain, beyond unbearable, collapsing blackness swallowed her hole and oblivion carried her away.

"Thane and Saffron secured the Drake residence. Run continual sweeps of the area in teams of two." Malik would take no more chances.

"All Kindreds without assignments, I want all the family members home immediately." Everyone needed to be accounted for.

Malik turned his full attention to Delaney. She had lost consciousness. The moment stretched as he watched her life flicker before him.

"Stay with me. You can't leave now. I'm so damn sorry I wasn't there. Keep breathing." His voice broke in places, shattering and reforming into scratchy pleas.

I am losing her.

Malik realized the other Kindreds were witnessing his loss of control, but didn't care. The idea of losing her nearly crippled him. Delaney had to live. Malik refused to waste one more minute not holding her, touching her, or claiming her for his own.

"Tryst, take everyone and find Peyton," Malik whispered.

Spyder stood next to the car, peeking around his shoulder was Daphne.

"What the hell happened? Why is she the only one jacked up?" Daphne's accusation rang out.

Delaney's breathing had deflated to shallow and labored wheezes.

"Fellene and Asher, man the scene until a Roq team can arrive and clean things up."

"Already on the way. The fates are setting up a place to treat Delaney." Bast spoke as she fell in line beside them.

"Ask Dane to come too. He should be here if things… Hurry." Malik link-spoke.

Each time she whimpered, his stomach burned with worry. The ride home took a lifetime to complete.

The garage door opened and, Fezz pulled in.

Malik hurried in with Delaney helpless in his arms. Daphne chanted something Malik didn't understand as they moved through the house. Kindreds stood everywhere waiting to assist in any way they might be of use. The kitchen island had been cleared off and they were directed to place Delaney's lifeless body there.

Vivianna gasped at the sight of her child.

Malik had told Vivianna he would always bring Delaney home, but he never meant like this.

No questions from anyone on how it happened. If someone would have asked, he wasn't sure what he might say. His sense of responsibility squeezed his insides flat.

"Everybody out, except Daphne and Vivianna. We need room to act." Ly stepped closer and Malik realized his eyes were boring into her. Viv put her arm on Malik.

"You too, Malik." Ly spoke.

"Work around me," Malik replied in a quiet yet determined voice.

"If you're going to stay, you'll need to be useful." Ly handed him a wet washrag. In slow soft motions, he ran the cool cloth over Delaney's face, gingerly cleaning all of the dried blood away from her mouth and nose. He finger combed her matted hair and brushed strands from her cheeks.

Sensitive nerves twitched and jolted her limbs in the unconscious state. The way she laid still, helpless near extinction, made him sick to his stomach. Malik's insides had been reduced to the emotions he experienced while his mother and father had died.

This is the end of my world.…

The sitting on the sidelines, never being able to stop the progression, Malik didn't think he had it in him anymore to continue on his chosen course. To sit idle took concentration on his part. He was compelled to do…something. He needed to expel the energy. Break every piece of furniture, beat everyone into a bloody pulp, or bring down the house with his bare hands.

When Delaney did move of her own volition, she moved closer to Malik. He longed to link with her, to find her and force her back from the darkness. Grab life and wrap the precious gift in a tight embrace and this time, nothing would tear him away or loosen his grip.

Malik hadn't slept much in the last few days and his patients ran thin; the combination fuel for an impossible outcome. Whenever Delaney regained consciousness, he wanted his face to be the first thing she laid eyes on and if by some shitty twist of fate she was leaving him, his expression would be the one thing she took with her to the other side.

When Viv and Daphne cut away most of Delaney's clothes, Ly began healing Delaney from the inside out. She shivered violently, almost knocking herself off the counter top.

Hours went by, and no change in Delaney's condition took place either way. She lied still as stone, as quiet as a church mouse, and as lifeless as a mannequin in the Macy's store window. Malik kept feathering the washrag over her face.

In his head, he told her their story. The whole sordid tale of why he aspired to do the right thing until she stood next to him. When she looked at him, his mind went blank except for all the pure male-like thoughts standing at attention. Three days alone with her in a cave had led him to realize he wanted her for the rest of his life. He needed her calling out his name again and again.

There is nothing that could sound sweeter to me. This is the truth she should have heard from me from the onset.

Malik left nothing out, not how long he had craved her, or how much, or how he would only exist if she were to leave him now. Malik told her things he'd never actually considered, even when he was alone. Dreams he'd always figured were foolish to hope for, but hungered for like food. He wanted a child.

Bent, Not Broken   237

He watched the Drake's and the glimpse of what life could be; it had made him want more. A family had never occurred to him before. Now, the thoughts plagued him same as only addiction might.

And I want it all with you.

When the Fates were finally finished with her, the clock read after midnight.

Delaney laid still as the dead on the kitchen island. Malik's back was stiff and his legs asleep. Tiny needles poked his limbs from inactivity.

"Malik, you need a break. I'll stay with her." A part of him understood Viv wanted time alone with Delaney.

"Delaney getting hurt wasn't your fault. No one ever suspect Lola. Rourke had her checked out. What does matter is you got to her and saved her life." Viv hugged him.

Malik stiffened. "She's hurt because of me."

"She needs you." Vivianna's eyes were pulled back to her child.

The thought of company didn't bode well with Malik. The backyard was still and secluded and the one place he could think by himself.

"Tryst." Malik waited for him to come online.

"Nothing yet." Trystan replied.

"What about her Finder?"

"She's out of range. I have no idea how Peyton turned invisible, but her GPS is off-line. Like Rourke, she's just…gone." He gritted the words out as the connection went silent.

Malik's anger grew with each step carrying him out to the backyard. Without much thought, he threw a punch at the block wall at the edge of the backyard. Concrete disintegrated into dust as his hand fractured under the pressure. The pain felt good and Malik held onto the emotion.

"A true mark of aggression." Dane's voice should have startled Malik.

I think I've been waiting for you. Hoping you would confront me, condemn me.

"Son." Dane stood beside Malik. Tonight, the term of endearment grated over Malik's skin. Anger flared within Malik once more. He couldn't let go of his self-loathing; he didn't want to.

"The tightrope will break under too much pressure, if you do not provide some slack." Dane said as he turned his head toward Malik.

Why those words should sooth him, he had no damn idea. The anger began to taper off, though the guilt remained as strong as any force Malik had ever felt.

"I screwed up. Rourke would have made sure she was safe. Maybe Isabeau counted on the closeness of us and Peyton. Isabeau knew I'd come for Peyton, no matter the cost." Malik's voice trailed off.

Dane's silence screamed at him.

Malik stared into the night sky, watching a lone bat fly around the streetlight. Moments crept past in the stillness, refusing to remain silent in his mind.

"How can you not berate me for my insolence; the complete irresponsibility, stupidity, and neglect?" Malik needed Dane to react. "Say something."

"Any word on Bannan, Bowe, or Peyton?"

"No." Malik shook his head.

"Life is short, yes? What I would not give to have just a handful of carefree moments with Dasha once more."

The idea of how much a woman changed everything struck Malik. Dane had loved Dasha with such a fierceness Malik thought him mad then. Dane watched Dasha constantly, with an attentive interest he couldn't comprehend.

"We wasted precious moments, Dasha and I, on petty arguments that mean nothing to me now. Time escaped us, leaving nothing but an old man behind. The future is lost to me now...forever. I would charge the ocean and render the deep a wasteland if I thought I might reclaim my bride, even if only for one moment in time." Dane's thick french accent was full of passion. "I wish now I had enjoyed the time allotted to us with more voracity. Let me offer a piece of advice. The hardest course of action usually offers the most resistance and is probably what you're fighting for to begin with. The war isn't only on the battlefield, and fighting for what you believe in should not solely be a militant stance. Perhaps you might apply the same unyielding passion to more personal endeavors."

Dane sat in one of the chairs as soon as their pacing brought them near the outdoor dining table closer to the back door of the house. Malik leaned with his hands on the back of one near Dane, unable to settle down enough to sit yet.

"I need to join Tryst and search for my son-in-law. I need to be useful once more. Can this be arranged?" Dane said.

"Bast." Malik's gaze held great admiration for Dane. His elder's words made him not feel alone in dealing with inner turmoil, and that gave him some peace and calmed him.

A minute later a tall women with a mane of yellow sunshine braided down her back appeared next to them.

"Bast, take Dane to Trystan. You are to shadow him until he is either in this house or home on Naroke." She nodded and followed Dane to the shallow water of the steps into the pool. She held out her hand and they disappeared beneath the surface of the water.

It didn't take long for Malik to head into the house and directly to the kitchen, but he discovered the island was empty. He wandered upstairs and found Vivianna standing in the doorway of Delaney's room, watching her little girl. Not wanting to intrude, Malik stayed out of sight and drifted inside.

"I love you, baby." Vivianna pulled Delaney's door shut with a quiet click.

Malik tossed a pillow on the floor and settled down next to the bed. Exhaustion plagued him. His head hit the cushion and his mind willingly swam into the darkness.

Chapter
TWENTY-FOUR

elaney's arms felt like heavy weights she couldn't lift. She yawned so wide the action made her eyes water and her jaw click. A faint glimmer flashed through her mind. Excitement roared up inside, forcing some of the sluggishness away.

"Am I fusing? Is that why I'm so tired?" Delaney asked Malik. *I can stay with him. I will live the life I am meant to with him.*

Her heart stopped and somewhere inside a horrible awareness blossomed. "Yes."

One simple word crushed her hope into nothing more than rubble. The way he answered with hesitation in his voice was what broke her heart. He understood there was to be no hope. His silence after that one word gave it away.

No! They are sending me away again. Tears burned Delaney eyes and she wanted to scream. *Not only am I denied my life, I am denied him. I am meant to be with him. He's all I want... He is my echo.*

"You're a bad liar." Delaney whispered back at him while tears burned her eyes. She folded her legs up against her chest and laid her cheek on her knees.

I can fight, I've proven myself, and none of my actions matter even in the slightest degree. Every moment of my past will still be obliterated.

Joss laying her hands on Delaney's arm was what set the binding in motion. She had muttered in her ear as the two embraced like family only moments ago. Delaney wasn't sure how Joss created the binding, but the processes had already begun.

"How long?"

"A few minutes maybe."

Minutes to live my whole life with him. Minutes to fight. Why? I only wish to stay.

"Our life together will always be like this, right?"

Malik crawled into bed next to her. She curled up into him. Her hands weaved into his shirt and she wrapped the material around her fingers, holding on, even though she knew she could never hold on tight enough.

"I want to stay with you. Don't let them take me away."

He pulled Delaney closer to him. *Can you hold me tight enough to keep me from disappearing?*

In his own way, she understood he wanted to resist the inevitable. An ending they both accepted no matter how much they continued to resist. Malik had to go on. He had to witness Delaney fade away against every instinct he had. He couldn't keep her. They were never supposed to fall for each other, never supposed to want the other more than anything.

But we do.

"We could run." Pain tore through Delaney. "Moments, nothing more than moments." She murmured. Her throat ached from trying to hold back her tears.

"No." His voice was velvety soft and shredded thin. *We will never have more than this.*

"We can't continue to live like this. You should leave me behind and move on." Saying the words out loud seemed right, though they ripped at her heart like vicious claws. "Run from me." The words came out in a painful rush of held breathes and faltering syllables.

"I'll be here when you wake up," he whispered.

His words pulled at her, piecing the thin surface.

"I will always love you." Malik's voice faded as Delaney began losing the fight.

Her eyes were so heavy, her body so tired. Delaney knew all would be lost the second her eyes closed. The helplessness consumed her as she let him go.

Delaney kept her eyes closed. She didn't want to be release from the dream. *No yet.* Pain shot through her, popping her tightly shut eyes wide open. Slow motion blinking only intensified her wish to retreat back into the sleep world. Delaney's line of sight found Mars, Neptune, and Jupiter floating just over head, through the moonlight dancing along the textured paint of the ceiling.

Her tongue stuck to the roof of her mouth.

Delaney's head slumped off to one side, sliding down into fluffy quicksand. Confusion wrapped its tentacles around her. Darkness swayed in the soft, primrose light of the streetlamp just outside the window. The smell of burnt hair and grilled skin lingered in her nose. Delaney surmised these sensations should be accompanied by an all-consuming agony. That they didn't because of a state of numbness enveloping her could not be known by her.

She attempted to drag herself up, but found only resistance. Delaney thought she might vomit. She wiggled and stiffly danced around until she was able to sit up and put one foot down on the ground, with lethargic hesitation.

"Ouch."

Malik grunted. His slumberous eyes found her. "What's wrong?" He focused on Delaney through a languid gaze. His mind grew cognizant of her bandage and fresh blood seeping through. He hastily sat on his haunches to face her.

"Wha...?" Her brain shut down and she went blank.

Delaney's head bobbed and weaved. Her eyes stared at Malik, or more aptly, through him. She appeared like a little kid with feet dangling off the bed. Messy hair with loose tendrils hanging down into her eyes and brushing her cheeks. He tried to push the wisps back, so they wouldn't itch her skin.

"Water." Delaney croaked in a voice unfamiliar to her.

"You're thirsty?"

Delaney nodded her head, closing her eyes at the same time the room began to spin. She reminded him of a bobble-head doll. Her brain was function much slower from the pain killers. He handed her a bottle of water as he scrutinized the damage her movements had caused. Delaney shivered every few seconds, oblivious to the fact.

"You're hurt. Do you remember?"

Her face crumpled as more tears slipped down her cheeks.

He caressed her forehead with his knuckles while taking her temperature. Malik understood touching her, in even the simplest way, would be a mistake. One touch could never be enough.

Delaney's head fell forward into him with a relaxed sigh. Her skin was so hot, he instinctively pulled back. He moved his hand down Delaney's brow to the curve of her face, resting on her cheek. She turned into his touch, settling her cheekbone right against his thumb. Her eyes slid shut and she murmured something he didn't catch. He let himself touch her just for a second before forcing his hand away.

"We need to talk," Malik said just above a whisper.

His lips moved, but the words were a jumbled mess. Delaney's head hurt and the more she tried to concentrate the more intense the pain grew. She blinked at him a half dozen times, then shook her head in confusion.

"Your dad, Peyton, and…Mount Hood yesterday."

She reached for Malik and he almost pulled back. He understood he should have.

Delaney placed clumsy hands on either side of his face. The soft pads of her fingertips traced his cheeks. Her eyes held his with concrete strength.

The touch became potent. The physical contact turned into more than touching; they merged into each other.

Her wonder-filled eyes never left the ever-present blaze growing in his.

Her reaction to him amazed her; she found herself drawn to him. Her fingers ambled down the bridge of his slightly crooked nose and across his face. A strong longing sensation spread with each whispery touch, need blossomed in every breath.

Malik couldn't hold back how much he wanted her. To experience every single thing to ever happen to her. He used every ounce of self-restraint he had to allow her exploration to finish, trying to settle for reveling in the way her hands caressed his skin. Malik witnessed her eyes change to a smoke emerald color. The flick of her tongue sweeping across her bottom lip became mesmerizing.

Delaney traced his jawline, then stopped short of his mouth. Her fingers raised up and he let them rest on his lower lip. The tips ran back and forth in slow motion, pausing on his bottom edge, like flames lapping at his mouth. She moaned.

He nearly lost his ability to resist.

Fatigue won out as her arm fell away. The loss echoed all the way through him.

He leaned closer to Delaney and raised her hand up to his lips. He kissed her palm, lingering until she shivered.

Delaney didn't want the delicious moment to end so soon. She tried to speak, but her words had been silenced with a kiss. His large hands cupped her face and he kissed her slowly. His perfect lips barely brushed hers as his nose grazed her cheek.

"God, I love you." He muttered under his breath.

The words seemed so important, but she couldn't hold on to them. The drugs, exhaustion, and desire all clouded her mind.

His lips released her and he rested his forehead against hers. He wanted to crawl in the bed with her and stay until they forced him physically to leave. Malik decided ripping the fingers from his hand would be a more pleasant experience than pulling free of her. Something so strong existed between them.

A sturdy and tangible 'it' and whatever 'it' was, had taken control of what they were not willing to.

Delaney grabbed at him with weak fingers and unsteady hands, trying to keep him right next to her.

He knew he should have left. The sentence repeats itself in his head like a scratched disc. A gravitational pull as strong as anything he had ever felt anchored him to her. Malik's forehead still rested against Delaney's brow. He took a slow determined breath, stealing hers. He held the pant for a moment, filled with regret, then pulled away.

She broke into pieces flitting through the air as his fingers released her. Sad eyes peered at him through loopy senses.

He stopped and lifted his face to hers. His wounded appearance told her that while she refused to let him go, he must have realized her effort and ceased pulling away. He leaned toward her, looking into her eyes with a bittersweet smile on his face.

The small gesture meant the most. *He doesn't want to leave me.*

"Your father is missing." Malik said the words slowly, and looked away.

"What? Where is my father?" She fought to clear the webs away from her brain.

"They were on Mt. Hood,"

"Why? Who?" The questions rippled through the fog over Delaney.

"Bannan, Bowe, and Peyton." Malik chewed on the inside of his cheek.

"Wait, no word from them at all?" Her head spun so fast she couldn't blink quickly enough to stop the twirling in her head.

Malik sat down beside her and let her lean into him for support. She was acting differently, needy. And he weakened to her.

"Are they dead?" Delaney whispered.

"We have no information yet." He wavered. The action was slight and barely noticeable, but present. He wasn't telling her everything and she understood he wouldn't.

"Are we going? When do we leave?" Delaney began making a mental checklist of the things she would need to bring and again attempted to move. She swayed and almost fell off the bed.

"I can't go, and leave this house with only four guards. I can't sacrifice all of your lives trying to find them. I have faith in Tryst."

"Why can't we all go?" Her voice rose a notch. Lucidity slammed into her.

"The operation presents too many dangerous variables. We are not familiar with the immediate area. I can't ensure your family's safety."

"Please, we need to go and get them back." She jumped to her feet and immediately fell back down on the bed.

Malik stared at her. She looked angelic in a bruised, battered, and burned up kind of way.

"Impossible. Your grandfather is helping in the search. I wish things could be different. I want them back too." If he thought it would help, they would already be on the mountain.

"Why won't you do everything possible to bring my father home?" Malik understood she attacked him out of frustration and fear.

"Please, Malik, help me find my father," she whispered. Tears streamed down her face.

He shook his head in frustration. The idea was stupid. Too risky and dangerous. He wanted to consider her proposal anyway.

"Get your strength back, then we'll talk again. I'm not saying yes or no, maybe...*if* you're strong enough to travel."

"Rest, and tomorrow if there's no news, I'll speak with your mother." Malik pulled the covers over her.

"You will?" She was bursting with hope.

"I don't want you to be unhappy. Other people's lives depend on the decisions I make. Can't you understand?" Malik felt the scope of his responsibilities were far beyond her grasp.

Delaney could only think of her father, but felt ashamed for trying to make him bend to her wishes by using guilt to her advantage.

"I'll check back in on you in a few hours." He reached the door.

"I'm sorry I'm so much trouble. I just want my dad back. Malik, thank you." Delaney smiled at him.

"For what?" He seemed confused by her gesture of appreciation.

"All the things you do every day." Delaney laid back against the pillow and closed her eyes.

Malik headed for the office, desperate to see if any developments on their missing had been reported.

"Will you stop pacing? You're making me nervous. Go workout or something." Fezz grumbled only a few minutes after Malik entered the command room.

Malik stopped in front of the world map and rubbed his eyes. He was suffering from severe exhaustion and needed to rest. He exhaled while trying to focus on anything but his emotions.

"Fezz, have some of the stuff from Turnberry delivered here. We need more manpower helping with research. Start with the maps and tools. Vivianna and the girls may be able to help identify and catalogue some of the items." Malik turned to face him.

"What are you looking for?" Fezz's fingers tapped away on the keyboard.

"No clue. I hope we missed something. Any information would at least give us a place to start."

"Seeley called Delaney 'the map' when he held her. Delaney fused and she had the same floating shapes and symbols Vivianna has. The marks resembled glyphs, or maybe pictograms." Malik shook his head. His gut told him the clue added up, but to what he wasn't sure.

"I'm tired and can't think straight. We're missing something and all the shit we found at the nest is relevant." Malik scrubbed a hand down his face.

"Why would Seeley and Isabeau care about anything else but killing them?" Fezz stopped and turned.

"They think they found 'the map' to something. The only reason Isabeau and Seeley didn't kill Delaney was because Caleb ordered them not to. All of this means something to him. Caleb wants to turn Delaney. Why her and not

Calliope? What makes Delaney unique to them?" Malik's head thumped in time with the beat of his heart.

"Seeley touched Delaney when she fused? Why didn't she fry him?"

"Find out as much as you can about Seeley and his lineage.

Get more information on the Demonoks too. I'm going to lay down for an hour. Afterwards, have Spyder keep an eye on the office and you get some rest. We'll rotate from then on." Malik half mumbled as he drifted to Delaney's room and passed out on the floor.

The dream of talking with Malik stayed with her long after she woke up. Fragments seemed clear, yet the rest was forgotten.

Delaney's thoughts turned to Malik.

"Where are you from?" Her voice sounded sleepy.

She glanced over the side of the bed. Seeing how worn out he appeared, guilt ate at her for waking him.

"What's the clock say?" Malik stretched his tired muscles back to life.

"Nine thirty." Delaney yawned. "You slept for about an hour and a half. Any news on my father?" She sat up, then gripped the edge of the nightstand to keep upright.

"Not yet." Malik sat up straight. He groaned as he repositioned himself. A popping sound from his joints made her laugh.

He yawned and stretched his arms over his head. She recognized the scar on his neck and noticed more when the stretch pulled his shirt up, uncovering his stomach and forearms.

"Age catching up with you?" She tossed the barb at Malik with a sheepish grin, trying to lighten the moment. *He is beautiful and maybe the scars were some of the reason why.* Malik had lived, survived, and even prospered when everything around him was in chaos. *I admire him.*

"Funny." Malik half smiled. Her heart grew warmer and threatened to burst right out of her chest.

"Wait, how old are you?" She laid back down.

"Which question do you want an answer to first?"

Bent, Not Broken   249

"Huh?" Delaney muttered.

"You asked me where I am from too." He continued to smile at her. Should he remain looking at her the way he was, Delaney would forget everything she wanted to say.

"Okay, where are you from?" Delaney drew her hands under her head.

"I'm the same as your mother. Our breed is the Leonawa Aquana Tallulah Waiths, the words mean 'Ghosts of the Leaping Water'. Over the years, the name has been shortened to Waiths. We settled in the Pacific Northwest of the United States many generations ago. I'm not sure about my particular family genealogy. My parents came to your family when I was a young child." Malik shrugged, remaining aloof and unreachable.

"Wait…anything else?" She tried to pull him out of himself.

"Okay. Um…our faction of the breed fled to South America. The humans began to hunt any divergent principles, anything differing from themselves. Their beliefs are far from ours. They think monsters are explainable by chemical imbalances and mental diseases. Heaven and hell are theories, not actually places. True evil permeates both worlds." The expression on his face explained more than his words.

"Homo sapien minds can't process the truth of our world. Myths and fairy tales are based in truth. When something terrifying or brutal happens to a human, they lie to themselves. In order to processes the facts, they create stories to help them cope. These accounts are told around campfires and soon take on a life of their own. Fairy tales manifest into legends. King Arthur, Zeus, Anubis, and Quetzalcoatl are all perfect examples.

"The Mayans and Aztecs were considered bloodthirsty for how they worshipped within their religion. They did what they believed must be done, or they'd be punished by their gods with disease, famine, and death. The people who feared what they didn't understand created a history they could comprehend.

"Should the human's discover our existence, they would massacre us. We are stronger, but the humans outnumber us." Malik smiled.

Delaney hadn't realized how knowledgeable Malik was. She found him well-read and highly intelligent, and became more attracted to him with each word. She maneuvered closer to him until she leaned her head against his shoulder. Pushing herself to stay awake, she fought the pain pill's effect to stay with him and his glorious velvety voice. Everything about him drew her in and held her still. He talked for a while, sometimes she slipped away but reemerged from her drug induced state and found him continuing. Her fingers played in his hair when she was awake. The touch was sensual and he leaned in.

"Malik, sorry to interrupt, I have questions," Delaney said, staring up at her ceiling and resisting how much she wanted to turn and face him.

"I like when you say my name," he whispered.

Her skin began tingling. A serenity surrounded her.

"Okay, ask away." Malik sounded more serious.

"What is a Kindred and why are you one of them?" Delaney nuzzled closer.

"My parents were slaughtered when I was an adolescent. They had strayed from the clan, searching for a chance at a normal life for us, for me. My parents even tried to live among the others in the Andes before distancing themselves from the breeds altogether. I was about twelve when I fused for the first time. We fuse around puberty. My first time happened in a public school, in my classroom.

"My parents wanted to protect me and attempted to run. We made it as far as the coast with a mob right behind us. They left me fused in a cave for my own safety. My parents ventured out to check if we could safely make it to the water." His voice trailed off.

Delaney remained silent, waiting.

That had been the worst day of his life, but Malik didn't want to appear weak. He fixated on being nothing more than a narrator to the story which meant everything to him.

"I looked on as the enraged mob beat my parents to death. They burned their bodies until nothing was left." Malik looked away from her. The pain was real and far too close.

Bent, Not Broken   251

Delaney wanted to ask so many questions. The chilly way he presented his story kept her quiet, though.

He stopped again, and the silence became unsettling to Delaney. She could only sense the distance Malik kept around himself. Malik's voice didn't change and he didn't move. He continued after a slight break, as if he were reading ingredients from a recipe book.

"I was left to fend for myself in the forest. Your grandfather and Fury found me in the Amazon years later. They decided I must be extraordinarily proficient at surviving. To endure the loss of my parents and persevere for years after was no easy task. They asked me to train for a guard unit being formed.

"I refused at first. Dane came back many times to talk. He became my friend. He explained the goals of the militant group and what they would be responsible for. 'The children of the Calia shore must come home,' he said. Until then, I had no idea there were more like me. Children who had been forgotten all over the world. Dane offered me a home, a purpose. It wasn't long before more of us began showing up. I reconnected with people I knew from my childhood. We trained together and bonded over our loss and our desire to change the future.

"A few years ago, an announcement came from Bannan. He was tasked with finding protectors for Vivianna's daughters. When asked, I said yes. By then, I had grown into a skilled fighter and assassin."

Delaney thought about how lonely his way of life must have been. The person he had become was much easier to comprehend.

"Where do you go when you're not here?" Delaney yawned the words out with a lazy sigh, still fighting the effect of the pain pill.

Malik wanted to tell her about the things he held important.

"Delaney, I never want to leave you. But if I do, you always will have a Kindred with you." Malik yawned.

"What about before, when Rourke guarded me? Where did you go then?" Her voice was growing softer. Malik hoped she would fight the drowsiness for a while longer.

"Six years ago, I was sent to fill in for Rourke. Eventually, I'd take over his responsibilities with your family when he chose to retire. When I wasn't needed, I went home and spent most of my time training new Kindreds. Sometimes I'd stay around here, in case I was needed. I'd stay behind when everyone went to the island in the summer for training, to keep an eye on you."

"Don't you ever want to go home? Wait, where's your home?"

"Naroke. I have a home on the island where we are from. You haven't been back in many years. Until you fused, it would have been far too dangerous." Malik answered.

"What's it like there?"

"My home is beautiful. The most spectacular beach in the world is in my front yard."

"Your grandfather can't wait for you to come home. Dane wants your family home more than anything. Then you may never get away, though." He laughed, a sound she wasn't familiar with, but one she liked very much.

"What's your home like?" Delaney pressed further. He was in such a giving mood.

"It's like your home. It's where my stuff is. I like the isolation. The other members of the tribe think I go out of my way to avoid them. My parents would have loved the bay. It reminds me of them. Nothing bad can happen there and no one else exists. I suppose my home is my safe place." Malik contemplated something for a moment.

"The Kindreds were disbanded centuries ago. When I returned with Dane and Fury, I was the first Kindred in a long time. Dane brought them back with the help of Fury. She's one of the original Amalgamates and the first Kindred. Fury trained me and a few of the others.

"As the wars became closer, reinstating the original guards for protection and resistance made sense. Peyton and Trystan trained beside me. They both came to live at my house because neither one of them had anywhere else to go. We added on rooms as we needed them. As the Kindreds grew in numbers again, they sort of migrated in until we all lived together.

"A state of the art kitchen, electronic gadgets, alarm system, everything one would need. Everyone brings different things with them, knowledge or a skill of some kind. Fezz brought in the future with his gadgets and electronic stuff. Peyton and Bowe are the painters and decorators. Trystan surrounds us with fine art. I build, anything and everything." He offered so much and Delaney greedily took all he offered. "You'll like it." He said confidently.

Malik had been careful to bring a piece of Delaney with him everywhere he went, especially at his home.

"How do you know what I like?" Delaney asked with a slight challenge to his confident nature.

"You don't know, do you?" He studied her. "I've read all your books. The ones you love are worn. Bookmarks sprout out like tree branches from them. Your favorite poems are 'Kubla Kahn' and 'Funeral Blues'. Your favorite novels are *Beautiful Creatures* and *Merdian*. Favorite books series are The Lords of the Underworld, Demons after Dark, New Species, and The Night Breed series.

"I've listened to your favorites list on your iPod, once Fezz showed me how to use the contraption. You enjoy classical, but you don't pay attention to the composer or the names of the songs. You listen and simply appreciate them for what they are. You love Etta James, Sia, Snow Patrol, A Fine Frenzy, and Beethoven's piano Sonata of Moonlight; they are played the most. When you're sad, you play Cannon in D by Pachelbel over and over. Oh, and you just now started getting into Colbie Caillat.

"When you run, you have faster paced music like The Blue Eyed Greens and someone who thinks he is a candy bar."

Delaney interrupted with a giggle. "It's The Black Eyed Peas and he's Eminem."

"Right, sorry. The art you enjoy, the beauty is everywhere around you. Alfed Gockel, Monet, Van Gogh, Giger, Edvard Munch, and Klimet. I'm not sure which is your favorite, you seem to like them all equally." Her mouth was open and she experienced a dumbstruck emotion as he waved around the room.

"How can you understand so much about me?" Delaney could hear the shock vibrate through her timbre.

"I wanted to identify with you as a person. You interest me. You hide yourself, much like we do. I guess I have experienced a similarity between us I only find with other guards." A light laughter rolled through his words. "When you chuckle, your smile reaches all the way into your eyes. You don't laugh much though, do you?"

"Can we die?" she said.

"Of course we can die. Some poisons can prevent us from healing ourselves. If a wound is purposefully kept open, we will eventually bleed out. Fire does a real number on us, as you have experienced. A Lunaires's blood will drive us crazy. When their blood reaches our brain, the chemical prevents fresh oxygenated blood from ever reaching our cells again. Rarely will it turn us completely. We can be blown to bits, usually explosions kill everything, though. If an appendage is lost, you can regenerate organs and limbs with help from the Fates. The process is horribly painful and requires rest and time. If your head gets chopped off, that's permanent.

"We do have to be careful of the other breeds. A Snatcher can switch places with you. The being can lock you up in a small part of yourself or kick you out entirely and take over your body. Snatchers are extraordinarily dangerous, perhaps one of the most lethal predators in the world. Others have the ability to crawl into your mind and make you commit acts out of character. Some can elevate your emotional state. Travelers can borrow your abilities if they are within range and you are actively using them."

So much material for Delaney to remember and understand. Malik wanted Delaney to have as much information as she could get. Knowledge would help her to keep her alive and defend herself.

"We don't breathe like the humans, but we need oxygen. We can slow down our bodily functions. Our respiratory system is similar to a bear's hibernating state, we need far less to sustain us than do humans. Once you learn how to slow your heart rate down, you can even appear dead. Hopefully no one buries you. Entombment sucks, trying to dig yourself out…freaky too." He shivered and scrunched his face as if memories were resurfacing. Ever since Cairo, he'd hated small spaces.

"Human disease can't hurt us. We can't get cancer or AIDS. We can have a type of heart attack, and even strokes. Your heart exploding, definitely a killer. A stroke would be similar to a Lunaires's blood exchange; the result could be fatal and if the medical condition weren't, you'd want it to be. Magical spells can mess with your head. Be wary of witches and wizards; they're vengeful when you cross them. Warlocks can also cause trouble because they're inherently corrupted. Enchanters, conjurers, and diviners naturally deceive.

"Doux La Roux can take a bite and usually the sting will only hurt like hell. Some full moons aren't as deadly as others. During the Animal moons, a Doux La Roux can turn whomever they bite. During the nature moons, the Doux La Roux are beginning their transitions and their bites are acidic and lethal. Once their saliva makes contact with our blood, our blood dies. The properties can no longer coagulate, so we can bleed out in about four minutes, give or take. You should be familiar with the moon chart, even though you probably will not remember it. Who knows what you'll take with you.

"The Harvest and the Hunter's moon are when the Doux La Roux gather to claim a mate; happens twice in a year. During this time, they are their most deadly. A mated male Doux La Roux is protective of his female, even more so if she is pregnant."

Many of the legends started popping into her head. Did elves, brownies, sprites, mermaids, and gorgons exist too? Myths, fairy tales, and folklore were all based in some part on fact. The possibilities were endless. She sort of liked the idea that humans weren't alone.

"Why would the moon phases be important to me?" Delaney shrugged her shoulders.

"Because you are half Doux La Roux. The traits could arise, even though Viv and Calliope display none of the signs. You could be detrimental to Amalgamates, and to me."

"My mom always says 'once in a blue moon'. Is that another name for a

Nature Moon?" Delaney said.

"The term refers to when three or more full moons dawn during a season. Two full moons in the same month, a third is a blue moon." She sank her full weight against him, snuggling closer.

"Are we immortal?" Delaney found this to be the most confusing part. Brody was still aging, yet her mother and father had stopped years ago.

"Age, trauma, and disease are the three things to kill a human. We can live forever. Age and disease are not a problem. Trauma is our only cause of death. So we are not truly immortal. We are subject to death." He took a deep breath.

"Can I see your Prints and Scripts, please?"

"Okay, I'll show you some." He pushed her up from him lightly. Turning to face her, his eyes were closed and he looked to be deep in thought. He slowed his breathing and then Delaney saw one of them. The grizzly bear on his chest peeked out at her. The green eyes were the same as Malik's.

"I call him Ranger because he's a protector, and in ancient Greece Rangers were guardians of the people. Originally, Rangers were forest caretakers. The name Ranger sort of fits him." Malik laughed. It disappeared and he got up off the bed to point at a large dog on his calf.

"Meet Jack. He's a character, protective too." Then Malik sat down with his back to Delaney to reveal a towering waterfall with flowing green moss. The backdrop was a dense forest and at the top was a grassy meadow. At the bottom, the falls fell away into a pool surrounded on three sides by lofty boulders. Then the water disappeared down into a large stream running out of sight. The scene was familiar to her.

"This is my own private Arcadia." His head twisted around to stare at Delaney.

"Why do you have more Prints than Scripts?" Delaney examined what she could.

Malik turned to face her, then settled with his body propped up against her pillows. Delaney was afraid to wait for an invitation, so she quickly laid down beside him. He opened his arms and let her fall right into place.

Bent, Not Broken 257

"I'm a guard. I fuse to protect more than anything. The falls give me some control over water. I'm limited, though. Halo traveling is a trip, but you'll like it should the opportunity arise." Delaney rested her cheek on his shoulder. She yawned and shook the clouds from her mind. Fighting the drugs was becoming useless. He raised his arm and pulled her closer.

"Are these all you possess?" The wide-awake dozing sensation felt like her skull belonged on a doll, wobbling with a rubbery neck.

"No, but the rest are private." He moved out from under her and stood up. "I need to go downstairs. Sleep and I'll bring you lunch later." Malik's way of ending the conversation was abrupt and took all the warmth in the world with him.

"Delaney, I do need to ask you something? Why did you go after Lola during the fight?"

"I realized when she get up and pulled her knife she was going to try to kill you, and I had to reach her first." Delaney shrugged her shoulders and looked away.

"Why get in between us? This…all the care we take, the sacrifices, are for nothing if we fail. Don't you understand you need to put your life first?" Frustration and anger rang in his words.

"Another stunt like that, Trystan or Peyton will take over my duties with you. Am I clear?" He yelled at her. Rage pulsed through him until he felt stir-crazy.

"I didn't want you to die. I had to attack her. I couldn't just stand by and watch you get stabbed in the back." She defended her actions.

"I will return around lunch time." He disappeared.

Chapter
TWENTY-FIVE

"We need to talk." Vivianna stood at the bottom of the stairs with an expression of defiance.

"Okay, but not here." Malik walked to the office. He had been expecting this argument.

"Has there been any news?"

Malik shook his head as they entered the command room.

Vivianna exhaled heavily. "How long am I expected to wait here?"

"I will contact Dane and forward a request to Ky to change their current orders and allow you to participate in the search. For the moment, you and the girls are on lockdown."

"You understand what she'll do to them. Screw the Counsel! Let's go now. They lost no one of importance, I have...you have. Why are you standing by, doing nothing?" Vivianna goaded Malik, and he comprehended her reasoning. But he no longer possessed the attitude of a hotheaded boy; he had responsibilities extending beyond himself.

"Delaney wants to pack and leave as soon as possible. I require you to talk the girls down. Regardless of what you and I want, we are stuck here. The situation is critical, you need to make them aware of the danger."

"You expect me to lie to them?" Vivianna had an edge to her voice.

"I prefer you to help them discern the reason behind the decision. Bannan doesn't require anyone dead on his behalf. Especially not the women he lives for." Malik hoped the logic had an effect on Viv too.

"I know you love Peyton. How can you sit by?" The edge of anger in Vivianna's voice grew.

"I'm not being idle, I am attempting to be fastidious. I trust Trystan to go to the ends of the earth to save them. I could risk us all, if I thought it would do any good. Isabeau isn't a fool. This might be what she's been waiting for. I can't take that chance. Can you put the girls in the line of fire?"

"I'll talk to them. You'll keep me posted?" Vivianna wiped her eyes.

"Of course." Malik's response wasn't reassuring.

"Yesterday, when we raided the nest, we found all sorts of historical things, maps, tools, a bunch of stuff. I had the bulk of the load taken to Turnberry. I'm having some more sent here. We need to figure out why the Stryders had the objects and what they planned on doing with them."

"How much are you referring to?"

"About thirty boxes and crates. You're the expert. Have the girls help you. Any evidence you find could be the reason the symbol on your neck is also at Mount Hood." He hoped this would ensure their cooperation and deter the talk of uprising.

After Viv left, Malik went back to staring at the map. Fezz took his turn sleeping and Malik watched the office. The room became too quiet. The energy traveling through him made his knees bounce against the desk.

Right now, Malik would give much to listen to Peyton razz him for whatever she came up with. She had already suffered enough. Malik slammed his hands into the table as he pushed up and paced the room again.

"Delaney, wake up." Daphne's frame slowly appeared. "You sleep like the dead. What did they give you?" Daphne sounded annoyed.

"Is she awake?" Calliope whispered. "I can't let Malik out of my sight. He's a fuckin' ghost." Calliope said in a frustrated murmur.

"Go, I'll tell Delaney everything. Brody needs to keep Spyder busy for a while. If they suspect anything, we're done before we can make the garage." Daphne snapped. The door closed with a soft click.

"Wake up. We need to talk. Delaney, please." She shook Delaney's shoulder.

"About Dad?"

"Keep your voice down. They might overhear you. If Malik thinks you're awake, he will be up here in no time." Daphne fell silent and listened carefully.

"What are they doing to find Dad?" Delaney asked, sitting up with Daphne's help.

"Nothing." Daphne quieted again. She leaned over until her mouth was near Delaney's ear. "We are."

Delaney had to strain to hear her.

"We're planning on getting him back with or without the Kindreds. Brody concocted a plan, and it's crazy enough it just might work. The Kindreds can't stop us once we're gone. They can't track us unless we let them." Daphne paused for a breath.

"You're still hurt, Delaney. We wouldn't fault you if you can't go, but I thought you might want the choice." Daphne glanced around the room.

"Why can't we just ask them to take us?"

"Malik will not let us go. They think the situation is far too dangerous. I asked Spyder and he said 'no way will our safety be compromised.'" Daphne talked so fast Delaney took a moment to follow her.

"Malik promised if contact hadn't been established by tomorrow... He lied?"

"He isn't going to risk any of us to go and get our dad back." Daphne hissed.

"He said," Delaney mumbled half to herself.

"Check your emails. We will outline our plan and send copies out. Daphne ascertained from Flynn that the Kindreds don't review our emails regularly. Tell

Malik you need to do homework." Daphne leaned over and kissed Delaney's cheek.

"Before I forget, stop taking the pain killers. Take the pills and hide them some place safe. They are our ticket out of here." Daphne helped her sister lay back down. "I'm glad you're okay. I helped Mom and the Fates the night they brought you home." Daphne moved closer to hug Delaney, then stopped.

"I'm good to go." Delaney let Daphne hold onto her for a while.

Malik had told her exactly what she wanted. Anger took the place of her pain and determination soon drove her.

"I have a lot of work to do." She walked to the door, Daphne turned to face Delaney. "Let's get our dad back!" Daphne mouthed the words.

A few minutes later, Malik wandered up the stairs and passed an obviously irritated Daphne. He walked into Delaney's room with a peanut butter and jelly sandwich.

"Feel better?" Malik placed the tray on the bed beside her.

"Yeah. Talk to my mother. We can leave tomorrow." She appeared weak enough to pass out at any moment.

Delaney understood needling him to be childish, but she couldn't help badgering him a little. She wanted her sisters to be wrong about him and to be able to trust that he was a man of his word and would help her.

"Delaney, you should take things slow. You have been seriously injured."

The sweetness sort of melted some of her anger away. She had to hold on her resolve. *Attractive Malik is currently the enemy, don't forget it! Great! Now I'm a hypocrite. I forgive my family for the pack of crap they spoon fed me. How can I hold his lies against him? I hate moral dilemmas!*

"I need him back. They may be hurting him right now."

Delaney needed to give Malik the opportunity to come clean.

"I'll look into what can be done." He circled the subject.

Great! So some of this is my own fault. I'm setting him up now.

"Eat your lunch." Malik sat down.

"Will you talk to her now? Please. I need to begin packing." She peeked around the room.

"Sure." He hesitated before answering.

He doesn't know what to say to me.

"Do you want to spend some time downstairs?" He glanced toward the door.

"Yeah. Can I take a shower too?"

"Of course. When you're ready, call me and I'll help you. Delaney, I'm sorry. I went to check on Peyton and her team. Seeley and Lola cornered you while I was searching for them. I promise I won't leave you in anyone's care again."

Delaney wasn't sure what to say back to him. She quickly changed the conversation. "I can't see clearly after I fuse. Everything is like a color signature. I just attacked everyone who came near me. Did I go after you too?" She remembered the door bursting open and bodies running in.

"You threw me and Trystan across the room." He smiled at her.

"I thought you were more bad guys coming for me." Seeley's words popped into her head. "What is Stonic?" She exhaled.

"Stonic? No idea. Why?" He examined her quizzically.

"Seeley said 'the dermic fonts marking me are the symbols from a language called Stonic,' I think."

"Stellanic??"

"Yeah, Stellanic."

"The dead tongue. You chanted the words the other night. No one has spoken the dialect in over 2,000 years."

"How would I be able to recite or even articulate terminology I can't recall?" She peered up at him.

Malik blinked and shook his head in confusion.

"Seeley is different than us. What is Seeley? He dazed me or something when he touched me. Wait, how is he able to touch me while I am all lit up?" She frowned.

"What did he say to you?" Malik stared.

"Um, he said I smelled good and we would meet again. Why does he want

Daphne?" Delaney subconsciously experienced the intimate caress of Seeley's warm breath on her neck. The words washed over her once more and she shivered. Delaney couldn't understand her awkward reaction to Seeley. He was someone to fear, though terror was not the emotion he instilled in her.

"I wanted to go with him. Why would I want to accompany him anywhere?"

"Seeley Delacroix is a Demonok. His father was a Sisolak demon. I have no idea what he wants with Daphne, other than to torture and kill her." Malik gritted his teeth as he spoke.

"Why didn't he burn like you and the others when he touched me?" Delaney put down the remains of her sandwich. She'd lost her appetite.

"He's half demon, that could leave him unresponsive to you as a hybrid. I'm not sure how to protect you from him." Malik stood in front of her, dragging his knuckles across her cheek.

When his hand dropped from her face, Delaney grabbed his fingers before he could get away. "Don't go." Delaney stared up at him.

For a moment, he fell silent. "I always want to stay with you. But your dad, Peyton, and Bowe are in trouble. I have a demon far too interested in Daphne. I'm shorthanded here. Call me when you're finished." Reluctantly, he pulled away and left her alone.

Delaney had a million things to pack. She needed time to formulate a plan of her own.

Delaney grabbed her Mac and headed to the bathroom.

Walking slowly down the stairs, Malik caught a glimpse of Calliope waiting at the bottom. Her hand gripped the railing with a tight fist made of white knuckles.

"Have you heard from Trystan? Is he all right?" She was fidgeting back and forth on her feet. Her face was clearly tear streaked and she looked as if she were about to throw up.

"I can't call him until later. He's scouting, and I could unknowingly give away his position. Fezz will relay any news immediately. After dinner, I'll attempt to contact him and maybe he can drift home for a few minutes."

Calliope adored Trystan and had begun figuring out just how much every second he stayed away. Deep black circles surrounded her eyes and Malik realized she had lost weight from her already thin frame.

The worst events set people straight, she thought to herself. "Malik, please explain to him I'm sorry. He'll understand why. Tell him," she cleared her throat, "I made a mistake." Tears rolled down Calliope's cheeks as she passed him.

"Calliope." She stopped and turned to face Malik.

"He wouldn't leave you unless he had no choice." Calliope left without looking back.

Chapter
TWENTY-SIX

Sisters,

Calliope will collect the last of the bags tonight after dinner. Only bundle essentials and bring every weapon you can use and carry. The area is colder than Vegas, so pack and dress accordingly. I printed maps of the surrounding areas and stowed them away in my gear. I'll grab the navigation equipment. Daphne's got the camping supplies. Brody's heading to the bank to get cash. After the money run, Brody can disable the GPS on the Xterra. This should isolate us.

Throughout the day, Calliope and I are going to be loading up the car. I told the Kindreds we are donating old clothes and shoes to a shelter. Stick to the truth. When the lies become too elaborate, you screw up. We're going to use Delaney's pain pills to put in the Kindred's food and need to do all this before anyone goes for her after dinner dose.

Pack your own snacks and drinks for the drive, they'll probably fall asleep before we get to eat. After everyone is sedated, we will finish packing the staples. Mom needs to be drugged along with the others. Once they are all out, we hit the road. Bring your iPads and cell phones, but turn them off. Left on, they can be traced. Remember to delete this email and clear the browsing history. Any questions pertaining to this plan, use the word "serendipity" and head to the upstairs bathroom and wait.

Be careful, the Kindreds aren't stupid and will not be fooled. Don't take chances with your guards!

END.

Delaney grabbed a piece of paper and jotted down a few notes of things she couldn't afford to forget: extra ammunition, clips; every dagger, sword, and knife in the house; boots, Mt. Hood would be cold, which is self-explanatory; iPad to keep Brody from making me want to bang my head against the car window; silencer, a dumb thing to forget; shotgun and bullets; gloves designed for hassle free movement; G-Shock watches.

Delaney sat staring at her writing as the words started to blur. A tear fell from the tip of her nose and the paper quickly soaked the moisture up. Her family was in turmoil and all the shit launched itself at her, smacking against her frail exterior with a painful force.

"Oh, Dad." The notepad slipped off her lap and she buried her face in her hands.

This is real. My father, the mild-mannered college professor who turns the lights off when he finishes, unplugs appliances no longer in use, and recycles everything, has been kidnapped by the Stryders.

Her fingers began to twitch and tingle. Delaney shivered with understanding. The temper she had been trying to control was about to set her ablaze with a raw energy that had a will of its own. She tried to calm her crazy thoughts with deep breaths. Her rage cooled and the reduction in emotions seemed to slow down the process, but the action itself continued and she had no idea how to stop or control the potential.

Delaney slid to the floor and sat, quietly thinking. To master the conductivity became imperative to her. She didn't want to hurt the people who were there to help.

Raising her hands, she saw the pale blue webbing connecting one fingertip to the next. She moved her fingers and they sent small flashes expelling into the air. They danced in sapphire twinkles finally bursting in little pops of sound and light. Delaney realized her eyes hadn't changed yet. Her visual acuity still registered in vivid live color.

She decided to push her luck further and attempted to stand on her own. She wrapped a towel over her hand to turn the faucet, and expelled a thankful breath when nothing exploded or melted. Once in the shower, her body started to cool. Delaney's head began to clear as the anger subsided.

Delaney grabbed her list, headed back to her room, and went to work after a quick shower. An hour and a half later, she had three backpacks of weapons and one of clothes and toiletries. On the way out of town, they would need to hit the Walmart for extra ammunition.

Malik walked into the office and found Spyder manning the helm.

"Malik, you got a second?" Spyder folded his arms behind his head.

"What's up?" Malik settled into one of the chairs at the large table.

"Updates from the field units have been coming in and Fezz told me to make sure you take a look at them. Now a good time?"

"Okay." Malik kicked his feet up into the chair right next to Spyder.

"Neith and Talon are awaiting instructions on how to proceed. An excavation is being conducted at the base of Mount Hood, near where the symbol was found. Very organized and well funded. A young blonde man is running the site and seems experienced. The workers are afraid of him; even the Stryders keep their distance. Neith doesn't like the guy or the situation." Spyder raised an eyebrow. Both men understood following your gut.

"Talon should continue to survey the archeological location under surveillance while Neith tracks the blonde. He is not to be out of her sight."

"No word from Riven and Poe for two days. Fezz sent a team to find a trail this morning. Last confirmed position is Marmaris, Turkey." Spyder glanced up, searching his expression. "No way is this a coincidence. Basil and Devlin are inquiring about Sebastian in the same area. Too much interest in Marmaris? Should I have Bardot and Serket look up old friends and find out who has been stopping by?"

Even as Spyder spoke, Malik's mind filled with memories. Marmaris had been important for a long time. For some reason, Isabeau continually returned to the beginning.

"Find them. We lose no more of our own. Send an additional team for safety purposes. Who's left?"

"Rail and Valkyrie will be dispatched immediately." Spyder continued to jot down notes from the conversation. Malik waited for him to get back to the reports, his mind wandering to Marmaris.

I once loved Turkey as well. Isabeau, with her alabaster flawless skin and ebony colored hair falling straight down to her hips. She sat on the second floor of a Russian Tea House overlooking the bay. Mid-March, the rainy season made the day blustery and brooding. The ocean burst over the levee in violent, white waves eating up the streets.

Alone in the back of the pub, Isabeau waited with a steaming cup of coffee hugged tightly between her hands. She scowled as the mug touched her lips.

Peyton, Trystan, and I filed in descending on a table too small for the lot of us. Laughter and tall tales of which brigades had accomplished and surpassed their goals swirled around the room like steam.

"Malik, how should I direct them to proceed?" The question drew him back to the present. Relief sped through Malik's body. Memories of Isa and the rest needed to be left in the past.

"Advise them to explore the area for the symbol or anything similar. Distribute copies and instruct the teams to search for variations as well. The city has ties to other cultures. I would bet at least one figure is present."

Spyder turned to the computer screens and began tapping on the keyboard.

"Malik." Delaney's voice sounded in his head.

"I'll be back." He wandered out of the office, heading for her location.

A minute later, he stood next to her. He stopped to look about the space, sucking in a deep breath.

Delaney experienced his frustration as he exhaled.

"Oh, you've been busy." He sounded shocked. "What's all this?" Malik mumbled as he looked around the room.

Three backpacks sat by the door, ready to go. Malik had figured she wouldn't be well enough yet to be this prepared.

"I told you I would be ready to leave. I'm going to ask Calliope to take my stuff down to the garage for me in a little while." Delaney carefully sat down on her bed.

"What did Mom say?" She struggled with dizziness and had to hold her breath for a few seconds, for the nausea to pass. Though no way Delaney was about to admit this to him, she hadn't healed enough to travel, let alone stage an attack. Her health would be his excuse for not letting her go and she refused to give him one.

"I haven't spoken to your mother yet." Malik sighed, then sat down next to her.

Delaney exhaled. Dark circles encased her eyes. She had fallen down on the bed from exhaustion, and it hadn't escaped Malik's notice. Delaney wanted him to believe she was fine and he didn't have the heart to call her on the matter.

"You are going to talk to her, right?" Her voice shook.

"I will. I accept how much you need your dad home, but I can't let you put yourself in a position to be captured or killed. Bannan wouldn't want you to die on his behalf." Malik glanced away.

She didn't realize not coming back was the least of how awful it could be should she fall into Isabeau's custody.

"This is important to me. If the situation were reversed and I was lost, my dad would find me. Don't you understand? He would search for me with or without your help." Her voice quivered.

Malik's hands gripped the mattress with white-knuckled fists. He gritted his teeth so harshly she heard the grinding. "I won't let you go. I have no way to protect you. Every time you're away from me, you almost die. I can't be everywhere you are once we're on the mountain. I am responsible for many things. What if I lost track of you?"

Malik pushed up off the bed and went to stand by the window.

Guilt seized her. *Will he forgive me for the betrayal? I want to be honest and confide in him, to tell him the plan and beg him to come with me as my friend, though I comprehend why I cannot.*

"Trystan is determined to track him. He won't stop until they are all home. You don't understand. We have rules we live by...a code. None of them will come back until the three of them are found." Malik wanted her to accept his logic and thought the only way was to tell her why.

"Trystan, Peyton, and I...we are family. The distance he has to take this isn't material, Trystan will find them. No one could search as hard as we would for one another." His back still faced her.

He peered through the window, wishing everything were different.

"I'm sorry. I wasn't aware of how close your relationship with them was." He tried to do the right thing by everyone and she was about to drug and ditch him for all of his selfless work.

Both intertwined in impossible situations. Should Delaney refuse to go, the odds of her sisters succeeding would drop. She couldn't out them and disclose their plan, but she didn't want to betray Malik's trust any further.

What do I do?

"I need them to be safe as much as you do." He sounded sad.

"Can we drop this argument for tonight?" When no response was offered, Malik turned to stare at Delaney. "Did you hear me?"

"What did you say?"

"I asked if we can avoid a disagreement for tonight? I don't want to fight with you."

The way he made the request encouraged her to surrender. She flew off the bed and straight into him before he could consider withdrawing the offer. Cinnamon swirled around them in a thick cloud as they stood tangled in each other.

Malik pulled her so close, he crushed the life right out of her. He wanted to experience every curve of her body and each breath she took. Another memory he could sear into his mind for later. His head rested on the top of hers. He inhaled deeply and tugged her closer still.

Being held tightly by him became a deep sigh of relief. For some reason, Delaney discovered hope and solace inside the cradle of his arms. She encountered something in him no one had ever offered, more than a safe harbor, more than a tender embrace. Within him rose a future she longed for.

Delaney weighed the situation and realized she couldn't make everyone happy, but she must try to keep them alive.

"I want us to have a new beginning." Delaney breathed into his chest.

"I'm fighting you to keep you here so we can figure things out between us. If we go to Mount Hood, one or both of us might not be coming back. I can't lose you now, not after I have watched you leave me before. Be patient. We'll find your father. I'm the best tracker the Kindreds have, if I think I can help, I won't hesitate to," He whispered into her ear.

Delaney shivered at how his breath caressed her skin. His scent danced in her nose. A shiver ripped down her body and Malik reacted without thought. The coconut and lime shampoo mixed with the Juniper encircled his senses, gradually coming alive under the images and the memories he couldn't stop from flooding his mind.

The night could be frosty cold deep in the arid canyon, and with little to build a fire, the chill embodied them. The parched sandy region was known for playing tricks like this. The near infertile ground gave the illusion that the sand knows no reprieve from the scorching summertime heat. But of course, it does and, when darkness falls in early spring, the warmth of the desert is nothing more than a pleasant memory. The wind howled across the smooth face of the elevated summit like a banshee awaiting the dead she had come for. The frigid temperatures were carried on swift reptilian wings.

I fought the darkness for as long as possible. Spots danced in front of tired eyes rolling around in my head as I searched for a safe place for us to hide. I half carried both of us to a small opening mostly hidden by fallen rocks. The space offered some shelter from the environment. The cave was dark, dank, yet luckily, not filled with any scorpions or snakes. The drop in temperature ensured the reptiles were still hibernating. The small mouth expanded into a deep cavern with an opening at the cap allowing moonlight to flicker down and cast an eerie glow.

We sat next to each other, her head on my shoulder, mine balanced on the top of hers. I had only meant to close my eyes and regain a little strength, but I must have passed out. I awoke to a warm curvy cocoon around me. Delaney had crawled back into my lap, her body burrowing into me. Delaney shivered and I wrapped about her.

"Malik, where are we?" Delaney breathed the words across his neck.

"No idea. We made a run from the Stryders. There was a car accident and we headed off on foot. We limbed halfway up The Prince of Darkness when you lost your footing and slid back down. You must have smacked your head while falling, because as I got to the bottom, you tried to bash in my skull with a rock." She shivered and Malik felt the swell of her breasts pressed hard against his chest.

She squirmed in his lap and the friction added to the unbearable aching that seemed a permanent fixture in his life. The coconut lime shampoo wafted up to his nostrils, his body stirred underneath hers.

His brain clouded with memories.

"Sorry." The hint of humor unmistakable and even though her laughter came at his expense, Malik smiled.

"Um, Tryst took Calliope and continued on to go for help. I was too disorientated to continue on, so now we're stuck. I tried to drift a little while ago, but I haven't healed enough to travel yet." Malik's head balanced on the rocky wall behind them. His vision swam through a sea of stars.

"I have been incapacitated for a while, I'm not sure how long." Malik could barely stand when he had gotten them to the shelter. Once he had succeeded in laying her safely on the ground, he must have collapsed beside her.

"What do we do now?" Her lips hovered over his skin. Another shiver

Bent, Not Broken

ripped up his spine as warmth spread throughout him.

"Don't worry, Delaney. I'll always keep you safe—" Malik barely stopped before 'or I'll die trying' busted out.

He kept his eyes closed and tried to remember all those feelings he was experiencing.

"Malik, I'm not afraid. I'm always safe with you." Her teeth grazed his chest. The sensation made him jump. He had grown hard from her sitting on his lap. Now, the bugle had become a painful erection straining against his zipper.

"Delaney." Her name became a throaty growl on his lips.

"Mmmmm." She nipped again, her tongue darted out and skimmed from his ear downward.

The breath caught in his throat. "You called me by my name."

"You're right, I did." She giggled softly as relief barreled through him.

"I was dazed as you descended to the bottom of the face. I didn't recognize you from the angle. When I saw you lying flat on your back, the past came alive and our life rushed into my head." Delaney kissed along the tender skin of his neck. She shifted her weight and faced him.

"I like being on top." Delaney mumbled as her mouth teased his. The joke becoming painfully funny.

I was in her bed. My hands have roamed her body. But she was a virgin and I wouldn't take that from her unless I could be sure she understood being with her was more than sex for me. I wanted her, all the things that made her who she was. Delaney had become something I couldn't resist, nor did I want to. Without her, the reasons for basic survival appeared senseless. I will force myself to perform the day to day as Dane did, but it would never be living without her.

She is more beautiful than any woman I have ever seen. Long blonde hair falling down her back like a river of honey. Eyes the color of milky chocolate.

"I missed you." Malik uttered breathlessly against her mouth.

"Am I fusing this time?" Delaney pulled back and spoke excitedly. Her eyes grew wide and an enormous smile claimed her lips.

"I don't know…trauma might account for your reactions. The binding may have been damaged when you hit your head."

Please, don't let it be the injuries. Allow the transformation to begin. I need her back dammit, just give her to me. To raise either of our hopes seemed cruel; they had been dashed in the past before, but hope was all I had.

Regretfully, painfully, I set her beside me. How much I needed her occupied my every thought. Her body right there, yet I understood once I started kissing her, I wouldn't be able to stop, nor would she ever deny me what I wanted.

"What's wrong?" Her voice sounded so unsure. Malik sent her too many mixed signals and felt ashamed. She had witnessed his erection and knew he wanted her.

"I'm going to scout out the area and see if I can figure out where we are. Stay in the cave. I'll check back every fifteen to twenty minutes." Malik turned to escape her.

"You're leaving me?" The hurt echoed off the cavern walls and punched Malik in the chest.

"No, I'm not abandoning you. I need to figure out how lost we are and if the Stryders are still searching for us." Dark spots dotted his vision and he swayed. He leaned into the wall, catching himself before he went down.

"Really? Are you crazy? You can barely stand up. Sit down until you are up to moving around. Should you suffer any more injuries, we're both dead."

Malik needed to wait.

"Have you changed your mind about us? Don't try to bail on me because of the sex thing. I want to be with you."

"You are mistaken." Malik sagged against the rock, then lowered himself slowly.

"Why are you running from me?" Delaney pinned him with a glare.

"Delaney, let the topic go." Malik hoped to silence her with his hostile tone. He didn't have the strength to do this right now.

"Like hell, I will. We have gotten close before. You act as if you desire me. Has something changed? Did you meet someone?" Delaney whispered the last question as her eyes fell away.

Bent, Not Broken   275

Malik hadn't given much thought to their situation from her perspective. As she is locked up in her head, he remains awake. Delaney had no clue what she may wake up to next, when the binding gave way. Time passed while she lived another life. Malik never realized how tortured she was.

"You will not lose me. The idea is ridiculous… impossible. I want no one else. I love you, Delaney. You are everything to me." Malik's eyes pled with her.

"I have so little of you. And if I'm not fusing—" Delaney's voice broke and tears streamed down her face. "I lose you again. What if it takes too long…and you move on? You can't keep going on without someone and I can't ask you to wait for me. You have no idea when I'm coming back. You're lonely and I am the reason. How can I bring you happiness?"

Malik pulled her into his arms and held her. He let his hands smooth her hair from her cheek and he wiped the tears away from her eyes.

"Delaney, I'm used to being alone. I can survive. Besides, while you're gone, it's not really living because I'm just waiting for you to arrive. Until you, there has never been another person like you. Casual sex isn't anything more than a bodily function. I passed time until you arrived. I need no one else. It's been you since…before I knew you existed." Malik placed a tender kissed on her lips, trying to sooth the fears and self-doubt.

"What's wrong with me? Why am I not changing? I wish for the transition. I don't want to leave again." She cried into his shoulder. Delaney's fingers dug into his arms.

How tight would we need to hold on to stay where we are?

"I hate the waiting too. Your transformation will happen. We have to be patient. I love you and my feelings are not going to change. Ever." Malik wondered if he were lying to her or to himself.

All Malik had was hope, but even optimism was quickly fading with each passing year she didn't fuse.

"You believe I will keep you safe, right?" Malik pulled her chin up to see her face. "Believe I will keep your heart protected as well." An uncomfortable silence smothered the space.

Delaney stared at the gritty dirt floor and tried to understand. "What is it like with her?"

"Who?"

"The other me."

"She's every bit of you. Once you fuse, the memories will merge and you are still going to be you. We'll work through the technical difficulties. Who cares? We'll have forever to figure us out. I'll have you, nothing else matters to me."

She collapsed into him.

Moments like these were fleeting and he tried to deny his exhaustion. He wanted to hold on to her and the moment, make them both last as long as he could. Malik's head hurt, he was hungry, thirsty, uncomfortable as hell, and happier than he had been in months. Their breathing evened out and soon they slept a peaceful sleep.

"Malik." The whisper bounced around in his mind. His eyes fought to open.

Delaney sat in his lap, again pressing herself against his chest. Malik liked waking up with her in his arms. She pulled her legs over and straddled him, nuzzling his neck with warm kisses. Malik's hands rested on her thighs. The breath caught in her throat, forcing out a whistling noise.

Malik shook his head trying to wake up as blazing fever wrapped about his groin. The heat from her pierced through his jeans to coil around him. She ground herself down hard on his growing erection and he swelled with excitement. Malik groaned in appreciation. His rigid length jerked up in response as she began grinding against him in a slow rhythm. She rounded her back, pushing her legs farther apart to press her core to him.

Her breasts rested so close, he lowered his lips and took one of her nipples into his mouth through her shirt. Delaney gasped and arched higher, threading her fingers into Malik's hair to cradle his face and force him farther into her.

His hand slipped under her top and kneaded the other breast. She pulled at his jeans. Malik latched on her nipple with his teeth, biting the tip. His tongue stroked the growing peak while she moaned and rocked back and forth, pressing herself down hard against his body.

Bent, Not Broken   277

Malik's hands devoured her skin. Slowly, he rolled her hardened point between his fingers. The heat coming from the inside of her thighs made him jerk. He had to touch her. Malik caught her half closed eyes clouded with need. She licked her lips and kissed him.

The moment was being conjured from pure lust. Pent up passion erupted within them.

"Delaney…you…" Malik tried to talk while her tongue slid over his.

Her hand mapped his chest and across his trembling stomach. Her finger dipped down and traced the crown. The bead of moisture sat on top was now being worked around with her fingers.

"No stopping." Delaney whispered as she undid the button and slipped her hand down his shaft. It had been so long since he had been touched, Malik almost lost it in her grip.

Her palm felt lava hot and she held him tight. When she released him, Malik nearly shouted "don't stop."

I needed her withering and begging for more until she was satiated. I will be burned right into her memories even with the binding still intact. I demanded my name be stamped on every inch of her. Her taste on my lips, so when this night ends I am able to relive how incredible her orgasm was. I could take my cock in my hands like she was touching me and imagine her there while I cum alone. I wanted to pull her down and plunge deep inside her until I lost myself in her beautiful perfection. I needed her wet and out of control so she would be too busy to dwell on the temporary pain. She needed to be in the same frenzy overtaking me.

Delaney slid back to straddling him, took hold of his erection, and rose up enough to push herself down on him. A definitive need to fill her swallowed up every single thought of resistance.

I required her to want me as much as I always desired her.

She fed his tip inside of her and all rational thoughts fell out of his brain.

Her body was incredible. The feel of her… I wanted to drive up, into her. It took such self-control not to pull her beneath me and pump my hips into her until

I exploded.

She had become so wet, she glided down. Malik grabbed her weight and tried to make sure she went down slowly. Her eyes held his in a vise grip, never breaking contact as she raised up and then slid down.

Malik saw the flash of pain cross her face and froze. After a few seconds, she exhaled and pushed farther down until their bodies were flush to one another. He couldn't have looked away if he'd wanted to. Delaney scooped her hips under and pulled up, rocking her body back while taking him in again. He grabbed her around the waist, tried to force her to stop moving.

"I don't want to hurt you. Give yourself time to get used to me. I want this to last." Malik convulsed upward.

"Malik." His name slammed him back into the moment. He realized where he was. They sat on the edge of the mattress and Delaney straddled him; the two points so close they submerged into one for him.

Malik couldn't recall how they had gotten to the bed. He stared at her for a long time.

Finally, I realize you are meant to be mine and I will fight to keep you by my side.

Malik had tried to wait until her memory came back, but here she was, like the first time.

At this moment, I'm weak. I'm so lonely for her.

Her fragrance, a rich aroma dancing his senses into a frenzy. Her hands tangled in his hair, she kissed him. Her tongue ran across the seam of his lips. The tiny bit of self-control he had left vanquished in an instance.

"I am lost in you, Delaney Drake. I used to think the waiting was the hardest part. Being with you every day and—you had no idea…complicated torture. I wanted to be a part of your life. I needed you to see me, to remember me. Turns out that had been the easiest part of my existence. Every time I was forced to let you go after I knew what we were like together nearly destroyed me."

Bent, Not Broken

In a few hours, Delaney would realize he lied about taking her to find her father. Delaney was tenacious and unforgiving. She might never let the betrayal go. This would become another obstacle to overcome.

Malik made this decision time and time again, but his choice never got easier. He had to put her safety foremost, even over his desire to have her. A growing part of Malik wanted to be selfish and take Delaney away from there. He wondered how much longer he could deny his instinct on how to keep her safe.

"Don't push me away," she murmured.

Malik heard words that had been voiced before. As if he would ever let her go.

"All directions guide me to you. I get that now. Whatever is between us is absolutely not going to let me go and I never want you to." Malik waited for her declaration of love, though acknowledgement refused to yield.

An uncertainty resided where none had been prior.

Chapter
TWENTY-SEVEN

"Malik." The voice breezed through his head, taking him back to the night they said good-bye the last time.

The Kindreds should be closing on their location. Delaney was close and I wanted her to finish while I remained inside her, before our lives returned to our version of normal.

Tryst found us, Delaney laying naked in my arms. I moved to conceal her from being seen by Tryst as he entered the cave. He figured out what had transpired, but kept the information between the two of us.

"Malik," Tryst stood off to one side, "we need to talk. You have to give her up. This isn't the first time, right?"

Malik shook his head in stoic silence. They had already drifted back to the relative safety of the Drake residence. Delaney was in the kitchen with her Vivianna and Joss.

"I'm sorry, man. I understand what you are going through."

Malik's anger peaked, emotion raged, and Tryst was the only thing in the direct line of fire.

"No, you don't. At no time have you ever had to give Calliope up. Had to let her go, when all you want is to keep her. By the end of the day, she will stare right through me like I've never existed. Again. A few hours ago, we…" As soon as the words left his mouth, he regretted them.

"Calliope has no idea I have feelings for her. She's too young and immature. So, I do understand." Tryst walked away without another word.

Malik went to find Delaney. Joss had already seen her.

Maybe this is how our life is supposed to turn out.

He had been too late to stop the inevitable. Malik surveyed Delaney from the shadows of her room. Tears coursed down her cheeks as she curled into a ball. Her petite figure shook from the sobs.

Malik had made the crazy relationship work so far, and he would continue to as long as he knew she fought to get back to him. He realized how lucky he was, seeing her every day was better than the alternative and being without her was unacceptable.

"I'll be here when you wake up," Malik whispered to her. "I love you. Find your way back to me."

Delaney slumped against him, relaxing further with each passing breath. She fought for a few seconds, twitching and moaning softly. But the finality set in and all was quiet except for the tornado of emotions spiraling through Malik.

A fierce raw energy ran within his body. His hands trembled, teeth ground tight until his jaw ached, his mind struggled with thoughts of the past and hopes for an uncertain future. The waiting by her side, the stillness while she slept like the dearly departed, and the moment reminded him of watching someone you love die. As the spirit fluttered from their body, he experienced the most profound sense of loss, of being lost himself. Her breathing shallowed, her heart slowed, and her mind began the process of forgetting all about the two of them.

Malik held her for hours. Until he was cutting it too close and she could wake up and find him beside her. He carefully pried himself from her, pushed off the bed, and stood staring down at her. The worry lines had disappeared from about her eyes and she seemed peaceful. The juncture was too hard to live with.

Delaney sat perched on Malik's lap, wondering where his thoughts had taken him. Questions filled her head and she tried to force herself doubt far, far away. With only a few hours until they put their plans in motion, she feared this time would be all she had left with him.

Her worry over betraying him and him not being able to understand and forgive her for it, made her want this moment to be the most perfect she could create for the two of them. A pinball game played under her surface, every touch ricocheting into a jolt of electricity. The sensations rippled through the entire length of her.

His lips were soft and when she opened her mouth, his tongue searched for hers. With one simple connection, her body came alive as if his hands had already begun roaming her torso. His kisses had a direct line to each nerve ending and as they blazed a distinct path down her skin, she combusted like wildfire.

She threaded her fingers into his silky hair, using the strands as leverage to bring him closer still. Delaney marveled at every line and curve her palms ran over. The powerful, dangerous assassin who had probably murdered more people than she could count was tender when he touched her, creating a pooling heat and an aching need deep within her. She wanted to be lying naked beneath him, to enjoy his body pressed against her.

She sucked in a shallow breath while he stared at her for a long moment.

The need to tell Malik she loved him became so strong. The simple phrase didn't seem to convey her feelings though. "I love you" was never going to be enough. All the emotions swirling and seething in her were more powerful than three simple words.

She had found her way this far, to be here with him, he should understand she was trying to find the way back home. Delaney accepted they had been here before. She believed him when he said the two of them were together, and sensed the truth of his word in everything she did. She was familiar with him intimately, in ways only a lover understood.

"Delaney, you ask too much of me. If we begin, I can't stop. I'm sorry. But I want…I need to be lost in you." Again Malik tried desperately to pull her free of him, before his arms hopelessly fell to his sides.

Delaney wrapped her legs tightly around him, defiance cemented in her posture. The expression on her face told him he could fight this conflict all he wanted, and he would lose at every turn. His pensive stare met hers, the strain of his emotions shown in the tight set of his jaw.

Delaney saw the fierce battle being waged inside him. Malik explored her eyes for some trace of emotion other than lust, but couldn't find what he searched for. He wanted her, but he needed her love.

Delaney shivered and his body sprang to life. This scene, so similar, had occurred once before. He wondered, if everything about them was destined in some form or another to be repeated. Even how they made love seemed to be preordained.

"Wait, this is not a good idea." He tried to escape. Malik sat unmoving with jagged breaths as his only sign of life. He began to tremble; Delaney knew his control teetered on a slippery slope.

"You always want to save me, and then save me for yourself." She receded and without hesitation grabbed his hands and brought them between her thighs. Her skin was burning through the material of her pants.

Delaney was trembling. The only heaven Malik had ever known was separated from him by cotton. His angel sat on his lap, hot and wet.

One of his hands moved around to the small of Delaney's back, though his gaze never left hers. Slowly his fingers worked up her spine until he reached her ponytail and worked the scrunchy out. He fisted her hair, pulling her head back with enough force to prove his self-control had truly vanished. Her shield fell down around her and for once, she didn't want to hide herself behind anything, not from him.

No clear thoughts held her mind; her whole existence revolved around his touch.

Malik ran his fingertips slowly over the cloth covering her already slick center. Delaney gasped when he pressed his finger against her. A moan escaped her mouth as her head fell forward. She trembled, her eyes at half-mast, glowing like rich emeralds with a fire he wanted to match. She gasped.

He moved his palm back and forth over her. The provocative display was more intense than anything she remembered experiencing. The rush of emotion coupled with the flare of pleasure slammed into her. Malik pulled tighter on the grip he had on her hair and deepened his kiss.

Delaney's nails scored his shoulder as her body jerked. Delaney tried to hold on as the sensations rocked through her insides.

"Beautiful Delaney, do you know what you are doing to me? You are playing with a fire that will consume us both." His finger slowly found their way inside her sleep shorts and pushed inside of her. He withdrew them only to drive back inside to her velvety softness.

Her eyes fell closed as she reveled in just how good it felt.

He is mine, the prospect resonated though her.

"Say you want me. I need to hear the words come from you." He nipped his way down her collarbone.

"I...I want you, Malik." Words spoken through broken breaths and cloudy thoughts.

"Look at me. Don't turn away." His eyes glowed a deep, brilliant emerald green.

Delaney couldn't pull her gaze from him.

The flames lapped at her with each slip of his fingertips. His other hand traced a scorching path across her rib cage, finally laying his hot palm against her breast. Delaney arched into his kneading touch.

"I'm with you. I've never been anywhere else." Delaney clutched at him out of a deep-seeded fear that she would never have the opportunity to do this again.

Her eyes flickered with something he couldn't identify and disappeared to soon.

Please, don't let me leave. Delaney wanted to shout at him. She tried to pull him closer. Delaney had this moment, this very second, and maybe this was all she was ever going to have with him after tonight.

She fought her shame. The emotion had to wait until tomorrow.

"Are you crying?" Malik stiffened and tried to pull back to face Delaney as his hands froze in their exploration.

She had to push the disgraceful feelings away. It was an act of pure selfishness on her part. Delaney knew he loved her and she was about to betray it, whether she wanted to or not.

Finally, they would have their moment and she reveled in it. She couldn't let him see her face, not until she concealed what was going on in her head.

Cruel, crazy laughter echoed through her head. What Delaney wanted the most in her life but had been reluctant to search for was right here. *Someone to find me beautiful, interesting, and formidable and he does. To him, I am already more than all the things everyone else was ever aware of.*

With trembling fingers, she finally got the nerve to push back and stared at him.

"Are you sure?"

"Don't stop."

Delaney grabbed the edge of her t-shirt and pulled the fabric up over her head. She needed to be bold, to take control of the only thing she had been allowed to—her own actions at this moment.

His gaze burned right through her bra and caressed her skin. He wanted to devour her. Malik had become beyond hungry for her.

Delaney wished to experience his reaction as he looked at her. She slid her hands around and unhooked the clasps. Anchoring her eyes to his as the material fell into her lap, she studied his every response. She considered him with absolute fascination.

He took her nipple between his fingers and rolled it slowly between them.

The pleasure shot straight through her. Malik's hips jerked upward and he sucked in a deep breath. His fingers tortured Delaney's nipples into taut crests and her spine arched. Air sat trapped in her throat as the pleasure seemed to increase with each subtle movement of his hands.

They examined each other. The closeness created an intimacy holding them in place, connecting them beyond touching.

Malik leaned closer until his breath tickled her chin. His tongue slid across her bottom lip as they parted for him.

He stood up abruptly, though he never released her lips.

Malik waited no longer.

His fingers crawled around to Delaney's back as her legs slid down to the ground. His shaft settled hard against her belly. Her knees wavered as he clutched her closer.

"Are you sure? I can still stop, if you want." His voice strained as if he were at his breaking point.

Without a word, she grasped for his jeans and undid the button, pulling down the zipper. His erection pushed forward. She stared at him. Confusion filled her eyes as they reached for his. She wasn't sure how to touch him.

Malik took her hand and wrapped her palm around his shaft just below the head. Delaney hesitated and glanced up at him, waiting as the air vacated her lungs in a burning sigh.

"Please, touch me," he whispered hoarsely.

Delaney took his length in both hands and squeezed gently. A shiver ripped up his body. She peeked up and found him staring at her hands, mesmerized by what she did to him.

He pushed up between her clenched fingers and drew in a harsh breath. How much he wanted her became incredibly empowering. Delaney's confidence grew as he trembled. He thrust up through her hand again; Delaney tightened her grip this time.

"Delaney." He rasped her name. Even his voice had become erotic.

He pushed at the top of her pants, hesitating for a second. Delaney let the

Bent, Not Broken   287

material fall to the floor. He nearly tore his clothes from his body, though his hungry eyes never left her.

Malik stopped and just examined her. Shyness swept over her as his eyes moved slowly over every inch of her body. He fell back on the bed, dragging her on top of him. His palm claimed one breast, kneading hard. His tongue traced warm circles around her nipple until he bit at it.

She climbed astride his body, taking him in her hands once more. She slid slowly down on his length. His eyes were locked on hers as he inched his way farther in.

"Okay?" He choked the question out.

Delaney shook her head yes. Words couldn't have made it out; she was biting her lip to keep from crying out. Delaney wanted to scream with how good he felt moving within her. Her body trembled with each sensation. When he was seated fully within her, he paused.

"Don't stop," she gasped between shallow breaths.

"Impossible." His voice faltered. He swiftly rolled her on her back. They stared at each as he started to move inside her with gentle thrusts.

He dropped a kiss on her lips as he pulled back from her warmth. He was already so close to the edge, he wouldn't last through much more. Lost in their rhythm, she matched him thrust for thrust. Her nails dug in to his shoulders as the pressure erupted within her. Her legs still firmly wrapped around his waist contracted, pulling him closer.

Their pace came faster as she experienced his erection thickening against her walls, stretching the snug harbor. She cried out softly as the sensation reached a peak and clenched him tighter. Delaney was dizzy and panting as bliss spread throughout her body. She studied his expression as he spent himself inside her, and a wildfire tore through her. It was erotic to watch him take such pleasure from her.

He crushed her to his chest and she bit his shoulder to keep from crying out. Her legs pulled him closer. His hips continued softly pushing into her as they lay together, tangled and content.

"My heaven," he mumbled to himself softly, but she caught it.

The thought warmed her further.

"You'll remember me this time." He breathed against her ear, a gentle stream of laughter hung from his breath.

"I'm not sure how the hell it was possible to forget you."

After a few minutes, Malik pulled himself up and stared at Delaney. He smiled as he looked at her face, then traveled down to his body. "You are perfect in every way."

Delaney was overcome by his words, the feelings, and the understanding that she was beyond in love with him.

He couldn't stop looking at her. Malik found every inch of her beautiful and already wanted to claim her again.

Malik stood and took in how perfect her body was to him.

"I love you, Delaney." His voice was barely a whisper. "Don't move."

He slipped on his pants, quietly cracked the door, checked the hallway, and snuck out. He came back a few minutes later with a wet washrag. He cleaned her thighs and gently wiped between them. She shivered as his hands pressed against her sensitive flesh. A tear slipped down the side of her face.

"Did I hurt you?"

"No."

"Don't cry. This is the beginning." He caressed her cheek with his fingers after he wiped the teardrop away.

"What the hell?" The scream echoed through the house and startled them.

"Mom!" Brody screamed again.

"I'm so sorry." He pulled Delaney upright.

They yanked on their clothes and ran for Brody. Malik raced after Delaney as she reached the bottom of the stairs. Once Brody was in sight, Delaney fell down beside her. She held Brody's hand while she screamed in pain.

"Brody, let me see." Viv was trying to force her to lie still.

She was on the ground flopping around like a fish out of water. Muted black symbols resembling floating clouds covered Brody's legs just under the skin. Brody kept grabbing at her lower back. Viv pulled up Brody's shirt and found something forming in an intense, deep, dark purple with a blue center and hot pink tips. The emblem wasn't any symbol. This particular character was comparable to Viv's. Swirls marked each of the three intersecting ends.

"What the hell is it?" Viv stared at the mark.

"It's stinging like a burn," Brody screamed.

Delaney sat staring at the entwining marks.

We are all being pulled into the eye of the storm. Not that Delaney believed solely in destiny, but it was damn hard to argue with at the moment.

Delaney thought about what just happened between them only moments ago. She glanced at Malik and his eyes were already on her. The butterflies fluttered through her stomach. She still felt him buried deep. It took a long time for their eyes to let go of one another's.

"It's….Brody, you need to hide this until we can find out more. Do you have any additional symbols similar to this one?" Viv had taken over talking.

Malik stood there, confused.

"Fezz." Malik moved away to stand in the hall.

"That is comparable to the symbol I faxed to the other guards. She's an element of this now, right? A bigger component than anyone assumed she'd be. Where does that leave us?" Malik paced the small hallway as he ran his fingers through his hair.

"She goes nowhere without you. If she has a problem with that, handcuff her to the bed." Malik commanded as he turned his attention back to Viv.

"Are all of the girls marked? But why? They aren't blood, why…how are they being chosen?" Viv was thinking out loud the same question Malik entertained in his own head. "Malik, I need to talk to you concerning the boxes from Turnberry. Lots of maps, some weapons, drawings that appear to be underground aqua ducts, and some family lineage papers that catalog not only Amalgamates but Doux-La-Roux, Benders, Pikes, Shells, Routers, and Rainers. Some of those I have never even heard of.

"How far back in history are the Styders searching? What could they want with the long dead?"

"Malik…." Viv's voice trailed off.

Malik quickly walked up to stand next to her. She sat stunned, with her mouth agape and eyes wide open.

"They are hunting for Relics. Caleb's inquiring about their sanctuaries after they were disbanded and fled their homes. Some must have headed north." Vivianna's voice softened.

"He wants something they had," Malik mumbled. "But what?"

"And why the Northwest? Caleb is exploring entire ancient sites trying to piece it together. What did the Relic have that would mean anything to Caleb?" Vivianna tilted her head as her mind worked through the clues.

"Isabeau and Caleb wanted the Stellar to narrow down the possibilities. They are chasing ghosts. A symbol at Mount Hood, but nothing more. They don't know that you have the correlating figures. The Stryders are searching for a way to find the exact locations."

"They search for the maps. We already have them; it's the girls and I. We must be…a type of key. If Isabeau and Caleb figure this out, there won't be a safe place to hide us, ever. What the hell do we do now?" Vivianna again spoke words that were already spinning around in Malik's head.

Flashes of understanding hit him.

"The Spirit People were never known to have traveled as far north as that. Why should the Relics have?" Vivianna continued.

"Calliope, will you help Brody up so Fezz can take a picture of the mark. We need to get it to the other Kindreds as soon as possible. They should search for specific symbols." Malik stopped. "Viv, the night Isabeau came to take out Delaney, she said 'Delaney showed the way.' Shit, Isabeau may as well have called her a map. They already know."

Chapter
TWENTY-EIGHT

At five p.m., they started the last supper.

Calliope, Daphne, Brody, and Delaney stood in the kitchen arguing about everything from what to cook to the dosing amount to add without killing the Kindreds and their mother. Unprepared and disorganized should have shown them how underqualified they were for a rescue operation.

Brody and Delaney almost came to blows on three separate occasions. Delaney tried to reason with Brody because she currently called all the shots. If Delaney got Brody to understand, the others would fall in line.

Calliope and Daphne acted as though Delaney had banged her head and gone crazy; they listened to her and then politely decided to ignore Delaney and her arguments. They didn't get that lying to him would cost her everything; she'd never told them just how attached she had become to him, or what had happened between them only hours earlier. Delaney kept attempting to recruit Daphne and Calliope as allies.

Calliope wanted to find Trystan so much she was one hundred percent on board and waited for no man, or sister. If Calliope had to, she would depart by herself.

Logic and reason were replaced with rage and retribution. Delaney's family was falling apart in more ways than she could count. Delaney had an appalling premonition that this was only the beginning of how terrible it might get.

Daphne wanted to retrieve their dad and the determination in the way she spoke made Delaney stop bugging her altogether.

"Delaney, would he leave you behind?" Daphne's voice held such contempt, the words bit into Delaney's skin.

"No." *But...*

The situation had become impossible. Delaney was giving up one of the two men she loved no matter which decision she made.

No-win situations are my specialty.

Delaney cried the entire time she diced peppers and onions and her assault on the veggies had nothing to do with their pungent odor. Brody, Daphne, Calliope, and Delaney watched them consume the home cooked meal and the drugs hidden inside. They listened to the compliments on their cooking and joked around exactly how dinner was supposed to be.

They lied and manipulated like professional conmen. At this fundamental moment, Delaney hated herself for being so convincing and less forthcoming.

Malik stared at Delaney while he ate. His demeanor appeared more carefree than she had ever seen.

Delaney avoided Malik's gaze. After the first few bites, she understood any chance to make things right had just been swallowed down.

The four men and Viv seemed more and more relaxed. Malik laughed and smiled, which he rarely did. Undoubtedly something weird had been going on between Flynn and Daphne. Something in the way he watched her every movement while joking and laughing beside her.

Brody continued to be mean as hell to everyone, making her part believable.

Calliope sat silently by their mother.

The night progressed according to the plan.

Delaney needed to be alone with Malik, to try to explain.

"Help me to my room?" Delaney said quietly from behind Malik.

Bent, Not Broken   293

"Of course." Malik yawned and nodded agreement to escort her, then sluggishly moved down the hallway.

The day had been a long and he was more exhausted than he was willing to admit. Malik tripped up the last stair almost knocking them both down. He smiled and shook his head.

Delaney forced her reluctant legs to move forward. She stuck as close as possible to his side.

"Here, let me help," Delaney said as she tucked herself under his shoulder.

Malik tried to resist her efforts, but his heavy limbs disagreed. He wasn't going to last as long as she had hoped. It took all Delaney's strength to get him inside her room. She dumped him on the mattress, nearly falling down on him.

"Just rest." Delaney pulled his shoes off and hauled his legs up, attempting to make him as comfortable as possible.

"Come. Be with me. Not done with you." The way he spoke made her want to turn away and hide as her breath caught in her throat.

He tried to pull Delaney down to him.

"You shouldn't worry about me. Everything's going to be fine, promise."

"My Delaney." His words were slow, slurred, almost unintelligible.

She wanted to fall into bed beside him.

"Why sad, beautiful?" Malik's sentiment brought tears scorching a path straight down her guilt-ridden face.

"Please don't be so nice to me," she whispered.

"What's goin' on?" He saw through her; she felt relieved.

"Don't be angry with me or the others. You left us no choice." She brushed the hair from his forehead.

"What have you done?" Malik's words were slurred and his eyelids flickered. Betrayal shone brightly back at her. When he glanced away in disgust, Delaney's hopes fell. "Why?"

"You had no intentions of taking me. You lied to me, to the others, buying yourself time to invent another excuse, and another after that. I knew. I gave you the opportunity to come clean, but you said nothing. How could you do that to me?" Delaney tried to sound as if her anger was justified.

In a few hours, the idea of a new beginning would be nothing more than a memory to him. Delaney had chosen her sisters over him.

"It didn't have to be this way. We could have gone together," she murmured against his lips. Delaney pulled away. "I tried to reason with them, they won't listen. They will leave with or without me. We have a better chance if I go too. I wanted to come to you and ask for help, but you lied." Delaney's anger swelled. She needed to be irate to make it easier to throw it all away.

"Wha' has you don'?" He would be unconscious soon. The flicker of love in his eyes dwindled.

Delaney had to let him go. She couldn't stand for it to be the other way around, to see him walk away from her.

"It was the chili. We put pain pills in the food. I didn't what to do it. If I let them try alone... This isn't my decision."

"Don't...go," he pulled Delaney down to him by her hair, tugging her closer until her lips sat against his. He tried to tighten his feeble grip. Malik's fist weakened, his strength waning from the drugs.

Tears flowed down her face—a river of them Delaney wished she might drown herself in.

"There's no choice for me. I am going." Her heart ached.

"You'll all die." The thought stung as if Malik had struck her. Words covered in spikes and razors shredding everything in their path, ripping at Delaney.

In an instance, she knew he was right too. It was a suicide mission. She wanted to look away, but knew she deserved to face her own actions head on.

"I...I know." In truth, she had suspected.

Fists of rage at those who had taken her father became hands clenched from anguish and hopelessness. Delaney dug her fingernails into her palms, trying to keep her pent-up emotions at bay.

"Stay. Will take you, prom..." He spoke the truth, though the moment had already passed them by.

She believed him, regretting even more that she hadn't been able to stop her sisters. He would have found a course of action to help her, even if it wasn't the way she wanted, which only saddened her further. She feared if her gaze reached his, she might disintegrate into a trillion pieces. She slowly glanced at him anyway, straight into those deep, dark, stormy eyes. The two of them were inches apart, but a million miles away from each other.

"They won't wait. They don't trust you now." All trapped by their imperfect decisions, their lack of faith and bubbling anger. "It's a trap, isn't it?"

He had been trying to tell her. Isabeau had their father, and was using him as bait.

"I'm not coming back." Delaney's words burned like blue flames colliding in her head.

"Don't come after us. There will be enough loss and death." Delaney wanted him to live, to experience happiness, even if she became excluded. "I apologize for all those things I don't remember. I grieve for their loss. I am giving you up and I hate myself."

"Can' le' you go. Love...," he slurred.

Delaney stood staring down at him, longing for a future she couldn't have. Malik fought to keep his eyes on her. He knew the next time they opened she'd be gone.

She laid down beside him, curling into him like a newly sprouted part. Delaney cried so hard his torso shook with her.

"You'll...you'll...be out soon. I'll st-stay until you're as-asleep."

She stared at him. She wanted to remember every hard line of his body and each curve and subtle plain of his face.

If he had more strength, the things Malik would do to change her mind. Delaney wouldn't leave the bed until he passed out from exhaustion and not from drugs.

"Don't come for me. Please, Malik, don't follow us."

"You smell good." His voice filled with longing.

When Delaney glanced down, he had passed out. She went to dress, load the last of her gear downstairs, and get the rope she would use to tie Malik up.

Delaney avoided the others. Daphne and Calliope tied the Kindreds to the chairs in the dining room. Brody finished packing the car. All was going according to plan.

Chapter
TWENTY-NINE

"Let's take him with us. We don't know what we're doing. This is a suicide mission, can't you understand?" Delaney's anger climbed and Brody continued to ignore her, adding fuel to her flaming temper.

"He's not coming. Did you tie him up? Do I really need to check?" Brody loaded the last of their stuff in the car.

"He's secured for right now. He'll drift when he comes to. The rope isn't going to hold him."

"Yes. The restraints will only slow him down. We gave him the largest dose. He'll be out for hours longer than the others. By the time he regains consciousness, Malik won't be able to stop us." Brody turned and faced Delaney. "We've got to go."

Reluctantly, Delaney moved into the house.

"You had no right to make me feel unimportant, you jerk." Daphne pushed Flynn's shoulder so hard his head bobbed like a doll in his unconscious state.

"Brody wants to leave. Where's Mom?" Four guards all tied up together, but no Mom.

"She's coming with us." Daphne answered.

"She's awake?" Delaney asked.

"Not exactly, I told Brody she wants Dad back too and would go along with us once we ditched these losers." Daphne sneered.

"What's going on?" Delaney stepped farther into the room.

"Nothing. Check on Malik. Make sure he is tied up tight," Calliope shot back. Delaney walked up the stairs, dread filled.

"Can you hear me?" Delaney stared down at him.

Malik appeared peaceful, still and beautiful in her bed.

Her gaze fell on the note she left tucked into the waist of his pants. In the back of her mind, she understood it was a mistake. Once he read that Delaney didn't want to leave him, he would come for her, potentially charging in and getting himself killed.

She grabbed the stationary, ripped the sheet up, and tossed the pieces in the trash.

She turned back towards the bed. She remembered his neck scar and decided to take advantage of being able to look at it closer without him withdrawing from the attention. It looked like he'd been hung. Rope-torn skin left the ripples of scar all around his neck. She couldn't bind him up after realizing that. She tossed the line to the ground and left the room thoroughly disgusted with herself for even considering the stupid idea.

"Delaney, we're leaving," Calliope called up to her.

A backward glance from the door and her chest tightened. *How do I do this without you?*

Delaney slept for a while. A haunting dream chased her from restless slumber. To be racing down the highway at eighty miles an hour with her mother passed out next to her seemed surreal.

She thought a lot about the daydream. Malik had always been a staple in her life, whether she knew the fact or not, and now he wasn't. Her nose stung from swallowing back the cries aching to come out. She fought them to appear calm.

The SUV remained quiet, and the darkness surrounding them swallowed their headlights. Each of the girls was isolated by their own demons, their every thought screaming dread and regret. Calliope bit at her fingernails until six of them were bleeding stubs. Brody gripped the steering wheel with white knuckles. Daphne crooned along with her iPod in a mournful tone devoid of hope.

"Anybody hungry? We gotta stop for gas anyway." Brody's voice shattered the silence.

No one made a noise. Food was the last thing on anyone's mind.

At the filling station, Calliope and Daphne used the bathroom while Brody filled up and got snacks. Delaney stayed with Vivianna and stared hopelessly out the window.

"Delaney, what the hell is going on?"

Delaney's mouth dropped open. "How long have you been awake?"

"No idea. Where are we?" Vivianna's voice still sounded groggy.

"I'm not sure, exactly. A couple of hours away from Mount Hood, I believe." Delaney noticed the sun was starting to dawn, its long reaching fingers crept across the sky.

"Where are the Kindreds?" Viv yawned. "And why am I tied up?"

The light filtered slowly in between Malik's heavy lids. His head ached. His tongue seemed pasted to the roof of his mouth. When he cracked his eyelids open, a mild earthquake vibrated through his brain. A ray of sunshine caught him straight in the face.

Daylight.

He couldn't move his arms or legs; they seemed weighted down by tractor trailers. Blinking didn't fully clear away the blur to everything. The soft scent of coconuts and limes wafted up from the pillow, and he relaxed and burrowed farther into the comfort of Delaney's bed. He reached for her warm body, wanting to lose himself in her lush curves.

"Delaney," he rasped her name. "Delaney." He waited. "Fezz."

"Finally. Want to come down and untie us? The little heathens drugged us and left us bound to chairs."

"Drift." *Why hadn't they drifted out of the bindings?* The situation befuddled him.

"Well, I'd love too, really. But Flynn, in his pathetic attempts to win the fair pain-in-my-ass Daphne, told her we could only drift alone or we needed water. They tied us up touching, so we're stuck. Get up, Malik, they're all gone. Viv, Brody, Daphne, Calliope, and Delaney are all MIA." Fezz's voice raised with each name.

Malik pulled himself up to a sitting position. A wave of nausea and dizziness pushed him back on his elbows. Out of the corner of his eye, he noticed a rope laying on the floor.

His mind stayed hazy, struggling with hindered awareness.

"They left me in Delaney's room." Malik drifted to stand in front of Fezz, Spyder, Flynn, and Shane with a sullen expression on his face.

"How long have they been gone?" Malik began untying the four angry Kindreds.

"Why would they tie us up?" Fezz's annoyance sounded tangible.

"We're here to help." Spyder shook his head.

"Where did they go?" Shane stood and stretched his hands out in front of him.

"To find Bannan," Spyder and Malik responded.

"I'll check LoJack on the car." Fezz walked to the office.

"It's the X-terra." Flynn yelled from the garage entry door at the far end of the kitchen.

"Brody said she was packing the car full of boxes for a homeless shelter donation. Bullshit, liars! They were planning this." Flynn picked up the chair he'd just spent at least a few hours in and threw the piece of furniture into a wall.

"They conned us. Daphne told me she was helping Brody, all the bags on their way to charity." Spyder sighed.

"The girls are smarter than we assumed. They dismantled the GPS. Best I can do is read the garage access log, which was accessed at five last night. They've been gone for over thirteen hours. Drive time to Mount Hood is... sixteen. If Brody is driving, I'd shave off at least sixty minutes...maybe more. I put them on the mountain at between seven and eight this morning. We have maybe an hour before the situation explodes." Fezz shook his head in disgust.

"They drugged Viv too—she ate with us. So why take her?" Shane stretched his arms out in front of him.

"I asked her to tell them waiting was our best option. I thought if the explanation came from her, the girls would listen, see reason." Thinking back, Malik realized it was stupid to think anything would dissuade them.

"They are very smart, the five of them working together. Didn't see that coming." Flynn's mouth formed a thin angry line.

"Tryst." Malik found Trystan had just drifted into the back room command office.

"Malik, what's going on? Why has no one been answering?"

Malik took a deep breath and explained the situation.

"Where the hell is Dash right now?" Tryst yelled. The sweet nickname he had given Calliope sounded desperate on his lips.

"No idea. They drugged us, when we woke up they were gone. If I had more information to tell you, I would. Don't you think I want to know where they are?" Malik bellowed back.

"They are on their way to you. They wanted to search the mountain for Bannan." Malik spoke through gritted teeth.

"Malik, we're not on Mount Hood." Tryst paused.

"Symbols were found at the base of the Three Sisters, Baker, and Shasta. We're scouring Rainier now. I sent teams to the Cascade Mountains. Malik, you need to find them." Tryst stormed out of the office.

"Gear up, we leave in twenty." Malik link-spoke the order as he walked down the hallway.

"They raided the office too. Maybe Viv was in on it with them. She's the only one who knows the code." Fezz stared at an empty weapons cabinet.

"Take Spyder and Shane with you to get more gear. Hurry." Fezz disappeared.

Malik doubted Viv had been a willing participant. The Kindreds underestimated what the girls might be capable of accomplishing on their own.

"Even the test items Bannan was working on are gone." The audacity filled Malik with pride and resentment. He had taught them to be prepared, to think things through, and to walk into a fight knowing the shit may go south.

They had no idea what they are going up against, though. Christos, Seeley, Isabeau, Caleb, and he didn't even know whoever else. Anger coursed through Malik and the image it conjured was of them making love the day before. He remembered standing by the window with her clinging to him, kissing him, pulling him closer. She knew then she was going to betray him and had set him up. Delaney realized he was in love with her and used his feelings against him.

I meant nothing to her. What we did represented nothing. I was a means to an end. Fool!

Malik stalked about the office, his temper flaring higher with each step. He kicked chairs out of his way.

Fuck, how could she do this?!

Finally punching a hole in the wall close to the map, he expelled some of the raw energy. The awareness of betrayal remained burning in his gut.

She used me. What angers me, is I let her do it. I made the deception possible.

"Um, I can come back, much later." Flynn turned around on his heels and strode out of the office.

"Wait. What is it?" Malik glared at the door through clenched teeth.

"I'm sorry. This is my fault. Daphne had been asking me questions. I thought she was interested in me and wanted to understand what we do. She was using me for information, even about the weapons and how to get in here. I always have to push women off of me, but it's not that way with Daphne. The one I want, doesn't want me. She set me up." Flynn picked up one of the chairs Malik had sent flying across the room and fell into the seat.

Bent, Not Broken   303

"Let the guilt go for now. We need to get them back." Malik wished he could take his own advice.

"I am a fool. I have put you in this position. I'm sorry." Flynn shook his head.

"Flynn, when they are all safe, we'll deal with them." Through narrowed eyes, Malik surveyed him.

Flynn shot him a look of apprehension, nodded and left.

Delaney and little Daphne will be lucky to leave this house ever again if they live long enough to get back. Brody will be on lock down until she reaches thirty, and Calliope, Tryst is going to kill her.

"Dane." Malik's link reached out.

"Malik," Dane answered.

Malik thought for a moment, then finally blurted out the truth.

"How long?"

"They dismantled the car's LoJack system, so we only have a time frame. Fezz ran some scenarios. He puts them on Mount Hood between seven and eight this morning. The five of us should be on point within twenty. Out."

"Leaestra."

"Malik."

"I need you back running communications at the Drake's."

"Copy that."

"Here." Fezz handed Malik his gear.

"Drift to the southeast base. With no direct roads leading after the highway, this position is our best bet," Malik said. "Okay, we are changing things up a bit. Spyder and Shane go after Viv. Fezz, you take Brody. Flynn, find Daphne. I'll search for Calliope and Delaney. Activate your beacons immediately. Leaestra will be running point from here." Malik pulled on his pack.

"Once there, split up into groups of two. Radio silence until you have a visual. There are eyes on the mountain, so the minute we drift, Isabeau will know. Don't forget Isabeau is a Traveler. Your fuses are useless against her." Malik drifted out of sight, and every member followed.

The trees stopped direct sunlight from reaching the forest floor, so they appeared in the shadows. Without a word, each man started off in a direction. Once their targets were located, they would drift to them. Malik hunched down as he moved to keep hidden in the underbrush while trying to avoid pinecones littering the ground like pebbles.

Am I still so angry I would try to hurt her? Or do I just do my job and walk away from her when this is all over?

"We drugged them and bound them up. Daphne and Brody decided to bring you along at the last moment, otherwise you'd be tied up with them." Delaney stared through the window at Brody pumping gas.

"Why are you crying?"

At first, Delaney didn't say a word. "I tried to talk them out of this. I wanted to get Brody to bring Malik along, but she refused. I lied to him, conned him, and left him. Malik will hate me for what I did." Tears slipped free and barreled down Delaney's face.

"He's going to be beyond mad at you, all of you." Viv sighed.

"You don't understand. I…" Delaney fell silent.

"Oh, you're in love with him." Viv shook her head as she realized the problem.

"He'll never forgive me for this. I set him up. He'll know the minute he wakes up." Delaney stopped talking when she heard the click of the door handle.

"Brody, Daphne, and Calliope Drake, get your butts in here," Viv's voice boomed out of the car.

Everyone filed back into the vehicle without a word.

"What the hell were you all thinking? You tied them up. How can they get to you if you need them? Do you even understand the chances you are taking?" Viv yelled as Brody pulled away from the snack shack.

"If you out us and call for anyone or give up our location, we'll stop and leave you in a bathroom," Calliope lashed out. "Trystan and Dad are out on the mountain. We're going to get them back. You can either help us or sit it out." Calliope didn't sound like any part of the sister Delaney knew.

"Calliope!" Vivianna exclaimed in pure shock.

"I want Dad and Trystan back, don't you?" Everyone fell silent at Calliope's question. She had just backed all of them into a corner.

"How much farther?" Vivianna asked.

"About an hour, according to the map," Daphne answered. "Are you hungry or thirsty?"

"Is anyone aware you have all escaped?"

"No." Brody glared through the rearview mirror.

Viv decided it wasn't a good time to be asking questions after that. They all went back to living in their heads and wrestling their own thoughts. The miles seemed to melt away behind them as the sun grew higher in the sky.

"We will split up once on foot. Delaney and Calliope go north. Daphne and I will take the south. Mom?" Brody looked at Viv.

"I'll head east." Viv's voice was thin.

Brody pulled the car off the highway at a rest area. Everyone grabbed a bag and started changing into black cargo pants and combat jackets. Even their mom suited up. They looked like they were going off to war.

Brody showed them the experimental ammunition created to take down Stryders. They divided the ammo up between them. On the back of their blade holders stood clip housings for ten clips on each side. Every pocket of their clothing was filled with something: a Leatherman, additional ammunition, cell phone, weapons. Brody had made sure to bring everything she found in the Kindred's office. Their dad had constructed sleeves and gloves to house new sleeker blades.

"I got us walkie-talkies. We all understand Morse Code, so use it. No conversation, if you talk on them assume whoever is talking is compromised." Brody handed each of them a handset and a tactical flashlight. "Once we are separated, stick with the flashlights and radios using cryptography to keep in contact." Brody fell silent, studying them.

They made last minute checks before they ventured out and more than likely got themselves killed or captured. Tugging on sweatshirts to cover up their gear, no one spoke until Viv broke the long silence.

"I can't talk you out of this, so…," Viv took a deep breath. "I never thought I'd be sending my little girls off to war. Be careful. Only trust each other. Don't tell anyone who or what you are. Are you still sure about this? Isabeau is out there waiting for us. She will hold nothing back." The concern poured through Vivianna's voice and mannerisms.

Delaney kept her eyes focused on the asphalt.

"Okay then, good luck."

Brody and Daphne embraced Viv and started off. Delaney and Calliope hugged her too, then she watched them walk away. Calliope and Delaney both kept looking back to the place where their mother stood watching. Viv got smaller until they no longer saw her clearly, then the magnitude of their actions began to sink in.

We're all alone.

"Calliope." Delaney pulled her to a stop. "Call him. Then he can help us find Dad."

Calliope looked at Delaney. "Trystan." They waited.

Delaney walked around for a few minutes. They remained still for a while, each realizing he wasn't coming. No one was.

"I should have left the note," Delaney thought out loud.

"Huh?" Calliope said, suddenly interested in anything Delaney had to say.

"Nothing," Delaney muttered back. *What would be the point?* Calliope didn't want to hear about her plight earlier.

"He isn't here. He has to know by now we're on our own." Calliope had become so upset she no longer paid attention to where she walked. "He still didn't come. I threatened our mom." Calliope stopped and faced Delaney. "I forced you to lie. I even made you cry. And none of that matters because he isn't coming for me." Unanswerable questions swept across Calliope's expression and her eyes swam in thick pools of tears.

"Why wouldn't he try to find me?"

Through her anger with Calliope, she understood. Calliope wanted to see him, to be near him. She desired the same things Delaney craved, but nothing was ever easy.

"Maybe he can't." Delaney's heart hurt and she wouldn't have wished the pain on anyone.

"Try yours," Calliope pleaded. "He always comes for you. He'd kill himself to get to you." Calliope's words made Delaney's temper flare.

Delaney shook her head no. *He isn't a toy. I'm not going to pull him into this after I forced him to sit out when he wanted to help. I can't do that to him.*

"Why won't you call him? He will find Trystan for me." Calliope pulled at Delaney, but she shook Calliope off and continued to walk.

Delaney wanted to do what she had come to do and go home.

"You wouldn't help me as I fought with Brody about drugging Malik. You kept silent when I wanted to bring him with us. He's not a damn party trick. Leave him out of this. I'm not going to drag him into this now." Delaney's temper got the best of her and she ended up screaming.

"I'm sorry. I need to find Tryst. I must talk to him."

What in the hell are we doing on the side of a mountain? Who's going to save us from ourselves?

"Shhh." Delaney noticed a vibration run through her pant leg. The Walkie-Talkie jolted her aware.

The clicking noise held the worst news. Their mother had been taken into custody by Isabeau and the Stryders at the top of Multnomah Falls.

"That's too far. The hike back to the car will take us more than an hour and another to drive to the falls. Even if we leave now, we'll never get to the meet in time." Calliope spoke while Delaney began pacing in small circles.

"Hey." Tryst stood behind Malik.

"Anything?" Malik looked over the landscape ahead.

"I found them."

Trystan drifted; Malik followed.

For a moment, relief pulled at Malik's heart. He remembered how stupid he'd felt only a few hours before. Then his resolve came back with a vengeance.

Calliope walked in front, Delaney close behind, and both at a steady pace. Calliope had tears streaming down her face. Her legs wobbled and her steps were shaky as she stumbled over uneven earth, muttering to herself.

Tryst caught up with Calliope and Malik fell in step beside Delaney, who immediately glanced at Malik as if she knew all along that he was right next to her.

"Move." Delaney pushed Calliope. "Stop feeling sorry for yourself. Pay attention and maybe we'll get out of this without getting anyone killed."

"Spyder."

"Malik."

"Multnomah Falls."

"Copy that."

"I'll go, Tryst. You stay with them." Malik drifted to Spyder's location.

"We can't get to her. The Luna Noviter Resurrexisses are guarding her," Shane said.

"Daphne and Brody are separated. Multiple attackers." Flynn's voice boomed through Malik's head.

"Stick with the targets." Spyder nodded to Malik and the three of them drifted to back up Fezz and Flynn.

Flynn and both girls are MIA. Four Stryders are down and Fezz has more in hand-to-hand. Spyder went up behind one and Malik took out the other.

"Flynn."

"Malik."

"Does anyone have eyes on Brody and Daphne?"

"They're both gone."

"Fezz, find Brody, lock her down. Flynn, locate Daphne. Too many people running around these damn woods with no supervision."

"Copy."

Turning, Malik drifted back to Viv's location. Spyder and Shane remained hidden next to him a second later. They stood on the Benson Foot Bridge, staring up at the falls. Larch Mountain wasn't an impressive sight like Hood, Baker, or Rainier, but Multnomah Falls' beauty was breathtaking. Malik feared they would know soon enough why Isabeau had chosen that specific location.

"Where is she?" Dane's voice came through loud and clear.

"Multnomah Falls on the Columbia Gorge." Malik felt Dane next to him a moment later.

Kindreds followed, popping up everywhere.

Tonight would be a battle and they were all ready for what lay in front of them.

They made better time back to the Xterra than Delaney hoped. She pushed Calliope the whole way. Calliope wasn't a runner, she was a slow-paced walker. Today, Calliope learned she was capable of running three miles in under forty minutes, which in all honesty was a terrible pace.

Delaney's cell gave them the coordinates to Multnomah Falls. Her stomach burned and the pain had nothing to do with running. Her father was missing and now her mother also, both probably in Isabeau's clutches.

"What will they do to her?" Calliope whispered as they raced down a deserted interstate.

The road was so empty, it was as if all the people in the world knew better than to be anywhere near that highway.

"They will kill Mom." Delaney finally started crying too.

We brought her here, delivered her right to the Stryders. Stupid little girls. We do need the Kindreds. We had no idea what to do or how to handle this.

"Malik." Delaney whispered his name. She had promised she could leave him out of this, and would if the help she needed were only for herself. *But this is my mother. This is so much more important than I am.*

But, Malik wasn't the one that came.

"Delaney, we are aware of the situation with your mom. Malik and some of the others are already on site, planning out how to rescue her." Trystan spoke from the backseat.

Delaney saw his grim expression in the rearview mirror as she drove. He appeared worn and exhausted. Calliope whipped around to face him from the passenger seat.

"Calliope, not now. We'll talk later."

She froze at the chill in his voice.

"How bad is this?" Delaney asked.

"You grandfather and the Kindreds will do whatever it takes to get your mother back," he stared straight ahead.

"What about our father?"

"There has been no sign of Bannan." He didn't even glance at Calliope.

Delaney thought of Daphne and Flynn, of this whole other thing filled with complications between each of the couples. Brody was lucky nobody liked her.

Chapter
THIRTY

The three of them sped past mountain peaks eclipsing the midday sun. Delaney continued to glare at the unbroken white lines with her mother's face dancing in her peripheral vision like a ghost. No word on her father or whether Brody and Daphne were alive or captured by Isabeau.

Malik was waiting for a breach in security to exploit. That he was trying to fix the problems her stupid sisters and she caused added to her feelings of guilt.

They had put all the Kindreds in danger, signing some of their death warrants by their actions. Amalgamates, men and women Delaney had never met, would give their lives in place of the people they protected. The weight on her shoulders pulled her down.

The Xterra pulled into a parking lot at the base of the falls.

The waterfall was split into two sections. The map showed a trail off the Benson Bridge leading up to the lookout on top of Larch Mountain. Delaney doubted Trystan would let them use the direct path…*too easy to pick us off.*

"Tonight will change everything" echoed through her mind. A foreboding sensation crept along Delaney's spine. She sat in the car for a few minutes. The allure didn't escape her; under any other circumstances, she would have loved visiting there. It was like a dream with the sights, smells, and sounds of beauty personified.

Delaney exited the vehicle and caught a glimpse of the old stone lodge off to the side of the gift shop. She fought to prepare while walking to the left of the quaint building. Her hands clenched in anticipation and mixed emotions spilled through her.

I am not ready to fight a battle, facing off against well trained killers, and I'm not sure how to be ready. So I choose to storm the gates and worry about the rest should I survive.

"Delaney, stay off the trail. Our path is through the forest." Trystan put his hand on her shoulder as he spoke.

She looked back at him with wild eyes.

"This is not a drill or an academic exercise. This is real life. Should we become separated, call Malik. He can find you. If no one comes, run. Get as far away as you can. Head for Portland. When enough time has passed, appeal to him again. If he doesn't answer, signal every name you know until someone appears. Understand?"

Delaney nodded numbly.

"Delaney, this is a war. Some of us…" He grimaced. "Most of us will not walk away from tonight. Just be careful and don't be one of the dead, okay."

Fear gripped Delaney.

"Tell Malik I'm sorry." Delaney grabbed Trystan's arm.

"You'll find each other." Trystan stared down at her with a haggard expression. "Apply your training. You know how to fight and you understand how to use the weapons. Don't stop fighting. It would be better to die in the field than be taken."

I won't survive torture. Am I to take my own life should it come to that? Dragging her gaze away, she glanced up at the falls. The situation seemed like such an oxymoron. Surrounded by beauty and evil ugliness at the same time.

Trystan, Calliope, and Delaney went deeper into the woods and farther out of their way to avoid detection. Trystan led the girls over fallen trees and

Bent, Not Broken   313

stomping through muddy brush and slick rocks in creek beds. Thick, rich, green moss grew wild over every surface, making it appear like the forest was famished and attempting to consume itself. Life was in abundance everywhere with flourishing shades of luxurious greens, rich browns, vibrant blues, and shimmery yellows. Even the thick undergrowth had long, winding fingers reaching out to trip them up. The girls' hands had splinters from the fallen trees they climbed over, and their knees and elbows were scraped and bleeding. Mud caked shoes and the constant drizzle of rain soaking their packs became burdensome. Balmy moisture from the falls made everything slippery, and the girls struggled to keep traction as they pushed forward.

A thick, dense fog hung over the treetops like eerie phantoms patrolling the sky or guiding the way. The roar of rushing water blotted out every other sound, thundering angrily as they grew closer to their destination. The setting sun was covered with dark, angry clouds threatening to erupt into a thunderstorm; the weather seemed fitting, given the circumstances. The lightning and the thunder would cover up the battle noise of the coming night. Whatever the clamoring water missed, the other sounds of nature eagerly swallowed up.

The woods were deserted, animals seeming to just be absent, the closer they got to the top. The air smelled like a mix of flowers, pine trees, and clean linens, reminding Delaney of how her dad always smelled fresh. She wanted to see him again so badly.

The legend of Multnomah Falls suddenly came to Delaney's mind. Millennia ago, a small tribe lived at the bottom of Multnomah Falls. One day an illness ravished the people, leaving many ill and more dead. The mighty coyote appeared to the chief's offspring while she prayed for her husband's speedy recovery. The spirit instructed her how to deliver her beloved clan from their death sentence. To ensure the tribes existences, the woman was told she must throw herself off the cliff from the highest point.

In order to emancipate her people, she did what was asked of her without hesitation, hoping her sacrifice would save her new spouse who lay dying. When the tribe awoke in the morning, everyone had recovered. The Chief and his daughter's new husband ran to the cliffs and found her broken body. They demanded the ardent spirits show them a sign that the sacrifice hadn't been committed in vain. At that precise second, water poured forth from the falls and has never ceased falling since then.

Legend said that when you stared up at the right time of the day, a woman's profile proudly overlooked the Columbia Gorge. A face was etched into the rocky surface and the rushing water became streaming tresses of hair around it. Tears seemed to fall from her eyes in the form of smaller streams cascading down the smooth rocks.

The serenity of Delaney's moment suddenly shattered by chaos erupting. A booming male voice whipped through the tall pines, leaving Delaney confused and terrified. Vivianna's screams became horrific. At the sound of them, Delaney barreled forward with little thought as to what she would face. Three Stryders talking in a small clearing came into sight. They were the only adversaries Delaney saw and the first thing she went for.

"How did Caleb find all these people?" Shane asked Malik while they shadowed the Stryders from the drifter's plane.

"I don't know. I'm not sure what Caleb is anymore. He's was a Death Dealer at some point," Malik replied in a bewildered tone.

"How do we defeat him if we don't understand his origins?"

"He's a Psychopomp, or he was. There are other names too, Sparrows, or Death Dealers. Caleb would escort a person's consciousness to the next destination, like a guardian. The ideology is dependent on which belief system the dead advocated. If they believed in hell and were a despicable human being, then fire and brimstone became their final station. One who subscribed to the idea of an afterlife, he took them to the other side. If you believed in nothing, you became extinct.

"He was the first of his kind. The angels created Caleb to work with humans. He was allowed to traverse all realms and possibilities. When Caleb became in need of help, nine companions were established to assist him. The ten of them directed spirits off the plane of the animated and kept the balance between the living and the dead. He helped free the world of malevolent spirits who wanted revenge, harming the living physically or just with humans inability to deal with ghosts.

"From the way my mother used to tell me the story, he was guiding someone to hell and something happened to drive him rogue. Caleb made a deal with the demons to help them escape and build an army, and they became known as Stryders, serving only him.

"He brings the vitality of people who don't want to die into Abaddon and their spirit is merged with a demon. The newly formed union is then escorted back to reclaim the carcass. Sometimes the experience is too agonizing for the human corpse and the demon can't transcend and the body combusts before the process can be completed, sending the malignant spirit back to hell for punishment.

"Some demons manage to overpower the vitality and altogether take control, allowing the soul to expire in a corporeal form."

"Do Stryders die when we kill the physical form?" Shane's posture slouched.

"They don't cease to exist like you and I. They are recycled, I guess. The demons are dispatched back to hell until a suitable replacement is found. Nothing like the Demonoks, or like Seeley. They are as immortal as we are." They walked the perimeter at the bottom of the falls.

"This war is pointless. We can't win." Shane stared at the ground.

"Oh, the battles can be won. Caleb is the one who sets the souls free. If he's stopped, the demons will have to find a new way of escaping. As for defeating the Demonoks, that may take more time and research."

"Is it true that the Demonoks are the heirs of Dahlia?"

"I have no idea. Demonoks are half human and half demon. I don't think it matters where they came from. They have free will, as free souls. They can choose to be human or demon."

"But, I thought all Demonoks were evil. None can be trusted." Shane glanced up in surprise.

"No. Every free soul has a choice."

"How can you be so sure?"

"Because Candace, Sebastian's wife, was one. She died protecting Daphne. I don't think any person is inherently nefarious. The acceptance of free will encourages each to decide moral right or wrong for themselves. Anyone can choose to be principled." Malik hated remembering Candace's sacrifice; it brought pain and frustration to him. He had seen the anguish and guilt her death caused. It destroyed Bannan's brother and two little girls became orphans in a single moment. "Daphne and Brody are mixed Demonoks."

"Yes, though they don't know that truth. They lost their mother, then their father right away after. Why burden them with more? Brody and Daphne believe they are half Gabled Amalgamate and Tracer. They have never asked why they don't have any animal totems. Or why neither can fuse."

Most of the older Kindreds knew what the girls would become. The subject was simply never discussed.

"Daphne is angelic." Shane spoke in a soft voice.

"You're in love with her?"

"She's beautiful."

"Malik." Trystan link-spoke.

"We're near the falls, a click and a half away from you."

"Copy."

The two began moving to meet up with Tryst.

"Malik!"

The frightened scream drove Malik to drift without a word to Shane. He was relieved when Shane followed because they had drifted right into the middle of a brawl.

Delaney ran forward, dropping Stryders with the poisoned bullets her father created. Their bodies combusted as she flew by one, then the next. She realized she had lost track of Calliope and Trystan shortly after encountering the first three Stryders.

Delaney caught a glimpse of her mother tied to a tall column ahead. Her head flopped forward and she passed out as Delaney surveyed the area from behind a tree trunk. Viv's beautiful hair was tousled with big tangles floating off of her scalp like feathers in the wind, and blood stained her face. One eye was swollen shut and her lips were puffy with cuts. Gashes covered her arms and legs. Her hands had burns all over them and her fingers appeared to have been scorched similarly to hot dogs forgotten on the bar-b-cue.

Four large men guarded her. One whipped around as Delaney advanced. The snarl on his face revealed long, sharp fangs, reminding her of a tiger mid-yawn. He had a knife in one hand, a blowtorch in the other. Delaney guessed what happened to Viv's hands.

Lola had been right. She'd learned how to torture from the best.

Delaney moved faster. The need for immediate vengeance unfurled within her like a flag on a battlefield and fear fell lost along the way. Two additional Stryders tracked her. Delaney shot one in the chest. Similar to firecrackers on the fourth of July, he burst into flames against the moonlit night. The second one was quick and avoided her first shot. Reaching to reload her gun, Delaney didn't see another Stryder moving in from the far right until it was too late. He leaped and they tumbled to the earth. Delaney clutched for a blade, then drove the knife into his chest, and pointed the gun at the other one as she rolled to her feet. He raced towards her and was only a foot or two away when Delaney shot. She dove into the dirt as he passed over her in a rain of falling fire.

Stalking back to its smoldering remains, she retrieved her blade. A scream in the distance attracted her attention. She realized her mother and the four guards were gone. Delaney approached the column, finding it coated in blood splatter and spray. Shreds of Viv's clothing littered the ground beside clumps of her beautiful dark hair.

"Mom!" Delaney screamed into the darkness enveloping everything. "Mom!"

"They are moving farther up the pass. Move fast," Malik said as he ran past her.

Delaney sprinted to keep up. They rushed down the stone path following the four guards. The hair on the back of Malik's neck stood on end and a disturbing awareness refused to be ignored.

The Stryders are going to sacrifice Viv in order to bring the girls out of hiding.

As Delaney rounded the corner, he grabbed her and forced her still. She struggled until he whispered, "This is a trap. They are waiting for us." The words froze her in place. "Can you light up? I'll stay out of your way when I get past you. Don't stop once you're moving." Her body shook as he held her against him.

Malik wondered if adrenaline or fear had taken over. One thing he was certain of was that she was nowhere near fusing mentally. She had no control over her emotional state. Malik waited for Delaney to tell him she understood, and then backed away.

She'd never fused on command, and though her emotions had reached a lethal point, no heat registered at her fingertips and tunnels had yet to encircle her vision. Delaney wasn't sure how to make the change happen. She knew her mother was being tortured and that should have been enough, though her body remained quiet.

"Do what you can." Malik drug his knuckles down her cheek before bursting forward and disappearing around the corner.

He went in first to buy her time. Stryders laid in wait everywhere. From the edge of his peripheral vision, he caught Kindreds popping up. Shane, Mia, and Thistle were already engaging the enemy. Delaney followed close behind and began shooting as fast as she could reload. When the space between them became too small for her to fire her gun safely, she went for her blades, slashing at the never-ending supply of Stryders.

Delaney blinked and her vision became narrowed and circular. Her fingertips burned white-hot as her head began to pound. The tunnel vision turned specific; Delaney no longer had normal perception and instead experienced hot and cool signatures like before. Her fingers ignited with scalding heat under pyroclastic flowing pressure. Delaney's skin grew sensitive and she attempted to cultivate the energy, forcing the power to hold until she released the momentum.

"Malik!" Delaney screamed.

His name was carried on a swift breeze nearly throwing him off his feet.

If Malik was anywhere in front of her, surely this time she would kill him. Her temper gave way to the intensity. She raised her hands above her head, the stratosphere crackled like violent thunder and lightning were all about her. White-hot energy soared through the darkness and Delaney followed her light. Her mind swam in the luminescent flow engulfing her.

"Drift." Malik link-spoke to the other Kindreds.

Screams and growls filled the night as they left the Stryders far behind. Malik came up behind Delaney. The action always required so much of her, she would need to be cared for when the response ceased.

White lightning crackled and ebbed around her. A roaring howl fractured the envelope. Delaney inhaled a deep breath and drew her arms down and back, preparing to push the energy out. She brought her hands up over her head and the air began to fiercely swirl more severely than an F-4. This time was different from the mall; the blast lasted for only a few seconds, but the damage was catastrophic. Bolts of blue electrical surges hit the Stryders and lifted them up like floating sparklers.

Delaney fell to the hard earth on all fours and threw up. Her body quivered and convulsed. Sweat streamed down her back and limbs as the chilly air bit into her skin and eased the sweltering heat pouring off of her. She knelt, motionless and confused. Blood dripped from her ears, nose, and mouth. Her vision refused to clear as fast as she desperately needed.

Delaney noticed Malik kneeling beside her just as he jumped up and jerked her to her feet.

Stryder corpses littered the ground. She'd managed to level the majority of their forces, but the stragglers—Hollowers and other assassin—began closing in from all sides.

Delaney staggered, still regaining her senses.

Malik raced forward to engage the immediate threats. He tore through the first two, then glanced back to find Delaney reloading her guns. She fired rapidly and her hands never wavered. The dead dropped all about her.

Delaney was hit from the left. The Stryder's outstretched arm knocked her off balance and she smacked the ground hard, then scurried to climb to her feet, grabbing for whatever she had remaining to work with. Once she was upright, she slammed her Sig Sauers against the clip holders at her back acquiring full clips, and moved forward.

Malik was nowhere to be seen.

Malik was covered in snow. The woman before him was a Traveler. She smiled, laughed, and then charged, hitting him square in the chest with her shoulder. The force knocked him to the snowbank, forcing the air from his lungs with a loud grunt.

The idea of Delaney alone with the stragglers drove him up. Malik grabbed her throat and ripped. She fell against him, blood covering his hand. He tossed her to the side, and drifted back.

Delaney was sprawled on the ground fighting to get up.

The shot came out of nowhere. She heard the crack but never perceived the penetration. Delaney flew forward from what felt like an out of control subway train hitting her. She tightened her grip on the Sigs and waited for the impact of the ground. Her head smacked the packed earth and she was momentarily dazed.

Delaney soon realized someone was laying on her back. She fought to breathe under the heavy weight. Forced to lie flat on her belly, she pushed hard to get her knees underneath herself for leverage, shimmying and scooting as she spotted two Stryders bearing down on her. One last push and the body fell to the side. She grabbed for the blades holstered on her thighs and let them soar. One knife pegged a Stryder dead center and tumbled to the ground. The other one bobbed left and she caught him in the shoulder.

"You have lost, little girl." He roared horrid laughter.

The Stryder was almost on her when it burst into flames like the head of a match. She searched the area for Malik. Delaney knew he wouldn't leave her, so when she didn't find him, she took a longer, slower look. She glanced down at the body she'd pushed off her back earlier and realized Malik had been shot instead of her. She rolled him over on his stomach. Blood poured from his side. Her eyes flew to his face only to discover a man she didn't recognize.

A stranger had taken a bullet for her.

She ripped open his shirt to locate a hole, and then rolled him to his side to see if the projectile was lodged in him or had exited. Delaney blew out a sigh of relief when she found an exit wound near his spine.

"Taloula."

The name startled her and she dropped him on his back. Air rushed out of his lungs and his eyes rolled around in their sockets. Delaney panicked.

"Call for help." His eyes rolled again.

Delaney shook him. He didn't respond, so she jolted him harder. He needed to stay awake until someone came to their aid.

Malik heard Shane and drifted to his location. Delaney leaned over a body. She frantically tried to move the torso. A second later, Malik kneeled beside Delaney.

"Help me get him up." She pulled at the downed man's shoulder as Malik wedged himself under Shane.

"Come on, we have to move," Malik breathed heavily under the weight.

"Is he going to die? He took the bullet for me," Delaney ran behind Malik. She rushed to keep in time with him through a maze of corners and vertical straightaways. Without the sun, Malik became turned around in the forest and had no idea where he was speeding off too.

"He'll be okay." Malik moved as quickly as possible under the burly man's burden.

"Malik, Mia said you have downed Kindred. I'm coming to you." Dane's voice echoed through Malik's head while relief flooded his insides. Shane's breathing had become almost nonexistent.

"Copy that." Malik glanced around.

Dane appeared out of nowhere holding a canteen. Malik traded Shane for the bottle. The man now holding the Kindred nodded and Malik threw the canteen's contents into the air. Dane stepped into the spray and disappeared with the injured Kindred as the water drops cascaded back down.

"What just happened?" Delaney remarked in disbelief.

"Move, the Sinera are almost on you." Mia must have been tracking them.

"I will explain later." Malik grabbed her hand and began running.

Their pace quickened with each step. Sinera came from behind them, forcing them farther into the forest. A hail of bullets whizzed past their heads as they approached the tree line.

"Half-a-klick, one o'clock." Tryst directed Malik.

"Copy." He had no choice but to run them harder.

Malik jerked Delaney forward and to the right. She fell on top of him, curling into him as his arms shielded her, bullets still whizzing past.

When a lull came in the firing, Delaney glanced up to face Calliope and Trystan staring down at her. Malik rolled out from under Delaney and pulled her to her feet while talking with Trystan.

"There are more than Stryders on this mountain." Malik spoke first.

"I have seen Travelers, Hollowers, and a Zepho. Caleb sent the most talented breeds he could assemble," Trystan said.

"Where are Brody and Daphne?" Delaney interrupted.

"There has been no contact with Flynn. He is in pursuit of Daphne. Fezz is tracking Brody. That's all we have."

Trystan tossed an oversized duffel bag at the two girls. Calliope handed Delaney additional full clips and more blades, which she stashed in the empty holsters designed for them. A tear slipped down her face as she gathered up her gear. Delaney silently prepared for what was still to come.

Chaos erupted with yelling and a burst of bright light. Mia, Thistle, and half a dozen Kindreds appeared. The Sinera had surrounded them. Malik turned to grab Delaney, but she was already gone. The Sinera realized more Kindreds encircled them from behind and began dispersing. Trystan and Malik drifted down the trail to the falls to find Calliope and Delaney.

Calliope grabbed Delaney and took off toward the falls, and where they believed Viv had been taken. With a dagger in one hand and a sword in the other, Calliope went first. Delaney had both Sigs drawn and guarded their backs.

"They're coming," Calliope yelled as she crouched down preparing to strike.

Delaney fired around her as a Stryders charged forward. They kept their backsides to one another and the Stryders closed in around them.

"Delaney!"

Her head shot to the side. She saw Malik approaching them and Kindreds surrounding them on all sides. The Stryders were given an obstacle to overcome before getting away with the prizes. Malik pulled Delaney to the right. She stumbled over uneven ground and they both went down.

"It's too late," Malik yelled.

Delaney shot him a bewildered expression.

"Delaney, it's too late." His voice broke. "Viv's been infected. She's already changing. Delaney, I need your weapon."

The words screamed in her ears but made little sense in her mind.

"What?" She glanced at him in confusion, then toward her mother standing within a small group of Stryder's several yards away.

He took her hand in his and gently pulled the Sig free.

"What are you going to do?"

He raised and pointed the gun at Viv.

"Isn't there another way?!" Delaney begged.

"No." The word went through her brain like a drop in still water.

Malik held Vivianna's tortured face in the sights. Emotions clouded his better judgement. The Lunaire had condemned her, but it was Malik who was about to take her life.

Delaney would never have the opportunity to understand her mother. All she had was the last few days.

His throat grew tight and his hands trembled enough to worry him the bullet might be off.

A shot cracked through the air. Someone hit Delaney from behind. Out of the corner of her eye, she caught Seeley walking out from behind the trees. He had Daphne imprisoned in his arms and a gun dangling from his fingertips. Daphne was crying and her eyes met Delaney's. She struggled to free herself from Seeley's grasp.

"Let me go, you bastard! I'll fuckin' kill you, Seeley." She thrashed about in his tight hold.

Seeley murdered Daphne's mom, and now the monster had her.

Delaney pivoted and found Flynn standing beside her.

"I will get you, Seeley," Flynn spoke through a haze of anger.

"Don't follow us. You'll only put her in danger." Seeley and Daphne were gone as quickly as they had appeared.

Flynn cursed as he stood helplessly watching them both vanish.

He twisted around to face Delaney.

"I heard a gunshot." He bent down beside Malik's still torso.

"Seeley shot Malik." Delaney kneeled.

"Delaney, your mom."

Though Malik's words reached her, she only stared at him, then reluctantly dragged her gaze back to her mother's twisting figure.

"Are you sure?"

Bent, Not Broken   325

The hope in her expression, in her eyes, broke him. He wished for another way, but knew better. *Viv is lost to us.*

Delaney took the gun from the ground where it had fallen. These Sigs had been her weapons since she had learned how to shoot. Now, staring at the guns, they felt all wrong in her hands. Delaney twisted towards Flynn and he stared at her with an odd expression.

"Lunaire infected her."

"I can't shoot." Flynn spoke gravely.

Malik could barely lift his arm until he finished healing, which would take longer than they had in order for Viv not to suffer unduly.

It's up to me.

Delaney turned towards her mom, watching her becoming something else. When Viv roared like an animal, Delaney jumped. Tears streamed down her cheeks as reality sank in.

Not only was Delaney losing her mother, she was going to have to pull the trigger herself.

Delaney turned, gun in hand, and focused on her mom. Viv bellowed again and erased all doubt that Malik told the truth. Her mother began changing and if she waited much longer, Delaney wasn't sure what she would have to do in order to help her from the misery.

"I'm sorry," Malik stared at her.

Delaney couldn't look at him, refused to think about him or what the old life held; that was nothing more than history. Her hands were shaking as she took aim. Delaney tried to square her shoulders, but her body wouldn't respond. Another horrible, pain filled wail from Viv shook her to the core.

A stifled sob came flooding from Delaney.

Her mother's screams quickly became deafening. Delaney swallowed stiffly. Viv's head flailed around, and her muscles convulsed so hard she barely stayed on her feet.

Delaney shook herself, trying to clear the image. She stared down the sights and found her mother at the other end. She checked her aim once more.

Releasing a gradual breath, she squeezed the trigger. Her upper body jerked from the kickback.

She watched her mother's head fly back and then whip forward in a lazy movement lasting forever. Viv's hair swept around her cheeks. Her thin, graceful arms flew out in front of her. She collapsed like a broken marionette to the ground.

Delaney's hearing became crisp. Her own breath in her ears, the blood pulsating within her brain, the breeze whispering through the tall pines were clearer than ever before.

Viv's crying and screaming, nothing more than an echo now. The crumbled shell of her mother lay at the Lunaire's feet.

Delaney's arms sunk to her side, unbelievably heavy. Tears that would never fall burned inside her gaze.

The gun dropped from her side with a thud. She fell to her knees, never taking her eyes off Viv's body. Malik wanted to turn away and avoid seeing Delaney destroyed, but he couldn't. He peered at her expression intently. He stared into Delaney's face and saw her change right before his eyes, hardening like cement.

"Delaney, no!" Calliope screamed her name.

She wouldn't turn to Calliope, not now.

"Get them the hell out of here!" Delaney screamed to Flynn, then didn't try to stop it. She welcomed the power to destroy everything in her path and hoped to include herself as well.

Delaney wanted them all to die, to suffer. She needed to burn the flesh right off of the Stryders and their cohorts. Anger bubbled up like boiling water inside her, clouding her judgment and ability to reason. She raised up to stand, shaking with rage. She couldn't control her fuse. Delaney needed vindication and revenge, and she would have them both.

Her hands grew pale starting at her fingertips. Electricity flared high and cracked across the sky as bolts of lightning bouncing off trees and dancing on the water.

Bent, Not Broken   327

Calliope's eyes expanded as she stared back at her in astonishment. Delaney had only begun the destruction. Calliope reached out to touch her. Delaney barely moved fast enough to avoid her.

"Don't. I can't control this!" Delaney hurled the words at Calliope.

The light overpowered her. Throwing her head back, a burst of white energy broke free and shot up into the atmosphere like a funnel cloud. The jolt knocked Delaney down on all fours. The earth exploded up and around her. The impact forced Malik to his hands and knees as dirt erupted into the air. Trees and rocks flew into the sky like pawns off a chessboard. A wall of water whipped around, tossing up the Stryders and slamming their bodies back down to the ground.

Malik lost Calliope and Flynn as damp soil covered his face. Delaney had become a searing pale blue light moving across the meadow, lightning still dancing off her.

Delaney exploded with the power. There was no fighting the energy or gaining control over her emotions. She didn't want to try; she wanted to burn.

"Delaney, please!" Calliope tried to sound soothing. The comfort only doused her angry flames with blazing hatred for herself.

Malik carefully walked towards Delaney. She glowed with the glyph moving over her skin like puzzle pieces trying to assemble into the correct order.

Delaney stared up at the midnight blue blanket with not a star in sight, saying something under her breath.

Calliope and Malik stood watching her for a moment, neither of them spoke.

If Delaney continued to gain electrical strength, Malik would have to restrain her and give Calliope time to escape.

"You have no right to comfort me!" Delaney screamed wildly in Calliope's direction. She teetered on the fringe of more than just the falls.

Malik stepped closer, but stopped when he witnessed how badly she shook with unyielding rage.

"Delaney."

"Don't say my name." She thundered at Malik.

He decided to keep quiet; the decision seemed wiser than to argue. She was no longer only trembling from the anger and shook uncontrollably. They remained still. Delaney turned her attention back to Calliope, but something else caught her eye.

Suddenly, the movement struck all of them. Delaney heard cruel laughter just behind her; the taunting sound made her blood broil in her veins. White hot liquid metallic tears scorched Delaney's face. She stiffened and lost her fuse. The witchy cackle boomed again.

In part, Malik was relieved that Isabeau had shut Delaney down before she could do any real damage to herself.

"How did it feel, poppin' Mommy? I didn't think you had it in you." Isabeau sneered only a few feet from Delaney. Her cackling sounded more like ghastly shrieks than laughter.

Delaney put her hand on Malik's shoulder, stopping him from moving forward to challenge Isabeau. "You're already hurt. Please, save the rest of my family. Tonight needs to end here with me, if I can do it." Delaney tried to gage his reaction. Her voice broke, but she didn't appear afraid, just haggard and lost.

"I can't…" The words died in his throat.

She asked him to leave her. Isabeau had been trained as Kindred, instructed to take men apart and keep going. Malik knew Delaney was no match for her.

"I have managed to betray all the things I think I am, everything I aspired to be. Even my mother." She remained calm as she spoke. Her eyes became unresponsive and her mannerisms slow and controlled.

Malik became afraid for her more than he had ever been before. Delaney wobbled on a tightrope. He feared a chunk of her wanted to fall and the remaining part needed to jump. Delaney had resigned to death.

Delaney's voice shattered as she said, "You should go now. Please. Walk away." A small, sad smile played on her lips.

Malik wanted to tell her how none of this was her fault. *War takes everything from you and you must resign to letting the pain go to survive.*

A bullet whizzed past Delaney's head. Flynn glanced from her to Isabeau. An expression of shock crossed his face. He fell down to his knees and then over on his back.

The fight between the two women would end in a rush, but it might buy Malik enough time to get the others off the falls.

"Go." Delaney twisted away. She hated goodbyes and this wasn't going to be an "I'll see you soon."

Delaney glared at Isabeau. She was striking in the light of the full moon, her clothes sprinkled with the blood of her enemies. Isabeau's hair blew in the mountain breeze. If only she had been strumming a Dulcimer and singing out for her demon lover. Delaney thought of Coolridge and Kubla Kahn.

Malik went to Flynn and hoisted him over his shoulder. He knew he had to act fast and get back to Delaney before it was too late.

"Tryst." Malik grabbed Calliope and made his way farther into the forest. Placing Flynn on the ground, Malik waited for a response.

"Stay with Flynn, Calliope. Where is Tryst?" Malik spun around to face her.

"I shot him." Calliope stared at Malik.

"What?" Malik took a step forward.

"He tried to restrain me, to take me off the mountain. He is safer where I left him."

"I have to get back to her. Find him, Calliope." Malik began yelling as he turned away.

"Thistle."

"Malik."

"Flynn's down and Calliope's alone. I need him escorted to the Fates." Malik jogged out of the woods, remaining in the shadows. He never saw Calliope coming up behind him.

"This is our fight." She hit him in the head with a tree branch she found on the ground.

Chapter
THIRTY-ONE

"What are you waiting for, Isabeau?" Delaney asked, tilting her head and half smiling at her. Delaney raised her hands in invitation. "Why do you want Malik dead so badly? Jilted lover? You didn't even get that far, huh? Unrequited crush, maybe?" Delaney had been told Isabeau obsessed over Malik. She didn't understand why, but guessed love was the reason Isabeau had made him a personal project.

Isabeau flew at Delaney, her sharp nails grinding into Delaney's arm, ripping and tearing her skin. Fumbling for one of the knives, Delaney drove it into Isabeau's stomach.

I may not be able to kill you, but I can hurt you.

Isabeau stumbled a few steps before turning on Delaney with unveiled fury.

"Why have the Lunaire's go after my mother? Too afraid to take her on yourself?" Delaney stilled as Isabeau moved closer. Out of the corner of her eye, she caught a glimpse of Calliope's silhouette on the edge of the tree line.

"How else would I have divided you? She is—*was* the center, the one with the pull. With no more family to worry about, the takeover becomes much easier. Seeley captured Daphne and he is going to break her. Brody is being brought to a secure location as we speak." Isabeau disappeared and turned up beside Calliope faster than Delaney could blink. "And I will be taking Calliope with me. I planned on kidnapping you, but now, I'll let you live knowing all of your sisters are gone. Oh, and with the knowledge you murdered Vivianna in cold blood. If this doesn't end you, nothing I can do will break you anyway." Isabeau ripped a hole in thin air, pulling Calliope and herself through the fissure.

Anger coursed within Malik as he grabbed the back of his skull. His hand found a slick, soft spot with gentle probing. His heart's pulsating beat drummed so loud nothing could penetrate his hearing. He looked around in confusion as he pulled himself up to his knees.

"A forest?" He turned and vomited, then forced his feet underneath him and wandered forward. His shuffling footsteps required all of his concentration. His ears rang like school bells chiming in his head. He reached the tree line and watched Isabeau disappear with Calliope. Helpless for having found them too late to intervene, he turned to Delaney. The air around her no longer buzzed super charged with electricity. A sad, smothering comprehension had stifled her energized state and replaced the hum with knowledge that her life as she had come to understand it was over. There was an undeniable chaos in the subtle tilts of her head as her new reality settled over her.

Malik imagined what Isabeau had said to her before stealing Calliope away. All of which would have been hateful lies or mean-spirited spin-offs of the truth. Isabeau lived to make people suffer at every opportunity.

Anger because of Delaney's betrayal had long since evaporated, but all the questions remained. Not that they mattered now. At the moment, he feared for Delaney's sanity.

"No!" Delaney screamed into the clear night sky. Isabeau had trumped

Delaney's plan.

From the corner of Delaney's eye, she caught a glimpse of Malik. She couldn't hold back the waves of tears any more than she could prevent a volcano from erupting.

Malik was all she had left now. She experienced the strongest raw need to run to him and bury her face so thoroughly in his chest she would be lost forever, confined to some safe place where the actions of the day would be forgotten, forgiven. Delaney understood the desire was unrealistic, but for a split second, she thought of how beautiful things might have been for them. She managed a smile for him. The facial expressions small, probably sad, and undoubtedly hollow.

Malik slowly moved closer. She began to laugh like a crazy person, crying hysterically at the same time. She tried to hold on, but her body sagged from exhaustion and her sanity slipped further away.

Isabeau was right; she had broken Delaney.

"I'm sorry, Delaney. You shouldn't have had to pull the trigger." Malik approached carefully. The last thing he wanted to do was set her off. She was on the fringe, and he didn't want to push her off or give her reason to fall. Even as pain clouded his expression, Malik tried to keep his speech steady and soothing.

"I did have to. Should you have killed her, I would hate you forever. This way, I only abhor me." She glanced around the forest, her bottom lip trembling.

Delaney searched for something. Her expression hardened as her gaze returned to him. She tried to don a brave face and he questioned why.

The earth convulsed, and rocks peeled off the wall supporting the falls and tumbled over. The tall pines became uprooted and tossed around like toy figures in a children's army battle. The mountain reacted to everything Delaney experienced.

I will end here, one way or another. If this is a good day to fight to the death, then this is a beautiful place to die. Can I ask for more? For the type of person I have become, this is certainly a gift. Is redemption possible for someone like me?

Bent, Not Broken   333

Fear of what awaited her on the other side crept up Delaney's spine. She had given little to no credence to religious ideas or belief systems, never succumbed to the idea of heaven and hell as religion perpetuated, until this moment. *One is coming for me, and I am afraid damnation is only a breath away.* Delaney composed a façade of strength, figuring she would talk to whomever was in charge, go straight to the top. Why waste time with middlemen?

She attempted to straighten her back, to be confident in her decisions, and tried not to flinch with all the thoughts stomping on her senses. She finally had memories, the kind that would stay with her forever, haunting her like a relentless ghost in a house not meant to belong to anyone. She stumbled around, confused and broken, reached the mouth of the watercourse, and then fell on the rocky edge of the fast-moving water before it jetted over into oblivion. Delaney sat at the brink of the waterfall, motionless.

She had to see Malik, if only for a moment. She needed to catalogue the exact color of his eyes; the jeweled green drove her to all sorts of dim-witted acts, the quiet plains of resistance falling below his cheek bones, the curvy slopes of determination encasing a dazzling smile rarely seen by anyone.

Delaney leaned over and took a long look into the darkness.

Malik reached her, but didn't rush toward her for fear of startling her. He moved with grace and outstretched hands until she turned and noticed he was there.

"So many reasons to walk to the edge and slip over. Please let me go." Her head fell into her hands. Hopelessness surrounded her, despair hung thick in the rolling dark clouds, and bit by bit, she gave in to the pain.

"You have to calm down or you're going to bring this mountain down." He shouted above the roar of the waterfall.

Her every delicate movement was mirrored by the nature surrounding her. The earth bent to her will. The water began to boil with frothy bubbles as she shimmered with a silvery glow. Her unhinged emotions complicated the integrity of the bedrock, the woods, and the summit itself. Energy spiraled off of her with such intensity the hairs on her arms stood on end. Delaney's lips tingled and she didn't know how to stop the fuse. Her pain seemed to be everywhere, reaching further into the mountain forcing it to groan and fracturing under the duress.

Malik was beside her before she took her next breath.

"You've saved me enough. Please, let me go." Her voice became so calm the serenity within surprised even Delaney.

Malik heard the finality in her words. "I can't make the hurting stop. But I swear, I won't leave you alone with the guilt," Malik's throat seized up.

The earth rattled again. More trees fell and Malik lost his footing, reached out for her, and she quickly moved away.

"I don't want to live with what I've done." Delaney realized there was more to her decision than just escaping. "Not even for you. I'm a monster." With a shaky hand, she wiped her nose. "I'm broken, you can see that now. I'm barely hanging on."

"I can't give up on you."

"You're not holding on for me, you're clutching for yourself," Delaney lashed out at him. He wasn't the one deserving of her anger, but he was the only one left.

"No, Delaney, you're wrong. I hold on for both of us. Because this anguish will take time to pass, the pain will lessen. I promise you." His tender sentiment was so filled with hope it sucked the air from her. She didn't want to experience his love, not right now.

Delaney played music loud in her mind, pounding his words into oblivion. The wind blew her hair about, dancing all around her, swaying in the breeze to the final Swan Song.

Tight fists at her sides, she blocked everything out except her music.

Canon in D, play for me, Pachelbel.

Delaney allowed the flutes and the strings to pull her higher, they let her soar as she shoved him back and fell over the edge. Delaney's descent was immediate. The air was rushing over her when she felt him hit her from behind. He wrapped his arms around her, molding himself to Delaney's back.

He flipped them over, pulling her on top of him, so he fell beneath her.

She squinted from the rush of air stinging her eyes, and witnessed a kaleidoscope of silver. The sound of the falls grew louder by the millisecond. Still, he tried to hold on to her, even under dire conditions. This time he wouldn't be able to save her.

I've finally brought us both down.

He continued to talk to Delaney, though many of his words were lost in the falling water. What she understood was not to be afraid.

I'm not. I am filled with regret, overwrought with guilt and sadness beyond compare. Fear hasn't placed yet.

This journey, my brief exploration of life and love has come to a resolution before it ever had time to blossom. All I want is him, now I'll have him forever and never acquire him at all. Our paths have been forked and we force them to intersect, in the process demanding what isn't ours to take, a future joined at the cost of everyone.

The end was encased in crashing water, hard ground, and sharp rocks. Together in the last moments, but always apart.

Closing her eyes, Delaney decided she'd seen enough in her short lifespan. Instead, she chose to picture each one of the people she loved in those final seconds. Even a glimmer of Lola appeared, just before the darkness won out.

She expected him to let her go. Leave her when she was in over her head and speeding towards earth like a missile.

The only chance she had to live was if Malik took the impact. Her body wouldn't find a Halo and fall straight through as his could. Nor would it withstand the pressure. Malik held on with a grip ensuring she couldn't get away from him, not again, not now.

The water exploded with the strike of an atom bomb against his back, ripping his shirt right off, throwing them forward while gravity pushed them down. The force of their entry slammed into them as a Halo gaped and they hurled through the water tubes interlacing the crust of the earth. Delaney collapsed against him. He began to swim in the deep end of the spectrum while his own consciousness hung by a sliver.

Halos are a form of travel reserved for Kindreds. One of the few gifts from the Creator to give them fair footing on the battlefield. The pressure outside squashed his extremities down and his insides spread, pushing to escape the restrains. Malik's head pounded on the verge of exploding; his body gained momentum as they spiraled down the water slide.

Malik tried to concentrate on where he needed to be. He clung to her as if his life depended on it. Because, in all actuality, it did.

They finally punched through and came full throttle out of the ocean and on to a pebbly beach. Propelled onto the sand like two rockets from an underground silo. The earth ripped at the skin on his back, pulling chunks free as they skimmed along the sandy edge of the surf.

Malik fought to hold on to her while the pain wanted to steal his wakefulness.

"Daan." Malik barely gritted out the one word.

"Malik?" Dane sounded rattled.

"Daaaa…." The single syllable was the only utterance he pushed out. He prayed it was enough for them to be tracked.

As the exhaustion began to win out and his limbs became heavy, Malik attempted to remain in the moment. If they were caught in the tide, they would be drug out to the open sea. He fought to anchor them on the beach and to each other. Grounding his back into the salty water as the sweeping liquid came up to flow over them, the ocean stung and bit into him, keeping him focused. A price Malik willingly paid to keep his wits about him and Delaney intact.

"Son." Dane reached down and pulled Delaney up and off of him, holding her gingerly against his large frame.

She is safe and Dane will guard her.

His head smacked the ground and the world fell away.

Chapter
THIRTY-TWO

Malik pried his eyes open to clean, white tile shining back at him. His head poked through the massage table style bed. A pair of mens shoes caught Malik's stare.

"Tryst?" The name got stuck half way out.

"Bout time." Trystan blew out a sigh of relief.

"What the hell is wrong with you?" Peyton's voice came from somewhere beyond the bed.

"My head." Malik's mouth still found forming words difficult.

"What did they give me?" His mind functioned too leisurely, and not characteristic of who he was.

The air whispering over his skin became angry fingers ripping at gaping wounds spread along his spine. The pain, though dulled by medication, pierced his senses.

"Is she okay?" Malik forced his head up and to the side catching Trystan eye to eye. He almost threw up from dizziness grabbing hold and refusing to let go.

Deep breath, slow exhale.

Malik repeated the action until the terrible nausea began to subside.

"She's in a coma. Delaney's a tough kid, she'll be fine. Right now, you need to get your strength back. Delaney needs you to be in working condition when she wakes up."

"How long was I out?" Malik resumed staring straight through the head rest at the cool tile floor.

"About a day. You need more rest." Peyton's motherly tone came out.

"Help me up."

"Wait for another few hours. I'll assist you then." Tryst shook off the request.

Malik wanted to argue, but couldn't. His eyes slapped shut as his breathing became even and calm.

"I'm heading out. I'll be back in an hour." Peyton pivoted to leave.

"Peyton, what's happening to us?"

Trystan's sad words stopped her mid stride. She turned to face him, but stayed silent.

"I don't know." She shook her head.

"Do you believe in redemption?"

"I believe you're redeemable. I think you served The Spirit People without question and you deserve to experience some happiness for all that you have sacrificed." Peyton moved to stand in front of him.

"Find her. Run away with her and be happy. No one will blame you." She embraced him, swallowing down the sting of her emotions.

Trystan's arms wrapped around her and his head found comfort on her shoulder.

"You should get back to work." Peyton swallowed hard.

"Yes." She pulled away and exited the room.

For a long time, Tryst stood above Malik's still figure.

We are getting too old for this shit.

He stared at his friend's battered body, realizing Malik would heal. *The never ending, impossible-to-win war has stolen our childhoods, our families, and our friends. We will pick up our arms and fight some more.*

Tryst sat back down in the uncomfortable metal seat next to the bed. He scrubbed a hand down his face, over blood shot eyes and the bristly reminders of how long he had been there. Without meaning to, he yawned.

"Either you can help me find her, or get the hell out of my way."

"Well, when you ask so nicely, how am I to refuse? Give me your arm."

Malik groaned as pain hit him anew. The wounds on his back were only partially healed.

"Any word on Peyton, Bowe, and Bannan?" Malik asked.

Trystan stepped back after Malik was stable on the bed, then answered. "Man, you were out of it. The symbol at the base of the mountain marked an opening. When they were attacked by the Stryders, they forced the obstructed aperture open and waited inside. A small passage led them to a large cavern. Bannan believes they found an ancient burial site. Mass graves of what might be extended families.

"With no indication of how they died, the possibility of foul play stands out in his head. The ground is littered with literally thousands of bones. They're at the museum undergoing Carbon dating and Potassium Argon testing.

"Mount Hood sits on top of hundreds of catacombs. At some point, a small city existed and may have flourished under the peak. From many of the artifacts they brought back with them, Bannan thinks the area hasn't been inhabited in over 10,000 years, maybe more. We found no evidence of Relics or even their descendants. Bannan, Peyton, and Bowe are heading back up there once Delaney comes out of the coma. I think additional Kindreds should be dispatched. Whatever is to be learned, needs to be found by us. I'm leaving tonight." Tryst paced as he spoke.

"Do you understand where she is?"

"I'm waiting on Intel. Should the information pan out, I'll be out of here within an hour." The checking of the wristwatch and the constant jerky movements now made perfect sense to Malik. Trystan thought he had found

Calliope's location.

"Where are they keeping Delaney?" Malik hobbled with Tryst's help.

"She's under guard down the hall. Come on. They may not let you in. They have orders that no one goes in or out of her room."

Tiel and Simon guarded the dark brown door with stern expressions. Malik nodded to them as he and Tryst continued to advance. Relief washed over Malik when they allowed him to pass without question or comment. Seaton and Chance stood just inside the door. Two sets of guards encouraged him to relax.

Delaney laid still in the center of a princess bed with sweeping, shimmery brown curtains dangling on each of four posters. She wasn't broken this time. She didn't appear as if someone had used her head for a punching bag and her body for kickboxing. Delaney appeared peaceful.

"How is she doing?" Concern filled his voice.

Her small frame against the huge king bed reminded him of how fragile she was.

"Can you excuse us, please." Tryst spoke to Seaton and Chance as Malik sat on the edge of her mattress.

"Will you help me? I just want to be with her." Malik scooted back, but found the position unbearable with his injuries.

"Do you think getting into bed with her is a good plan?"

Tryst is right. Probably a stupid thing to do.

"I'm not leaving her again, unless Dane or Bannan tell me to. Please, help me."

Trystan recognized pure determination in his expression.

To get settled beside Delaney without agony took about ten minutes. His busted and torn up body hurt like hell, but he didn't care. Malik pulled himself over and snuggled her into his side. The position was uncomfortable, even painful, though this was the only thing he wanted.

"Will you go to the Drake's? In Delaney's room, on the second shelf of the worn bookcase are all her favorite books. Bring them here for me, please."

Bent, Not Broken   341

Trystan nodded and drifted out of sight.

"I missed you." Those are the words that began the one-sided dialogue. A conversation followed, a free flowing stream winding on for miles.

He spoke out loud for everyone to hear about how she was chaste like the light and he was anything but. The horror stories of all the things he'd done flowed as if always waiting to be heard, as if absolution might still be possible.

He asked for forgiveness in a round-about-way, because he wanted to be worthy of her.

Because he would probably die in the war and she deserved more than he could give her, he apologized. Then he told her about his mom and dad, how he'd grown up, and his time in the Amazon, hoping she understand why he was the way he was.

Maybe if she recognized the voice, realized someone was waiting, she'd hurry back. Somewhere in the stillness she was trying to get out.

Bannan came in and out about a hundred times every hour, fussing over Delaney with anxiety plastered to his features. When he walked in the first time, he paused in the doorway, then went about checking on her without so much as a glance Malik's way.

After Bannan left, Dane came.

"I'm sorry. I tried to get to Vivianna. I was too late." A hundred more apologies wanted to come out.

Dane stood nearby, staring off into space.

"Do you believe your will to be strong enough for both of you?" Dane finally spoke.

"My determination has to be. She's lost in her head. She can sense me when I am in the shadows. Delaney feels me, realizes I'm here. She'll find me because she understands I'm waiting for her." He felt the truth run all the way through himself.

Malik only left Delaney for bathroom privileges. His back burned from the hours of immobility. Malik wanted to be the first face Delaney saw when she woke up. He needed her to know he never abandoned her.

At night, Malik scoured Delaney's mind, entering her dreams to find nothing more than inky darkness. He searched, but came up empty-handed. After hours of getting nowhere, he switched tactics and started with Samuel Coleridge's Kubla Kahn. He recited the verses slowly and just above a whisper, the way she would have liked. Then he turned to Frost and Auden. She loved Beautiful Creatures, so he read that too.

Tryst brought Delaney's Mac. Malik combed her playlists and played for her Enya, Deep Forest, and Immediate Music. He rummaged for something to bring her back. He held her hand, raising the soft skin to his mouth, and kissed her palm about a thousand times. He traced circles on her arm with his fingertips.

Malik awakened to Trenton standing over him.

Trenton scrubbed a heavy hand down his face before he found words. "The Counsel has convened at Nacea Waith. They insist you attend because of your position."

Malik frowned in understanding. "Okay. I need thirty minutes."

Trenton left the room.

"Tryst."

"In three." True to his word, he stood in front of Malik only minutes later.

"The Counsel is convening. They have issued an order of appearance. When Delaney wakes up, I want her to be with people she is familiar with. Can you stay?" Malik pulled himself out of her bed. His wounds had healed and the movement no longer hurt.

"Peyton." Trystan shook his head no with a comforting grip on Malik's shoulder while suggesting the alternative sitter for Delaney.

She appeared in the room and Malik grabbed her. He hugged her tighter than he ever had.

"What are they calling a meeting for?" Trystan said.

"I'm not sure." Malik said

"I think I found Calliope. Talk about a female prisoner Isabeau takes a special interest in came from Shane before we lost contact. I'm heading to New

Zealand within the hour. I am going to be captured by Isabeau, then wait for an opportunity to get Calliope out." Tryst had never sounded so serious.

"She will kill you both." Peyton moved closer to Tryst. Her brow furrowed in worry.

"Calliope's hurting and alone. How can I not go to her?" Trystan was so determined to have her or die trying to find her. Knowing there was no way out for either Trystan or Calliope, he was still willing to walk into hell and sacrifice himself.

Trystan pulled Peyton into an embrace. "Don't worry. I'll leave my Finder on until I'm inside. Once you have a signature, come get us." Tryst made the process sound so easy, too simple to be authentic.

"I hope I find someone as amorous of me as you are devoted to her. It will take my breath away." Peyton whispered as she laid her head on his shoulder.

"You'll have no back up. You don't have to go alone. Let me come." Malik asked.

Tryst smiled at him.

"I'll see you before you know it."

"Peyton, will you stay with Delaney for me?"

"Of course." She leaned in to hug Malik. Peyton had never been one to show her emotions.

All of us have changed, moving in different directions.

"I'll wait to leave until you return."

Malik arrived at Nacea Waith to find an empty room. Fury sat alone, off to the side of the room.

"We need to talk, you and I." Fury motioned for him to come closer.

Fury proceeded to tell Malik a story about the Creators. Malik's mother had always referred to them as the Spirit People during a time when the tribes all lived in peace. When the balance became disrupted by territorial disputes, power struggles, over depletion of the animals needed for food and shelter, the gods stepped in just short of a tribal war.

"Each tribe had a plague set upon them as a test. In order to determine if humanity was worthy of the world, they approached one clansman from each tribe and gave an ultimatum. If they could prove to the Creators that they deserved to continue on and prosper, then humankind would not be destroyed.

"The Spirit People confronted Lahaylia, Princess of Shallow Waters. She was told of a way to save her populace, her father and new husband, from an agonizing death. She was instructed to climb to the top of the Multnomah Falls and jump. Her sacrifice alone ensured a cure to be distributed directly. Without a thought she did what was asked of her. Selflessly, she hurled herself off the cliff and gave vitality to her people with the sacrifice of her own.

"The Spirit People became rather impressed with the act of unconditional love and selflessness, so they resurrected her and granted her immortality, if she so wanted. She asked to resume her life, but the Creators denied her request. Lahaylia could come back, though not as the girl she was. Lahaylia had died and I was born as Fury The First."

"Her people would no longer be known as Shallow Waters. They became the Derma Relics. I was appointed to be the custodian of the woodlands, and able to fuse with whatever animals I choose. My tribe was allowed one totem to fuse with. I am the first protector, the initial guardian. The original Kindred to be chosen." spoke with a wounded pride Malik didn't understand.

"I accepted the primary component of the Creators' offer and stood watch, keeping my tribe safe. I protected all creatures from becoming over hunted and the forest from being over consumed, and watched over everyone except my husband. I asked that they prevent him from learning I still lived."

She explained how painful it would be, should she be forced to observe him each day knowing he could never be hers again. She preferred him to be encouraged to go on with his life. He left the tribe without ever hearing the truth.

Fury told the Creators she'd had her one love and couldn't imagine another.

"The Spirit People decided if I could be devoted so unconditionally, then every person should be irresistibly drawn to a fundamental core value, regardless of breed, beliefs, even the laws of nature shouldn't interfere. They created the Echo Law to honor my sacrifice." Fury stared off at nothing as she spoke and Malik watched her expressions change between pain and pride and some combination of both.

"Next, they went to the Snowhawks and appeared to the chief's firstborn daughter, Soaring Eagle. She was told if she went to the top of Mountain St. Helen's and threw herself into the Volcano, her clan would all be cured. Without hesitation, she dove into the steaming hole.

"The Snowhawks were allowed the antidote. The Spirit People posed their question again and she requested to remain with her tribe as their protector the same as Lahaylia had. Soaring Eagle became Night Star Showing The Way. The Spirit People granted her and her society the power of fire and they became the Relic Dares, keepers of the flames.

"The Creators then approached the Broken Streams. They went to the chief, telling Ny to go to the water and stand within the depths and wait for the lightening to find him during a violent electrical storm. After Ny died, the Creators reanimated him and posed the same offer they'd given Night Star and me. Ny asked to be allowed to watch his daughters grow up. He became known as Horizon And Infinite Light. His tribe would fuse with voltaic conductivity and the Rafe Relics were born from the power of air, keepers of cataclysmic energy.

"Two additional tribes were approached, but rejected the Creators proposal and chose their own lives over their responsibility. First was Staass, the son of the Clan of the Hunting Stag who was banished for his flight. Staass was to be ruled by a sunless sky and bitterness swam in his veins like poison. He was singled out, ostracized from everything he had ever known. He was the father of the Lunaire.

"The second was the Northern Wolves. Chief Neen'aaton, abandoned his tribe. He was expelled and the Kelpies were born. He existed with help from apparitions. The People of the Northern Wolves were saved by the chief's wife, Field Mouse, who volunteered because of the shame of her husband. She infused with the squall and charged forward as the guardian of wind, power of the Tempest. Thus, was born the Hynts. Field Mouse became known as Fatine The Warrior Of All.

"The Clan of the Stag were saved by the second child, a daughter named Kaaw. When she was brought back and given the offer, she requested to become a protector and she and her society were fused with the Earth. Given the power of Magique Relics, the Tracers came into being. They were converted to the caretakers of the Rites and bore the mark of the Fates. Kaaw now would be addressed as Sigh The Fearless.

"Once each person's fate was decided, it became a binding agreement between the gods and the inhabitants of this world. The Creators left the Earth to the breeds and allowed them to flourish. But as with all deals, there are those that search for loop holes.

"Neen'aaton and Staass united and searched for the doorway to Nubi Sereum. They believed that on the other side, they would find the resting place of the Spirit People. They wanted revenge. The two stumbled on the corridor to hell. What became of Neen'aaton isn't clear, but Staass made it back from the underworld. But he wasn't alone. He'd been bound to a demon, a Succubus named Dahlia. Once loose on the world, she mated repeatedly and the Demonoks were born. Dahlia is the Mother of Chaos.

"Tobias of the Clan of the Turtles and Serafina of the Seraphims of the Nile asked to be left as mortals, but there was a catch and their people could have no protectors assigned to them. The Creators decided because Homo sapiens were multiplying faster than the breeds, they should be made to forget about the differences between themselves and the other world. The tribes had become Amalgamates—humans who could fuse with different elements of the universe. Each had a protector standing watch. The original guardians who had given up their lives for their clans were formed as the first Kindred Relics. They were trained to hunt down the Lunaire, the Kelpies, as well as Staass and Dahlia.

"When the Spirit People had this more active role, countless breeds co-existed peacefully. The territories were divided up equally and life went on as before. Each breed was given a choice on where they would like to inhabit.

Some chose Europa, others, the roving sands, one group asked for the glaciers and two groups were allowed to be nomads.

"I think the glyph you have witnessed on Vivianna, Daphne and Delaney are the Creators making contact with us once again." Fury pulled the long dark grey cloak from her shoulders. Closing her eyes, she took a deep breath and the same markers floated just under her skin.

Chapter
THIRTY-THREE

Delaney woke up disorientated.

Heaven?

She blinked a few times to clear the fog, realizing the pounding headache wasn't going away. She tried to surmise what had happened, only increasing the thumping in her brain with each muddled thought. The pieces wouldn't fall into any logical order.

Shadowy yellow luminescence danced and swayed like campfire light eating at the shadows. Delaney lay curled up on her side and didn't move right away. Instead, she let her senses tell her a story. A crackling sound came from a fireplace at the edge of the space. The aroma of tobacco flower wafted through the air. For a moment, Delaney wondered if she had died, but figured her head would hurt far less.

She rolled over onto her back, then noticed the sound of ocean waves crashing against a shore. The clashing sounds seemed to encircle her. Off to the right, stood large cherry wood French glass doors set in an elegant entryway. The room had a stone fireplace, and she was laying in a fluffy bed with mosquito netting draped from a wood canopy. She cocked her head up and saw water through the bay windows. Waves rolled in the moonlight of the clear midnight sky.

So heaven has a fantastic beach? Or hell has been underrated.

Repositioning herself, she stared at the room's rock walls. Primitive drawings of hunting scenes with various weapons dotted the artwork bows, daggers, swords, and spears on the jagged stone cliff side. The drawings showed different animals and a variety of other characters; some may have been hominids chasing bipedal creatures she couldn't identify.

One depicted a chariot race, which she found odd because the chariots had been hitched to something that had no resemblance to horses. Two images incorporated pyramids she'd never seen before. They appeared to be from MesoAmerica, but had attributes of Egyptian culture too, some included an Asian influence.

The pyramid's surfaces were covered in limestone and connected by two long footbridges coming out of the middle of each. Even the Sphinx got a spot on the wall, captured in mid-flight, its golden wings with scarlet edges reached for the sky. Three different scenes interconnected the ancient Greek gods, the Egyptian deities, and a group she failed to recognize.

Depictions of a bird and a snake mixed together. One had a reptilian bird-man with a headdress of vibrant Polynesian feathers with rich reds, sunshiny yellows, electric blues, and forest green. People bowed down before the figure the same as they would a priest.

Delaney felt intoxicated from the surge of overwhelming sensory information. She pushed herself up to a sitting position and more paintings came into view. Most of the images had been painted in a reddish clay color; only a few appeared in varied pigments of basic colors like blue, black, red, and green. She peered from ornate scene to intricate landscape, her exhausted mind spinning into murky confusion.

Where the hell am I?

A surge of nausea gripped her and she tried to breathe through it and not think about how much she wanted to vomit from the spiraling room. She turned over to her side, facing the adjacent wall. The surface was covered floor to ceiling with symbols reminding her of a cuneiform writing system. The tiles communicated natural features of waterfalls, palm trees, and shrubs. Others seemed reptilian, like alligators and crocodiles, and insects like dragonflies and mosquitos.

"Trenton, she's awake." His voice was rich and warm, similar to espresso sliding down your throat.

Two intimidating gentlemen stood in the room with her; each wore identical black linen-like pantsuits and serious expressions. Both men appeared to stand at least six feet tall, with dangerously handsome bronze faces.

Delaney listened to the two speaking in a language she didn't understand, though she was certain she had heard the dialect before, somewhere.

A prisoner? "Why am I here?" Delaney asked them.

"Someone is coming to speak with you. You are safe with us," one of them said as he bowed his head and his shoulder length auburn hair fell like a curtain over his eyes.

She considered his youthful and pleasant features. Though the man wore a serious expression, something stood out in the way he glanced at her. When he realized she was sizing him up, he smiled a warm and reassuring smile before averting his gaze.

The other man had a buzz cut and a deep rigid scar two or three inches long marring the side of his face. The blemish did not take away from his handsome appearance. It made him look more dangerous, alluring in a frighteningly attractive way that had an irresistible pull. His eyes were a violent gray, like storm clouds threatening to unleash a tornado any second. They were warming by the moment as he stared at her. When he realized Delaney's interest, he flashed a pleasant smile, setting her at ease just that much more, then he looked away.

Another tall, attractive man walked in, wearing a similar black linen-styled pantsuit with red stitching. He carried himself like an authority figure and there was an air about him that said commanding officer. He had an expression of keen intelligence with piercing eyes and a hawkish gaze seemed to take everything in. He communicated to the two guards in the same language they'd spoken to each other, then turned to Delaney.

"You may call me Trenton. This is Seaton." He pointed to the guard who had answered her. "This is Chance." He gestured to the man with the scar.

Each smiled at her again and she couldn't help but return their warmth. Especially Chance, who had bedroom eyes. Something about him made him extraordinary and downright irresistible.

"While you're here, they'll care for you should you need anything. Will you please accompany me? Clothes have been laid out for you in the corner." His voice was detached and cool.

Trenton, Chance, and Seaton turned to face the door. She strolled to the corner and the sarong style frock of muted onyx with blue trim hanging from the dressing shade in the far end of the room. Rich coffee brown leather sandals had been placed off to one side. She'd never been the dress type. Delaney liked her jeans, t-shirts, and Mary Jane's. She got up and rounded the privacy screen.

Someone had taken excellent care of her. They'd included underwear and a bra. Her hair even smelled like lime and coconut shampoo. Peeling off the purple pajamas, she dressed. Returning to the bed, she perched on the edge as she laced the leather sandals up to mid-calf.

"You are expected." He turned and extended his hand when she approached.

"Of course, thank you," she replied in sheer bewilderment.

"Thank you for taking care of me, Seaton, Chance." Each man smiled at her as she thanked them.

"This way." Trenton stepped in front and she followed him with no idea what to expect next.

She kept quiet and trailed closely behind him as he led her out into the moonlight and up a rocky trail. In the inky darkness, she found it difficult to maneuver the stony path. Delaney fell and scraped her knee, then watched it begin to heal and disappear. Trenton offered his hand to help her up, then to steady her every other step as they continued. Saying thank you every other second felt silly, so she stopped and the climbed on in relative silence.

All she could hear was a gentle breeze blowing. The scent of lilies and salt swirled around her and an eerie glow cast down by the stars and the full moon helped light their way.

They reached the top and the view opened up to the ocean. Barren earth with sparse patches of tawny yellow grass danced in the salty breeze. Basalt rocks littered the landscape like pepperoni on a cheese pizza. They walked by colossal black monolithic figures whose daunting frames made her shiver with apprehension. The carved volcanic stone configurations, sometimes three or four times their size, had wide foreheads over faces with sharpened, angular features balanced by giant white disk eyes and elongated ears. Strong jawlines sat on truncated necks with prominent noses and sunken eye sockets. The figures had no arms and were half buried in the dry soil. Large torsos or oversized noggins, appearing like a bunch of disembodied heads, made up some sort of bizarre stone graveyard.

It was creepy and mystical at the same time.

They were commanding structures. Their enormous white globe eyeballs seemed to follow her. Everything she'd experienced since waking made her feel at a loss for words. But she decided to jump right in regardless.

"May I ask you a question?" Delaney shifted from one leg to the other.

"Of course." He stopped and faced her.

"What are they?" She gestured back toward the stone figures.

"They're called Sentinels, and are the island warriors. Down below is the Counsel. The Sentinels are guardians to the court of Nacea Waith. They keep our people safe and protected." He gestured below, then continued leading her down the sharp incline.

He seemed to Delaney as a well-educated man, with impeccable manners. She followed behind him, thoughts racing.

They passed several more figures that appeared discarded, abandoned in a rush, and never finished.

"Why are some laying down and others standing facing the ocean?" Her head pivoted, constantly turning to witness something new.

"The ones overlooking the water are called Pickets. They protect us against seafarer attacks. Our way of life has become a sad thing. Many of our homes can only be partially maintained or restored. Full restoration will be unwise, or we might give our position away.

"Humans are inquisitive. Their nature is to destroy before requiring answers. How would we clarify what we are? So we hide our existence well in our ancient homes. The inhabitants of this island have suffered in order to maintain our secrets. They're proud people who we as a populace are indebted to." He spoke with such high regard.

"These mighty Sentinels and Pickets were revered warriors. They fought unsurpassed for thousands of years before retiring here and lying in wait, resting while the lull allows them time to. They slumber until they are needed once more." As he pointed toward the eyes following them, their massive heads turned and followed their decent.

"Where are we?"

"We are on Naroke, better known as Easter Island, about 2,000 miles off the coast of Chile. This is a sacred place with a rich history of our people. Because this haven is so isolated from the rest of the world, it's easy to maintain our anonymity here. This land has been our home for close to a thousand years. A stronghold we escaped to when they destroyed Maripesa." Off in the distance a large bonfire lit up the late-night sky with eerie luminescence.

"What is happening?" They continued down the slope.

"Everyone is preparing for the burial." His voice was solemn.

"Whose funeral?" she asked.

He glanced away.

The Waltz of the Mariners. The phrase sounded romantic, serene, even enchanting. How could something so ugly as last rites be referred to with such beautiful words?

Delaney awoke with no memory of her failed attempt to end her and the man she loved after she shot her mother. Malik nor her family entered her mind until the memories of the mountain flooded Delaney's head like rushing water from a sudden glacial thaw just as she asked Trenton whose funeral was being prepared ahead of them.

I can't face the unspoken accusations. I have to keep them at arm's length for as long as I can. The memories alone are already eating at me, picking me apart.

Nothing could be forgotten and everything would be relive a hundred times an hour. Delaney couldn't face what she'd been a part of, the things she had done.

So many gathered in respect of her mother, her family. The people all wore flat black linen-like pantsuits. The soft fabric swayed in the gentle ocean breeze like rolling wheat in a field. Her grandfather stood in the same dress suit as the others, though his had gold accents and embroidery. Delaney's father was dressed in black trimmed in Maroon. Malik's black suit was trimmed in royal purple. She matched them with an ocean blue border.

Daffodils had been placed everywhere, a shower of bright sunshine yellow that somehow lightened the moment. Bannan had made sure to place hundreds of the flowers all around her, inside the casket. Vivianna had loved daffodils.

Viv laid in a rich dark cherry wood casket. The darkness enveloping her mother was brightened by the vibrant flower buds. Ebony wood chairs were set up in the shape of a crescent moon surrounding the coffin and overlooking the ocean. Daffodils even hung from their tall backs.

Such acute attention, so much time invested.

Why am I here?

She sat quietly with her hands intertwined in her lap. Through her façade, she fought to breathe, too afraid to move because the guise might fracture and leave her vulnerable for all to scorn.

Life seemed to slowly, irrevocably pass right over her.

Her knuckles were white from clenching them. Waves of nausea threatened to burst free. Delaney's palms were damp and bile rose up, burning her throat.

Bent, Not Broken   355

She sat between Malik and her father, at least his body. Her grandfather sat next to him. Both had red-rimmed eyes surrounded by dark circles. Her dad looked physically ill, gaunt and brittle, and emotionally distant, broken. Bannan hadn't spoken more than ten words since he'd come back. Even now, he seemed dazed and confused as to why they were all gathered.

I might as well have killed him also.

Dane seemed to have aged overnight. Like the day Dasha died, the life seemed to have been ripped right out of him.

Delaney's lower lip quivered. A harsh sob escaped, despite her best efforts to hold it all together. She sniffled and dabbed at her nose with a tissue Malik handed her. Every time he grabbed for her hand, she was still for a second until finally shrugging his tender touch away.

Malik handed Delaney another tissue and asked her again, "Are you okay?"

She knew he meant well. She couldn't explain why the inquiries inflamed her, but they did. She never uttered a sound.

The rest of their row was empty. There'd been no word from Daphne, Brody, or Fezz and Calliope was being held by Isabeau. That was all they would tell her and she knew they were hiding things from her. At the moment, she didn't care; her mind refused to handle anything more.

Her mother's death, and her hand in it, was already too much to bare.

The people were all gathered by sunrise. Her grandfather rose and walked slowly up to her mother's coffin.

A closed casket. How do you cover up the monumental hole in her head? Her body jerked with wild laughter that crackled only inside her mind.

Dane's face was a mask of tightly pulled skin that Delaney feared would crack when he spoke, tearing into shreds and swallowing him up whole. He reminisced about her.

Delaney forced herself to stop listening. She didn't want to see Viv through his eyes.

After a lifetime, he returned to his seat.

Delaney stared off into the sea.

Redemption, a loaded word, one with connotations of forgiveness, understanding, a chance at atonement. I could be hopeful of deliverance, though I'm not foolish enough to expect anything. To me, the sentiment is like trust— something earned, not freely given. Based on the choices I have made, both redemption and trust are out of my realm of understanding.

Her father's feeble form rose and walked up to the platform. "Delaney, do you want to say something about your mother?"

Malik shook his head with an expression of concern, trying to tell them she should remain in her seat.

Delaney didn't feel her legs carry her. As she got closer, a silhouette appeared wearing a deep sea blue, off-the-shoulder frock. Her dark tresses caressed her face and a peaceful hint of a smile played on her mouth. She stood off to the side of the platform, and a slight breeze made the hem of her dress dance frivolously around her long, slender legs. Her arms cradled her body as if she were chilly and she stared at Delaney.

Delaney turned away from the ghostly appearance of Viv to find an arc of strangers, and their eyes all pinned on her. Delaney's mouth was so dry and no words sprung to mind. She opened her lips and figured something heartfelt would flow right out, but nothing came.

The movie began to play in her head.

She shook herself, trying to make the craziness stop. The film had played enough in the hours since she'd woken, and remembered, and sat numbly watching people gather to honor the woman she'd killed. The spider web of faces blurred behind tears cascading down her cheeks.

Malik watched as Delaney fell apart before his eyes. She kept pulling to the left, like someone was to her right that she wanted to avoid.

"My mother is…. She was…." Her voice died. A poem she once heard flashed through her brain. Before she knew what she was doing, the words poured out.

When my demise here comes,

I will leave word,

to throw my ashes to the wind,

in the same place as yours.

We can run through the meadows,

stopping only to smell the purple flowers,

while dancing under the stars all aglow,

through the springtime showers.

We shall play among the seasons

No bounty on time will rest overhead.

We will toss away all thoughts of reason

We shall claim forever together instead.

Before I knew Vivianna as my mother, I loved her. I am left with so many unanswered questions. Things I wanted to say or have said to me. All those opportunities are gone.

"Go ahead, Delaney. Tell them about murdering me. Explain how you shot me in the head." Viv pulled the hair away from her lovely face. Bugs crawled out of her nose and mouth and her eyes became shiny black spheres with red interiors.

"She shrieked as the venom took her, flailing around like a fi-fi-fish out of water. I rem-remember raising my g-g-gun, finding her in the s-s-sights, and pu-pulling the trigger. Her head snapped b-back. Her cu-curly hair swept about her. Then she just fell to the ground like a b-broken doll." Delaney's voice sounded unrecognizable to her as the words came tumbling out.

Malik drifted to her side causing his chair to fall backwards. He tried to grab her, to hold on to her.

A unified gasp echoed around her. They were shocked.

What did they think happened?

Delaney looked out at them, seeing accusations in their eyes. People were standing up and pointing at her, the murderer.

"This is what I remember from the night I murdered my mother. I killed her. I shot her in the fuckin' head!" She screamed at them. "Daddy, I'm sorry."

Bannan had already begun moving toward her.

She stood shaking and screaming like a crazy person, then stumbled backwards. She tried to get to the coffin, but couldn't see where she was going through her tears.

Malik grabbed her, forced her into him, blocking the path to her mother. Delaney began punching him with angry fists. He held on until the fight fizzed and she collapsed against him. He picked her up and she clung as a toddler would. He carried her out of the sight of the crowd and farther up the meadow. Her feet hit the bare earth and she wobbled on weak knees. He didn't pull away. If he had, Delaney didn't believe she could stand alone.

He sat down cross legged on the ground, pulling her down with him among the long wisps of meadow grass, effectively hiding them from view. She crawled into his lap like an infant seeking protection. They sat together in the yellowish grass for a long time, silence doing all the talking. Her forehead rested against his cheek. Tears fell and soaked the sleeve of her dress. She turned her face up to his and stared into green shimmering pools. Malik closed his arms around her and tried to make her feel safe.

"Why did you follow me over the falls?" Delaney searched Malik's expression.

He didn't say anything.

She closed her eyes. *I don't blame him for not knowing. I can't face you looking at me.*

"What am I supposed to do now?" Delaney choked on the words.

"Learn to live with your actions. There's nothing else you can do. You have to let it go. You did something ninety nine percent of people couldn't have done. You put Vivianna first at the cost of yourself. Find a way to live with the repercussions or they will consume you." His fingers touched her cheek, wiping away the tears. Malik glanced towards the water.

"It's time." Pushing up from the ground, he offered her his hand.

"For what?"

"To say good-bye. This is important, come on."

Delaney froze on her feet. *I can't....*

Bent, Not Broken

"It's the Waltz of the Mariners. You need to wish her a safe journey." He gently tilted her head up to look into her eyes. "Come on. I won't leave you."

"Why not?" The words were soft and maybe Malik hadn't even heard her. He didn't respond.

They walked to the rocks at the edge of the sea. Malik and Delaney stood off from the others. A small wooden boat carried her mother's coffin drifting farther away with each wave, heading for the horizon.

The Waiths took flight. The air filled with graceful giant wings, all paying homage to Vivianna. Others ran into the surf, reemerging as large grey whales, seals, and sharks. They swam beside her while birds patrolled the sky and fish encircled Vivianna's vessel.

"They will stay with her until the Mariners come and take her home," Malik whispered.

One by one, each person threw island flowers, daffodils, rocks with notes wrapped around them, photographs, or other mementos honoring Vivianna into the ocean. Meaningful objects would go with her mother and she found comfort in this. Her father cut open his hand and let his blood fall into the water.

"What is Dad doing?"

"Some are sending her good wishes, others are saying good-bye with memories they held dear of her. Each person will give something they value. Your father loved your mother very much. If I had to guess, he is giving his heart to her for safe keeping. Bannan offers himself," Malik said, with tears in his eyes.

"He will hate me forever," Delaney murmured to herself.

She paid close attention as the vessel became smaller with distance. People began to gather in smaller groups. Everyone stayed and kept an attentive eye on the horizon, as Delaney did. They started to talk about Viv, remembering her with nice words and loving sentiments.

Bannan remained behind on his knees, letting his hand rest in the salty water. The alkaline must have burned, but he never moved. His face was empty and quietly wept alone. Watching him grieve so publicly only made her guilt heavier.

Delaney couldn't go to him. She feared the accusations.

I tried so hard to protect my family, and in the end, the sacrifices were all in vain. I managed to destroy them instead.

"Why do they refer to this as The Waltz of the Mariners?"

"Ghosts of the Leaping Water, from where we come, we return. To be reunited with those who have gone before us. The ocean depths take you to the other side, like a gateway." He inhaled deeply.

"To heaven or hell?" Delaney asked as she leaned her head against him.

"Both, I suppose." Malik waited with her, sitting on the ground.

Delaney cried until no more tears would come. Finally, she got up and went to make her offering. Malik stayed by her side. She cut open her arm with a jagged rock, following her father's example. The blood dripped over a dandelion she found a few feet away, her atonement meant to stand out in the field of other flowers and mementos. She dropped the petals and studied them as they floated, finally sinking below the blue surface.

Malik pulled an old, worn photograph with a corner missing out of his pocket. Delaney wanted to ask what the picture was, but refrained.

Chapter
THIRTY-FOUR

Delaney's strength finally gave out and she passed out in Malik's arms. Only four people remained on the beach hours later. One sat alone, hand still dangling in the water. Another stood swaying in the night breeze high on the bluff. Malik bundled Delaney up in his arms and left the two to grieve in private.

He took them back to his house, listening to Delaney talk in her sleep as he carried her. She whimpered, jostled, and pushed violently to get away until he almost dropped her, then clung to him as if he was a life preserver.

The war had just begun for her. She would fight a battle within herself, and one with Isabeau and Caleb. Both of which could cost her everything.

Malik tucked her into his bed.

Bannan and Dane should realize where he had taken her. He wanted to keep her safe until they were more capable to do so themselves. For now, he would make sure she had everything she needed.

Malik watched her sleep for a few hours. Worry creased his brow as he studied her restlessness.

Delaney woke up alone in a bed larger than she had ever seen before. The decor reminded her of a dream she once had. The room was enveloped in a blue like the Mediterranean sea, beige the color of sand from one of the beaches on Mykonos, and creamy vanilla similar to a blood moon.

"You're awake. Are you hungry?"

Her gaze found Malik sitting in a corner with a stack of papers, smiling back at her. She pursed her lips in response and he nodded in understanding.

A steaming cup sat beside her on the nightstand.

"Apple cinnamon?" she mumbled.

Malik nodded. He wanted her to feel at home. Wanted to ask her if she would stay with him if he could show her how safe she would be.

She knew by the sadness in his smile, the lines of concern etched into his forehead, that the night before had really happened. A shallow breath filled with fresh raw pain caused her to avert her eyes and study the comforter, though her gaze never quite met the fabric.

"Where are we?" Her voice was thick and gritty.

"This is my bedroom. You were so upset last night, I brought you here. I went this morning and informed Bannan of your whereabouts."

Delaney stared at him, making him visibly uncomfortable until he spoke from the agonizing silence.

"What do you think?" He gestured around the space, the pride in his expression obvious.

"Your room is nice." Delaney attempted to sound interested, but knew she had failed.

"I wanted you to like being here." His eyes were watching her so carefully.

I need to get lost in him again. He is a safe place to hide.

"Thank you for yesterday." Tears broke free and flowed down her cheeks. Delaney tried to smile at him.

"You won't always hurt as much as you do right now. I understand the instinct to push everything away, how running seems like the only answer. But, punishing yourself will not bring her back. Nothing except time can lessen the pain or the guilt. For your own peace of mind, let her go. When you lose someone you love…it's…it's easy to allow the anger and sadness to consume you."

Malik had watched his parents die. He understood the overwhelming sense of impending responsibility and the impotent rage rearing up, always threatening to bubble to the surface.

Delaney wanted to lie still until numbness came into her heart and all else was driven out. She turned away, unable to face him.

"Please, give yourself some time." Malik crawled in bed next to her.

Delaney curled into him. He pulled her close and let her sob. When the tears finally dried and no more came, she began to calm.

"Come on. I'll take you home." He had an odd expression on his face.

"I can't…I don't…. Can I stay here for a while?"

"As long as you want."

"Malik, we need you." Leaestra's voice whispered though his mind.

"Copy that," he said, gazing down at Delaney. "I have to go to work. I won't be gone long. Food's in the kitchen. The other Kindreds will stay away. I'll be back soon." He leaned down, kissed her cheek, and disappeared before she blinked a second time.

A moment later, Malik stood behind Leaestra in the office the Kindreds kept on Naroke. She reminded Malik of Fezz, typing as fast as inhumanly possible.

"Hey, Malik," Leaestra said.

Malik walked around the conference room sized table and said, "Fezz, where have you been?"

"I've been searching for Brody for days. Every lead got me nowhere. She's gone." There were deep circles around Fezz's eyes.

"Get some sleep, Fezz. I want a full update when he wake up, Leaestra."

"Trystan's Finder has been disconnected. I was tracking him until about five minutes ago." Leaestra stopped typing and turned, glancing up at Malik.

"Where?" Malik scrubbed a hand down his face.

"Maripesa." Her brow furrowed in disbelief.

Malik was too stunned even to wrap his head around the facts.

Why would he have gone home to search for Calliope?

"Monitor his Finder twenty-four-seven. Find Bannan and Dane, I need to talk to them. Tell Bannan to bring the weapons he's been working on over to my house. I'll leave soon after to track Tryst." Malik gathered up his gear and drifted home.

Isabeau would go after Tryst with a vengeance. Malik had to find him before she killed him, and time was already ticking away.

Marble, granite, slate, hardwood, and rock created most of the surfaces in Malik's house. The decor was eclectic with modern flairs. On the walls hung prints Delaney immediately recognized. He'd collected all the artists she admired. Every book she loved filled the shelves along one long wall, as if Malik had cleaned Amazon out.

He understands me. He has taken so much time to see who I am. He did all this for me.

Tears poured from Delaney's eyes as the realization settled into her.

A man who hears all I say and everything I don't.

She moved room to room, admiring all of his personal touches. A large Mango wooden desk decorated with only a Mac and some papers on top sat alone in a small room. Delaney imagined him sitting there, doing paperwork or staring at the Mac paperweight and wondering what it did. Imagining the trained assassin, nonhuman creature, beneath his incredibly attractive exterior working with a computer didn't seem to make sense to her.

In the kitchen, Delaney fixed something to eat, but left it untouched on the red and gold marbled granite countertop. She was trying to keep herself busy with anything to help her move forward, or at least forget. After a shower, she sat before the large picture windows overlooking the ocean, watching the water sweep up and pull the sand away.

Every time Delaney closed her eyes, Viv's head bounced from the impact of her bullet, slim arms whipped through the air, and her body crumbled to the ground. A gruesome horror flick she couldn't stop from playing over and over again. Cold space always seemed to fill a space next to her, as if Viv was there staring at her.

Delaney saw her mother's reflection in the glass just behind her whenever she stared into the windows too long or too closely. In every shadow, she was there, pointing an accusatory finger straight at her killer.

Malik drifted to the side of his bed and found Delaney had vacated the bedroom. As he went to locate her, he spotted an uneaten sandwich on the countertop. An eerie silence persisted in every a room and each corridor, heightening his uneasiness.

I shouldn't have left her. I knew she wasn't okay. His heart seemed to skip every other beat.

When he reached the front room, he found her sitting in a rocking chair facing the windows overlooking the beach.

"I'm so sorry." Delaney was repeating the words in pain filled whispers, with tears running down her blank expression.

Malik kneeled down next to her, placing his hand on the arm of her seat. She never glanced over at him. Her eyes were glazed and her thoughts a thousand miles away.

Fear gripped Malik like boney fingers digging into his skin.

"Delaney."

She turned her head and gazed blankly at him.

"I need to speak with your father and grandfather, but didn't want to leave you alone too long. They will come here, soon."

A few moments passed before she slowly nodded in understanding.

"You need to eat. What can I bring you? How about your favorite, some pizza?"

She remained still, locked in place as a prisoner in her own mind. Delaney's entire being felt tired and she barely moved. Malik's voice smoothed the rough edges of her emotional upheaval, though words barely penetrated her understanding.

She resumed staring out the window.

A knock on the glass french doors jarred Malik.

Delaney never even blinked. Her demons waited for her just beyond the edge of dark created by the interior lights reaching out through the window. She understood they waited for her to lower her guard.

He'd said her father and grandfather were coming. She had managed to avoid spending time alone with them since she'd woken up in the infirmary.

I need to dodge their finger-pointing glances. How can I face them?

Her actions had taken less than a split second to transform their lives forever. Vivianna had told Delaney she would be extraordinarily powerful, and yet with all her power, she couldn't prevent any of this sorrow.

She heard the knock at the door and froze in panic. She wanted her dad, needed to talk, to listen, and to be connected with someone she once had such a strong bond with.

Without a sound, Delaney slipped from the chair and went to hideout in Malik's room. She braced her back against the wall, listening to them talk about Calliope and Trystan. She hadn't let herself think of Calliope or the others. The spacious room began closing in on her. Viv's voice echoed in her head. The walls became concrete pillars wound tightly with barbed wire and iron bars.

Delaney put on a sweatshirt and slipped out of the bedroom. *Malik is no fool, there must be another way in and out of this house.*

She quietly opened all the doors at the rear of the structure until she found one opening to a hallway instead of a room.

"Do you know where Calliope is?" Bannan inquired as he dropped two large duffel bags to the stone floor.

"Trystan's last confirmed location was Maripesa. As of forty-five minutes ago. If Isabeau has him, I need to hurry. What do you have?" Malik heard a second knock at the door and waved Dane in. He turned to check on Delaney, but the chair sat empty.

"Where's Delaney?" Bannan glanced around.

"I'm not sure. You should talk to her." Bannan's eyes told Malik he missed his daughter. He realized they needed to be together now more than ever before.

Malik was relieved Bannan went to find Delaney.

"Leaestra told me about Fezz. She said nothing of Brody's situation." Dane said in a gravelly voice, then his lips stilled in a grim straight line.

Malik noticed subtle differences about him immediately. Dane's face was gaunt, eyes bloodshot. Malik never imagined Dane as anything but viral, energetic, and alive. He grew worried for him, as well. When Dasha died, Malik thought he had willed himself to die too. Viv kept him from giving up. Malik wasn't sure how to do that for him.

"Fezz is the most determined man I have ever met." Malik sat on the edge of the sofa and gestured with his hand for Dane to join him. "Brody tricked us all with her little drug and ditch stunt. He'll take her actions as a personal attack on his ability to perform his job competently. Fezz will leave soon to continue searching and won't stop until he finds her. Once he has her, he'll torment her until she cracks like an egg. He'll need her to understand she screwed the wrong guy over. If I were lost, I'd want him trying to find me."

"What of Daphne? Seeley will tell her the truth…use the information to break her. The knowledge may destroy her." Dane stood staring out at the sea.

"Can you go after Brody and Fezz? If there was another way, I'd never make the request. I must get to Tryst. He won't last long while they're torturing Calliope in front of him. The Kindreds sustained many losses at the falls. We're spread thin trying to decipher the puzzle and still provide protection, as well. I need help." Realization struck Malik with a metal jolt. Dane needed a reason to keep going and helping more actively than usual might help him.

"You are worried." Dane took the same chair Delaney had vacated.

"I am. Those girls had no idea what they were getting themselves into." Malik ran his fingers through his hair as he spoke, and began pacing the room.

"I meant you are concerned about me." Dane extended his hand and waited for Malik to respond.

Malik moved to the outstretched hand and they shook as Dane said, "Thank you, son."

He was saddened by Dane's expression. This man was like a father to him, his mentor and friend. He was in pain. On the edge of choked up, Malik suddenly became that little kid in the Amazon.

Dane released Malik's hand and smiled. "I think you might be correct. This would be good for me."

"You will need to partner up with someone. Any preferences?"

"The choice is yours." Dane waved his hand with indifference.

"Leaestra, send Mia to my house. Tell her to ready herself for accompanying Dane to Oregon. They leave before morning." Malik exhaled as he sat in a rocker next to Dane.

"Delaney!" Bannan's shout echoed through the house.

Malik left his seat so fast he knocked the chair backwards.

They found him rushing through the hallway between the bedrooms.

"She's gone." Bannan appeared stricken.

"Where the hell did she go?" Malik bellowed.

"I figured I would find her in one of the rooms. I checked them all, she's gone."

"She couldn't have gotten far. Bannan, will you head to the dock? If she's trying to get off the island, she'll need a boat. Dane, search the beach please. I'll track starting at the backstairs. She must have found the other exit today while I was out."

Malik found no sign in the stairway or outside. He drifted up to the bluff to look over the area for her, but saw nothing. Delaney had become skilled at ditching him and it was beginning to piss Malik off.

The corridor was lit with gas style lamps. A sensor picked up each of her steps, illuminating the next one and extinguishing the previous light. The cut stone was more uneven than in the house. The passageway had doorways every twenty feet or so.

She emerged from the tunnel, the wind howled and whipped Delaney's hair. Strands stung her face and eyes. The cold bit right into her and she shivered. She pushed forward to the rocky cliffs. The thundering, crashing din coming off the water kept Viv's voice at bay. Delaney had been begging the spirit to go away, but also wanted it to stay and torture her. She felt she deserved no less.

No one to intervene this time.

Delaney stumbled over the rugged landscape. Her muscles ached with exhaustion and every little thing rubbed her the wrong way. She wandered into the quiet darkness, forcing her reluctant feet to keep going regardless of how much they wanted to find Malik. She had become proficient at slipping away unnoticed, and refused to turn back from her goal of reaching the cliff's edge.

The accusations repeated in her head like from a scratched CD. He couldn't free her from this or from herself. Malik was a fixer; he needed to fix her, to save her. Some things aren't meant to be saved.

The hurt was so overpowering, overwhelming, it weighed her down, swallowed her whole, and left her feeling lifeless. She was feeding off of the misery.

A ghostly movement caught her eye, blue silk and chestnut tresses blowing around the female figure. Delaney stood at the cliff's edge, gazing down on the water far below.

"Leave me alone! Go away," Delaney screamed at the star filled sky and full moon.

She dropped to sit with her legs dangling over the cliff. Below her, the swells crashed over basalt rocks littering the beach. Angry wind chased the surf right through the gauntlet, never letting up. The crashing swells called out to her, summoning her to the soothing sound just below.

Can those waves pummel me into the rocks? Or will the power suck me under and finish me quickly?

"Please, go away." Her voice a soft breath.

The gusts whistled across the bluff as Malik moved higher up the trail to the cliff's edge. He was almost knocked off his feet as a flurry whipped around the parched earth. Naroke was beautiful as a whole, but barren like Mars in many spots. The wind stung Malik's eyes as he searched for her. He finally found her small silhouette, and as he neared, heard her pleas. Malik wondered if she knew she was talking to herself.

He realized Delaney couldn't be left to her own devices in her current state and didn't know how he would search for Trystan and protect her.

"What's going on in your head?" Malik wasn't sure how to help her.

The voice forced Delaney to be quiet, but she refused to acknowledge Malik.

"I am afraid to face them." She blew out her breath slowly. "They must loath me for what I did. I want their forgiveness, but am I unworthy of the absolution? I slaughtered her. The woman my father loved. Dane's only daughter. How does someone forgive you for something like that? She had no weapon, no chance. Do you hate me too?" She choked each word out in a steady pace, leaving no room for him to answer her.

"I don't know how to help to you." He released a frustrated sigh.

Malik knew there was less time to save her than to get to Tryst. He sat down directly behind her, encircled her with his legs, and drew his arms around her. Her position on the cliff's edge made him need to have a firm grip on her.

She resisted briefly before succumbing and pressing back against him.

"You're so far away, Delaney, and only drifting farther. I will help you if you'll let me. I promise to stay by you until we figure this out. Is this what you believe you deserve? Would your mother want this for you?" His words made a sob rumble within her.

"Do you think she saw me?" Delaney ran both hands over her face.

Malik hadn't given any thought to what was going through Viv's head, what she may or may not have been aware of in her last moments.

"I doubt Viv was present when the end came. I think you put her out of her misery. The act was a kindness. I shouldn't have let you accept the responsibility." He took a deep breath. "What you did was incredibly selfless."

"I'm so sorry." The apology felt right and empty at the same time for Delaney. "My brain replays her death continuously. I can't sleep, nor breathe without reliving the moment. I can't make the horror movie of the moment I shot her stop. Why can't I force an end to the memories?" Delaney wondered if he understood her through broken words and gasps between her tears.

"You can't let this destroy you. This war is far from over. Your sisters are still lost. We need to find them. A reason to move forward is a positive step." His breath kissed her neck as he spoke. "Let her go, Delaney."

"Leave me alone," she whispered to the wind. "Tell her I'm sorry." If only the breeze might relay the message.

Malik hoped the sentiment made her feel better. For a perfect moment, they sat together on the cliff watching the night play out. Delaney nuzzled up against him and their lives seemed to be going in the same direction. She may not remember their past, but new feelings had begun to grow. The path between them was something that would not be denied.

Delaney clamped her eyes shut, but didn't want to visit the movies again. She needed the darkness and craved to get lost in Malik. Cinnamon swept about her and she let the scent comfort her, just for a while. She longed to relive the moment they had been together.

"It was always you. Every direction comes back to you." She bit her lip hard after saying the words.

His arms tightened around her and he nuzzled his face into her neck.

It is safe here, safer than I deserve.

"I'm sorry. To find happiness with you after what I've done, feels wrong. I don't deserve your acceptance." She crawled over his body, pulled herself up, and forced her legs to walk a few feet away.

"Delaney, you need to stop this." He sounded angry.

"Maybe I deserved you before, the chance at a happy life together." Delaney turned to leave, but Malik caught her arm before she could getaway.

"Your mom was the last tie I held to my own parents. The only person I remembered who knew them on a personal level. She was all I had left of them. A thousand questions I still wanted to ask her, memories she may have been able to explain to me. We all lost someone we loved, but you are the only one who blames you.

"What's between us isn't just about you. It involves me too. You can run from me, but I won't stop searching for you. Escape me and what we have, however, you will never be free of yourself. Stay here and face this with me." He pulled at her chin, forcing Delaney to meet his gaze.

Loud laughter buzzed inside her head.

"Stay with me. Fight this. Let's get your sisters back. We can exact vengeance."

"At least avenge my death." The ghostly whisper rippled through her, sending a shiver down her spine.

Delaney understood the fight was far from over. They needed to find the others, dead or alive. Everyone had to be brought home.

The best way to tell an author that you liked or disliked their work is to write a consumer review. Love it or hate it, I want to know what you think. This is the only way for self-improvement and growth, so please take a few minutes and tell me what you thought.

Acknowledgements

There are so many to whom I owe some form of thanks.

Joanna Penn: Without The Creative Penn website, I would never have found Debra L. Hartmann, The Pro Book Editor. She is the most amazing person and I feel so blessed to have found this wonderful editor who encouraged me to move forward. She also connected me with Indie Author Publishing Services' EM Tippetts design team. Without you, I know this wouldn't have been possible, so from my heart and family, thank you!

Michelle Rinehart, who has read more copies than she probably wanted to, gave the love of reading back to me, and inspired me to not only write the book, but dream that it would be published one day. I admit you were right and *thank you*!

Mom and Dad, I have no idea where to even begin. Thanks for the trips to the library; it all started there when I was five years old.

Willa Jemhart, fellow author: Thanks for getting me started and sticking by me.

Ashley McGarry: Thanks for reminding me to go have fun, just not Bingo.

To every library, librarian, used book store, Barnes and Noble, and Amazon: I have spent thousands of hours wandering halls and internet pages searching for perfect books, and in my saddest moments, these places have lifted me up and reminded me that life is beautiful even after the ugliness.

UNLV counseling department: If I hadn't had to go back and take Physical Anthropology 1, I never would have developed a love for myths, cultures, and dead civilizations.

Upcoming Books

Damaged, Not Destroyed (Calliope)
Book Three Title TBD (Daphne)
Book Four Title TBD (Brody)

For book five, I can't decide whether to tell Peyton, Shane, or Troy's story. If you have a preference, just find me on Facebook, Twitter, or www.sukisather.com. Maybe you will be the one person who can help!

CPSIA information can be obtained
at www.ICGtesting.com
Printed in the USA
FSOW04n0838131015
12111FS